summer of the hungry pup

summer
of the hungry pup

by   byrna barclay

NeWest Press
Edmonton

First Edition.

Canadian Cataloguing in Publication Data

Barclay, Byrna.
    Summer of the hungry pup

        ISBN 0-920316-19-0 (bound).
        ISBN 0-920316-21-2 (pbk).

        1. Riel Rebellion, 1885 — Fiction. I. Title.
        PS8553.A73S8   C813'.54   C81-091349-6
        PR9199.3.B37S8

Published by NeWest Publishers Ltd., "The Western Publishers,"
204-10711-107 Ave., Edmonton, Alberta   T6C 0W6.

Manufactured in Western Canada.

This Book is Dedicated

to

The Cree Elders

and

My Own Elders

to RHW who showed me the way to vision

to RK who showed me the way to voice

and especially

to Donald K. who showed me the way to believe

Acknowledgements:

I wish to thank the following for their assistance:

The Saskatchewan Department of Culture and Youth; The Saskatchewan Arts Board; Jean Goldie of the Saskatchewan Archives, Regina; the staff of the Helena Historical Society, Montana; and especially Ho Chin of the Old Military Branch, Smithsonian Institute, Washington D.C.

For their critical comments, support and faith:

Stan Cuthand who taught me more than Cree; the writers at the Saskatchewan School of the Arts — summers 73-77; Ken Mitchell who taught me how to laugh at myself; The Prairie Factor: Lois Simmie, Bob Currie, Pat Krause, Barbara Sapergia and Geoff Ursell, David Carpenter; Charlotte Weiss who believed in Old Woman and suggested the end; Maria Cambell who prayed to the grandmothers that this book might be given to People; and always Ron, Julianna, and Bruce who lived through it all with me.

In Cree there is no way to say Thank-you; there is only *Tapwe Ki-tatamihen:* Truly, you please me.

All the characters in this book are novelistic. Although I have adhered faithfully to Cree history, the people who lived it, such as Poundmaker, Little Bear, Lucky Man, Bowboy, Major Sanno, Lts. S.C. Robertson and J.J. Pershing of the U.S. Cavalry and Supt. Richard Burton Deane of "K" Division, N.W.M.P. are portrayed, not as they were, but as I imagined they might have been perceived by Old Woman, herself a dreamed character who belongs to all People.

Although I have borrowed some of the beautiful names of my own ancestors, in particular that of my grandmother Johanna and the Bjorlings, none of the characters are representative of the real people, nor are the events of this story in any way parallel to their lives.

THE CREES
1885 — 1896

March 30, 1885   Poundmaker's Crees loot Battleford.

May 2, 1885   Battle of Cut Knife Hill.

May 26, 1885   Cree Surrender at Battleford.

June 2, 1885   Lucky Man, Little Poplar, Little Bear and followers leave their reserves for Montana. Marquis of Landsdowne reports to Secretary of War in Washington that 60 Crees have gone south.

July 10, 1885   Little Poplar and 28 warriors cross the South Saskatchewan River between Swift Current and Red Deer Crossings.

January, 1886   Lt. S.C. Robertson and 32 men of Troop A., U.S. Cavalry sent out from Fort Maginnis. Little Bear and Little Poplar found camped on opposite sides of Missouri.

Cavalry drive Crees north from Rocky Point, 123 miles to Fort Assinniboine. At Fort Assinniboine, Little Poplar is arrested. President Cleveland grants political asylum to Crees. Crees camp on south fork of Sun River.

Little Bear joins Rocky Boy and his band of wandering Chippewa.

Subsistence Department refuses to

	pay cost of food for Crees because they are not prisoners of war.
May, 1886	20 lodges of Crees at Fort Assinniboine. Col. Otis sends 8 lodges of Cree to Fort Belknap to help with spring planting. Crees join Crows, Assiniboines, Gros Ventre in making Sundance.
August, 1886	Cavalry at Fort Assinniboine receive orders to keep Crees away from American bands.
Winter, 1887	40 lodges camped in Collins Ravine in Silver Bow County. Crees look for work in Fort Benton. Hundreds of steers downed by blizzards and Cree eat frozen cattle.
October, 1888	Crees spread throughout Sun River Region, Halfbreed settlements at Big Spring Creek, near Judith Mountains. All rations stopped.
1889 — 1891	120 lodges at Fort Assinniboine. 73 lodges on Teton River at Willow Creek, Dupwyer Creek, and Piegan Agency at Fort Shaw.
1889	Letters and petitions from Montana citizens request deportation of destitute Crees.
1890 — 1892	Spiritual revival led by Wovoka. Ghost Dances performed by Sioux stopped by cavalry.
April, 1896	Governor Rickards petitions Secretary of State for removal of Crees. $5,000 appropriated by Congress for deportation of Crees back to Canada. Major J.M.J. Sanno of the 3rd Infantry appointed to conduct general round-up of rebels.
June 1, 1896	Indian Commissioner A. Forget, Supt.

Richard Burton Deane of N.W.M.P., and Interpreter Peter Hourie travel to Montana to meet with Governor Rickards at Helena. They present him with Amnesty Proclamation of July 6, 1886, carefully pointing out that it does not apply to Indians guilty of cold blooded murder.

Detachments of soldiers begin state-wide round-up.

June 18, 1896 Lt. J.J. Pershing of 10th U.S. Cavalry arrests 110 Crees near Great Falls, Montana.

June 20, 1896 Supt. Deane of "K" Division returns to Coutts, N.W.T. from an inspection of Milk River detachments, arriving in time to meet the 2:30 train containing the first shipment of Crees.

June 21, 1896 Bowboy shoots himself at Great Falls, Montana. Major Sanno starts the trains for Canada before the law can intervene.

June 22, 1896 60 Crees and Halfbreeds born in U.S.A. hire lawyer J. Hoffman who petitions Montana District Court with a Writ of Habeus Corpus. Lt. J.J. Pershing called as Defendant. Crees ask Commissioner at Havre to intercede for them. Several obtain Certificates of Intent to become American citizens. 70 members of Belknap Reservation and Chippewa without reservation are illegally caught in the search.

Hoffman argues that the Act of Congress only fixed the sum of $5,000 for removal of Crees and did not authorize it. The Law read "Canadian Crees" and 60 American citizens are being deported contrary to the Constitution of the United States.

Judge Benton decides the Montana Court has no authority to overrule an Act of Congress and no jurisdiction over a federal officer: cavalry are to continue the deportation.

June 23, 1896   2nd Lt. W.S. Wood of 10th U.S. Cavalry arrests Little Bear and Lucky Man.

June 25, 1896   Little Bear and Lucky Man discovered among a consignment of 71 Crees delivered at Coutts, N.W.T.

July 8, 1896   Little Bear and Lucky Man appear before Supt. Perry at Regina Police Barracks in a preliminary hearing. Evidence produced is insufficient to warrant a trial. Accused are released and sent to Onion Lake.

     Little Bear returns to Montana and Rocky Boy Band. (In April, 1916 land, including 30,900 acres of Fort Assinniboine is set aside for homeless Cree.)

July 22, 1896 $5,000 allotted by Congress spent. Last batch caught in Missoula. Cavalry march 192 Crees north.

August 6, 1896   Last batch driven into N.W.M.P. camp 3 miles from border. They had walked 350 miles. Column of route led by Lts. Pershing and Fleming.

     Outbreak of Measles.

August 7, 1896   Dr. Mewburn travels 72 miles from Lethbridge in 10 hrs. He and Corp. Bullough, the hospital steward, take immediate charge of the camp. Crees isolated 3 miles from N.W.M.P. camp on Cattle Quarantine Grounds beside White Mud River.

September 2,
1896

Camp declared free of infection. Remaining Crees returned to their former reserves.

My Other-Granddaughter,

I am Old Woman, humble woman, poor woman, but I try to speak to you.

Before, when your grandmother was here, I did not go inside white house. Now she is gone, and you drag me inside. It is like winter house on left-over-land. All first houses the same.

Long time ago your grandfather cut down spruce trees, stuck them together with river mud and straw. Long time ago on left-over-land my Horse-dance-maker cut trees for house too. I remember how it hurt him to strike a living thing. He prayed to Spirit-of-all for forgiveness. I remember how I was forced to wash brown walls white by wife of man who handed out flour.

You think I am dying and you drag me inside white house. For four days I turn my face to crumbling wall. Between logs old clay is cracked. It peels under my twisted fingers. I close my eyes and smell old trees, old roots, older earth. I see passing of more winters than walls hold or can ever shut out.

For four days I turn my face to log wall, away from you, but my ears are not so old I do not hear you. For four days I have thought on it. I speak now.

My Other-Granddaughter,

You say you will take me home to *reserve*. Left-over-land belongs to people of Thunderchild, Little Pine, Lucky Man and Sweet Grass. It was set aside as places where People would die out like buffalo. Left-over-land is only part of home. Home is prairie: Great Four of east and north and west and south.

I have seen white men change face of land. They build homes of sod, then wood, now steel and concrete. Now I see how they have changed and hardened faces of all my granddaughters. New way of painting face is not good.

So it is better that you tell me how you love your old grandmothers. You say you did not go to your grandmother's funeral. Now you do not want to dance at my feast-for-dead. You want to see me living. So I tell you. Do not cry for the living. Do not cry for the dead who are happy dancing in night lights of sky.

Who is this person who tells you I am dying? What does he know of medicine? I tell you about medicine.

Are my bundles there? Move them closer to me so I can touch old deerhide.

It is good now. When you are ready to hear the Way of it, I will tell you how to take away weeping-eye-disease, how to make coddle of Company-rum for new mothers, how to loosen tight chest of baby with coughing sickness, how to shrink swellings behind old man's ears, how to undo foxpaw curse, and how to crush loveplant seeds to rub on your young man's leggings. I will tell you where to find herbs and roots. What must be ground to powder. What must be turned to liquid. I will show you medicine.

I will show you how to see as far as place where earth meets sky. You will know meaning of vision, how to dream, and how to live as He-who-is-alone-above intended from the time of remaking of earth.

Who tells you I am dying? When I tell you I am dying, then you will know it.

14

My Other-Granddaughter,
        You have forgotten what I taught you,
how it is done, how to lower your head and show respect
for People, how to say it without words: yes, I listen well
to all you say.
        You look at me, eye to eye, the way of
your white people. You ask me to speak my name and
names of my fathers. Elders have said it: never speak
Name of father or grandfather, Name of mother or
grandmother. You show no respect. You say Name of
dreamspirit, Real Name, and that is going against all we
believe.
        I am only Old Woman. I have seen
too many winters on prairie to want to remember what I
was called before I met Horse-dance-maker. I was his first
woman. That is how you must know me: First Woman.
He had four wives, but I was first. I followed him beyond
place where earth meets sky then back to Valley of Battle
River.
        I will tell you how I went away after
Rebellion and returned. I will tell you what happened to
me and all alienated-ones.

My Other-Granddaughter,
        You are not Exact-speaking-person.
You do not dress Cree, think Cree, speak Cree. You have
forgotten all I taught you. But do not bring to me an
interpreter to change my words so you may understand
what I say.
        I have seen sounding creatures before,
many times, and I know them by their brown hats.
Sounding Creature is a dragonfly who hovers over people.
He twists words to give them different meanings so Queen's
men will be happy with black marks they scratch on paper.
He sweats. But meanings for men of first Queen and our
ancestors do not come together. Promises do not hold
same meaning for men of her grand-daughter, this
Elizabeth, and for my children's children. Even name of
first Queen was never interpreted right by sounding
creatures. Victoria was Okimaw-iskwew, *Woman Leader*.
There is no other way to say it. But people who came

across water called her Great White Mother and the name was used by redcoats and missionaries and Indian agents who said we should think of ourselves as red children of Great White Mother.

Naaaaa! I used to laugh at such foolishness. Now it brings pain to my heart. People are forgetting that they are Iyiniwak, *Real People*. White men have told us we are red children so many times we have become children who cannot say what is best thing to do. People can say who they are only by remembering what they have always been: Prairie People.

There are more changes that must be made, by People this time, but I will not live to see them.

I have seen sounding creatures at trading posts and forts on both sides of dividing-line. Dragonfly translates five beaver skins into one Company-blanket-coat. At Battleford, when Poundmaker and all leaders give up their Names, he cannot find a way to tell us what this means: *treason.* Eleven summers later, long knives deliver us into hands of redcoats. At dividing-line, Sounding Creature hovers over people's campfires and he tells redcoats who is planning to escape.

Sounding Creature does not speak exact way of it. He cannot speak with hands. He translates word to word and cannot interpret how People see and hear and feel changing of earth in their hearts. I do not like him. Do not bring him here.

It will do no good if you scratch my words on paper. You say you want me to tell you my story, tell you how I became medicine woman, so it may be put away in place of stone where old totems and yellow papers are saved for all people. So words will not be lost.

Naaaaaa! I know nothing of this place or of that way of keeping things. I trust memories and stories of oldest grandfathers and grandmothers. They see long distances, see in four directions, and they speak the Way.

Do not take up scratching stick or you will forget how to write things down in your head.

My Other-Granddaughter,

Elders have always spoken in one voice. The memory goes back long before white men came across water in wooden boats.

I listened to elders as you are listening to your Other-grandmother now. I heard words flow like strong currents of Battle River. Words turned to water and fell from elders' eyes until they carved channels down sides of their faces.

I heard ringing voice of Speechmaker, that one, Poundmaker. His words smoothed and softened stone.

I knew power of Big Bear's voice. He was too-much-bear. He made Thirst Dance for four days and four nights. His Song was so strong when drums stopped thunder began. It made sky tremble. Thunderbird sent slashes of rain. Big Bear made drums sound in heads and hearts of People.

I listened to prayers of Pipe-dance-maker. I saw how he made all things run well for Prairie People.

I heard whistle-call of ancestors dancing in northern lights. I knew somewhere many People were dying of Covered-with-sores disease.

I knew fear of not knowing where to find food. I heard wolf's long howl and unending growl of summer's hungry pup. I sucked rabbit bone when there was no lard or pemmican. I fell asleep to sighing of another grandmother telling stories to hungry children.

So do not ask me to put words on paper. How can songs run well on paper? How can paper hold sounds of this old heart drumming move-along-dance? How can it interpret story-painting I draw behind my eyes? I say no. It cannot hold taste of buffalo tongue, colour of sky, silence of underwaters in Battle River, or softness of albino calfskin. These things I know, and scratching stick cannot capture turning of poplar leaves, changing of my seasons.

Put paper and scratching stick away from me. I want nothing between us. Come closer to me. Fold your hands between mine. So we hold each other and close distance of different ways.

It runs well now.

My Other-Granddaughter,
I tell you I have thought on it for four days. This is true. But I have dreamed on it for four nights. Also. My dream is why I have chosen to speak the Way to you.

I tell you my dream. But first look through window. See how Battle River turns swift and sharp, westward from Poundmaker's into Little Pine's land. See how black poplar roots push out of dark earth and reach for water. They like to get their feet wet. Sap will be running again in time of budding leaves. You will peel bark, scrape white sap with knife. Then we will make many-berries-feast. Also.

Water is low. Fallen poplar is caught on sandbar, leafless branches jut from spilling waters like white deer antlers. See, stones washed white and smooth, they stretch across water and join shores at bottom of steep banks. They were placed there to make weir of fish baskets by grandmothers. Here, grandfathers snared skunks in time of disappearing buffalo and again in time of fight at Cut Knife Hill.

When I was a child I jumped naked in water. I chased frogs up steep bank. My mother poured water over my muddy body, wrapped me in Company-blanket, and carried me home to share bannock and tea.

Now you see it, how well it runs in my place of belonging. Waskicosihk! Here is Place of Deer's Rump Hill.

Long time ago, war party of Crees followed Song of strange young man to this place of good hunting. They and their children's children have always been known to all Prairie People as Deer's Rump People. This happened long time ago, so long ago, it was before white people came across water in wooden boats.

18

My Other-Granddaughter,

I tell you my dream. I see Man-of-all-songs. He waits for me on Deer's Rump Hill. I am ready to follow him on last four day walk to place of eternal dancing.

But look there! See how blue the hills, how blue the color of woman's spirit, how clefts are touched by light of worthy man's spirit.

Deer's Rump Hill touches sky. See how earth rushes away from neck of river, how thick poplar bluffs spread up and over hill. Now look at back of Deer and see how it stretches from east, across horizon, to west; it joins two homes of sun.

I see dark cloud shading down from place of belonging. It takes the shape of a hand that seems to brush ancient hide of Deer, sweat of hand dampens and darkens hide. Yellow poplar leaves turn and bristle like old hairs, so hand must smooth back of Deer to round Rump.

My Other-Granddaughter,

For four nights I wait for Man-of-all-songs to come to me and speak of these things. On fourth night I am falling asleep and I see him standing on Deer's Rump Hill. His feet are bare, but he has deer hooves strapped to his ankles. They make music for deer's song. Deer robe falls from his shoulders. His arms stretch wide, so his hands touch two horizons and bring them together for me. I am dreaming and I think he is holding out his arms to me, that he wants me to come to him. But he says, "It is not time for last day walking." I want to go to him, but he says, "No. That is not the way to do it now." I must wait longer. Wind is not blowing in the right direction.

Man-of-all-songs has said it. I must tell my Other-grand-daughter of the Way. So it will run well after I am gone.

My Other-Granddaughter,

         Four days and four nights have passed. In dawn of new day I will speak to you. I will tell you my story.

         Maybe. I do not know.

Annika

North Battleford and the surrounding Battle River reserves are located at the junction of prairie and woodland. Ninety miles north and west, the town of Livelong struggles to survive. Rich prairie gumbo is forgotten here. The land turns rocky, and the buildings of the town, tar-papered and false-fronted, huddle together against encroaching spruce and poplar and willow. It is a wild and rugged land, populated with bear and beaver and coyote. It hasn't changed since my Swedish grandmother arrived in her oxcart.

I am living in the original homestead, five washboard miles north of Livelong, on the first quarter section my grandfather bought for one dollar per acre in 1896. The rest of the family land was acquired through the years by my Uncle. The Reed Place, the Holst Place, the Johnson Place, all named for original settlers, belong to my cousins. But this north quarter was left to me by my grandmother. At the south end of Turtle Lake, across the road allowance from Thunderchild's Reserve, it is close to Patchgrove School.

I am living with a grandmother, not my own Swedish one, but a Cree woman known to the townspeople as the Medicine Woman. She has adopted me, in the Indian way, and she calls me her Other-Granddaughter. Old Woman came to live with me on the morning of my Swedish grandmother's funeral.

I was washing the breakfast dishes in rainwater heated on the old wood stove, thinking about the consequences of taking my lardpail and hunting for chokecherries instead of taking my place among the mourners. I didn't want to go to the church. I didn't believe the coffin or grave could contain the spirit of Johanna of Hannas, milkmaid and gleaner.

I stacked the plate, cup, and frying pan to dry on a cookie sheet.

The town would talk. "Annika didn't have enough respect to even go to her grandmother's funeral," Mrs. Hultman would say.

I ladled some warm water from the reservoir into the wash basin and had a sponge bath.

"She's never been the same since she ran off to the city to get schooled." That from the Welshman's wife.

I pulled on my jeans and sweatshirt.

"She's losing it," Beta Tangleflags, the hired-out squatter's woman would say, "here!", tapping her forehead.

"Screw the town!" I said aloud. I decided to make my way downriver today.

I looked out the long-paned window. A bright October day. A strong wind tossed poplar branches, tore the remaining brown shrivelled leaves, swirled them high, then swept them through the grandmother's garden of frost-burned woodflowers. The poplar branches nearest the house slapped the window. I would have to prune it or the first winter storm would force the branch through the window. Shutters fixed from the inside would make the house warmer. Frosted windows emanate a coldness the same way a stove radiates heat. I must not forget to pack the base of the house with straw and mud. I was thinking of jobs to keep myself busy, of the winter-proofing the house and my life needed.

The poplar branch smacked the window with such force it almost shattered it. It swayed, then struck the window again. I heard a small cry, "eeeeee!", a human cry, then something bumped against the log wall.

Colors spinning: blue and flashes of red.

Again the cry: "Eeeeeeeee!"

I ran to the door, yanked it open, and tripped on the step. I fell on the stoop, banged my right knee. I scrambled to my feet and darted around the side of the house.

A tractor tire was suspended by a stout rope from the strongest branch of the large poplar as swing for my cousins' children. A small incredibly old and mis-shapen Cree woman was stuck in the tire. She was spinning around and around, the rope twisting above her. Her hair was unbraided and hid her face like a white shroud. It had the texture of cornsilk. I did not understand the sign of her mourning, the unbraided hair.

The rope twisted out of itself, turned the woman, and swung her in the opposite direction. Her hair swept across her wintered face like cobwebs unravelling.

"Eeeeeeee!" she cried. "Eeeeeeeeee!"

The woman was drunk or crazy, maybe both. She was weeping and not enjoying what I thought of as a regression to childhood games. Swinging in trees from tractor tires was not a game Indian children ever played—was it?

"Eeeeeeee!" she screamed. "Annnnnn-eeeeee!"

She was calling my name. The skin on my face and arms was prickling. My breath was short, and I was beginning to feel dizzy too.

"Eeeeeee! Annnnnn-eeeeee!"

Annie. My grandmother's Swedish cronies called her Annie, a diminutive of Johanna. I was named for her, Annika, which means Little Annie. This Cree woman must have known my grandmother, and she was calling her name.

"My grandmother died," I said, "three days ago. You won't find her here."

"Annnnneeeeeee!" The woman was spinning around and around in the tractor tire. "Annneeeee!" she screamed. Wisps of hair looked damp and clung to her sunken cheeks.

She was grieving. How could she have known Johanna had died? This woman wouldn't read the *Turtleford Sun*. Why would she grieve for Johanna?

She pushed her leather feet in ruts gouged into the earth by the feet of my cousins' children. I stared at the deerhide moccasins. Moccasins. Lined with rabbit fur. Moosehide mittens. Warm leather leggings. They were traded for chickens and flour and sugar.

Yes, there was a woman. She didn't come to the farmhouse on my Uncle's land with the Crees he hired to clear the Hood Place. She came to my grandmother's house. Alone. Every week. To see my grandmother. Without the leather clothing she gave my grandmother, my mother and aunt would have frozen hiking three miles down the railway tracks to school. My cousins and I wore moosehide mittens made by this woman now spinning in a tractor tire.

We went berry picking together, and she showed us

where to find wild turnips and onions. At harvest time, she beheaded and plucked chickens. We carried sandwiches and sealers of tea to the men in the fields. She told us stories. In Cree. She taught me to speak Cree.

Then I remembered how my grandmother had run away, long before my mother and aunt were born, and how this old woman had found her running wild across the prairie and had taken her to live on the reserve—then what? I couldn't finish the thought, couldn't remember all my grandmother had told me about her fear of gophers that she thought were large rats or how she was so afraid of the thunder and lightning she rocked her daughters in her chair all night and sang hymns to them.

Johanna of Hannas was a Swedish homesteader. In 1896 she left her village near Malmo, left her artist lover with a locket of burnished hair, and followed my grandfather, her Scanian woodsman, across an ocean and then a continent in an oxcart. She was terrified by the northern lights, the night drums of the Indians and the distances of the new land. Twice she ran away and twice she was found by the medicine woman. From her she learned the prairie secrets of how to conquer the settlers' fear of being alienated from homeland, family and friends. It was the medicine woman who helped her resolve all her fears of this new unending land and eternal sky. Of course, their friendship went beyond the sharing of bannock and tea and a trade in leather goods.

I dropped to my knees beside the ancient woman. "Old Grandmother," I said in Cree. I didn't know her name. The townspeople and my family always called her the Medicine Woman.

There was a large bundle of bright new cloth beside the swing.

I caught the spinning tire in my hands and stopped it. The grandmother hung limp, her arms dangling, head waggling.

"Don't," I said. "Don't do this."

She lifted her withered head, the old eyes were closed, but she said, "Annie."

"I know," I said. "I know." I eased the feathery body out of the tire. A child would have weighed less, but its baby fat would have given it a solidness. This small body was light, buoyant, and I was afraid she would float up from my arms and be carried away by the wind. "I'll carry you inside," I said.

"*Namoya*," Old Woman said, "I do not go inside white house."

She understood my English. She opened her eyes. Her pupils dilated. "Annneeeeee!" she screamed. She twisted her body, feet kicking, arms flailing. "Annneeeee!" she cried again.

I couldn't know what she saw when she looked at me, but I think she must have seen the young Johanna. "Annika," the family always said, "she takes after the grandmother." The medicine woman must have been afraid of what she thought was the spirit of her friend she had called back from the dead. That was the only explanation I could think of. She certainly was terrified by the sight of me.

"I'm not Annie," I said, "and I'm going to take you inside where it's warm."

Her body sagged in my arms, her head falling back. I shifted her weight so her head was supported by my right shoulder.

I thought she had lost consciousness, but she said, "My bundle."

Beside the swing, a large bundle of bright new cloth tied with rawhide thongs. Holding my back rigid, I bent my knees, slowly lowering both of us to the ground; I managed to catch hold of the thong with my fingers, scoop it up, then slowly, straighten again.

Old Woman was breathing through her mouth, unevenly, and rattling sounds erupted from her chest and throat.

I carried her around the corner of the house, up the three steps to the door, balanced the light body on my knee, and opened the door.

"Annie," Old Woman said, and the word became a sigh that floated over my shoulder behind me. The word was almost tangible, Annie, it was caught and lifted by wind; it disappeared over the rough edge of the road allowance and drifted away through the spruce and poplar on Thunderchild's Reserve.

The homesteader lane, lined with a shelterbelt of hedges, was cut across by the washboard road. On the other side of the ditch, a wagon trail wound into the bush country and land belonging to the first people.

I carried the medicine woman into my grandmother's house.

Death is white. When it enters a room the air seems to thicken like fog hanging heavy over the flats along Turtle River. It leaves nothing untouched. Cats sleeping under the stove will scurry to the door and scratch to get outside. And, that white morning, when Old Woman lay on my grandfather's sheepskin rug before the homesteader range, the log walls seemed to be calcimined rather than varnished brown.

At first I thought she was suffering from shock. The pallor beneath the brown face was deep, and her forehead was beaded with sweat. I wrapped her in quilts and built up the fire in the stove. Kettle on the front burner to make tea.

I knelt beside her.

Old Woman was well over ninety. If she was approximately sixteen years old in 1885, as she said several days later, she must now have been about ninety-six. She had seen the passing of a century, and now she had a beauty that I had never seen when she was seventy. Her sun-dried and wind-toughened skin had worn thin as old rawhide. It was almost transparent, but shining, as if the spirit of the woman would break through the body's barrier and find release. A filmy veil covered her eyes, but the pupils were still dense and dilated. Her eyelids were crusted. A thick mucous clogged her nasal passages. Her beathing sounded like the plugged drains in the sink I once had in my Saskatoon suite.

It was either bronchitis or pneumonia.

What to do with her? She needed a doctor. I had no telephone. The power lines, installed in 1951, were never extended north beyond the flats. I could take Uncle's '46 Fargo and drive down to my cousin's farm to call Old Doc MacRaw, but I was afraid to leave Old Woman alone. Her breathing was too shallow.

Under the quilts, the small body jerked, then stiffened. Her face twisted. "Oiiiiii," she said.

"Where?" I said. "Where do you hurt?"

"Pain," she said in English, "here in my heart."

"I've got to get you to a doctor," I said.

"Medicine," she said in Cree. "Open the bundle," in English.

I placed the bundled cloth on the table. I was afraid to open it. It looked like a medicine bundle, and although I didn't understand the full significance of totems or the power of Indian medicine, I felt I had no right to touch it. I placed my ear against the bundle. I don't know what I expected to hear: the ticking of a time bomb or the hiss of a garter snake. Maybe it contained a drum or dancer's rattle.

If the bundle contained a medicine of some kind there would be nothing dangerous in it. I had to open it.

I fumbled with the knots, untied the rawhide, and jumped back.

No jack-in-the-box. Nothing leaped up from the bundle.

I folded the cloth back. Only more cloth. Layer upon layer of new cloth. I wondered if the different colours meant anything.

In the centre of the bundle I found some braided sweet-grass, a clay dish, a small woman's pipe, yellow ochre folded in waxed birchbark, and tobacco. There was also a large hard object wrapped in blue cloth that must have been her totem. I have since learned that no one is allowed to look upon a totem. I must be kept away from all eyes, especially white ones; it is only worn as a protection in times of danger.

Inside the larger bundle there were many small deerhide bundles, each tied with a different colored ribbon. They all looked alike to me. "Which one?" I said. I held them up, each in turn, so Old Woman could see them. She shook her head.

"Red," she said in English, meaning the bundle tied with a red ribbon. "Make tea. Strong."

Water was boiling in my grandmother's singing kettle. I filled her blue cup with water. "How much?" I asked Old Woman. "A teaspoon?"

She tossed her head.

Quickly I dumped grains of a crushed plant into the water, stirred it, and knelt beside her. I eased my arm under her shoulders and held her up. I wanted to spoon the medicine tea into her gaping mouth, but she grasped my wrist with surprising strength and pulled the cup to her lips. She took a great gulp of the steaming tea, then sank back, and I gently lowered her onto the rug.

Immediately, her face smoothed out, body relaxed. She breathed easier, deeply, and it was as if I had given her a shot of adrenalin.

"Old Grandmother," I said in Cree, "It is good medicine!"

"Foxglove," she said in English.

Later I learned from MacRaw that it contained digitalis and was used by the Indian people for heart disease long before it was discovered by us.

"Well, I've got some homemade remedies of my own," I said.

I filled every pot I had with water and set them to boil on the stove until the steam was so thick in the house water ran in small rivers down the inside window panes. Sweat dripped down my own face. My hair was damp.

I made a mustard plaster and put it on Old Woman's chest.

She scrinched up her nose, twisted her mouth, and turned her head to the wall.

"Annie used to do this for me when I had a cold," I said, "and if you complain like I did I'll get out her wintergreen ointment. Try a whiff of that if you don't like mustard plaster!"

"Son o' bitch," she said. "Got some vanilla?"

"Yes," I laughed, "but I won't give it to you."

I gave her the rest of the foxglove tea, one sip at a time, from the spoon. When the cup was empty, Old Woman looked at me for one slow moment. "You," she said, then turned her face to the wall.

The crisis had passed, the grandmother was sleeping, her breathing even although phlegm in her chest rattled.

It was noon, and I was starving. I heated some *vetebröd* in the oven and cooked a pot of coffee in the Swedish way, dumping grounds in an enamel pot and letting it boil until it was thick.

I sank into my grandmother's rocker, in front of the windows, and I tried to think it through: what to do with the

28

medicine woman.

She was talking in her sleep, a chanting, and I thought she was delirious. Old Woman's medicine tea had helped, but she needed a doctor. I decided to risk leaving her and take the '46 Fargo up to the farmhouse on my cousin's place and call Old Doc MacRaw.

My parka was hanging on a nail at the back door. I shrugged into it, then stepped outside.

The Fargo was huddled under a snow quilt. It had snowed all morning, the first fall of the season, but I hadn't noticed because of the steamed windows.

Inside and outside of my grandmother's house the world had gone white.

Uncle's Fargo was so old it had a running board. The wagonsides were bent and battered, but my cousins still used the truck to haul cords of wood, fence posts and barbed wire. The battery was dead, so I returned to the house for the winter one stored under the stove and lugged it back to the truck. I hit the hood with my fist. Snow slid away on either side, and the latch spring gave way. The hood bounced up, and I hoisted the battery into place, attached the wires. "Blue is for north pole," I chanted, "red is for south." That was the only way I could remember which was negative and which was positive. I slammed the hood down, hit it again, and the lock held. I climbed into the cab, turned the key. Something rolled over under the hood, and it sounded like an old man groaning in his sleep. Then something else caught and the motor churned. I let the oil surge around wherever it surged, the motor warm itself.

Clutch in, squeeze and pull down for first gear. The truck rolled down the lane, cutting a new path and leaving a snow swath on each side.

I had left the gate open. The barbed wire would freeze into the newly-banked snow and I wouldn't be able to drag the posts back from the lane for the rest of the winter. I allowed the truck to coast to a stop, looked both ways for cars and trucks, a city habit. The municipal grader had already been by, the road was cleared, and I thought it strange that I had been so absorbed with the Cree woman I had not heard it roar through the flats.

Across the road allowance the trail into the reserve was so buried in snow I couldn't see where it began. I had lived most of my life here but I had never visited Thunderchild Reserve. I hesitated, wondering if I shouldn't take the main road into the reserve and find Old Woman's relatives. No, I had to get medical attention for her immediately. MacRaw might want to hospitalize her, and the relatives could be notified later.

I shifted gears, turned left, and pulled over a dip in the road. The truck strained as if it were a horse pulling chained logs to the sawmill. It slipped sideways, over a patch of wind-cleared ice, and I braked. Nothing happened, nothing held firm, the wheels were not aligned, and the nose of the truck veered to the right. I swung the wheel to the left, remembering how Auntie always yelled, "Pump 'em! Pump 'em!", meaning the brakes, at Uncle. So I pumped the pedal.

The old wheels found last summer's ruts and locked into them. The Fargo found her way slowly southward. The gas pedal was frozen, maybe the gas line too, and I gripped the wheel, sweating now, letting her coast downhill.

A map was shaping in my head, not an R. M. map with dots for towns, triangles for farmhouses, and rectangles for grain elevators, but a relief map of the Turtleford District. The log house I just left faced the road in the Nordic way. Auntie's house, three granaries nailed and plastered together with mud, was built in Uncle's American style. On the Reed Place, the two-storey English house backed onto the river. The out-buildings on the Holst Place leaned into the wind, and Johnny Tangleflag's shack just squatted on the flats.

Three miles away, Patchgrove School seemed to be perched on top of the timberline. Five miles beyond, the station house, thick-set as a matron, had a swaying sign: LIVELONG, a wish more than a promise. The elevators sprang up from the earth and scraped the sky. All prairie structures were squared off unimaginatively like the farmers' fields.

I wondered where Old Angus MacRaw would be this time of the year. He spent his summers at his cottage at Turtle Lake, he might be there now, but it was late in the season even for him. When I thought about it I realized that he sought refuge from his practice at the lake every time of the year. I would try to get a call through to him from the pavilion. Someone in the beer parlour there could cross the lake in a canoe and take the message to him: Emergency. Go see Annika.

To my right, reserve land was shaped by natural boundaries of river and bush and hills. No fences were needed. Before the federal government built log and tarpaper shacks, all things were circular like the prairie itself. The base of the lodge was round, fire stones were laid in a circle, and the camp was protectively closed in a circle of lodges. An Indian can always see as far as the place where earth meets sky. I could see no opening into the reserve, the solid line of spruce and poplar unbroken by road or rails.

What did I really know about the medicine woman, apart from what the townspeople said of her? She was born on the hunt, somewhere, and she was one of the few Cree who had never taken Treaty. She wandered from reserve to reserve, living with relatives everywhere, but she disappeared into the bush before winter and emerged again in the spring.

Then I remembered her telling my grandmother, one hot dusty August afternoon while we shelled peas on the front stoop, that she had lived on Thunderchild's before the North West Rebellion, that she had visited Poundmaker's Reserve during the outbreak, but she belonged at a place called Deer's Rump Hill, a landmark on what is now Little Pine's Reserve near Old Battleford.

It is not unusual for an Indian to move from place to place, and there has always been a close association between the people of Thunderchild's and those living on the Battle River reserves.

Old Woman must have family everywhere, and I could imagine all of them visiting her in the Turtleford Hospital. Their chanting and story-telling and joke-making would disrupt the hospital efficiency and drive the nurses and Old Doc MacRaw as crazy as long-eared dogs spooked by a porcupine.

I had reached the CPR trunkline. It was laid across the ridge separating the reserve from the squatters' flats. A white cross was nailed to a peeling post, one arm missing, the letters long ago worn away, but no one had replaced the railway crossing sign. Everyone in the north country knew where the crossing was, and anyway, only Indians from Thunderchild's traveled this road, except for my cousins when they worked the north quarter.

In winter, when storms made the roads impassable, the crossing was where my family used to wait with the caboose for Old Angus MacRaw to come from Livelong on the railway jigger.

I tried to slow the truck for the crossing, pumped the brakes, but nothing held. The truck slid toward the cattle ribs, pulled for the ditch. I seemed to hear an airplane landing, the brakes now screaming and pulling back and roaring. Something snapped under my foot, and the Fargo shuddered to a stop in the middle of the tracks. It coughed, spluttered, and died.

"Move it!" I yelled, remembering the carload of Indians who had tried to beat a train and how the coroner had listed sixteen possible causes of death to the driver.

I turned the key, floored the gas pedal. Nothing. I jumped out of the cab, imagining fenders flying, glass shattering, and the Saturday train zooming into oblivion. It was Sunday. No train coming for another week. The old grasshopper could lie on the tracks if it wanted to.

What to do ? It was three miles down the tracks to Livelong, but the garage wouldn't be open on Sunday and probably no tow truck there anyway. Down through the flats, get warm in Johnny Tangleflag's shack, then cut my way up the pasture to the farmhouse.

No train coming until next week. Only an old jigger, its levers pumping, up and down, and Old Angus all tweedy and kilted, McGill University scarf around his neck, colors flying. He waved a bottle of Chivas Regal at me, grinning. His grey felt hat shoved back on his head was teased by wind but he caught it and held it fast.

The jigger was so badly rusted its wheels creaked and squeaked. It bumped into the Fargo, the old geezer toppled sideways, rolled off the jigger and didn't spill a drop of his best Scotch.

"Wanna lift, lady?" he said. "Or a drink? Or both?"

The old bottle-tipping doctor was Canadian-born, and the ancestral gaelic that crept into his speech when he was drunk was the result of too much hooch he made in his own still when Livelong's beer parlour ran out of Johnny Walker and Chivas Regal The Scotch was shipped up north from Saskatoon by bus. For the doctor only.

The box of groceries from Ernie Sommer's store lay on the jigger platform. MacRaw had obviously gone into town, picked up his groceries, had a few drinks in the beer parlour, then stumbled across the street to the station house where he found his old jigger and instead of returning to the lake he abandoned his Studebaker and went down the tracks for a ride. This time he had no purpose, no baby ready to be born, no farmer caught under an overturned tractor; only this ride through what used to be.

"Up at the cabin this late?" I said.

"Ha'e to get awa'," Doc said.

"I was on my way up to the farm," I said. "I need your help, and I was going to call you from there."

"Well, here I am," he said.

I wasn't sure how to approach it now, remembering the winter of '46 and the trouble over an Indian baby he had refused to admit to the Turtleford Hospital. In those days hospitals were strictly segregated and Indians were allowed admittance only to Indian hospitals. Thunderchild's people had to go ninety miles by horse and wagon to Battleford. The Indian baby died, and the town was divided between those who said the law must be changed and those who supported MacRaw.

"I've got a sick person at my place," I said. "Will you come?"

"Don't ha'e me bag wi'me - do I?" MacRaw swayed, tilted the bottle, took a long drink, and wiped his mouth on his tweed sleeve.

The black bag was perched on top of the box, between loaves of bread and a brown package that was suspiciously shaped like a bottle.

"You do," I said, "but I don't know how we're going to get back to my place. Fargo's broken down. Unless you can walk?"

MacRaw twisted up his mouth, corners turned down: his best dour expression. "Well, noo," he said. "No sense buyin' a new one when fixin' the old will do." He reached for the edge of the jigger platform and pulled himself up. He was steadier on his feet than I would have believed possible, boney knees poking almost through the plaid, but then Old MacRaw walked that way drunk or sober.

While I toted his grocery box to the truck and settled it on the cab floor, Old Doc tinkered with something under the hood. I'll never know what he did to the truck, but I'd have believed it if he told me he gave it a drink of the Scot's finest. The Fargo's motor seemed to sneeze. "The choke!" MacRaw yelled at me. I pulled it. The gas pedal floored by itself, the truck shook, then the motor roared. MacRaw was chastizing the Fargo, and it seemed to be talking back.

MacRaw did a Scottish turnabout, he called it a "twinkle", arms raised in the highland fling, feet taking him backwards, forwards, then sideways, and finally to the truck's side. He climbed into the cab. "We're in business again," he said. He pulled a bagpipe chanter from the inside pocket of his tweed jacket.

I slid into the driver's seat, backed the Fargo across the cattle ribs, swung her around onto the Livelong road, then turned her right again, and headed north to the homestead.

"Too-oo m'baoo," Angus MacRaw sang. He twiddled his fingers on the chanter, blew into it, then repeated the sounds made by the chanter. "Tah tah m'bagaaaaaah!" He called it mouth music. The only imaginative expression I'd ever heard from the Scot. "Unemotional people na'e allooo themsel'es anything but work," MacRaw said. "We live in a grim land. We ha'e need o' the plaid to warm the body. We ha'e need o' the pipes to warm the heart."

"What's the name of your song?" I said.

"Marrrrrry's Weddin'," MacRaw said. "Me an' Marrrrry. Wedded to the day." He lay his shaggy head on the top of the worn leather seat, too close to my shoulder.

"I'm not your Mary," I said. "Watch it or I'll roll your rrrrr's reet back at you!"

"You ha'e the smell o' heather aboot you," he said.

"And you smell like an old goat," I said.

"Toooo-oooo m'bagoo!" sang MacRaw. "Tah tah m'bagaaaah!" His scraggly beard tickled my neck.

"I've got the medicine woman at my place," I said.

"Tah-wah-hallla-ooooo! MacRaw bolted upright so

quickly he bumped his head on the dashboard. His can of MacDonald's tobacco slid into the corner and was stopped by the window.

"That old witch has evaded me for theeerty years! Halla! Halla! An' noo ye've foond 'er, Eh?"

"She's very sick," I said. "I'm afraid she's dying."

"Are you certain she's the medicine woman?" MacRaw said. "Do you know what her name is?" He was suddenly sober and the Scotch was gone from his speech, but not the smell of it.

"She calls herself First Woman," I said, "but I don't think that is her real name."

"She knows a lot about herbs and roots, eh?"

"How do you know?" I said. I steered the Fargo around last summer's potholes. New ice in the ruts. It wouldn't melt until spring.

"That's her!" MacRaw said. "The same old woman my patients always called the Medicine Woman. For years they told me about the most remarkable cures. Treatments that worked when mine failed!"

I was afraid MacRaw was going to launch into one of his stories about the Old Days. MacRaw sober was almost worse than MacRaw drunk. Never stopped making up stories, but at least he had put away the chanter and his mournful mouth music.

"They say 'old woman in the bush did it'. One man came to me with mastoids. Two days later he showed up again, the swellings behind his ears were gone and there were no scars. 'Medicine Woman did it', he said. But like all the others he refused to tell me who she was or where I could find her. I sent some of the white mud she packs into gunshot wounds to the lab in Saskatoon. Annika, there's streptomycin in it."

"I know," I said. "The Indians knew about penicillin long before we discovered it. Put mouldy bannock on infections. But, do you know anything about foxglove?" I told him how immediate the effect of the tea was on Old Woman.

"It contains digitalis," MacRaw said. "But I'd like to know what herbs and roots this woman has that we still don't know about. Until recently there have been no histories of malignancies in Indian people."

I took the turn into my lane.

"I must talk to her!" MacRaw said.

"I can't promise that," I said, "only if she is willing to talk to you and tell you what she knows."

I braked the Fargo in front of the stoop, thinking that MacRaw never wanted to be a doctor. He followed the calling of his family and spent his life treating the people of the north country. He took to the bottle to nurse away his homesickness for a land he had never even seen. I couldn't help drawing a parallel between him and the old Cree woman: the last of the oldtime country doctors and the last of the medicine women.

Inside my grandmother's house, the pots were still steaming on the stove.

"Good girl," MacRaw said, "steaming's no good unless you can cut the air with a knife."

Old Woman was still rolled into blankets before the stove.

"Well now what've we done?" MacRaw said, adopting his crusty bedside manner. "Gone and got ourselves feeling poorly, eh?"

Old Woman refused to answer in English or Cree. She understood everything he said, and she gave him her best insult by staring at him.

MacRaw knelt down beside her, took his stethoscope from his black bag. "Let's have a listen to the old heart," he said.

Old Woman clutched her blanket, pulled it closer to her neck. "Who is this person?" she said to me in Cree.

"Doctor MacRaw," I said, "he's come to see you."

"He smells," she said in Cree. "Expensive scotch," in English.

"And you smell like mustard," MacRaw laughed. He took the withered hands in his own arthritic ones, lay them on each side of her, then peeled away the layers of blankets. Earplugs in, he blew on the steel end of the stethoscope to warm it with his strong breath, then listened to her heartbeat.

"He listens" Old Woman said to me, "but he cannot hear drumming of ancient move-along-dance of women."

"How long have you had pain?" MacRaw asked her,

but Old Woman refused to answer until I translated the question into Cree.

"I do not know," she said to me, "it is many summers older than this white house, than shacks foodgivers built along riverbank."

"Doesn't she speak English?" MacRaw said, folding his stethoscope and tucking it back in his black bag. "Only words like beer and scotch, eh? Know them well myself."

"You do not give me away," Old Woman said.

"Ask her how long she has had pain in her chest," MacRaw said.

"It is as old as papers my fathers gave their names to," Old Woman said, "as old as those forgotten and broken promises. I tell you it does not belong to me but to all People. Naaa! White man cannot understand."

"A long time," I said to MacRaw.

Old Doc attempted a physical examination of the old Cree, but it became a tussle of blankets and fluttering hands. They reminded me of two old dogs fussing around an abandoned fox den.

MacRaw checked her ears and eyes with a penlight.

"What can he hear and see?" Old Woman said.

He stretched and bent her twisted leg. "When was it broken?" he said.

"He wants to know about your leg," I said.

"I fell from cattle car of the *train* we called iron horse," Old Woman said. "That was eleven summers after the Outbreak. Long knives drove us out of Montana across dividing-line back to Valley of Battle River."

"She fell from a boxcar and broke her leg in 1896," I said. "Something about the cavalry driving Crees over the border back into Canada. She must have been in exile for ten years after the Rebellion."

"Old wounds coming back to haunt us," MacRaw said. "Well, nothing we can do about it now. Too late to rebreak it and reset it. Probably was set with splints in those days. Interesting." MacRaw reached again into his well-travelled bag for his prescription pad. It was yellowed and tattered at the edges. Scribbling in the secret language known only to medical people and druggists, he said, "I'd like to do a blood count on her, but I wouldn't risk moving her to hospital. Keep it up, Annika, with the foxglove tea, the mustard plasters and steaming. I'll leave some penicillin pills with you—one every three to four hours—got to clear up those lungs. So often its the pneumonia that takes the old ones in the end." He handed me the paper. "Get Ernie Sommers to fill this when you need it."

"He has some medicine for you," I said to Old Woman.

"What does this man know of medicine?" she snorted. "His medicine cannot take away pain of remembering what happened to People."

"Will you tell me what happened to people?" I asked, "tell me what happened to you?" I was so strongly aware of how much history Old Woman had lived, history that was never revealed to me in school books, and I wanted to hear it from her.

"I do not like him," Old Woman said. "Send him away. Then I tell you my story. Maybe."

"What will you do with her?" MacRaw said. "Tell her to go and live with her relatives on the reserve. Or, if she pulls through, I can arrange to put her in an old folks' home in Battleford that accepts Indians."

"Where do you live?" I asked Old Woman. "Do you want to go back to left-over-land?"

"I am not looked-after-person," she said. "I do not know what this means: *welfare*."

"She never took Treaty," I said to MacRaw.

"I want to go to my place of belonging," Old Woman said. "I want to live near Battle River where I can see Deer's Rump Hill."

"Then I will take you there," I said, "when you no longer have coughing sickness."

"What's going on between you?" MacRaw said. "What're you up to now, Annika?"

"I can't turn her away," I said. "I'm going to look after her."

"Always takin' in stray cats," MacRaw said. "They messed in the clothes cupboard and your aunt used to chase them and you out of the house with a broom."

"I'll drive you back to the crossing," I said, "or into Livelong if you prefer."

"Annika, Annika," MacRaw said, shaking his wooly head and lifting his black bag. "See if you can talk to her. Get a list of herbs and roots if you can." At the door, he said, "I'm goin' back the same way I came. On the jigger."

"An' there's noo changin' yer mind aboot it," I laughed.

I drove MacRaw back to the crossing. The old doctor pumped his way back to Livelong on the jigger, and I went up to the farm house to get the cot and mattress for Old Woman that I knew was stored in an unused granary.

When I returned home, Old Woman turned her face to the wall and refused to talk to me. She was silent for four days.

It was the morning of the fifth day. I was burrowed into my quilts in the sleeping loft, only my nose sticking out of the covers, and I stared at icicles hanging from the central beam of my grandmother's house. The first log hewn, she once told me, is the guardian tree of the home.

It was too cold to get up, and I thought of how Crees called January the month when frost explodes on trees. It was only October, and I renamed it the month when frost begins to crackle in the joints of the house.

My jeans and sweaters were stiffening on a nail hammered into the wallboard above my bed. I reached up, pulled my clothes under the quilts to warm them, then dressed under the bedcovers. I pulled on extra socks over my bed stockings.

Ice on the rungs, and I slid down the ladderway to the wooden floor. Overnight, frost had thickened on the windows. Water was frozen in the washbasin.

Old Woman was a buried lump of blankets next to the stove.

I rattled the grates so last night's ashes fell into the iron drawer at the bottom of the stove, promising Old Woman I would empty it after breakfast. She turned in her sleep and sank deeper into the quilts.

I blew on my hands. They were chapped, the skin dry and scaling, and so cramped with cold it hurt to grasp the lifter and remove the front lid from the stove.

Weekly newspapers were stacked beside the kindling box. I crumpled the first few pages of *The Western Producer* and shoved them into the stove, remembering pen pals and comics and poetry I once found in those pages. Now I was about to start a fire with an article on the proposed Gardiner

Dam and Diefenbaker Lake at Outlook. I wondered what Old Woman would say about engineers dynamiting tons and tons of rock and making a lake on the prairie. I decided to ask her during breakfast, maybe provoke her enough so she would speak to me.

"*Moniyaw*, they are changing face of land!" The remembered voice belonged to Old Woman. We had toted chicken sandwiches and sealers of tea to the men repairing the bridge over Turtle River. The grandmothers spread their skirts over large boulders and watched Uncle, other municipal councilmen, and hired Crees heave wooden beams on their sweating shoulders and lift them into place under the arch of the bridge. They were reinforcing a structure first built by my grandfather and his brother in 1904. During the break, they talked about destroying the beaver dam, about building a culvert, and straightening the road.

"Earth does her own changing," Johanna had said, and the medicine woman told us both the story of *Mistasinē,* the big rock near Outlook.

According to legend, Kind-old-man-buffalo had found a lost boy. He gave him a kidney to eat when he was hungry, wrapped him in buffalo fur when snow and wind blew them across the prairie, and taught him how to fight during the mating season. Kind-old-man-buffalo had finally turned the lost boy into a big rock that looked like an over-sized buffalo lying down. For centuries, the Plains Indians had left offerings there.

Now, engineers found the rock had iceberg dimensions and extended beneath the earth to such a great depth it could only be blasted out of the ground with TNT. The Federation of Saskatchewan Indians had raised thousands of dollars in an attempt to save the sacred site, but the project was going ahead as planned. The big rock would be destroyed, but *Mistasinē* would live in pieces.

I stacked poplar kindling around the crumpled paper like tipi frames and added three pieces of split birch. I struck a match on top of the stove and touched flame to the black and white drawing of Blackstrap, the first man-made mountain soon to be raised near Saskatoon.

I put my grandmother's singing kettle and a pot of coffee on the back burners: tea, of course, for Old Woman, but the Swede in me couldn't start the day without strong coffee.

Frying pan for bacon and eggs on the front burner. A tin rack for toasting bread over the fire.

"My Other-Granddaughter."

I jumped. My knee hit the latch on the oven door.

Old Woman had spoken to me, the first word uttered in four too-silent days. She was lying on her back. Her face was turned towards me instead of the wall.

"Well!" I said. "Good morning!"

She tried to sit up, lifted her withered head from the pillows.

"Feeling better today?" I said, stacking the pillows against the wall and propping her against them. "I've got a surprise for you. Guinness Stout to help your appetite."

Old Woman didn't answer, and I thought it was because I was speaking English.

"You look good," I said in Cree. I ladled some warm water from the reservoir into the washbasin. "You look good in dawn of new day," I said again. I washed her face and hands.

The deep pallor remained beneath the brown skin, but her eyes were bright and no longer crusted around the lids. She coughed. Her chest was looser, breathing easier.

The coffee was cooked. Yes, cooked. Swedes never percolate; they dump ground coffee into a pot of boiling water and wait until it is thick as molasses. I poured myself a strong cup, set it on the reservoir, and buttered the toasted bread. "I still don't like cardamom seeds," I continued, "but I guess my grandmother was right. It wouldn't be lifebread without them." I munched like a true *Kaffa Chera*, hoping my references to Johanna would evoke a response from Old Woman.

I fixed her breakfast plate, pulled a chair close to her cot, and fed her.

I remembered my grandmother's annoying habit. She never said thank you or that's enough when I poured coffee into her blue cup; she just pulled the cup away and coffee spilled onto the oilcloth. "Remember Annie and her cronies around the table?" I said to Old Woman. "Always harping on the same string." They cried when they met and cried when they dunked the *vetebröd* in coffee and cried when they parted.

"Remember Mrs. Hultman?" I asked Old Woman.

" 'Annika is a northlander,' she always said, 'she wrangles and bangles about the same thing.' 'Yes,' Johanna answered, 'but whose granddaughter is she?' "

"And you are my Other-Grandmother," I said, "I'll fry bannock today instead of baking *vetebröd*."

"I am Old Woman, humble woman, poor woman. But I will try to speak to you."

Those were the words she always used to start a story. I ladled water into the dishpan.

"Before. When your grandmother was here. I did not go inside white house. Now she is gone, and you drag me inside. It is like winter house on left-over-land. All first houses the same."

I nodded, swirled soapy water over the plates with a dishrag.

"Long time ago. On left-over-land, my Horse-dance-maker cut trees for house. I remember how it hurt him to strike living thing."

Old Woman coughed. I gave her my grandmother's china spitting bowl. She hunched over it.

"It's time to take your medicine," I said.

"Naaaaaaa!" Old Woman said. "That is not medicine."

"Is that why you wouldn't talk to me for four days?" I took the penicillin pills from the cupboard.

"Take medicine," I said in Cree, "and I'll make rosehip tea."

"Pine needle tea stronger," she said.

"Okay. Pine needle. Now open your mouth. That's it. Now the water. Swallow!"

Old Woman took MacRaw's medicine, spilled water on her chin, then turned her face to the wall and refused to speak.

I sat down in the rocker, propped my feet on the open oven door. "Want to go back to the reserve?" I asked.

"When you are ready to listen," she said.

"I'm sorry," I said.

"I have seen white men change face of land. They build homes of sod, then wood, now *steel* and *concrete*. Now I see how they have changed and hardened face of my Other-granddaughter."

I had no answer for Old Woman. English is my first language, but I understand Swedish and Cree. Johanna spoke to me in all three languages, but I was allowed to answer only in English. She sent me to university in Saskatoon, and like Old Woman now, she found, when I returned, I had forgotten the old ways of doing and saying things.

"Naaaa!" Old Woman yelled. "You asked me to speak my name and names of my fathers to this person who tells you I am dying. Elders have said it. Never speak Name of father or grandfather. Name of mother or grandmother. You show no respect! You say Name of dreamspirit, Real Name, and that is going against all we believe!"

"Ni-matahten," I said.

I listened to Old Woman, and I felt how language erupted from landscape, how the name for a bird imitated its song. Her sentences flowed strong and deep as the long curve of Battle River, and I began to think in sentences instead of words. *"Miyopayiwin,"* she said. "It runs well." *Miyopayiwin.*

I allowed Old Woman's words to shape story-paintings behind my own eyes. I lost myself in a memory that didn't belong to me but was full of promises for me.

Old Woman held my hands between hers. "I tell you I have thought on it for four days. But I have dreamed on it for four nights. My dream is why I have chosen to speak the Way to you. My Other-Granddaughter, I tell you my dream. I see Man-of-all-songs. He waits for me on Deer's Rump Hill. I am ready to follow him on last four-day walk to place of eternal dancing. . . . For four nights I wait for Man-of-all-songs to come to me and speak of these things. On fourth night, I am falling asleep and I see him standing on Deer's Rump Hill. His feet are bare, but he has deer hooves strapped to his ankles. They make music for song of deer. Deer robe falls from his shoulders. His arms stretch wide, and his hands touch two horizons, bring them together for me."

On the windows, frost was shaping prairie patterns. Outside, there was a shelterbelt of caragana lining the lane and a wall of tall northern spruce beyond the north quarter. But I shared Old Woman's illusion of Deer's Rump Hill and her dreamspirit. She carried us both through frosted glass and tree barriers to her place of belonging.

I remembered my grandmother telling me how those same blue spruce had reminded my grandfather of his home in Vastergötland. While he lay dying in this homestead, years before I was born, he told stories of his youth in Sweden. It is the occupation of the old to live in the past.

Old Woman was tired. I was about to insist that she have some soup, then sleep, when she finished what had become an ancient speechmaker's oration by saying:

"My Other-Granddaughter, four days and four nights have passed. In dawn of new day I will speak to you. I will tell you my story. Maybe. I do not know."

Ahtokwe! It was a typical concluding remark. She couldn't say *Ēkosan* because she hadn't said it all. Her apparent indecisiveness was not unusual. Crees have always said "Maybe" even when they have reached a decision. It was maddening to government agents.

That afternoon, Old Woman slept deeply. No chanting or groaning, with only intermittent coughing.

By evening, the temperature was dropping again. After supper, I built a fire in the stove, then changed into night clothes quickly. I pulled my flannelette night gown and chenille bathrobe over my head before stepping out of my jeans. Winter dressing and undressing is a functional art to farm folk.

I shoved the rocking chair close to the stove again, propped my slippered feet on the open oven door, and settled in for an evening of story telling. Old Woman told me how she left Canada after the North West Rebellion of 1885. It was more than a remembering.

Old Woman

This is happening long ago. So long ago, this is happening, there are now, no True Leaders to show us the Way.

Outbreak is over, Riel hanged in place where bones lie. Poundmaker and Big Bear are shut away behind stone walls in place called Stony Mountain. Wandering Spirit tried to shoot himself, but he lived to feel rope tighten and break his neck. Man-without-blood, Coat-turned-inside-out, Miserable Man, Round-the-sky, Iron Body and Bad Arrow were hanged at place of the forks of Battle River, ropes cut so bodies dropped through trap door into wooden boxes. They were carted away and buried under sand.

River People do not understand what is happening.

In last days, before Metis were defeated at Batoche, providers searched for small game and looted settlers' cabins. Runners carried messages to Leaders all across prairie. Warriors fought at Frog Lake and Hobbema, at Duck Lake and Frenchman's Butte. So we were all part of it.

At final surrender, there were people from every piece of left-over-land. Thunderchild hid with Woods People, Star Blanket and Big Child took shelter with white-collars; they were the only Cree Leaders who did not take part. So River People say this Soldier Leader, Middleton, should build stone walls around all left-over-lands and hold all people prisoners instead of just our Leaders and those he thinks did the fighting and looting.

River People do not understand. It is true there can be no more fighting without War Leaders. But how can there be peace without our Peace Makers? If Woman Leader and her headmen want to blame someone, they should look to men-who-hand-out-food and the power behind them. They should look to themselves for causes of Outbreak.

After he took our Leaders away, Soldier Leader sent us back to left-over-lands. But people in Battleford want to teach us that rights of belonging did not pass into our hands when we looted stores. So redcoats are rounding up those they think did the looting and are taking them back to Battleford. Those who are not accused of going against Woman Leader are told it is bad for them to go away from left-over-land without a foodgiver's paper saying they can go. Some are put away in redcoats' guard room, but most are being sent away to Stony Mountain for as long as fourteen years.

Even so, white people are not satisfied. They raid our camps and take what they want. Soldiers from the east are going home with ceremonial dress, furs and trinkets.

So Outbreak is over. Buffalo are gone. Promises are not kept. We have no way to make a start on left-over-lands: no hoes, no rakes, no cattle, no medicine chest, no school. Nothing has changed with the fighting. Our horses were taken away and we are confined to left-over-lands. We cannot sell a load of hay or wood. Soldier Leader says we have broken promises and there will not be Treaty-payment-time. Treaty money will go to pay for damage to white people's stores and homes. So we still have summer's hungry pup visiting our lodges. He will never go away now.

We are so afraid of this punishment. We are afraid of hanging rope. We have decided to go across dividing-line and live in Montana. We will go to live with Crow People, Blackfoot, Sioux, Deer-robes-people; all Other and Different People.

We are moving south in Red River carts, in wagons, and on foot. We travel in small family groups to avoid suspicion. Redcoats are searching for more *rebels* and we are afraid of them following us, capturing us, and taking us back to Battleford for hanging. Any man found off his left-over-land without a say-so-paper from his foodgiver will be arrested and punished on suspicion of being a *rebel*. That one, Dewdney, who thinks cod liver oil will cure covered-with-spots-disease, he says he will give any loyal Indian fifty dollars for telling him names of people who are running away. But no one will betray River People.

We are defeated. We shall be known as Alienated-ones, estranged from family and friends and tribe. Many times we traveled to Land-of-cactus, but never before without thinking about returning. Going away is a bad thing. Elders have said it. By leaving we gain freedom to wander and make our own Way, but we lose freedom to live as one people and right to return.

We will search for a new Way, without buffalo, but also without foodgivers and white-collars and redcoats to tell us what to do.

Black shadow was drawn over prairie with killing of buffalo. It was defined by scratching stick of Woman Leader's men at time of signing promises. It was stretched by barbed wire fences around settlers' lands. Black shadow falls over our Way again. We have lost our Leaders. All of them. Those who were not hanged or put in prison are flying away to Montana.

This is happening to People, long time ago.

So long ago this is happening to me. It is time of hatching eggs and flying up of young ducks. I have seen four-times-four summers in Valley of Battle River. I am making my first child in my belly. But I must leave my place of belonging. It is wrong time for going away.

I am alone in centre of summer camp that slopes down from Story-teller-hill. Above me lights of night-sky-dancers circle swallow-tailed cones of **People's lodges.** They drop closer and closer to ground. Departed-ones-dancing are calling River People to join them.

Protective circle of lodges is broken in five places. Five lodges are missing. Five fireplaces are cold. Families of Lucky Man, Little Poplar, Fox, and Bowboy left at different times to avoid suspicion. Lucky Man said we must stay away from river landings where redcoats will look for us. We will join together four camps from now and cross Saskatchewan River where current runs swiftly.

All night each head of family made Give-away-dance and presented small bundled gift to those departing. There was no farewell song, no crier racing around circle of lodges, no dogs nipping horses' heels, no children jumping up and down and waving to painted warriors going on horseraid.

Now we are last to leave, mother, Horse-dance-maker and I. It is wrong time for going away.

River People have disappeared inside tents. Those who stay behind are unable to sleep, some weeping, others praying. My eldest sister's son howls for his mother's milk, the cry sharp and cutting through deeper and steadier chant of elders. He is Poundmaker's newborn son and he is Speak-often-person like his father who was Speechmaker. I hear cry of one who will always be too-much-hungry. I feel angry fists of my own unborn child beat against my soft skin walls, but I hold him safe inside. I think our sons, brothers who may never meet, they will always know what it is to be too-much-hungry.

My eldest sister, I will miss her. She is Poundmaker's youngest and last woman. She will wait for him to come back from Stony Mountain. She leans over her child and her shadow leaps out at me from skin wall. Her lodge begins to move away from me. It is shaped like a woman.

All lodges are moving in a circle around me, all are dancing, all the shape of women making feast for departed-ones. They dance with bundles belonging to the dead. They leave spaces in circle for those who have departed.

I am not alone now, but feeling of being alone is growing into feeling of being apart, and it is so strong in me, I feel as if each time I said "Ēkosan!" to departing-ones they became departed-ones. It is the same as if they are dying and part of me is dying. Also.

Night-sky-dancers above me and around me. Lodges dancing all around me. Earth and sky are circling together. I kneel before cold ashes of my mother's fire, where her lodge once held my family. Anchor ropes have been untied, lodgepoles taken down and lashed together with rawhide, skin coverings folded, winter and summer linings rolled up: all bundled into wagon.

All day I have been pulled in two directions. I want to go with Horse-dance-maker to a safer place for him. He is not a fighting man, but he went to Battleford with Poundmaker and he was there at Cut Knife Hill. He did not kill anyone, but he took part in a small way. He is afraid of hanging rope. So I want to go south with him, but it is wrong time for going away.

I am afraid of redcoats who search for people who looted Battleford. I think they know women went in wagons and did most of the taking away of flour and bacon and cloth. I was there, with my mother and grandmothers, and I am afraid of redcoats. Soldier Leaders do not put women away behind stone walls, do not hang them for going to Battleford to find food for their children. But they fired big guns on sleeping lodges. So I am afraid of redcoats.

All day I had this feeling of restlessness, but it is not the same as wanting to go travelling when young birds call People upriver. All day I felt it was time to put things in their place in lodge, to move proper things to isolating tent. I felt like nesting. I knew it was wrong time for going away. I should have been making ready to go to isolating tent with my mother and grandmothers.

I know my time is near. Child has dropped and I carry him low. His head presses so heavy between my legs I must often go to out-of-sight-place to release my water. I should be going to isolating tent, but I have been making ready to go in other direction. I have been moving camp, not making camp.

I curl in cold ashes of my mother's fireplace. I will give birth to my first child here.

Above swallow-tailed cones of skin lodges, far above empty winter shacks huddling along riverbank, northern lights shade up from grey into black of night. So I cannot see Deer's Rump Hill, but I feel it is there, and I do not want to leave my place of belonging. I want my first child to be born here.

"That is not the way to do it!" It is my mother. She is too-much-woman. It is the same as how it was Big Bear was too-much-bear. She wears travelling clothes: dress coarse as canvas and heavy as tent made of bad material that Company trades for five fox furs; long fringed shawl; bright new scarf made from blue silk she stole from Little Bearskin's trading post; and unbeaded moccasins.

I burrow into ashes, spread my arms and push my hands deep until I feel warmth of old fires. My toes press against stones circling fireplace. My body curves into earth. I will make a grey nest to have my child in. It will rise out of ashes and I will call him Ashes Boy.

"That is not the way to do it!" Too-much-woman grabs my thin arms with her bearpaw hands. She pulls me from dead fire.

My toes turn inward, knees buckle, and my legs will not hold me. I sag against her heaving breasts. "I do not go." That is all I can say to her.

She holds me. It is the same as if Bear has come, all grizzly and panting and holding me fiercely. I feel strength of Bear passing from her to and in and through me. I want to fight it. I want to sink back into my shallow grave of ashes.

Bear Woman will not allow it. "Earth is home," she says. She holds me away from her, props me up with huge hands. "No matter where we go. There is home!" She brushes ashes from my face, tucks my hair inside my scarf, and folds Company-blanket around my shoulders. "So we go to Land-of-cactus. Earth is Only Mother and She is the same on That Side of dividing-line as She is on This Side. Go! Go!"

I stumble, sway with wind blowing long buffalo grass. I do not fall back to earth, but I am stubborn too, and I do not walk. I fix my feet to earth, push my rawhide toes into sandy soil.

Bear Woman heaves her heavy body over wagon side, swings thick legs over, and she settles on top of bundles. "You walk behind!" she yells at me.

Horse-dance-maker smacks horses' rumps with rope. Wagon lurches forward. Horses strain. Wooden wheels turn. Wagon begins slow rumbling down old trail towards place where scaffolds are built for the dead.

"You walk behind!" my mother yells again. "It is only way to do it now. You walk behind! Long way! Going will be easier for you."

I take one step and stop.

"Walk through your sadness to other side of it!" Her voice is low and deep, but it carries through night and through wind making poplar leaves rustle.

I take long slow steps.

"Walk! Walk far! When you give birth it will go easier for you." Bear Woman turns her wide back to me.

Horse-dance-maker sings his Song to horses. He coaxes them away from grasses. Wagon hugs curve at lower end of Story-teller-hill. Wooden sides brush sacred cloth drooping from scaffolds for the dead. Each poplar pole is a trail man must take on his last four day walk, poles of scaffold crossing because many ancestors meet each man and help him on his way.

Wagon drops into valley, disappears into place where dark of land meets dark of sky. I follow sound of wooden wheels creaking and iron rims striking stones.

I will come back in dawn of new day. I will come back to my place of belonging. There is no word for it. *Goodbye* is too final. I will see people I leave behind in dawn of new day.

That is all for now.

I am last person in long line of departing-ones. Far ahead spaces between four families must be closing. Going is slow, but they will meet at lake where children dance when sun goes down. It is a long way to first rest camp, to meeting place. A longer way to dividing-line. Too long a way to Cree Crossing.

I follow wagon. Rough cracked ruts made by Red River carts are hard under my rawhide feet. I stumble, trip on unearthed root, fall, my hands and knees slamming against dried mud.

I am afraid my unborn child is hurt. My breath is lost, and I stay on all fours, panting to catch it back. My back sags, weight of child pulling down, so I feel like old sway-back-horse. I want to roll over on my side, roll into ditch and hide in long grasses. I want to let go of crying inside my chest and pain of going away too soon. If I start crying now I will never stop.

I push with my hands. I heave my swaying body up, balance on my feet, feeling dizzy again. My hands are scraped raw, but I brush dirt from my long skirt. My leggings are torn, both knees skinned and bleeding.

My mother signs: you ride in wagon now?

I wave to her: No. Go on. It is not time yet.

My back is young and strong, straight as lodgepole pine in centre of women's tent, but it is tired from carrying so long and so far my heavy belly. I lean backwards, stretch, and knead my back. Small and growing pain eases. Tight feeling loosens and flows away under my hands.

Child stirs in my belly, small hands pushing down, feet kicking high under my ribs. It is like flutter of wings and skittering of birdfeet. When he kicks like that and pushes against walls holding him, he makes breathing hard to do for me. I take in great gulps of night air until sky stops spinning around me. I think I will call him Flying-away-too-soon.

Small tensing under curve of my belly. New feeling I have never had before, not pain, but a tightening, as if a fist has grabbed hold of something low inside me, twists, then lets go.

I cradle my swollen belly with both arms, hold it and my unborn child. Go back to sleep, I tell him, because it is not time yet. Sleep until we make camp.

I trudge on, head down, not looking back, but a shadow lies behind my eyes:

I see long back of Deer's Rump Hill stretching away, behind me, and a grey upright form, a tall figure, the shape of a man with out-stretched arms. He walks down from Hill, follows me, coming closer and closer; until I feel he is near, behind me now. His arms curve around me but do not touch me. I feel as if I am wrapped in softest tanned deerhide. If I drop my arms to my sides I will feel fringes on his sleeves. He is holding me up, supporting me and my child, carrying us along. I think I hear a voice saying, "I will go with you. I am always here with you." Only later will I know who he really is, why he comes to me this way, and then I will know full meaning of my dream. But this is only first time he comes to me and I turn him away.

My belly seizes. My skin tightens. It is the same as if a rawhide rope has been tied under my belly, knot in middle of my lower back. Someone is pulling it tighter and tighter, tugging, then pulling me forward; so I want to run, taking small quick steps, but running hard behind wagon. I clutch my belly. I want to run in four directions, run in full circle until rope is cut and child finds his own way.

Now I understand why my mother made me walk behind wagon. I walk through darkness of night, through all my pain, and I know there will be light of new day and new child on other side of it. I walk. Soul of a person must walk through wind on night of coming into life. I walk my child.

Night air grows cool all around me. I fasten blanket

tighter around my drooping shoulders. I hold firmer my lengthening circle of belly. Wind plays with fringes, lifts scarf away from my neck, pushes hard against my back, flattens my skirt against my legs.

Tightening inside again. I cannot run in straight line behind wagon. I scurry around myself, trace circles in dust with rawhide toes.

It is not pain I feel, but a strange way of saying no to letting go of my first child. My body tightens against birth to come as if it does not want to give up child, but hold him forever against cold of night and fear of unknown things ahead. I do not know what circle of prairie holds for him on other side of dividing-line. If it will be safe for him there. Old Way is gone on That Side too. It vanished with buffalo. There will be no Way for my first child to become worthy. No horseraids. No battles against Blackfoot. He will not ride into camp singing of success in the hunt, an albino calf slung over his horse's neck. There is no Way for him to receive Real Name in ceremony. No Leader to make that Dance. I am afraid for my child.

Wagon has stopped. Horse-dance-maker hunches over reins. Sighing and rumblings are coming from under his black hat, and I think he is praying.

Bear Woman sits stiffly in wagonbox, staring into night, looking at point between north and east. I sign to her that I will find out-of-sight-place to release my water again. She nods, and I see that she is silently crying. Tears chase each other down smooth curves of her full cheeks. How can this be so? I have never seen my mother cry before.

I wade through long buffalo grass. Behind willows I squat. No water comes. It is not time for waterbag to break, it just feels like it.

I curl on my side, and my right hand touches stone. I tuck my skirts around my legs, and my left foot touches stone. I lay my hot face against Grandfather Rock, and my left hand touches stone. I grope forward, my hands rooting through grass. Stone after stone. Arranged in a circle. A forgotten fireplace.

Through grey night I see skeleton of lodgepoles reaching up to form swallow-tailed cone. Then I know why wagon stopped, why Horse-dance-maker prays, why my mother weeps. It is deserted Thirst-dance-camp where Big Bear made rain four season ago. Lodgepoles of his Spirit Lodge are bare. No sacred cloth flutters from Centre-pole. Thunderbird's nest is gone.

I crouch in long grass that leans over and almost hides cold fireplace where once Keeper-of-fire and Keeper-of-pipe made ready to dance. I stare at wall of poles, at shadows lengthening and wavering and bursting into Thirst-dancers obeying drums' call and dreamspirits' teachings. Big Bear sits at far end, naked except for his breech clout. He is painted with clay. Bundled tobacco tied to his braids bounce on his sagging shoulders. He is Thirst-dance-maker. There is power in his voice, power in his Song, and greatest power of all Parent-of-bear in his medicine bundle. For four days and four nights he makes rain.

I knew nothing, then, of his calling all Leaders together or how he wanted all People to join together so promises would be kept by Woman Leader and her headmen. I knew nothing of long council meetings, of bundled tobacco Big Bear and Poundmaker sent to Leaders all across prairie. I only knew the Dance.

I forgot buffalo were gone. I forgot how I had grown too thin to be beautiful, how children cried at night for food mothers could not give them. I only knew the Dance. I did not think, then, how short life is; I danced to make ancestors in next place happy.

I stayed on women's side of Lodge. I felt eyes of new-young-men upon me, but only cared that Horse-dance-maker watched me.

Power of drum moved me. I felt thunder in every part of me. I wanted to dance wildly, my feet skittering like bird, my arms dipping and swooping until I flew. But that was not how to make women's move-along-dance, grandmothers said so, new-young-women must dance slowly around circle.

So I was ready for Horse-dance-maker to crawl under tentflap and place blue marriage bead between my breasts. I did not hold back then; all wanting of him rushed together in me and I made the dance beneath him. I felt his strength surge through me. How could I think of food when Dance is made and Horse-dance-maker has chosen me to be his first woman?

54

Now he comes to me again, under cover of sky, but it is different this time. He does not speak. He drops to his knees beside me and folds me in his arms.

I lean against him, comfortable with him. I rub my nose under his chin. Smell of him is so good: leather, tobacco, sweat.

"How does it go with you?" he says.

"It is not time. But soon."

Unborn kicks against his father's forearm. Horse-dance-maker laughs. "He will be born fighting!"

"I think there will be no more fighting," I say, "and no more War Leaders."

"Even the unborn will not forget what happened." Horse-dance-maker is not a fighting man. He has never gone on raids against Blackfoot. But there is a struggling in him that I can feel when I am with him and not give name to. He will fight for people, in a different way from our Leaders, but he will find a new way for us to go on living on That Side of dividing-line. I do not know how this can be. It is something I can only feel.

I am his only woman, then, and I am enfolded by him, his right arm supporting my weakening back, left arm sliding under hills of my breasts. I know he too is remembering Big Bear's Thirst Dance and how it was with us then.

My underbelly seizes again, and I clench my teeth. I say nothing, but Horse-dance-maker can feel it. He lets his arms fall loosely to his sides.

"I did not want it to be this way," he says. "I should not be with you now."

"So what is new about children being born when People are moving around?" I say. "Children are always born on the hunt. They are born on This Side. They are born on That Side."

"We make camp here," he says.

"Not in sacred place," I say.

"Then you ride in wagon."

"No. When it is time I will tell you and my mother will put up lodge. Our child will be born in the exact way of it. Now you go."

"You ride in wagon!" Horse-dance-maker yells.

"It is easier to be walking!" I yell back. "Go!"

We have never shouted at each other before. He plows through long grass, and he beats low poplar branches with his hat. He yells, "Stubborn woman!"

I am kneeling in sacred place, and then, I find myself praying:

"I must go away. I must go away for a long time. I cannot know what I will find on other side of dividing-line.

"I pray that good things will go with us, so it will run well for People on That Side.

"I pray for my unborn child. May he never know Covered-with-sores-disease or coughing sicknesses. May he never hear growl of hungry pup. May he never see his belly swell and limbs shrink from being too-much-hungry.

"Elders have said buffalo disappeared underground to escape riflemen but one day their heads will reappear and they will rise up out of wallows. Bring buffalo back. So it will run well again for People. Bring buffalo back and end long visit of summer pup.

"Bring buffalo back so there will be a tomorrow for my child and for his children and for their children. Bring buffalo back so there will be a Way for him to become worthy.

"Bring buffalo back and I will dance. For four days I will fast. For four nights I will pray. This I promise.

"Bring buffalo back!"

At top of Centre-pole of Spirit Lodge, where once Big Bear placed Thunderbird's nest, dark storm clouds build into massive shape of angry face. It is not Piyeso, Thunderbird, I see, but Man-of-all-songs. He has followed me from Deer's Rump Hill to place of Big Bear's Dance.

Man-of-all-songs wears buffalo head-dress, horns pointing to direction I must take: south. His black hair grows shaggy down each side of his face. He rises above Centre-pole, arms lifting skyward, and great folds of his robe fall from his shoulders to form skin covering for Lodge.

I am only new-young-woman. I feel it in my heart's drumming that I am not worthy of this dream.

On night a child is born it is Old Woman who must dream of his future, who must give him a Name. I am only first woman of Horse-dance-maker.

I do not understand what is happening to me, and my fear is so great I tremble all over. I push myself up, using my shaking hands. I turn away from second visit of Man-of-all-songs. I stumble away from Spirit Lodge.

Behind me, Man-of-all-songs is calling me, and it is as great as first drumbeats of Thunderbird.

Bear Woman wails her fear of Bird, "Peee-yaaa-soooooo! Peee-yaaa-sooooo!"

I am running through long grass. My leggings are soaked, my rawhide toes stretch and squish in mud. I am new-young-woman running in rain, leaping over shallow ditch onto trail, running, holding my swaying belly. My skirt is torn and wet. I am running in rain, not knowing when it started or how long Thunderbird has been angry, but I think it has been for a long time and that it started before this night. It is raining. Water streams down my cheeks. My scarf and blanket are soggy. My braids slap my cheeks. It is raining, and I am running. Bird drums. Sky whitens all around in four directions; light streaks across horizon; lightning splits sky. Rain turns into pellets of ice that sting my face and stone my back.

Thunderbird is angry because people are defeated. He is angry because bellies are empty and buffalo are gone. He is angry because Deer's Rump People must go away and it is wrong time for going away.

Hailstones bounce in wagon ruts, fly all around me. I run blindly to wagon. I brush against someone with black and drooping hat. It is Horse-dance-maker. He grabs my arm so I spin around and fall hard against his buckskin chest. He steadies me. He shouts something I cannot understand because of Bird's drumming: "—but I won't let you!" His left arm grips my shoulders and his right sweeps under me forcing my legs to bend and he grunts against weight of me, lifts me up; and thicker arms of Bear Woman haul me over wagonside.

I sink into pile of bundles. My mother rolls canvas over us and makes it dark inside wagon. I am shivering. Bear

Woman wraps me in sleeping-robe. Her bearpaw hand gently probes under skins, presses against my underbelly.

"It has stopped?" she says.

I feel only cold and fear of Bird who is pummelling canvas with hailstones.

"Drink."

I feel tin rim of cup against my lips.

"Just a little."

I swallow, but dribble some on my chin.

Bear Woman coaxes: "A little more. It is good."

Liquid is strangely warm, not from being held over fire, but it has its own heat that spreads through my arms and legs to make them stop trembling. I fall deeper into bundles, burrow warmly. I am falling asleep.

Wagon rumbles on. Going is slow, but wagon sways and creaks and shakes. Bird's anger fades, grows distant. I hear horses snorting and sucking sound of hooves pulling in and out of mud. Going is slow. All night under raining sky.

I am held high above earth, between waking and dreaming. I see myself walking beside Horse-dance-maker, southward, between large rocks shaped like buffalo. Some standing. Some sitting. Some lying on their sides. We walk between stone buffalo.

Horse-dance-maker grips my elbow. His head is bent, his lips and chin set firmly. I have never before seen this in him. He does not speak. His forelock, braided with horsehair, twists down and over his long flat nose. His eyes are narrowed for seeing long distances. He sees so clearly things ahead. But unspoken things that always pass between us, so good we warm our hands on them, are gone. He is taking me away—from him.

Where buffalo are lying down, he leaves me.

I find myself on edge of place I have never before seen. I think it is lake where children dance when sun goes down, but everything is changed. It is not prairie. It is not lake country. It is not woodland. It is all of these. I am on edge of a lake and large white birds with long necks float on it. Short grasses grow away from green water and shape upward into long slopes and small hills. Wind turns grasses back towards me and I see undersides of such deep green I have never before seen it.

All is so new and strange, but I feel no fear, and that is strange, not fearing a change I have no control of.

Then children appear. They are all girls. They wear bright scarves, new shawls and many-colored skirts. They are happy-cheeked and fat; they have chunky legs and round arms. Bright ribbons stream from their hair. Some carry striped cones over their heads. I think new tent cloth is to keep out rain, but sun is shining. I shade my eyes. It is hard to take in so much happiness all at once.

Children are dancing around Centre-pole, but there is no hide or grass covering for their Lodge. It is a Dance I have never seen before, never heard of before, and only children, girl-children, may make this Dance.

I lower my head respectfully, turn my body away from them so they do not see me crying. What grandmothers say is true: there is always pain in loving.

Children are dancing when sun goes down. There are girls from north and east and south and west. I know them by colors they wear and designs on their clothing. They are dancing, and circle is broken by two tallest girls who make room for me, but I do not know how to make this new Dance.

I listen to their Song. It holds chatter of small animals, skitter of birdfeet, laughter of Mēmēkwasowak, Little People who leave arrowheads and spearpoints on prairie and upset canoes in rapid waters. I do not know all the words, only sounds of earth and sky, because chanting is coming from languages of Sioux and Crow and Salteaux and Blackfoot and Assiniboine.

I dare to lift my head, and I see a lodge so strange it makes laughter out of crying. It is made of river stone, roof shaped like a tipi but covered with sod. Small openings are covered with patches of colored cloth.

Inside, children make a feast. They pass bannock

59

and pemmican in a circle. Some are curled on Company blankets, and they sleep the sleep of those whose bellies are full.

Outside, Man-of-all-songs waits for me. He is dressed so strangely, I feel no fear, and my laughter almost brings me out of dream. He wears moccasins with creeping floral design. His leggings are made from grey horse blankets. His belt has a shiny buckle. Long stick with knife on end is thrust into scabbard made from another blanket. His shirt is made from brown rabbits turning white. His robe is long, falling from shoulders I have yet to place my head upon. It is not made of deerskin, fox fur, or buffalo hide. Fur is grey and matted and falling out in clumps. It is Wolfskin.

Man-of-all-songs is silent, but I know his Song is Wolf's long howl for those who go hungry. He grips a scratching stick and something large and square and bound in cowhide. It is not a Treaty-pay-list.

Laughter has left me. I dare to look at his head. No pelts tied to his hair, no status topknot, no horned bonnet. His head is bared. He wears his hair long and unbraided. He is in mourning.

How can this be so much so? Man-of-all-songs is silent and he mourns when children are making a new Dance. *When sun goes down.*

It is third time he has appeared to me. I must turn him away. But he will not go away from me. So I turn my back to him.

Man-of all-songs speaks:

My granddaughter,
> You must go away. You must go to places you cannot even dream about.
> Where you go, there will be no hunt.
> Where you go, I will go. There you will find me. Here you will find me.

My granddaughter,

        You are protected.

        I will show you how to make new Dance. I will show you where to find medicine. I will show you how to make new feast.

        Where you go, you are protected.

        I will give you power of words. But I do not give you song of your own. I give you Song-of-women. You must sing it for them and teach them new words. Song is for women and for children of children.

        Where you go, you are protected.

        I hear all words to all songs. I feel joining of all things under sun. My blue woman's spirit lifts. I am pulled towards this man who sings all songs. It is so great and so strong I see my blue shape stretch and rush out of me—to him. It snaps back to me so fast I feel like a bowstring, but I also see he folds me into his robe.

        I have never known anything so deep and strong before, nor will I ever again, not even in dreams I will have as Old Woman. First medicine is always strongest.

        This is only third time he has come to me, and there must be one more fourth and final visit. I am ready to receive him and take back that sense of myself that he now holds.

        My lower belly contracts so hard I lose my first waking breath.

        "Take in small bits of air," my mother says. "Pant. Like dog lying under bush on hot day."

        I yield to pain, go with it to other side of it. Then I open my eyes and see I am lying among bundles. My clothes are damp but I feel warm. Wagon has stopped. We have travelled through first night of our leaving.

Bear Woman rolls back canvas. First light of new day is grey and air is cool. It has stopped raining. I hear many dogs barking. I wonder what place we have come to and who is making camp. I hear low voices of women, one voice sharp and cutting, "—meat!", so clearly I can almost smell it roasting.

My mother offers me her bearpaw hand but I push it away. I roll over onto my hands and knees. This is how I get up: by stretching like dog coming out of sleep. I grasp side of wagon and pull myself up.

I really am at place where many children died during Blackfoot raid on sleeping camp, where many children may be seen dancing when sun goes down. I see three tents pitched near poplar, one moved apart and closer to water's edge. It is isolating tent. Women have made ready for me.

Fox and Bowboy are slogging into camp. Dead porcupine, food fit for Woods People only, is slung over Fox's long back. Two prairie chickens dangle from his right hand. Bowboy carries single-shot Snider. Fox says to Horse-dance-maker, "He fell into slough. So he returns with empty sack and gun jammed with mud. Better he should live up to his Name!" Fox passes by without stopping. He is lone man who doesn't like to go visiting. His totem swings on back of his head: foxtail.

"Ni-kwatisok!" Fox calls, but children do not run to meet hunters who hang their heads ashamed because there is not enough food for all five families. Children run to mothers crying: "Why no antelope?"—because there is not enough rabbit in Company-pot; "Why only two prairie chickens?"— because one small porcupine is fit for Woods People only.

Bowboy ducks under Lean-to made of poplar poles covered with canvas. Fox drops prairie chickens into lap of Lucky Man's grandmother.

Old grandmother is squatting before Lucky Man's tent, her arms around crying grandsons who press faces into her sagging breasts. Lucky Man's head appears under tentflap. He is Always-laughing-man, and he says, "So you make your poor old grandmother sit in rain and get wet?" He grabs his sons by their necks, one in each hand, and pulls them into lodge. Grandmother crawls in after them.

Then Lucky Man's silly face reappears. He is not laughing now. His eyes are small but growing bigger. He looks as if the grandmother has smacked him down. He ducks out of tent. He looks at me, once, more afraid of me than redcoats, then runs fast around tent. His sons are faster behind him. Both rub where the grandmother has hit them.

She totters through doorflap, complains about being too old to sit in rain plucking chickens. "Ahstum!" she calls to Lucky Man's four women. They crawl out of tent after her. She yells at youngest woman that she must do it, "Pluck chickens!"

So we have been stopped here for a long time, since dawn of new day, and women have left me sleeping in wagon until it is time. They have been making ready, and I am happy that it will go in exact way of it.

I see women gathering together, coming out of tents, slowly, coming towards wagon. Men must be sent away. But Horse-dance-maker does not do it right. He hands ropes tied to unhitched horses to Lucky Man's first son and tells him to hide horses in woods where redcoats cannot find them. He should go away from me now. But, he jumps over hitching post and stands under me. He holds his arms up to me.

Wagon is not so high and jump to ground so far. My legs are as long as they were before I bulged out in front and behind and sideways. I boost myself up and perch on rim of wagonside.

Horse-dance-maker does not do it right. He will not let me slide down to wooden wheel and jump to muddy ground. He catches me under my arms and lifts me down. If members of warriors' society saw him they would never get over making jokes. He has never done such a thing before, hold me close to him in front of others. He leaves me to giggling women. His head hangs in shame of showing feelings in front of others.

Women make circle around me. "It is good you have come," the grandmother says.

"We have isolating tent," Lucky Man's eldest woman says. She is Blackfoot. She likes to cook rabbits and eat them. I do not like her cooking.

Fox's woman giggles behind her shawl. She has never had a child. She wears her best clothes and paints her face as if she is going to Sundance. She smiles. Her teeth are stained blue. I do not see why so many new-young-men chase her into saskatoon bushes. I do not see why Foodgiver bothered with her.

I look at her, hard. It is not time for painting face and saying silly things. "Take pregnant bitch," I tell her. "Take from it, waterbag. Boil a long time. Bring it to me to drink." Fox's woman is eight winters older than I am, but she will do what I tell her to do after today.

Lucky Man's grandmother lowers her head, nods.

My mother shoves my shoulder, turns me to her. "How do you know such things? How?"

"I know," I say.

Bear Woman narrows her eyes to slits, but she cannot stare me down and make me speak of things I must never tell anyone. She cannot shrink me down to a child crying for forgiveness.

"You have had an experience," she says.

"I go to tent now," I say.

Women open their circle to me, then follow behind me. I have silenced them, and the only sounds in camp are yelping of bitch Fox's Woman is chasing down and her high voice, "Why me? Why do I have to be the one to do it?"

Fox's woman slips and slides in mud. She grabs for dog. She falls on her belly. Her pretty dress is dirty now. But she has hold of dog's ears. "Dog! Dog!" she yells, and it is not a naming. Dog is lowest form of animal, and there is no other curse in Cree.

Dog braces feet, growls, and tugs as if trying to pull a travois backwards. Fox's woman yanks dog's head back and swiftly slits throat. Blood spills to ground. Fox's Woman does not know how to do anything right. She will have to be told how to do it: to hang dog by neck from poplar pole strung across two tripods. I will tell her to stop throwing mouldy bannock to dogs. To soak it in hot water and place it on red swelling sores of children.

These things I am thinking for first time and happiness of knowing medicine makes me laugh. Women think I am laughing at Fox's woman and they join me, laughing not too loudly behind hands and shawls.

My steps are long and slow to isolating tent. My arms

cradle child in my belly who will soon be struggling for first breath.

Outside tent, my belly seizes. I yell at women, "Stand away!" I clutch pain and run with it, in circle. "Out of my way!" Circle made, pain is gone.

I duck inside isolating tent. Company pot hangs over smoking fire. Wood is too wet to burn. Lucky Man's Blackfoot woman kneels and blows on coals. The grandmother takes her place at back of tent. She pounds and mixes medicine in wooden bowl. I watch her for as long as it takes her to dump powder from leather bag into bowl. She uses her paddle and does not touch anything with her hands. She sighs. She chants. She is an old talker, never quiet, so I am glad of Her Song.

Lucky Man's eldest woman unfolds Company blanket, turns it high over fire, warms it.

Bear Woman strips away my damp skirt, unties my moccasins and slips them from my feet. She washes my legs and feet with water that smells of roses. She reaches for warmed blanket and wraps it around my shoulders. She tells me to lie on sleeping-robe and rest until it is time.

Before I can turn and move to back of tent, water rushes between my legs. I turn my flushed face away from women.

The Grandmother nods happily from her corner. "Waterbag breaks," she says. "It is good."

My mother lifts roll of cloth from women's bundles, tears long strip, wipes my legs. She looks up at me, "Have you eaten anything?"

"Only buffalo tongue," Blackfoot Woman says bitterly.

"Better than rabbits!" I say.

"Have you?" Bear Woman keeps at it.

"Only a little tea," I say.

"It is better anyway," the grandmother says.

I feel terrible urge to find out-of-sight-place, but the grandmother says no, that is not it, "It only feels like that; it is child pushing down."

Old Woman, the Grandmother, must see to birthing. She takes over, without a word, because this is understood among women.

But it is my first time in isolating tent and I do not know what to do. I need to find out-of-sight or over-hill-place. I cannot believe it is only my child that moves in me.

Old Woman spreads buffalo hide, fur-side-down, before centre pole of isolating lodge. Medicine moss tumbles out of large leather bag onto hide. Old Woman is careful not to touch it with her hands. She kneels on edge of mossbed, on north side of centre pole. "Squat down," she says, "on moss."

My feet sink in soft moss, in thickness of buffalo fur underneath. I squat before centre pole.

"Grab hold! Take pole in both hands! Hold tight!"

New lodgepole pine. Bark peeled away so pole is yellow and smooth. My hands are sweating; I cannot get good grip on it.

Old Woman asks me to hold out my left hand, and she sprinkles, from leather pouch, white grains of crushed plant in my palm. "Rub hands together like this," she says.

Scent of powder is sweet. Grains are coarse. They make my hands stop sweating so I can grasp pole.

"No!" the Grandmother yells. "Feet wider apart!"

I ease my feet wider apart.

"Bounce! Let your buttocks drop good between your legs! Ahhh! Better now." Old Grandmother has no teeth and her lips disappear into cave of her mouth when she smiles.

Everything inside me is pushing to get out. I cannot breathe. I clench my teeth and grip pole.

Old Woman rubs my back, low down, stroking and stroking. Her hands are so small. I wonder how they can be so strong and steady.

"When you feel pushing," she says, "take small and short breaths. When pushing stops, you take long deep breaths."

"Other way around," Bear Woman says. She laughs, and Old Woman scowls at her.

It begins again, not pain, but a bearing down I have no control of.

"Good. Good." Small hands press against my back, push down, rub and ease away tired feeling.

No one has to tell me to push. It is happening by itself, and I cannot say when to start or stop it. I forget to breathe. Such force takes my breath away. My chest caves in, my shoulders hunch towards pole.

It stops. I take short breaths.

"Rest between! Take deep breaths to rest yourself!" Old Woman wipes my sweating forehead and hot neck with wet cloth.

I am not working now, but child has not stopped moving inside me. Unborn kicks and small arms seem to be flailing; it seems to be swimming to get out—or no—fighting to be born. This child is never still.

The Grandmother's laughter is a deep rumble that makes her shapeless belly roll from side to side and her sagging breasts flap. She sends long look to my mother. "I do not think it will be a boy," she says. "This one is fighting to be born!" She chuckles and holds her own belly.

I do not understand what is so funny or how anyone can laugh now. But I am doing all the hard work.

"Boys are lazy," Bear Woman says, slow smile spreading across her wide face. "Even at getting born."

"Men like women to do everything for them," Grandmother says.

"Move camp for them," Blackfoot woman says.

"Move sliced meat back to camp from hunt," Lucky Man's youngest woman says.

"Move over in sleeping-robe!" Bear Woman cries.

"Move under!" the Grandmother yelps.

Their shrieks are flying up smokeflaps. I am afraid men will hear laughter and know what women are about. I think women will never stop laughing. Old Grandmother wipes tears away from corners of her eyes with end of her shawl. I think even my mother has forgotten about me. She flops backwards on pile of bundles and rolls around, holds her belly from too much laughing.

"Men go to fight Blackfoot. They fight each other in council when decisions must be made." Old Woman is not laughing now. "I have seen it. They fought redcoats. And power of Woman Leader's headmen."

Blackfoot Woman's laughter fades behind her shawl. Bear Woman rolls back up to sitting position. She pulls smile away from her mouth with fingers.

"But it is women," the Grandmother says, "who must do real fighting for life. They fight to give birth. They fight to keep child alive. Fight each day to find food when there is nothing for men to hunt."

"I will speak now," Bear Woman says. "My daughter, Old Woman tells you to work hard now. That is true. Giving birth is hardest work woman must do. It is work of women. I see that you know this, because you have felt truth of it. But I tell you now to fight. Fight hard!"

I stop listening. Pressure is so great this time, I feel my hip bones spreading, and I am afraid they will slip out of their sockets. I work pole, grip it, push hard against it. My arms ache. My toes curl into mossbed. My heels brace against floorhide.

Old Woman presses down on my lower back with both hands.

I hear summer pup growling. I am afraid he has crawled into isolating lodge. I hear grunts. I hear animal snorting like it is burrowing into earth. I hear long and slow and deep growl. My chin digs into my chest. I cannot breathe. I think my blood will burst in my face. Then I know that grunts and growls come from my own throat.

Pushing stops. I am sweating. My mouth is so dry. Where is that Fox Woman with dog broth? I will make her chase dogs for four days. "Water," I say, but there is no time to drink it.

Bearing down is long and hard. I take in short quick gasps of air. I push hard. I work at it. I fight for life of my first-born. I am afraid I will be torn apart. I dare to look between my legs: wet head of my first born. Black hair is thick and matted and flattened.

"Push! Push!" Women yell at me.

On other side of centre pole, Fox's woman stares at me, mouth open so I can see more stained teeth than I want to see. She spills broth from tin cup. I did not see her enter lodge, and now I have no time for her pale and stricken face or her wimpering.

I push. It is easy now. My child slides from me, slowly, dropping and curling on mossbed.

"I have no teeth," Old Woman says to my mother, "so you must do it."

Bear Woman leans over mossbed. Old Grandmother's hands take hold of twisted rope. Bear Woman bites, and it is quickly done, rope severed evenly. My child is no longer part of me.

Grandmother lifts my child and takes her away—yes, it is a girl-child—to be washed and wrapped in her mossbag. She points to purple birthmark at base of child's spine. "She belongs to People!"

Bear Woman takes place of Old Woman beside pole. "You are not done work," she says. "Push again. Hard!"

Something red and wet and pulpy falls from me. Bear Woman takes it outside to be buried and prayed over.

I fall over, sideways, onto mossbed. Someone, I think it is Blackfoot Woman, gives me to drink broth of pregnant bitch. I take small sips. Someone, I think it is Lucky Man's youngest woman, is bathing me. Old Woman stuffs moss wrapped in rags between my legs. Lucky Man's woman, one of them, folds new warm blanket over me.

I am falling asleep, but I think I have not heard my daughter cry yet. I lift my head. Old hands gently lower small bundle into my arms. My child is tucked into her mossbag.

A feeling warmer than blankets, than coals lifted from firebed with forked stick, surges through me. I must look at her.

Her eyes are not brown yet, but I think they are beautiful. I wonder if she can see my face so close to hers. Her ears are not flat to her head, they stick out like Bear Woman's, but a little spruce gum behind each ear while she is growing will fix them to her head. Her face is small and round like mine, but her cheeks are fat. She has her father's long and flat nose, and her eyes are close together. There is Blackfoot blood in this one that I did not know about. "I will speak to your father," I say. She is able to grasp two of my fingers in one fist. She has overly-large hands like Bear Woman. I feel where her toes touch mossbag. She is long of limb like me. "You look like mole burrowed out of its den," I whisper. I nuzzle soft hair. It is long and thick for a newborn. Old Woman has parted it in the middle because that is how a Cree daughter must wear her hair. It smells of crushed flowers Old Woman rubbed into her scalp. "Beautiful smelling mole," I say.

"Let her suck," Old Woman says. "New milk does not come for three days. But Lucky Man's youngest woman has enough for your child and hers." She cups my breast in her hand, teases small mouth with nipple. It is hard and small as raspberry. Child opens her mouth and bites down. I yelp. Old

Woman laughs, "Such a child I have never seen born before!"

My first child is strong. She is a fighter for life. She comes from me, but she is no longer part of me. What elders say is true: child belongs to tribe before it belongs to mother and father. Rope has been bitten off. She is her own person now.

I want to think about a name, but I cannot think of tall strong women, only about men like Night Traveller and Walks-through-wind who are not here to bless a child with Name.

I am tired. I am falling asleep.

There is growling at tentflap. "Out! Get away from here!" It is Bear Woman.

"I want to see her!" It is Horse-dance-maker. His black hat is stuck in doorflap.

Why does he come here? It is not like him to go against elders' teachings.

"Get away! It is forbidden!" My bear of a mother beats his ears, but his head does not go away.

"I don't care!" He ducks his head this way and that way. "Let me in!" He has one foot in tent. "I want to see her!"

"You cannot!"

"Everything has changed!" Horse-dance-maker pushes against yielding tent wall.

"That is not the way to do it!" Bear Woman hits him hard on back of his neck. She has never liked him for not being a fighting man. She fights him, with big words, through me.

I turn my head, lift it, so I can see better.

Horse-dance-maker is crying, but not from beating Bear Woman gives him.

"I will see him," I say, "so you let him in."

"Isolating tent!" Bear Woman yells. "He makes it unclean!" She will not allow any man into her tent who has tears on his face. When my father cried and prayed to his dreamspirit each time she put up lodge, she yelled at him too.

My father would cry now if he were here to see what is happening to People. He was Old Man. He called spirits of buffalo, and he died of broken heart when they did not rise up out of wallows.

"Stop fighting!" Old Woman has said it. "You break teachings by fighting this way!"

Bear Woman stops hitting Horse-dance-maker, but she does not move her massive body out of his way. Her fists dig into her heavy hips.

"A woman never speaks directly to her son-in-law." Old Woman has said it again.

Bear Woman backs up, but she is not cornered.

Horse-dancer-maker steps inside isolating lodge. His head hangs.

Bear Woman opens her mouth to growl again, but she has no words for him now. She will not speak to him through a third person, and that is her best insult to him.

My mother made warriors of three sons before I was born. She dared to go against my father when he wanted to teach them medicine. He said medicine men were true Leaders long before horse came to prairie and War Leaders took over. He said medicine men must be Leaders again, now buffalo are gone, because no one else has power to call them back. People cannot live without the Way. But Bear Woman traded ceremonial dress and beadwork for horses and sent her sons to fight Blackfoot. She traded fox furs for guns at Little Bearskin's trading post and sent her sons to fight redcoats. They are in Stony Mountain now. Her sons. My elder brothers.

Horse-dance-maker is not a fighting man. I think his face will crack into small pieces and peel away like birchbark.

Old Woman shuffles to tentflap. "We go and see my grandson," she says. "We see about feast for new child."

Bear Woman cuffs Horse-dance-maker one last time. She ambles out of tent. She is mother-of-bears. She shows them how to hunt for berries, smacks them from behind, chases them up tree. That is the way of it with my mother. She scolded Leader of Warriors' Society when he visited my father because he moved a bowl away from his foot without asking her first.

Fox's Woman brushes her body against Horse-dance-maker and passes out of tent. She does not know how to do anything but flirt with a man.

Blackfoot Woman snatches up her blankets and bundles. "Watch out behind you, little rabbit!" she says. She sweeps her long skirts out of tent . She is tall, even for Blackfoot woman, and I think she could be Fox's sister. If truth were known about how many raids Fox's father made on Blackfoot camps when men were out hunting.

Lucky Man's youngest woman scurries out of tent. She cannot hide her fear of what has happened, and she tosses her skirt over her head, crying into it and forgetting what she is showing Horse-dance-maker.

He does not look at her legs. He will not ever look at another man's woman.

"You!" Old Grandmother's shrivelled head reappears under tentflap. Wispy braids slap her cheeks. "I do not have a dream for this child!" Her old head shakes from side to side. "For child of a man who breaks into women's tent. For child of a man who speaks to his mother-in-law. I do not make Dream-of-name!" Tentflap falls under her crinkled but strong hands.

"See your child," I say to Horse-dance-maker.

He strides to fireplace, drops to this haunches, and sits cross-legged beside me. "It is too hot in here!" he says. His pain has turned to anger. He does not tell me why he has come to see me too soon, why he broke into isolating tent. I do not asks him to tell me what he cannot say.

I sit up, reach across mossbed to fire. I pour tea for him from black kettle into bowl. "If child were a boy," I say, "I would call him Breaks-into-tent."

Horse-dance-maker drinks tea. Trickster grin is on his face.

"You look like Wesakachak," I say. "Act like him too!"

"It is good child is a girl," he says.

"You want a son."

"I will have many sons," he says, "but now we need many girl-children to be born. So they may have many children."

I was born during Blackfoot Starvation Winter. I think of my sisters, Cree and Blackfoot, and how there are not as many new-young-men who have seen as many winters on prairie.

"She has your eyes and nose," I say. "You never told me you had a Blackfoot grandmother hidden in bush. But I see it now!"

He traces a line down her long nose with his pointing-finger, then a matching line down his own nose.

Our child's nose twitches, but she does not cry. She will never be a woman who is always crying too much. Not like Lucky Man's youngest woman.

"She is too much like your mother," Horse-dance-maker says. He leans over fire, pours tea for me. He holds my chin, helps me to drink, although I need no one to do this for me.

I have never known a man like Horse-dance-maker, never a man so gentle with women. Not even my father who hit back at my mother with words, lashed her with curses because he was too old and too weak to beat her.

"So!" he says. "What name shall we give her? Old Woman will not do it. Dream a name."

"Then I will dream on it," I say. I have had three dreams of Man-of-all-songs. When he comes to me fourth time I will have a Name for my child. I do not know why he did not appear during birth, why he is waiting, or what he is waiting for, but dream will be fulfilled. Then I will be medicine woman. Also.

"So!" Horse-dance-maker says again. He slaps floorhide. "So! Now we have a child. There is no food for feast. No gifts to give away. No horses or blankets or beadwork." He slaps floorhide.

Dust is flying up. Fox's Woman is not good at hanging things out to air. She is not good at sweeping out tents.

"Nothing left! Nothing! Lucky Man has traded everything he has for food too!"

"He has many women and children to feed," I say. Numbers of family members show how worthy a man is.

Now I see how it goes with Horse-dance-maker. He is shamed, but there is no elder to make feast for newborn. He is shamed, but there is no elder to give forgiveness, to blacken his brow. He has broken the Way, and there is no one to make it right.

"Maybe something of the old must be broken or taken away before we can make a new way?"

"When we cross dividing-line," Horse-dance-maker says, "we will find new way to go on living. I do not know how we will do it, but we will find a new way."

Women are beating fists against tentflap, wanting in, but not one shouts now.

Horse-dance-maker leans over me. I touch his smooth cheek. He rises, takes four unsteady steps to tentflap, lifts it, and disappears.

Women flutter in, all talking in one voice, but I hear Bear Woman above others: "Your husband agreed to butcher his horses!"

"My grandson says Great Deliverer is helping us escape," Old Woman says.

"We make feast for newborn," Blackfoot Woman says.

"Pretend it's buffalo," Fox's Woman says.

He is Horse-dance-maker. His dreamspirit will never forgive us if we eat horses. He sacrifices his horses so four families may eat and go on living to see other side of dividing-line. So we may go on travelling, go on living, and find new way.

"How can we travel without horses?" Lucky Man's youngest asks. She cries into her skirts again.

Without horses, redcoats will catch up to us. They will find us and take Lucky Man, Fox, Little Poplar and Bowboy back to Place-at-forks for hanging. Redcoats have been searching too long for them. Redcoats are never slow at giving chase.

It is too close in isolating tent now. Fire flares. Blankets are smothering me.

It is a long way to Cree Crossing at dividing-line. We have no horses, and redcoats are never slow at giving chase.

I am crying in smoking tent.

Annika

After Old Woman told me about her flight into exile, I felt as if I were awakening from a dream.

It was cold in my grandmother's house. The poplar had burned down in the stove. The gas lamp had gone out, but its heat had melted a circle in the centre pane of the long row of windows. A weak November light lay just behind the frost.

I looked through the glass. I saw myself as a child skipping down the washboard road separating my family homestead from Thunderchild's reserve. I must have been swimming in the Turtle River because I wore stretched and soggy woolen bathing suit.

Ahead, two old women waded through orange and black tiger lilies that struggled wildly for breathing space in the ditch. They were speaking sign language, gesturing as if they were mute, but sharing something that made them laugh together. They both carried lardpails full of saskatoons, and I believed they had met while berry picking. One would make pies, the other bannock.

The grandmothers heard my approach, for I'm clumsy in the bush and dry leaves crackled under my bare feet. They stopped and turned to me.

They were the same height, neither heavy nor slim, but shapeless as the aged are. They both wore fringed shawls and bright headscarves, but one wore beaded moccasins and knee-high leggings, the other thick cotton stockings and running shoes. Their faces were small and round, as furrowed and wind-blown as the land. I tried to read those faces as I would a map. One grandmother had eyes as blue as lingonberries, the other had eyes as brown as river mud. The

Swedish woman was as fair as the Cree woman was dark.

The calm that comes only with the acceptance of all things and people seemed to be an invisible bond between them, for they were turned toward each other as much as they were facing me. I expected them to join hands and offer that unity to me. But they seemed to be waiting for me to come to them.

I wanted to go to them, speak with them in whatever language—English, Swedish or Cree—that would bring us together, but I didn't have any words.

I turned away from the window. I felt as if I were on the edge of the Livelong Coulee, about to plunge into the most inportant discovery of my life.

The next morning I had to go to town to refill Old Woman's prescription, pick up my mail, and send in my Christmas catalogue order.

The road into Livelong runs straight east and parallel to the railway tracks. On the right side of the washboard road the station house is set apart from the loading platform, cattle holding pens and the inevitable grain elevators by long spaces of wild grass now hidden by shrouds of snow. On the left side, the white stucco church. It was built by the Anglicans, Lutherans, Baptists, and Catholics. Because agreement couldn't be reached regarding the shape of the roof, the steeple was not added to the bell tower until the Catholics built their two-steeple church on the other side of town. Then the corner church was converted and proclaimed the Church of England. Today, children are christened, young folk married, and the dead buried from this church, but itinerant pastors must be imported by the Lutherans and Baptist. The Mennonites keep to themselves at Fairholme, and the Crees hold their sundances on the flats.

The centre of the town is one block square, the business section established on the south and east sides. Across from the empty snow-filled lot, the post office, Ernie Sommer's store, the old livery barn, and the Red & White Store. The garage was built by Reed to provide gas for overland Fords. The hardware store was once owned by the Jewish family. The Chinaman is buried in a fenced-off section of the graveyard north of town.

On the remaining two sides of the square, the Harse house, Graham house, Bjorling house, and Opsal house represent the original builders of Livelong: Abrahamson, Johnson and Reed.

No one talks about that beginning, about dump carts pulled by mules, the surveyor's quick love affair with the blacksmith's wife, or Karna. Karna built the hotel, but the other townswomen wouldn't allow her a new respectibility, so she brought her girls up from Chicago and established her old business upstairs. No one remembers the midwife, Old Lady Harse, how her upper plate slipped when she said, "I may be called out," or how she curried rabbits for the new mothers. No one speaks about the handsome Grahams with hair the colour and texture of wheat, or how every generation of Bjorling women fell in love with them but none ever married.

The townspeople are more concerned with the comings and goings of Mister Hicks. The silver-haired Daddy of Livelong, the only man north of Battleford who ever owned a Cadillac, he wears a store-bought suit every day of the week. No one remembers the fight between the English and the Swedes over the location of the town and how it was settled by the coming of the railway. No one knows how much land Mister Hicks has or has not bought up since, but one thing they all know for sure: the devil drink and womanizing will take him in the end.

No one ever questions beginnings. Only the why of endings. And I was snowing and blowing at one time, thinking about how my grandmother always said, "We build on the wrong plan."

The old Fargo was idling in front of Ernie Sommer's store. I shook myself back into 1964.

An Indian car was parked beside the old hitching rail. I knew it was an Indian car, not by the battered fenders, dented bumpers and animal tail hanging from the rearview mirror, but by the swaying fishnet cradle slung across the ceiling in the back of the car. I heard an infant's angry yowl. A young woman pushed the cradle.

The brass doorknob was frosted. I yanked the door open and stepped inside Ernie's store. It smelled of last summer's ice cream, old leather and wet wool. Mittens were drying on the oil burner. In the middle of the store, counters were piled with denim overalls, flannel shirts and longjohns. Cotton dresses hung limply on a rack against the east wall. Flour sacks leaned against potato bins. Shelves were stacked with tins of coffee, canned soups and fruits and vegetables. Salves and ointments for horses and cattle were mixed in with aspirins and cure-all tonics. Comics, magazines, paperback books about the American wild west, nurse stories and Harlequin romances were scattered on top of thermal underwear, blankets and sheets.

Behind the counter, Ernie, one hand on the cash register, his myopic eyes widening behind thick lenses. He was staring at a man who was staring at a piece of paper on the counter.

"Hey!" I yelled the prairie greeting.

"You back?" Ernie smiled. "Guess you're too big fer cutout dolls now, aintcha?" By never allowing me my age, Ernie would never grow old himself.

Ernie's customer wore new hiking boots, green cotton pants and a Bay jacket with red and yellow stripes. He pushed his red hunting cap away from his forehead, but he didn't look at Ernie or me. His round face was scrubbed and shiny.

I was bushed. Bits of bark clung to my parka sleeves from carrying stacked poplar logs in from the woodpile. I hadn't washed my hair for ten days.

"Sorry," Ernie said, "you know I don't have that much money in the till."

The paper was pink, a federal government waterseal in the corner, and across the top: BAND COUNCIL OF THUNDERCHILD RESERVE. The cheque was made out for $18.92.

I slid the prescription across the counter. "Fill this for me, Ernie?"

"Sure 'nough," Ernie said. Behind the counter, he slid his fingers along the jars on the middle shelf until he found the penicillin and digitalis bottles. He dumped pills form the larger bottles into smaller ones.

"I haven't been able to get into the bank at Turtleford," I said, "because of the roads. Grader hasn't been by yet." I enjoyed the lie. "Can you cash a cheque for me?"

"Sure 'nough," Ernie said. "That'll be two sixty-four."

The councilman from Thunderchild's folded his cheque and slipped it into his wallet. His silence swayed in the close air like his child's fishnet cradle.

I touched his woolen arm, but he didn't look at me. He brushed past me. "Wait!" I said, but he didn't. I dug into my shoulderbag for my cheque book, hastily scribbled the date, my name and the amount: $21.56.

Ernie pressed brass buttons on the till, the cash drawer slid open with a ring, and he handed me a ten, eight ones and ninety-two cents. He didn't count out the change until the door banged.

"See you," I said.

Behind me Ernie said, "Strange kid. Stranger now she's growed up." I scuttled out of Ernie's store.

Outside, I caught up with the councilman from Thunderchild's. "Here," I said. "Give me your cheque."

His bottom lip curled down, and I was afraid he was going to spit at me.

"I know what you're thinking," I said. "Whites never give anything without wanting something in return."

He pulled his wallet out of his pant pocket, unfolded the cheque. "It'll bounce, y'know."

"I don't think so," I said. "Look. I want something and I know it's wrong of me, but I had to stop you somehow so I could ask you something. It's really important. I need to get in touch with some people."

"An' they're Indians," he said. He folded the money into the inside pocket of the Bay jacket and stuffed his wallet in his pants pocket.

"How did you know?" I asked.

"If they weren't you wouldn't be askin' me," he said.

"I've got an old woman staying with me," I said. "She's sick and I don't know if her family knows where she is. I don't want them to worry."

His eyes narrowed.

"She's a friend of my grandmother's," I said. "She's very old and I'm afraid she will—"

"Die," he said, and lowered his head.

"Then you know her!"

"Lot of sick people in winter," he said.

"Her name is First Woman," I said, knowing I was

being predictable by insisting on names. "*Iskwew*," I said, trying to remember the word for First, but only able to think of Top Woman, One Woman, and Leader of Women.

"I don't speak Cree," he said.

"Some people call her the Medicine Woman," I said. He nodded.

"I'm looking after her. I just wanted to know if you know any of her relatives. They might be worrying about her."

"What was that name again?"

"Old Woman," I said. "First Woman? Medicine Woman!"

He said, "I don't know anybody."

"But you must! You're on the Band Council. You must know who lives on Thunderchild's."

"Name again?"

"The Medicine Woman!" I yelled.

"Not there now," he said.

"I know that!" I yelled. "She's at my place!"

He hit the hood of his car, yanked open the door, and climbed into the driver's seat.

He hadn't even said thank you for the money. There was no word for it in Cree, but that man spoke only English.

My Swedish grandmother was right. Indians and whites were like two horses harnessed together but pulling against each other.

We are built on the wrong plan.

Old Woman

We are all travelling together now, four families of Lucky Man, Little Poplar, Bowboy and Fox. We are a long time walking from Deer's Rump Hill to place where children dance when sun goes down, a long time walking across prairie to Saskatchewan River where currents run swiftly. We have no horses, and we are all walking: four families spaced in long line of People moving south in search of water, small game, a way to go on living.

Lucky Man says when we make camp. He is leader breaking trail now. At feast for my newborn he sang long prayers and thanked Great Deliverer for helping us escape.

Behind Lucky Man walks Bowboy. He was scout for Big Bear, and wants to travel faster. He wants to leave us, find stray horse and travel faster. Redcoats are looking for him. He has not killed anyone yet, but he says rope is always swaying above him, rope is always trying to catch his neck in loop and drag him back to Place-at-forks for hanging. Bowboy wants to travel faster.

Bowboy carries gun. He has a few charges of powder, percussion caps, but no trade balls or shot. He leaves trail to go hunting for small game, but he returns with gophers he chases down with stick and woman's kettle full of water.

I ate some lumps of roasted gopher. Each piece seemed to make plumping sound in my belly. It tasted good, but there was not enough meat to ease cramps or make bellies stop swelling. I ate some to keep up my strength. So I can carry my newborn on my back. Solid bumping of her against me is comfort to me. She is too small to weigh heavy.

When she stirs from sleep I stop and give her milk. I have more milk than she wants or needs. She bites my nipples and kneads with her fists. There is anger in my child that I think will never go away.

I have more milk than she needs, so I share with children whose mothers' breasts have shrivelled. Giving is like that.

Before my own milk came in, for first three camps, Lucky Man's youngest woman fed both our children. But she was too-much-tired and too-much-hungry, and her milk dried up. So now I have milk for her child, but Lucky Man's woman cries into her skirts more than ever now. I suckle our children in out-of-sight-place where grandmothers cannot see her crying. I feed her child first because my newborn does not cry. We are good friends, she calls me Eldest Sister, although we do not share same man.

So we are all going along together.

I listen to silence of Horse-dance-maker. He goes ahead of me. He never speaks to me now. He drags his feet and carries bundles on his back. It is women's work to move camp, and it is hard for men to do this, but they all carry kettles and blankets and lodge poles and skin coverings on their backs.

Lucky Man's grandmother made travois for her dog. She is happy to do this, in old way of moving camp before horse came to prairie. She curses dog: "Atim! Atim!" She snaps willow switch at him. Dog flattens ears, strains against collar, and drags poles through long grass.

Earth is not sandy now. No foxtails blow in one direction towards Deer's Rump Hill. Earth has turned her back. Hard lumps of dark clay stick to travois poles. Dog twists head back at grandmother, grins at her like trickster.

So we are all walking with silence.

Fox looks over his shoulder. His totem's tail swings and bounces on his long neck. No redcoats coming.

Little Poplar clutches belly. He does not know why it hurts and it is getting worse. It better stop or he will not be able to fight redcoats. He turns head around like rabbit and holds belly's pain. Little Poplar looks over his shoulder. He is afraid of redcoats coming, but he is more afraid of summer pup coming at him from behind, and he does not see Fox until he bumps into lean man's back.

Fox is third man in line. His totem's tail swings above all men's heads. His eyes are so sharp he can see hatching birds in nests. He hears tiny beaks cracking shells.

Little Poplar drops back, ashamed for not watching for signs of small game.

Flattened blade of grass, paw print, turned stone, cold fireplace or hoof print left by passing horse would prod hope of finding food. Here, no circle of stones, burial ground or sundance camp.

So we are all silenced by fear.

Even Bear Woman does not speak. She looks behind her often. I see her driving wagon, and I think it is because we do not have wagon that I want her to be driving.

We are walking to meet sun. My scarf is damp from sweat. My skirt sticks to my legs. I need water. I want tea. Lucky Man says we will find duck eggs where river current runs swiftly.

We go long way around place of crossing river. Redcoats will look for us at landing. I do not know how we will cross river. We have no boat.

We are near water now. I can smell it. Earth slopes upward. A long rise. I think we will find mouth of Miry Creek soon. Wolf willow. Earth slopes downward. Cat-tails and red-wing blackbirds.

I see wagon, not ahead, behind me. It must be because my legs are so tired. Many days walking. My rawhide feet find stones to turn on.

"Awahe! Awahe!" I hear voice so clearly I almost answer.

My mother ambles on, her large head swaying from side to side. She carries heavy load. She has not lifted head to call to me.

"Duck eggs!" I think it is my eldest sister, but she is not here now, near creek that joins river, here, under slanted sun.

"Rabbits!" It is Blackfoot Woman.

"Ribbons!" Fox's Woman. Who else thinks of things to make her pretty when children go hungry?

Now I see women running to meet us. They wave scarves. The call to us in one voice.

I shut my eyes. I poke fingers in my ears. I have been walking under sun too long.

Raiders rush ahead of women. Lucky Man and Fox and Little Poplar and Bowboy, they are whooping and shouting and calling names. It is not the way to speak Real Names.

I am ashamed for them. I drop my head. I trudge over rise of land.

"Little Bear! Ho!"

"Kingbird!"

"He is My Little Brother!"

People swirl around me. Arms brush against me. Hands touch me here on my shoulder, there on my back. I sink to my knees. I fold hands in skirts. I dare to lift my head. Below me, here is good camping. Poplar and willow for shelter and making fires. Water to make tea. Lodges are scattered on lower end of river island. I am lifted and carried with rush of People. I dance down long slope. Leader strides over flat of land. He wears five-point blanket coat. Status topknot. He bears the Pipe. He stops, waiting, lifting arm in greeting. I want to run to him. I want him to hold me, lift me, carry me to his lodge.

Wind teases his braids. His face is full in cheek as if he has never known summer pup. His chin is thrust forward. His lower lip is heavier than upper lip. Corners of his mouth turn down. Eyes are slanted, dark and dense. Eyes of Bear. He turns large head to me. His face does not change, but eyes catch light, so I know he is surprised by me.

Lucky Man is with this Leader now. They speak sign language. Leader does not take eyes away from me.

I follow women down to camp. "Who is this Leader?" I ask Bear Woman. "Who camps here?"

"He is Son of Big Bear," my mother says, "and it will do no good if you look at him. He went against his father."

He is Imscees, aggressive-one, Little Bear, Little Badman. I have never seen him before. My eyes would remember that face. He must have been there, at Big Bear's Thirst Dance, but so many leaders and over two hundred lodges—no, I would remember that one.

Children race around camp. No dogs chasing them. I am afraid they were forced to eat dogs.

Lucky Man and Bowboy and Fox and Little Poplar and Horse-dance-maker go with Little Bear into his lodge to smoke and talk.

Women make camp. Bear Woman and I choose place sheltered by poplar. We untie ropes binding lodgepoles. We lay poles in circle for lifting. I do this without thinking about it. My face burns, but not from sun beating on it; I feel upon my face and breasts and legs—eyes of Bear.

I have been many nights without lying with Horse-dance-maker. I must wait until our child has seen three winters before I make another child in my belly. That is too long to go without a man.

I want to put up my own lodge.

In dawn of new day I work at finding wild turnips, grass berries, and wild onion. I have my own digging stick. It is long chokecherry limb, long because I am tall. I grasp round knob. I poke through grasses, searching for roots.

It is too early to find good roots, but peeled and strung on dried sinew, they will be good to carry in my grub bag for eating on the way.

I work sandy knoll. Blue carrots taste like fish and I leave them alone. Land falls away to river. I work on hands and knees. Child sleeps on my back. Always, all my life, I am hungry. I never stop looking for bits to eat. My fingers reach for fresh shoot. I dig deeper, thumb and pointing-finger curl around bulb. Tugging now, careful not to stretch plant, I pull it through loosened soil. I roll back on my haunches and sit on hillside. Below me is river. I loosen mossbag straps. I swing my child around and lay her on my lap. She sucks angry fists. She is hungry, but she does not cry. I take my breast out of Company dress and give her to suck. I brush dirt away from turnip, nibble it. I watch what is happening on lower end of island.

Whiteman has beached his boat below our camp. He is laying fire. I see kettle, axe, fish.

Lucky Man and his brother Wild Carrot, Little Poplar, Bowboy and his brother, Kingbird, they are walking in line toward whiteman. Bowboy carries gun, but I can see they will not harm whiteman because they are walking so he can see them.

Bowboy holds out gun and points at boat. He signs: trade gun for boat.

Whiteman grabs axe and kettle. He jumps into boat. He pushes off.

"Wait!" Bowboy's little brother yells. He tries to pull boat back to shore.

Whiteman swings arm high. Axe comes down. It chops Little Brother's head. Little Brother sinks to his knees in river water, his head drops between his arms, but his hands grip edge of boat. Blood spurts from his head and splashes boat. Whiteman chops Little Brother's hands so they come away from his arms but hang onto boat. Little Brother falls facedown in water, legs rising, and he floats like deadman. His blood spreads in water all around him. Boat is floating away from shore.

Bowboy shoulders gun. He shoots whiteman in belly. Whiteman crashes backwards into boat. It floats away.

I cannot hear Lucky Man talking, but I can see that he will not let Wild Carrot swim after boat. I read signs he makes with his hands: it is too risky. Whiteman might not be dead. We cross river tomorrow.

Boat is caught by current that runs swiftly. It turns circle, then drifts downriver. Whiteman lies in boat like sleeping child on his side, legs curled, holding his belly as if he is too-much-hungry. I think he is not dead.

Even so, I am afraid. Redcoats will never stop looking for raiders now.

I clutch child to my breast. I run down long slope to camp. I am afraid. I want to be in Little Bear's camp. I make fists. I pound my thighs. I pump my legs. Hot wind is blowing back things I want to forget.

I am afraid of redcoats, afraid they will follow us and take us back to Place-at-forks. I am afraid they will hang raiders by necks and drop bodies into wagons to be carted away and buried under sand. I am afraid they will find out it was women who took food and cloth from Place-at-forks.

I am afraid, and I am running.

Redcoats look for us at landings so it is not safe to cross

Saskatchewan River in those places. Lucky Man is worried about crossing fast-flowing-river. He smokes crushed minkberry vines and waits for sign from his Great Deliverer.

Sign comes to him. He finds stray buckskin horse on hillside above camp. Horse's front legs are scratched by barbed wire fence, one has fresh splint markings. Lucky Man says horse will make our trail easier for redcoats to follow. He shoots horse.

Now women are working at slicing meat and drying it for travelling. Lucky Man's four women build boat. They make willow frame and cover it with horse's hide. They seal seams with kidney tallow. They make horseboat to cross River.

I am gathering duck eggs. I tuck my skirts between my legs and wade through cat-tails and water grasses. I am gathering eggs and thinking about what happened to people and why we have to go away.

We are a long time walking to Montana. We traded most of our hides and ceremonial dress for food. Dried horsemeat, we ate last of that five camps ago.

We are carried along by heavy wind and prairie fire. Before me I see only smoking sky. Behind me only burned grassland.

I am weak from being too-much-hungry. I am afraid my milk will dry up. My skirt is damp from sweat. My teeth feel gritty.

Our moccasins are black from scorched earth. We lift our spirits by making jokes about our feet. We call ourselves Blackfoot. That is how we know Other People, as Blackfoot, but we are not enemies now. There are no horses to steal from each other.

Man-of-all-songs does not go with me here. There can be no songs in this place. I am afraid I will never find a name for my child.

I fight wind, and this is strange for me. I have always gone with wind from place of good camping to place of good camping.

We must make our way through wind and fire to battle hills on Oldman River. There, Bloods who work porcupine quills into their clothing will take us in and give us food and blankets. They are our enemies, but they will help us all they can. That is the Way: people in need are never turned away, not even enemies.

I fight wind and fire. I fight story-paintings that burn behind my eyes.

Fighting has driven us away from all belonging.

On this day, so long ago, I climb hump of battle hill above Oldman River. Grass is brown and blowing in one direction. Wind beats at my back and swirls my hair around my face. My rawhide feet find old trail between hills. I take hill sideways, down to clusters of willow bared to winter's coming. I gather dead branches for firewood. My empty waterbag flaps against my thigh.

Here is place of last great battle between Crees and Bloods. Here is where Bloods were camped. They were weak in fighting-men, so many taken by Covered-with-sores-disease. Our Crees thought they could end fighting that was old as northern-night-dancers. One last battle, and Crees would make scalp dance, the winning theirs for as long as Thunderbird drummed.

"Yei! Yei! Yei!" Wind carries ancient cry of Crees who rushed Blood camp. Leader made the sign: palms wipe out enemy. But over these hills was an out-of-sight-place where Bloods were camped in protective circle of three hundred lodges. They were roused by Jerry Potts.

Crees fought Bloods across flatland, across valley ridge and down into ravine. "Nipahikohk!" roared horsemen. Crees were called Cut-throat-people. They fought Bloods across these blue stones on riverline. They were killed on shore of Belly River. Blood flowed with water as if River's belly had been wounded. Crees were defeated by Red People.

Leaders made sign to Leaders: make peace at Wetaskiwin.

Women carved bodies and cut death marks on their own hands to avenge death of providers. Elders burned sweetgrass. Women made feast for dead. They danced with blankets, ceremonial dress, and bundles belonging to the dead. They left spaces in circle for fighting men.

These things I am thinking, not looking up at hills, at high places where scaffolds were built for the dead. I am afraid of high places. I might find bodies hanging from trees. I fill my waterbag and tie it to my rawhide belt. My back is tired from lifting and carrying heavy loads. I lean back and rub where it hurts. I lift my head.

Above me, wavering line of hill. It is not long and smooth back of Deer's Rump bristling with yellow poplar. It is not broad and flat back of Cut Knife Hill turned towards Battleford like sharp and shining blade. Battle hill is humped like back of buffalo. It reaches from flatland down to water's edge.

Wind pushes me. I rock on my feet. My lips are cracked and bleeding.

Bloods have been good to us. They gave us blankets and shared bannock with us. They remembered the story of Battle of Oldman River, and there is peace between us. But Little Bear says we move south with light of new day. Lucky Man prays to Great Deliverer.

No more walking. No more lifting. No more carrying. My throat is tight. I cannot swallow. My mouth is dry. No more hills. No more carrying around hills. Across backs of hills. Up hills. Down hills. No more trudging around hills where people died fighting. Wind screams through poplar, beats around my ears. I hold my spinning head in both hands. No more walking across flatland to hills where people are always fighting. "No! No! No!" I scream. I hold my head. Hills are turning circles around me. They chase each other around and around the joining forks of rivers. I hold down my own screaming voice. I hear hooves thudding. I hear Buffalo's last roar. I hear the Song.

Above me, on hump of hill, Man-of-all-songs stretches his arms and holds still the battle hills. Long buffalo robe falls from his shoulders. He wears horned head-dress. His mouth opens in last long roar of Buffalo.

This is fourth time dreamspirit appears to me. I do not turn him away. It is time for naming of my angry child.

I am riding humped back of hill. It moves under me. I cling to buffalo grass tufted like fur. I ride down, into buffalo wallow. It is dark where buffalo fled prairie fires, where buffalo escaped riflemen, where buffalo disappeared under earth.

Man-of-all-songs sings of returning herds. Buffalo rise from wallows and bring Miyopayiwin to people. It runs well again.

I soften tufted buffalo beard with crushed fireweed. I comb and tie status topknot. I spread sacred cloth over wallow. In clay dish I burn braided sweetgrass. At each corner of wallow, I place skygod stick.

Man-of-all-songs presents Pipestem to four directions.

to northwest blue skygod to peace and dream-life	to northeast thundergod to black forgiveness
to southwest red deathgod to firestick and war	to southeast yellow skygod to eye-of-fire and protection

Ni-wapitin aski
O-ma-aski-ay-wako
Ni-kawiy

	(I see
Earth	This One
That is	my home)

Wallow rumbles. Buffalo's lost roar erupts between hills.

Ni-sa-wayimaw:
(Bless this place
so close I will
with you open earth)

Out of my loving grows buffalo calf.

O-sawaysis: (Out of
fire's yellow center
comes Yellow Calf)

I followed Man-of-all-songs from Deer's Rump Hill to place where children dance when sun goes down. I followed him across prairie to place where Saskatchewan current runs swiftly. I followed him to battle hills on Oldman River and into buffalo wallow. He brings together all things under sun.

I am not afraid to go beyond Cree Crossing. I am not afraid to go to Montana now. I have dreamed and become a medicine woman.

Away from wind, between hills, I give milk to Yellow Calf.

We are crossing over into Montana. I do not know when we stepped on dividing-line. Sioux call it Medicine Line. Exact-speaking-people call it dividing-line.   Naaaaa! Whitemen call it *border*. Buffalo did not know what this means: *border*. They moved north and south. Prairie was the same to them on both sides. People followed buffalo north and south. Prairie was the same to them on both sides. At Cree Crossing I see them: stone buffalo. I leave offering of sacred cloth, tobacco, and sweetgrass. I pray it will run well for People on this side of dividing-line.

Long way behind me is Deer's Rump Hill. Long way ahead of me is Fort Assinniboine.

Annika

My Other-grandmother is a woman of many voices. The first voice I heard, that fifth morning, was the cranky chastising one of the elder giving lessons to a child. Old Woman speaks according to the role she is fulfilling, and her speechmaker's voice was formal, ringing and officious. When she prayed, Old Woman sighed and chanted. The second voice I heard was that of the young wife, lost and afraid, walking through the night and giving birth by morning. Even the hoarseness lifted from Old Woman's throat.

When Old Woman told the story of the last battle between the Crees and the Blood Indians she again adopted the voice of the storyteller. But it was the Medicine Woman who redreamed each visit of her spirit teacher. Then her sentences were choppy, she was often breathless, and her thoughts seemed to be fragmented. Her voice rose to a hysterical pitch and I thought she was delirious again. When she remembered the fourth visit of her dreamspirit she regained her calm.

"All my life, things that have happened to me have pushed me from place to place," she said. "All my life, memories have chased me from place to place. Earliest memories go after me hardest, but I look backwards so I may see directions. So I keep on going."

The next morning I did a little remembering of my own.

It was Sunday, a clear cold day, the air so still the smoke rose straight up from the stovepipe.

"There were so many other Sundays," I said to Old Woman. "Here in this homestead. Johanna never worked on the Lord's Day. On Saturday she prepared all the food, mounds of Swedish meatballs and pickled herring in sour cream. *Gufflebitter*. A dozen loaves of *vetebröd* she mixed in a cream separator. And stacks and stacks of pancakes with whipped cream and lingonberries. All just in case visitors came by on Sunday. And they always did come. From miles around."

Old Woman nodded, slurped away at her second cup of tea, but she didn't answer.

I was drying the breakfast dishes, pacing between stove and cupboard, wiping the cereal bowls so quickly they were put away damp. "I don't do a very good balancing act, do I?" I said to Old Woman, my arms tipping like the scales my grandmother used to measure fresh coffee grounds.

"You do good chicken dance," she said.

"I'm too much like my grandparents," I said. "I don't remember him, but my grandmother always told me grandfather was a loner, used to brood all day Saturday while she worked, and hid behind his Swedish newspapers on Sunday when company came. But Johanna cried when they arrived and cried when they left."

"You want to see people," Old Woman said. "What you going to do about windows?"

The row of windows along the south wall was frosted.

"White people have glass openings in houses," Old Woman said, "but they never look out. With so much frost no one can see inside. See who is at home to visitors."

"If someone comes," I said, "we'll hear the truck."

"If you don't clear windows I can't see People outside. Do it!"

At night, the heat of the gas lamp melted a circle in the centre pane. Now I pressed my palm against the day's new ice. Frost burned my hand but turned to water. I wiped the patch clear with my sleeve, and peered through it.

Outside, more than a dozen people along the caragana hedge. Most of them seemed to be women huddled in heavy jackets and all had bright scarves on their heads. They were silent. Waiting.

"How did you know they were there?" I asked Old Woman.

"People do not go inside white house," Old Woman said. "So you better go out and see what they want."

I ran to the door and yanked it open.

The councilman from Thunderchild's squatted on the front stoop. He stood up, turned to face me, shoved the hood of his Bay jacket back, and pulled the red hunting cap from his head. His clean and gleaming hair crackled with static electricity. He held out his right hand, offered me a small deerhide bundle.

"*Kinikinik*," he said, "and some good tobacco."

"Bring it! Bring it!" Old Woman cried from inside the homestead. She bounced on her cot, clapping her hands.

I took the bundle in to her. She snatched it from my hands. She weighed it in her own withered ones, sniffed it, then asked for her small woman's pipe.

"You can't smoke." I said. "Not with that cold."

"You tell him to come inside and see how white people live," Old Woman said. She reached over the side of the cot, trying to find her bundle underneath it.

I was afraid she would tumble from the bed. Her old bones were so brittle the shortest fall could break an arm or hip. "Be careful!" I warned, and caught her by the shoulders. I laid her back against the pillows. "Here! Have your own way again!" I untied the bundle and gave her the clay pipe.

Old Woman took tobacco from the councilman's rawhide bundle and packed her pipe. "Light it!" she ordered.

I struck a match on top of the stove and lit the pipe.

Old Woman's lips folded over the stem. She sucked on it, blew three smoke rings out the other side of her mouth. She closed one eye, tilted her head, and looked at me. Some kind of ceremony was about to take place and Old Woman couldn't make that ceremony without her pipe.

"You should be choking by now," I said.

She didn't inhale the smoke, but she coughed, cleared her throat, spat in the china bowl, then said, "I accept his bundle. It does not mean I do it. It only means I agree to hear all that he has to say. You tell him there is room for him in here. To come inside and sit by stove."

I was afraid the councilman had come to take her back to the reserve. Now it was more than a matter of not wanting her to go back to a poorly ventilated, unheated, shack. I wanted to hear the rest of her story. Without her, the winter nights would be too lonely. Old Woman was the cure for my aloneness.

"You are just a little bit spoiled," I said, "but I won't let him take you back to the reserve. Not even if you want to go."

"Naaaaa!" Old Woman said, grinning, "I go where I go. I stay where I stay. Tell him to come inside."

"You have the right to live where you want to," I said.

"So does my Other-granddaughter."

"*Tapwe ki-tatamihen*," I said. It was the closest way of saying thank you in Cree. "You never bother me about my decision to live alone in the bush," I said in English.

"Accept what happens to you," Old Woman said, "if you cannot say what is best thing to do." She shooed me towards the door like she was going after Johanna's turkeys.

I backed up, wanting to say more, not sure what that was. Old Woman said it for me: "Your grandmother. She say to me one time that English go back and forth. Swedes never go that way!"

"They go forth and back!" we laughed together.

"*From och tilbaka*," I said. "Looking after you has got me going around in circles, this way and that way, like sheep." I whirled around and ran to the door.

The councilman was twirling his red hunting cap in his mittened hands.

"She says to come inside," I said.

He ducked his head and entered the house. I shut the door behind him.

"Come," Old Woman said.

Councilman smiled, moved closer to Old Woman, stood before her with lowered head. "No wind today," he said. "But lots of sick people in winter. Lots of old ones. Many children come back from school sick."

"I cannot do it," Old Woman said out of the side of her mouth. Pipestem was stuck between her dry lips.

"How much?" councilman asked. "Some people have money."

"Naaaaaa!" Old Woman yelled. "You go see The Loon. He takes money!"

"Sure, some people go up there," councilman said, shifting his feet, "but Old Man is mixed up with bad medicine. He puts curse on some people. There's one outside who says only you can undo it."

Old Woman took the pipe from her mouth. She

smacked her lips and made sucking sounds. "You do not do it right," she said. "Go sit at feet of elders. Talk Cree. Dress Cree. Then come back to me. Then we make talk. Then I can do it. Maybe."

"By then it be too late," councilman said. "Too many sick ones this winter. People say only Medicine Woman can help." He pulled another small rawhide bundle from his jacket pocket and gave it to her.

"Ahhhhhhh!" Old Woman cried.

Councilman shuffled to the door, head lowered, and went outside.

"Now what?" I asked Old Woman.

"People will not come inside white house. I told you that before. So they talk about what to do now. No one wants to tell that one about trouble and how they are sick. No one wants to be first or show how much gifts they have for me. So we wait." Old Woman pulled the pipestem from her mouth and waved it at the windows. "Clear them!" she shrieked. "I want to see People!"

I dug through the utensil drawer, found the square aluminium egg lifter, and scraped the frost from the centre window. Frost curled like wood shavings, dropped onto the sill, and melted on the oilcloth covering the oak table. I thought of how Johanna always watched for the morning when there was no night frost on the windows. "It is thawing weather," she said.

As if she could read my thoughts, Old Woman said, "We watch changing moons." She flipped back her quilts, struggled to put her legs and feet over the side of the cot, then held her head. "Oiiiiii," she cried, "I have a swimming head!"

"You're still weak," I said. "Put your head between your knees." I ran to the cotside, but she pushed my arms away.

"No! No!" she shouted. "It is good now."

"I'll carry you to the window," I said, "so you can look outside." I wrapped a blanket around Old Woman, lifted her, and carried her to the centre pane. "You are getting heavier, I said. "You eat too much lard with your bannock!"

Old Woman didn't listen. She peered out the window. Outside, people were gathered around the councilman. Men were hanging back, heads lowered, faces pulled into parka

96

hoods. Women held leather and cloth bundles in their hands. Old Woman tapped on the window pane. Councilman heard her, turned his head, pointed. He said something, and heads lifted, faces beamed like suddenly-lit coal oil lamps. A young girl broke away from the crowd and ran to the window. She wore white crinkle patent boots and her legs, bare between the knee and her short mini-skirt, were red with cold. Her hands were shoved up the sleeves of a man's siwash sweater. She pressed her nose against the glass, pushing it sideways, grinning, her breath steaming the window.

"Naaaa!" Old Woman cried. "My granddaughter!" Her feet kicked under the quilt, and she beat the glass where the girl's nose was flattened.

"Stop squirming or I'll drop you," I said.

The young woman shrank away from the window.

I carried Old Woman back to her cot, propped pillows behind her, and waited for her to tell me what had displeased her. She poked more tobacco into the pipe bowl. "Naaaaa!" she cried again. "I do not want to see her that way. I tell her but it does no good. She will not listen. Wooden Ears!"

"Why don't I ask her to come in and see you?" I said.

"I have no medicine for that one!" Old Woman held out her pipe and I relit it. Furious smokepuffs escaped from the left corner of her mouth. "Tell Chief I am ready."

"Chief?"

Old Woman grinned, only one side of her mouth moving, so she looked like Wesakachak, the trickster. "You talking to Indian aristocracy," she said. "He is one of Thunderchild's great-grandsons. But somewhere in the bush there was a Scot—I have forgotten—grandmother or grandfather, but this Chief go to so many schools he does not speak Cree. Even so, he is Chief."

"Why are there more MacDonalds on the reserve than Frasers?"

"MacDonald had a bicycle!" Old Woman laughed, but she pointed the pipestem at the door. She had her medicine bundle open.

Again, I let the councilman in. Before the grandmother he bowed his head with respect. "Your granddaughter," he said. "She says she is sorry. All she has is money."

"Naaaa!" spitting in the cup. "I do not take money! I know what she wants. Tell her I say same thing as I say before. I do not have love potion!"

Old Woman sucked on her pipe, blew smoke rings again. "No," she said to herself in Cree, "that is not the way to do it now." She took sweet smelling grains of a crushed flower from her medicine bundle, retied them in a small square of red cloth.

"My granddaughter," she said. "She wears cloth of such bad material I have never before seen it. Fringes are not rawhide. Skirt rides up her legs and show more thigh than any man should dare to see. She piles her hair on top of her head in curls fat and round as horse droppings. Band around her hair is not beaded. Leather on her feet is too stiff, heels so high I am afraid she will trip and fall." Old Woman handed the small cloth bundle to the councilman. "Tell my granddaughter," she said, "to let her hair fall to her shoulders. To part in the middle, braid it, and tie it strong with rawhide. Tell her, when he is sleeping, to rub crushed flowers on his chest, heartside." She waved the councilman away, and he took the bundle outside.

Then a small face bobbed at the window. The granddaughter was jumping up and down, pulling bobby pins from her hair. Each time her head reappeared one more large fat roll of hair was let down, until her black hair was flying all around her face. Old Woman laughed: "Love is its own kind of good medicine."

Old Woman waved her pipestem at the door, and I let the councilman in again. This time he carried Bay blankets stacked on his arm. "From families of Old Horse," he said. "Children are sent home from school. They have measles. Bad colds too."

"I do not want blankets," Old Woman said.

"Old Horse had a hard time getting them," councilman said. "He take his sons and grandsons who aren't sick and they trap many weasels. Many beaver. They trade skins for blankets."

"You do not listen to me!" Old Woman yelled. "I do not take blankets!"

"One blanket for each child sick?"

"I tell you true story," Old Woman said, "then maybe

you understand. Maybe. But I do not think so."

Councilman carefully laid the blankets at the foot of her cot.

"Porcupine Ears!" she yelled in Cree. "Keep blankets!" she ordered in English. She puffed on her pipe, staring at him to show her anger and diminishing respect for him. "Long time ago," she sighed, "In that place. Regina." She twisted up her mouth, "Naaaaaa! Story is no good told in English. I tell it in Cree and you interpret."

"Then it will come out the same way," I said. "He will only hear the English version."

"You want to be Chief," she said to councilman, "but you do not speak Cree. You do not think Cree. How can you be Leader of People if you do not know the way of doing things? I cannot accept Old Horse's blankets because he needs them. I will tell you what to do for children, but you must promise to sit at feet of elders and learn exact way of it."

"I promise," councilman said.

"You do this for People. You do this for sick children. But you do this for yourself. Also!"

Councilman's face swelled red. His shoulders shook. He looked like a small boy chastised by a teacher, but he didn't make a sound.

"Long time ago," Old woman said. "Missionaries and teachers from reserves all over pick twenty children to go to new Industrial School in Regina. Children they say are best able to learn white ways. By time of freezing-up-moon, ten children are dead from measles. Whites are plenty scared and they send ten children left home to reserves. By January, they are dead too. Whites still keep at it. In Fort Qu'Appelle, children are dying of measles. Whites cut off their braids. To get rid of lice they say. This is happening too many times, and that one, Dewdney, he sends ten gallons of cod liver oil. It won't cure measles!"

"My wife's grandfather," councilman said. "He got measles once. At Day School. He got over it. But he is blind."

"Man-blind-in-one-eye," Old Woman said in Cree.

"My wife tell me," councilman said. "Her grandfather's grandfather goes up in attic and prays all night. He pray for protection. He promised to dance four days and four nights if life of his son was spared."

"Now you see it!" Old Woman cried. "Tell Old Horse

to wrap children in blankets. To keep them warm. Tell him to cover windows in house with paper, sacks, old skins, rags. Keep out light! Tell fathers of children to cut wood. Women must keep fires in stove going all night. Tell families of Old Horse to gather together and make feast. They must pray for healing!"

"Old Woman must do it," councilman said.

"Old Horse knows what to do," Old Woman said. "Now take back blankets!"

"Another family needs help of a woman," councilman said. "Charlie Smallface had bad accident at the saw mill and can't work no more. So his woman goes to work for the Welshman down in the Coulee. But there's no one to look after kids. They need a woman."

I shook my head at the councilman. Surely he didn't expect Old Woman to keep house for them.

"Sara can do it," Old Woman said.

"She ran off to Saskatoon," councilman said. "Some people seen her hanging around the bus depot. They tell her to go home. But she won't."

Old Woman sucked on her pipe. "There is a woman. On Little Pine's. Her children have left the reserve. Her husband died and she cannot get over it. Send someone to Eli Bear. He will get her to come up to family of Smallface."

Councilman went out again, conferred with someone who had a sty, brought beaded moccasins to Old Woman; after three more people were given advice through him, I realized this could go on for days. Each time he went out he let in a block of winter air. I was afraid of Old Woman catching pneumonia again. "How long is this going to go on?" I asked him, shoving more poplar into the stove. "Old Woman is tiring and I don't want her to catch cold again."

"Tsssst!" Old Woman said. "You fuss about nothing too much!"

"Only two more," councilman said. "People cannot go through winter without help of Medicine Woman."

"*Ki-nisitohten.ci?*" Old Woman said to me. The old head trembled, and her thin braids slapped her neck.

"I understand," I said. Then to the councilman, "If she won't take care of herself there won't be a grandmother to help!"

"*Moniaskwew ki-ka-patisew!*" Old Woman snorted,

turning her face away from me. "What else?" to the councilman.

He offered her an ancient skinning knife with a buffalo bone handle. "Very old," he said. "My great-grandfather's. I give it to my son but I have to take it away from him again. I tell him he can have it back when he goes trapping."

"Why not trapping now?" Old Woman asked. "Good time for catching beaver."

"He got into a fight in the pool hall," councilman said. "Got cut up pretty bad. Wound isn't healing. In his arm." He drew a long line down the sleeve of his Bay jacket. "Swell up pretty bad. Red. And pus coming out now."

Old Woman accepted the skinning knife. "It is good you took it away from him, but not so good about the arm." She gave the councilman a small rawhide bundle tied with grey ribbon. "This must be mixed with water," she said. "Boil water. Long time. Then mix in small bowl. Careful not to touch with hands! Then pack wound with it. Wrap arm in new cloth. After four days clean it out and do it all over again."

"This is from a woman with bad headaches." A silk shawl and blue headscarf. "The Loon put a very bad curse on her. She says she will do anything. Only you must help her. She's pretty crazy her head hurts so bad. She screams a lot too."

"How did he do it?" Old Woman asked.

"One time he comes sneaking by her house," councilman said. "He catch her dog and hit it on the head with something."

"Ahhhh-ha," Old Woman said. "It is true. If you hit dog on head you get headache."

"Can you undo it?" councilman asked. "She says only the Medicine Woman can help her. She goes to doctors in North Battleford. They give her pills, hook wires up to her head, but pain doesn't go away for her."

"This needs strong medicine," Old Woman said. "Where is dog now?"

"She give it away to some people. But pain stayed."

Old Woman searched through her bundle, pulled up one tied with dried sinew. "Magic bones," she said. "Shake them. Spill them out on table or floor. Tell her they are spirit bones. Ask her what she sees. Lie her down on bed. Put ice on her head. Place cloth wrung out in ice water on her eyes. Take cloth away. Put your hands on her head. Tell her you have power given you by medicine woman. Power to take away pain. Tell her you see her pain. It looks like small dog. Now it is coming out of her head. It is running fast up your arm. It jumps off your shoulder and runs out door. Tell her she will have no more pain in her head."

"That's all for now," councilman said. He left Old Woman sorting out her gifts.

"We've used up more wood than we do in three days!" I said. "Maybe you should have asked the Chief to split us some more poplar!"

"You do not believe," Old Woman said.

"Magic bones!" I said.

"*Moniaskwew,*" she said.

"Sure, I'm a dumb white woman," I said.

"If you believe in power of medicine—. Naa! You cannot understand. Only so much I can teach you."

"Herbs and roots," I said, "but I won't buy that magic bone stuff."

"I want to see People again!" she ordered.

I carried her to the window. Outside, people were huddled in an old buckboard pulled by a sway-back team of Indian ponies. Slowly, the wagon creaked and rumbled down the lane.

"It is good," Old Woman said.

"I've had enough of visitors for one day," I said and put her back to bed.

"You must learn to be alone with yourself," she said, "before you can live well with other people."

"You taught me that going away from family is bad," I said. "Elders have always said it," switching to Cree. "Even so. You go away from People and live in bush for long time. You went away from People after Outbreak."

"You must go away from people to find vision for your life," she said.

"Your dreamspirit," I said. "I understand that, but what I think and feel aren't the same thing." I knew my decision to live alone was right for me, but I still needed to be with other people as well. I missed my grandmother, the family arguments, the Sunday company. "I can't have it both ways, can I?"

"I cannot be more than what I am, more than woman who must always bend with wind," she answered. "I cannot be less than what I am. I must listen to my heart's drumming."

"And you are saying I must listen to mine."

"Dare to see long distances," she said. "Walk through bush to prairie. Bring all things together under the sun."

"Not tomorrow," I said. "Monday is laundry day."

Old Woman sighed, "You will never learn about time."

"Tell me more about going away," I said. By learning about her search for a new way of life, I was learning about my own. "You still haven't told me why you went to Montana," I said.

"You must go back to your own memories," she said, "then even beyond that to other side of horizon."

That night, Old Woman began remembering for me the main events of the Indian involvement in the North West Rebellion of 1885. She was there when Poundmaker's starving Crees looted Battleford, and she took part in the Battle at Cut Knife Hill.

"So I tell you about why we had to go away," she said. "I tell you about what happened to People on Battle River. There, all things were torn apart and taken away from People."

It took several weeks for her to relive that part of her life.

Old Woman

We were over two hundred lodges camped at Poundmaker's left-over-land. Piyeco, the crier, brought news to River People: "They hide in Fort! All of them!" He rode around circle of lodges. "Place-at-forks is deserted!"

There was no stopping Poundmaker's young men. Going to Place-at-forks meant powder and shot and guns. They were so eager to fight they went and took what they wanted with no thought of tomorrow and all tomorrows after that.

Poundmaker said nothing, brooding over there, not speaking to my eldest sister who combed his long hair. She braided it, tied his status topknot. He was Okimahikan, new leader of whiteman's making. He never would have been recognized as True Leader before white people came across water in wooden boats. Some leaders were set up by Company factors, others by Woman Leader's men at treaty-signing time, and many more by men who handed out food when we settled on left-over-lands. Most were chosen because foodgivers could tell them what to do. Poundmaker was one of these leaders and he was mistaken for True Leader.

When Big Bear made Thirst Dance, Poundmaker told Ballendyne who was interpreter for Dewdney all that was taking place. He was not strong enough to stop young men from going to Battleford. Going to Battleford made Poundmaker a *Chief.*

So young men gathered to go. Women hitched horses to wagons.

I was sweeping out my family lodge. My father leaned against anchor post laden with sleeping robes hung out to air. I pretended I did not see him. I never disturbed his prayers. He weighed a piece of lead, flat and square, in his hand. He slid it down to ends of his tense tapering fingers. His skin was slack and pale, veins sticking up and pulsing. Such a small piece of lead. Only one ball if he melted it down. He could whittle edges, polish it round, melt scraps—add them to what? There was no more lead. Only one bullet then. He worried the lead, turning and twisting it. He tested it with his thumb.

I knew he would not go. He could not go so unprepared.

Women gathered around my mother's wagon. They sang farewell song to men who were going to Place-at-forks.

"Bring back beef! Tea! Blankets! Some ribbons!"

Bear Woman's wide thighs spread over sitting boards on wagon. "Stop praying!" she yelled at my father. She refused to ever say it is just time to be old.

I dropped willow broom. It smacked earth. I fought my billowing skirts. I watched young men gathering to go. They pushed horses this way and that, rode circles around lodges, weaving this way and that through camp.

"They are going to Place-at-forks," my old father said.

Horse-dance-maker came, leading the fastest horse. "Awah-hē!" he said to my father. "You won't come with us?"

"You ride too fast for me," my father said.

Horse-dance-maker leaped onto horse's back. He kicked grey racer's flanks. He was too anxious to go, too eager. He was not a fighting man. He had never gone on a horseraid against Blackfoot. I was afraid for him.

"You won't be hungry when we get back," Horse-dance-maker said. He jerked rope, turned horse's head, heeled flanks and galloped away. He stirred up dust.

"Porcupine ears," my father said, "all day I can talk to young men but they hear nothing."

"Come on!" Bear Woman called. "Come on!"

My eldest sister, Fox's Woman and Lucky Man's four women crawled into wagon. Bear Woman bounced on the seat. She was as broad as blanketed rounding of grey racer's rump. My old father buried his fear of redcoats in dark studying of lead. He was not so old he did not hear young men mounting fast horses. Children jumped in dust, chased dogs, shouted at raiders. Women sang farewell song, waved and wished raiders luck. But this time we were not left behind to wait and see who came back from raid.

"We bring back beef!" Bear Woman yelled.

"I match your beef with my beef!" It was Fox's Woman, and all women shrieked with laughter.

Suddenly, something caught me up and lifted my feet and made me run to wagon. My skirts were flying up, but I did not care. I laughed. I slapped my thighs, running, and I did not think about tomorrow. Only about ribbons and dancing and feasting. Bear Woman grabbed my hand and heaved me up. I perched on seat beside her. My scarf was slipping, and I retied it. Bear Woman slapped horse's rumps with rope. Wagon rolled towards trail to Place-at-forks. It was safe to go there. Redcoats and townspeople hid in Fort. They were afraid of Riel and his promises, of Dumont and his fighting wolves, of Poundmaker's warriors ready to die for our children's Tomorrow. They were afraid of Big Bear who had called all People together to make show of strength. Wagon creaked and shook. It bumped women from side to side. Fox's Woman bounced up and down and waved at warriors. Her feet were dancing.

"Sit down!" Bear Woman yelled.

Women settled into wagon, but their chattering and laughter scared away small birds nesting in willow. Ahead, Poundmaker led line of raiders. His war leaders flanked his sides.

"Go fast!" Fox's Woman yelled.

They started out slowly, singing. Farewell song rose above flat of land that angled down to meeting place of Poundmaker's and Little Pine's land. It followed raiders, pressed at backs like wind, and rising again, it pushed them to turning where blue willows reached down steep and muddy banks of Battle River. Horses' heads swayed and tossed, stretched for clumps of new prairie wool. Hooves clicked on stones. Dirty winter snow yielded small runs of water to warm and insisting breath of Goose Moon. Tails swung easily. Horses left droppings in new mud.

Line of raiders dropped down, moved through poplars awaiting promise of leaves, horses' front legs disappearing first, then blanketed horsemen vanished. Earth seemed to swallow raiders, slowly sucking, to spit them back out of valley onto flatland at Place-at-forks. Two camps from now. I left my old father lighting the Pipe and praying for Miyopayiwin. Nothing would go well again for People.

Not if we sacked Battleford.

So now I tell you why we looted Battleford. I was there, in last camp pitched beside River. Poundmaker had called a council. He was always stopping here and there to make talk. He never could decide what to do even when he was doing it.

Raiders arranged themselves in circle according to their status among River People. Red Pheasant from Eagle Hills and his headmen were seated across from Poundmaker and his young men. They smoked and passed the Pipe. Outside circle, woman squatted near wagons and smoked their own small pipes. I was listening to all our Leaders said.

Fine Day started it. "Halfbreeds are fighting!" he said. He was a War Leader, not a speechmaker like Poundmaker. "We must fight for our own reasons," he said, "not Halfbreeds'!"

Poundmaker shook his head and long famous braids bounced on his blanket-coat. "When Riel's men came I sent them away," he said. "They cannot win but I hope it does not go badly for them."

"It is true Halfbreeds fight for their rights to land. We are brothers and we must join together." Fine Day clenched his teeth. "But I say if we join them without taking their hands in ours they will not fight for our cause. Paskwawiyiniwak! We are Prairie People. We must fight so our children do not go hungry!"

"Awahē! Awahē!" women cried in one voice.

"Wires have been cut at Place-of-settlement. Prisoners taken! Now Place-at-forks is empty of Across-water-people. I say let's go!" Bowboy spoke true to his Name.

The Pipe passed back to Fine Day. He never showed himself unless he was sure of his followers and he never disagreed with Poundmaker. Now he did not know what to do because he could not know what Poundmaker would decide. "Riel's men," he said, "they come to talk, then run away. Why don't they stay when they know we are going after ammunition?"

"They speak words tall as trees," Poundmaker said.

"But they are as much afraid of us," Fine Day said, "as they are of redcoats."

Poundmaker said nothing, and I knew that when he did speak it would be a long persuasion as slowly moving as summer rains. He would lead Fine Day to the decision he had already made: to do nothing but wait.

Red Pheasant's men were whispering to each other. Pamihakan. They were first looked-after-people who never did anything for themselves. They took foodgivers' flour and bacon as if it came from One-above.

I could see that it would not go well.

Lucky Man's four women built a small fire and made tea. Bear Woman refused to get out of wagon. She wanted to go on to Battleford. She smoked her woman's pipe, but I knew she would not wait long for men to decide what to do.

"Who will give us flour and bacon if I take up arms against whites?" Red Pheasant passed Pipe to Poundmaker. "Stonies killed their foodgiver and a white man who lives near their left-over-land!"

All council ways were broken. Raiders shouted in one voice: "We need ammunition! Guns! Food! What do we wait for? It begins!"

Red Pheasant faced his own men. "Halfbreeds are fighting! Stonies are starting to fight! Those who are not fighters take to woods!"

Looked-after-ones scuttled away, mounted horses, and headed for out-of-sight-places. Some would take shelter with white-collars.

Red Pheasant spoke again. "Since Treaty-signing-time Poundmaker has held out for a better way. He never stops stirring up foodgivers. He speaks to Woman Leader's headmen for us. He tries to get better things for our children. He must go on doing so!"

Sudden silence settled over council as if great and many-skinned lodge had dropped from Thunderbird's beak. Red Pheasant was centre-pole, his men staked tent pegs around outside circle. Poundmaker's men were inner linings. Fox, taller than even Poundmaker, his totem's tail showing his status as runner. Night Traveller who earned his Name four-times-four and more against Blackfoot. Iron Body. Piyeco.

All men silent.

Pheasant had no liking for Poundmaker from the time he took one of Pheasant's wives into bushes, broke away from Eagle Hill's band, and took to Cut Knife Hill strongest and boldest warriors. Poundmaker, once headman for Pheasant, set himself up as Leader and caused a split among River People.

Maybe it was the signing, as much as disappearing buffalo, that caused Outbreak. True Leaders like Big Bear would not take Treaty and so separated from those who were put on left-over-lands.

"I know what you want," Badger said at time of signing in Fort Qu'Appelle, "but I do not think it will run well." He spoke of Miyopayiwin, but Sounding Creature, that interpreter, could not find words to show Woman Leader's men what it was Badger saw disappearing from land whitemen said belonged to a woman who lived across water. It was more than buffalo.

Now Red Pheasant was making Poundmaker a Leader, but he placed all the blame for fighting on him. Poundmaker should have been medicine man like his father who gave him his Name, content to sit drumming beside pound and calling spirits of buffalo.

Poundmaker was making talk: "From the beginning I did not trust promises!"

At Fort Carleton there was no word for what Woman Leader wanted from People. Asotam was The Promise, and it had nothing to do with putting black marks on paper. Asoktsikew was one who promised to dance with bone skewers tearing his flesh. That Promise was made when life was threatened. Promise was kept when life was spared by He-who-is-alone-above. At Fort Carleton promises were made by Woman no person had ever seen. People gave away land forever and were given empty words. No life came from signings, and after there was no dancing.

"You all know how I told Star Blanket and Big Child that land is no piece of pemmican to be broken up into small pieces." Poundmaker waited for his words to reach outside circles. His words reached me. "Maybe they had no choice. They had to sign. I do not know. But now our children go hungry. We cannot go fishing and hunting where we find game as it was promised. Land belonging to Creator is cut into small pieces. Buffalo are gone. We are held down by words scratched on paper that will never rub out. I say promises do not need to be scratched on paper."

"Tapwe! Tapwe!" People cried in one voice.

"Everything Woman Leader's men do they scratch about it on paper," Fine Day said. "That is the only way they can remember to keep their word. Even so, they do not do what they say they will do. The only way now is to take land back!"

"We cannot win!" Horse-dance-maker cried. "We will all die!"

Listening, I was also watching a horseman riding fast towards us. It was Peter Ballendyne, interpreter and defeated rival of Erasmus at Fort Carleton. "Foodgiver sent me!" he yelled, almost falling from his horse, "because he wants to know why you gather in such large numbers."

Fox and Bowboy made room between them for Ballendyne.

"I will talk to Foodgiver," Poundmaker said.

"He won't come. He says to tell you he is worried."

"Tell him to cross River and meet with us."

"He feels it isn't safe to do so."

"So Foodgiver is afraid!"

"I must warn you," Sounding Creature's voice hardly carrying to outside circle, "Payne and Fremont are dead! Killed by Stonies! All Indians are implicated. You are caught up in it!"

"If he comes and is willing to talk we can settle it."

"He is willing to give up certain things if you—"

"Tell Foodgiver we will do what we have to do."

"Your last word?"

"Ahhhh-ha! Unless he comes."

"He won't!"

"Then Foodgiver decides for us." Poundmaker spoke to People now. "You want to go. I cannot stop you. But touch nothing until sun sets." Not wanting blood spilled, he said he hoped Foodgiver would come and give in to demands for better things, would maybe talk for People and get Woman Leader to give one large piece of left-over-land to all Real People.

Poundmaker had shown his weakness. Word returned to warriors.

"Yei! Yei!" raiders cried. They jumped onto fast horses. Women climbed into wagons. We were going to Place-at-forks. We would take what we wanted, with no thought of tomorrow. Women would do most of the taking away of food and cloth and furs.

Raiders raced ponies. They cried, "Yei! Yei!" They broke into strange square dwellings arranged in rows along deserted streets. All day women had stalked streets. We flattened noses against glass. We grumbled about so much to eat on boards along walls. Now we were taking food. We left guns for warriors. Lucky Man's four women, my eldest sister, Fox's Woman and I waited outside Little Bearskin's Trading Post. My fingers were tingling, palms sweating.

Beside me, Horse-dance-maker hammered lock with his war club. Fox was close behind him. Wooden door yielded, but not to Horse-dance-maker's club. It gave way to man pushing backwards and bumping his way out of dark post. Fox jumped sideways. Horse-dance-maker was thrust to ground. His club thudded onto earth. Cursing, inside man turned, his thick arms bunched around beaver skins and fox furs. He ran, knees bent, like old woman needing out-of-sight-place in a hurry. He clutched his loot and ran.

It was Foodgiver, one who told Poundmaker he could always get his body inside tent door if he could get his head in first. It was Foodgiver, one who always took best for himself and locked storehouse behind him.

Door to trading post was open now. Open to Poundmaker's raiders who always brought back ponies, beadwork, skins, and blankets from raids on Blackfoot camps. Horse-dance-maker leaped into darkness. Fox crawled on his knees behind him. Bowboy smashed window with war club. Splinters clung to frames and he knocked them out with fist wrapped in sack.

I boosted myself up and over sill. Behind me I heard more doors crashing, warriors yelling and dashing into stores. Inside, air was rank with tangy smell of tallow and skunky odor of weasel skins.

"I can't see!" I cried.

"Traps in corner," Horse-dance-maker said.

I bumped into something solid but yielding like Bear Woman's belly. Flour dust flew around my knees. I felt my way along wall, tore my shawl on nail. My right hand touched white saddle. More nails. Harness. Traplines. Smell of leather. Another harness. My fingers curled around long coarse hair of winter-killed fox. On lower shelves candy, hidden so People's children could not steal it.

Strike-him-on-back smashed boards with rifle butt. He swept candy boxes into pile at my feet. I grabbed glass jar, cracked it open on edge of counter, poked my fingers into honey; and I was sucking, melting sweet trickling out corners of my mouth. More. I scooped into jar again, found my mouth, and the sticky honey ran down my wrist.

I stuffed my lootbag with jars of fruit.

Fox searched for ammunition. He tossed lead and tin box of powder to Bowboy. Tin box flew over my head. I ducked, backed into something lumpy and broad and moving. It was Foodgiver. He had calf skins and fox furs over his flanneled arms. He dropped weasel skins, so anxious he was to take best of Trader's goods. *"Goddam squaw!"* he yelled at me. "Tell your fat old mother what's mine is not hers!" Then Foodgiver was running again, hunched over his loot, running to his tent.

"No guns!" Bowboy pulled a metal ring on floor behind counter piled with shirts and pants whitemen wore. "Dogass!" He hoisted wooden floor, let it crash down, and cold musty cellar smell rose: damp dirt and rotting potatoes. Bowboy jumped into hole.

Strike-him-on-back balanced bolts of red and yellow cloth on his head. Yellow-mud-blanket knocked jars off shelves. I caught one, unscrewed tin top. I wanted to take lard pails home. I crammed candy sticks into my mouth.

Bowboy dashed up and out of cellar. Lizard ran down potato sack slung over his shoulder. "Leave food for women!" Lucky Man's Blackfoot Woman dragged it out of post to Bear Woman's wagon.

"This way!" Horse-dance-maker yelled.

We followed him through hole in wall. Orange cloth

fell from hanging pole. It tumbled onto my head. Laughing, I made move-along-dance. Fox's Woman found a ribboned hat. She stuffed boots into her sack.

Horse-dance-maker stuck his head out window. He hooted and slapped his legs. "Your old mother does not bother with flour!"

I poked my head through his crooked elbow. My mother was hustling away from Foodgiver's tent with furs draped over her wide shoulders. Foodgiver stood under his tentflap, cursing, his fists waving at Bear Woman, but he did not go after her. There was not a man living under sky who dared chase Bear Woman.

Now Foodgiver was running towards post, coming back for more furs.

Horse-dance-maker squeezed me. "Your old mother knows how to clean out tents! Ho! She is too-much-woman!"

I found Company blankets piled on bed. Bowboy's head had disappeared under bed, but he was backing out. He bumped his shoulders on springs and his feet hit washstand. A jar shaped like penis had dry roses in it. It fell over and spilled brown water on Bowboy's head. He was dragging something heavy, something wooden, and it scraped along floor. A long box, top nailed down. He smashed it with his war club and tore boards away with his hands.

"Guns!" Bowboy cried. "*Sniders!*"

Singing and dancing outside. Someone fired rifle, wasted ammunition. Crashing sound in other room. "Let's go!" Piyeco yelled. "Fire!" He pointer towards River "Where Woman Leader's man lives! The one who puts men away behind stone walls!"

I swung my lootsack over my shoulder. I stacked blankets and lardpails on my right arm the same way I carry firewood. I tottered as if I had had too much firewater.

Bowboy threw rifles to Strong Body and Horse-dance-maker.

"Horsemen!" Piyeco yelled, waving his arms, "riding from Fort!"

We scuttled out of Little Bearskin's Post, left Foodgiver flinging fox furs over his shoulders. Outside, People were running this way and that way through darkness. They were afraid of whistling Dead who were hungry and wanted a feast.

Northern night lights of Departed-ones-dancing dropped closer and closer to ground. Black smoke rose from house belonging to Woman Leader's man. He might send raiders to Stony Mountain if they did not get away from horsemen soon.

Something small and furry ran between my feet. I laughed, no longer afraid, because Horse-dance-maker carried ratfood in his bundle so northern-night-dancers, even night fire, would not hurt us. I tossed blankets and lardpails and lootsack into wagon. Horse-dance-maker came galloping hard, his buckskin arm grabbing hold of me; and he swung me up to ride in front of him. Grey racer obeyed side kicks. Horse-dance-maker held me tight. I wound long mane around my hands. I leaned forward over horse's neck, pressed my legs against bunching shoulders. Horse-dance-maker curved his body around mine. Strike-him-on-back and Bowboy rode on either side.

"Look! There!" Horse-dance-maker laughed.

Foodgiver sat gloomily on pile of furs in front of his tent made of bad material. Guarding loot from Bear Woman.

"Otasahkew!" Horse-dance-maker roared, his smooth cheek against my damp one. His laughing breath smelled of firewater.

We flashed by sulking Foodgiver. Fox joined us, his totem's tail bobbing on his head and neck. Red Pheasant and his warriors swept down on us from steep bank of River, but dropped speed to ride behind Poundmaker and his War Leaders. Raiders from Little Pine's waited at end of last street.

"Yei!" Night Traveller cried, raising his Black Bess.

Raiders. Sudden rush of horsemen. Many People moving everywhere.

Long line of raiders formed protection before Leaders. Horse-dance-maker closed distance between raiders and Leaders. Space between Night Traveller and Strong Body opened so Horse-dance-maker and I, Fox, and Bowboy rode in center. Northward we flew. Long neck of street stretched back; Battleford was behind us and before us only flatland grew darkly in all directions. Many horsemen dashed across our trail. Leader turned south, and flowing wave after wave of horsemen was crossing current against rushing river of Cree raiders pushing north. "White raiders!" Horse-dance-maker yelled. Townsmen going to Battleford to finish looting.

Where prairie meets bushland Night Traveller and raiders from Little Pine dropped back, one by one, to ride behind Poundmaker and his followers. Behind them, Red Pheasant's men slowed. We were on Sweet Grass land now, cut our way through willows along Creek. Horses' hooves thudded on grassy banks. Small stones flying all around. We crossed Creek, and water splashed on my legs.

We raced along bottom of Battle River Valley. Patches of left-over-snow flashed by on either side. Night air was cold and damp. Horse-dance-maker held me tight. Long pull over hill and then, from behind, raiders rushed distance between them and Leaders. They swept down on us, long line split by Red Pheasant. He swerved and turned south, returning to Eagle Hills. His warriors followed, line of them spreading across valley floor and disappearing into darkness until I only heard diminishing thud thud thud of hooves.

We pushed on to Poundmaker's left-over-land, but slowed for long walk to Cut Knife Hill. I thought of feasting. Many days food. And Leaders had *Sniders* and lead for flintlocks.

River People feasted after looting Battleford. Raiders told stories for nights on nights and their daring grew with each telling.

Poundmaker was afraid redcoats would arrest raiders. But Goose Moon passed into Budding Moon, and no soldiers came. War Leaders wanted to fight, and Poundmaker sent scouts to watch soldier leaders and tell him about their marching. "If they want a fight we will give it," he said, "but redcoats must fire first shot." He sent tobacco to Leaders all across prairie, asking them to join us, but bundles were returned. So Poundmaker sent Horse-dance-maker to Crowfoot to ask Blackfoot to join us.

On first night of Budding Moon, my eldest sister and I were mending ceremonial clothes with bits of old rawhide. We huddled close to fire in my family lodge. We listened to hoarse voices of raiders telling stories around outside fireplaces. Songs mingled with higher shouts of warriors making fun beyond protective circle of lodges and fires. Raiders threw lengths of stolen cloth, tossed red and yellow bolts, hurled streams of blues and greens over dark budding poplar. "Awahē! Awahē!" they cried.

"Let soldier leaders come and try to punish River People," Bear Woman said. "We are better fighters than redcoats."

"Tssssst!" my eldest sister said. She listened to new-young-men sing Around-tipi-song.

Wasakamesimowin! Song sailed over swallow-tailed cones of lodges. Horse-dance-maker's voice rose above others. He strolled between lodges singing.

> "I walk around camp
> at night singing
> Ami Ami Nicimosis!"

Horse-dance-maker crouched around lodge towards doorflap. We watched his shadow creeping along skin wall.

> "I wonder who is this
> who is walking?
> She is my Nicimosis
> Ami Ami Nicimosis!"

"He is coming after you," my eldest sister whispered.

"We have fun with him," my mother said.

"Come on! Come on!" Horse-dance-maker groped on his hands and knees towards doorflap.

I wanted women to go visiting. I had not lain with him since the night we looted Battleford. My heart fluttered. My hands trembled. My stitching of cloth was poorly done.

"Come on! Come on!" Horse-dance-maker poked his head around anchor-post, whispering, "Come on!"

Bear Woman lifted tentflap and stuck her overly-large head outside. "I gave up *Come-on* long time ago!" Her laughter shattered promising night air.

Horse-dance-maker scampered backwards, around tent, away from Bear Woman. She rolled into lodge, kicking her feet and holding her belly from too much laughing. My eldest sister tossed bits of rawhide in air. She ducked out of tent, hurried to her own new man.

I rolled into my worn and frizzled sleeping-robe. I would wait until Horse-dance-maker had made talk with Poundmaker. Then he would come to me and lead me away from camp down to bed of Battle River. We would lie in long grasses and he would be my only covering. I would sleep in his arms all night.

"This time he is not so lucky!" Bear Woman said. She rocked back to her haunches. She added dry birch to fire. Wood caught, gave her more light for mending.

I lay on floorhide well below rising smoke. Waiting. It wasn't so late. Horse-dance-maker would come to me this night. He had been away too long, but raiders would not do anything until he said the word from Crowfoot. Poundmaker would stop them. I turned my back to Bear Woman. My fingers slid across summer skins lining lodge. I traced jagged curve, joining tears in deerskin with my fingers. Old lining would not last passing of Budding Moon, and my father had promised long wet summer. I reached into my sleeping-robe and pulled at my rawhide toes. I wanted to run barefoot to Horse-dance-maker.

"There isn't enough rawhide!" Bear Woman yelled. She threw bits of leather into corner where she stored winter robes. She cursed riflemen as though they could hear her.

She was always yelling. She screamed at my father that he was not a provider, it was his fault buffalo grass was burned. She was always yelling. She smacked my ears for going into bushes with Horse-dance-maker when there was wood to be gathered. Nothing pleased her. Not even a full pail of berries.

She settled again before fire, complaining about too much unused-to-food we had stolen from Battleford, about Old Women's Society. "Those old she-dogs! All they do is go visiting! They talk too much!" Maybe she was afraid of their medicine. They never asked Bear Woman to join in medicine feast. Maybe because she was too-much-woman.

Her fringed shawl and skirt were streaked with grease. She did not care about her hair, needed new ribbons and scarf. I turned away again, wanting Horse-dance-maker. Wanting fighting to be over. Wanting a lodge of my own. Night smoke spiraled around lodgepoles reaching for sky. Return of Goose Moon had brought warm wind. Left smokeflap was open to stars. Juniper branches burned down. Smoke hung low in lodge. It drifted through scorched smokeflaps. Through shimmering heat waves I saw Horse-dance-maker's dusty head in doorflap.

He came back. He had been away from me many nights, but now he was back. I wanted to cry out to him. I wanted to leap up and run to him, but I only burrowed deeper into sleeping-robe.

Horse-dance-maker carried medicine bundle. He took his place before fire, but didn't lean against willow back-rest. I could not speak to worthyman who brings bundle inside to make ready for battle. I stared at cloth-wrapped-bundle. I could not breathe. I was so afraid for Horse-dance-maker. He had never been a fighting man and now he was making ready to fight redcoats. I turned my head again to skin wall. I must not look upon totem. I did not know he had a dreamspirit, but a man does not speak of this to his woman.

Cloth was new. Did that mean he had had a vision when he was travelling? It would turn a provider and legender into fighter.

Horse-dance-maker was preparing the Pipe. Now I understood why only women and children had feasted on this first night of Budding Moon, why Poundmaker had not eaten stolen food. The fighting would start soon. But what was the word from Crowfoot? Would Blackfoot join us?

"Ayaw ota!" My old father lifted tentflap. "He is here!" he cried. "Poundmaker is here!"

"There is room for him by fire," Horse-dance-maker said.

Bear Woman curled into pile of winter robes like old She-bear stirring in winter sleep.

Horse-dance-maker leaned over me, his blanket-coat rough against my face. It smelled of many campfires and tobacco. He whispered, "Ki-kitmakayimitin." Then he made room beside fire for visitors.

Poundmaker ducked into lodge. "Tawaw!" Horse-dance-maker said. "Api!" Poundmaker took centre place before fire, Horse-dance-maker and my old father on each side of him. My father prepared Pipe and gave it to Poundmaker.

"River is high," Poundmaker said.

"Ahhhh-ha!" my father said. "Too high for weirs."

"It is wrong time for fish," Poundmaker said. He

passed Pipe to Horse-dance-maker.

"So we watch children grow thin and weak from eating bacon and flour Foodgiver hands out!" Horse-dance-maker said. "How long must we listen to them crying for food we cannot give them? How can a man eat pig when his belly wants buffalo tongue?"

There was a new anger in Horse-dance-maker that I never heard from him before.

"And how can a man stand noises his woman makes?" my father said. Bear Woman was snoring, but my father's words might waken her, and then even Poundmaker would be smacked down by her growling. Men laughed because my father was a medicine man who should have been able to cure such ailments.

"Stonies have joined us," Poundmaker said, "and some of Thunderchild's People. It is hard to feed so many camped together."

"It is good!" Horse-dance-maker said. Furious smokepuffs escaped between his teeth. "Sweet Grass People increase our numbers by many more. Now we fight!"

"People gather in numbers for safety," Poundmaker said.

"No! They come to fight!"

Poundmaker took the Pipe from Horse-dance-maker. "First I must think how are we going to feed all of them. Foodgiver will not give me food for People from other left-over-lands." He pointed Pipestem towards Deer's Rump Hill. Smoke circled his long head.

"Sikakosak!" my father cried. "Get providers to kill skunks!"

"We do not have enough ammunition for hunting and fighting both!" Horse-dance-maker tore rawhide bag from his belt and hurled it over fire. It hit tentflap and fell flatly on floorhide. It was empty.

Poundmaker said: "Foodgiver told Stonies, 'Go back to your own land and get your own grub. I do not have enough food for Poundmaker's People.' "

"So we make bows and arrows," my father said, "and killing skunks will kill our appetites!"

"Have you talked to Stonies?" Poundmaker asked Horse-dance-maker. "How many will fight?"

Horse-dance-maker held up his pointing-finger. "If we defeat redcoats *once*, others will join us. It is up to us!"

"How do we feed so many? We have more than two hundred lodges of our own and not enough food. We are chased away from hunting places. No small game!"

"We can snare gophers!" my old father said. His knees bounced on floorhide.

"We must do something," Horse-dance-maker said, "before we have no strength left!"

"Roast porcupine will give us strength," Old Man said, "and when river goes down we can set up weirs."

"Fish! Porcupine!" Horse-dance-maker yelled. "Must we live like Woods People?"

"Better than skunks," Old Man said.

Poundmaker shook his head. Horse-dance-maker reached behind him and squeezed my toes sticking out of my sleeping-robe. Glances circled, then it broke, my old father leading the laughter and all of him shaking. His toes wiggled out of holes in his moccasin like fish caught in weir. Poundmaker threw back his head, swallow-lump bobbing in his stretched neck. Horse-dance-maker snorted and pulled his long nose.

"We must think of children," Poundmaker said. His blanketed narrow shoulders drooped toward fire.

"Maybe buffalo will come back," Old Man said.

"We must decide what is best for children. It is time to be silent and think on it."

"Roast porcupine," whispered my father. Kind-old-man-buffalo always had last word.

I fingered tears in deerskin lining. Maybe my father spoke true, maybe buffalo would come back. After River People defeated redcoats and chased away Across-water-people. My father always said buffalo would come back, rise again out of wallows.

Then providers would build pound. Poundmaker would sit behind wall of poles and drum and call spirits of buffalo: "Paah . . . skwah . . . moos . . . toooos . . . . wak!" Beaters flap blankets. Skin drum calling and beating faster and faster. Providers drive buffalo through stone drive-line. Buffalo swerves towards opening, stumbles over Great-log, rolls into hollowed earth, then rolling back, hooves striking air, and on his feet running, head charging, butting walls, but finding no way out of pound. Herd follows, rushes against logs, hooves pummeling earth. Clods of dirt fly all around. Arrows fall from sky, bullets spraying between logs. Roar of buffalo. Thudding of bodies.

Old Man asked for Pipe. "Iska! Ni-mayapahten!" he said. "Long-time-ago I had bad dream. My dreamspirit pointed to Tomorrow and made me look at it. But it was dark and I could not see! Then I saw my daughter walking alone. I was afraid for her. She was alone. Night sky was all around her!"

I trembled in my sleeping-robe. I wanted to run to my old father, into his arms, be held by him. I burrowed deeper into sleeping-robe.

"I am Old Man. I am too weak to fight and too slow. But I think you must stop what is happening. Woman Leader promised good things. But land is changing. We are punished for killing buffalo and wasting meat. Maybe we try to raise cattle. Dig in soil. Maybe."

"Tapwe!" Poundmaker said. "Now we ask for one large piece of left-over-land for all People."

"Woman Leader will never give us land! She only takes it away! She wants it for settlers!" Horse-dance-maker clenched stem of Pipe between his teeth. "No! I say we take land back. We give it back to Rightful Owner!"

Old Man sucked his bottom lip, took deep breath, pointed at Horse-dance-maker. "There are four things we cannot give away. Land. Grass. Trees. Animals. They belong to Father-of-all."

Poundmaker seemed to be looking through summer linings. "Woman Leader promised we could hunt and fish as before. It is not so! Foodgiver demands a paper. He will not let us fish or hunt outside of left-over-lands. Without his Say-so we cannot visit relatives and friends on other left-over-lands."

"Now you see why we must fight," Horse-dance-maker said.

"What does my Other-father say? Will Blackfoot

help?"

Horse-dance-maker said, "Crowfoot will not fight. Too many people died in Blackfoot Starvation Winter. They are fed by Woman Leader's headmen. Beef is a bribe so Blackfoot will keep peace."

"We do not attack redcoats," Poundmaker said, "but if they come we will be ready."

"We will not be caught asleep!" Old Man said.

"It is good!" Horse-dance-maker said.

Were redcoats coming? Two moons had passed since we went to Place-at-forks and no soldier leaders had come. Maybe because redcoats were afraid to fight worthymen who knew how to slit Blackfoot throats. If they knew how raiders had found Blackfoot lovers humping beside Crowfoot Creek and had returned with ceremonial dress and beadwork and a great story of how lovers were so lost in grabbing-hold they never knew who lifted their heads, slit throats and let blood flow together; if redcoats knew that they would never come to Cut Knife Hill.

"We have guns," my father said, "but no bullets."

"We move camp often so place of fighting is to our side of it and not theirs," Horse-dance-maker said. "We are fighting wolves! We make too many surprises for redcoats. Never attack from same place twice! Never let them see where we are!"

I had never heard Horse-dance-maker talk this way before. Something was happening to him.

"So we shoot only when we cannot miss!" Old Man said.

"We are hungry wolves," Poundmaker said, his voice holding sadness heavier than stone buffalo at Cree Crossing.

"Ahhhh-ha!" Horse-dance-maker cried. "Stalk herd! Keep out of sight! Suddenly come at them from behind! Snap at weak! Cripple strong ones! Then wolves go for neck!"

Poundmaker shook his head. "Maybe we wait."

Horse-dance-maker rose without using his hands. His lips were stretched tight over his grinding teeth. He stood, left arm hidden under blanket-coat, right raised as if he would strike Poundmaker. Slowly, he showed his hidden hand,

122

drawing it away from Company blanket. He gripped a war club. He pointed it toward warm wind's home. He smashed hole in rotting skin wall.

Lodge shook with shock of disrespect. It swayed, top joints creaking. It leaned towards Battle River, then held by anchor ropes, it steadied. Night wind breathed through skin wall.

"That hole! When big gun fires on our camp this lodge will be one big hole! That hole is nothing!"

"If redcoats fire first we answer with fire," Poundmaker said, lifting his body to its full height. "I will tell People this."

Horse-dance-maker took rotting skin in his hands. He ripped it until hole was larger than Poundmaker's head. "Look! Out there! Can you see long distances! See redcoats coming?"

"I see only People's campfires," Poundmaker said. "Protective circle of lodges."

Horse-dance-maker thrust his head outside. "Peeeee-yaaay-choooooo!" he yelled. His dusty head showed again. "I do not go against you," right hand on heartside, "so I lead you to see longer distances."

"Redcoats coming! Redcoats coming!" The Cry was going around camp. "All warriors gather!" Around and around circle Piyeco, the Crier, galloped. "Notintokimawak! Notintokimawak!" Piyeco, the Crier, galloped. "Notin-tokimawak! Notintokimawak!"

"How soon do they come?" Poundmaker said.

"Soldier Leader has left Swift Current," Horse-dance-maker said. "I saw many redcoats. Not many camps behind me now. Maybe one sunrise they come. Maybe two."

"Call River People together," Poundmaker said.

"We must prepare them for the worst," Old Man said.

All night warriors painted faces, cleaned flintlocks and *Sniders,* and prayed for protection in battle. I worked with women. We stuffed shirts and leggings with grass and hid them. Buckskin warriors looked real behind poplar, slumped against willows, propped on logs.

Before sun rose Horse-dance-maker came looking for me. I saw him riding grey racer through deserted camp. He bounded over and around stones circling cold fireplaces. His all-night-watch at Creek's crossing, better than tossing in sleeping-robe, prepared him for battle. He was ready, wanting the the fighting to start, but first he was looking for me. I pushed through underbrush, hands sweeping leafless branches aside, toes digging into soft sandy soil. I started towards new camp, hoping he would follow me to my lodge.

Horse-dance-maker rested his horse where once clustered tents of women and children who had no providers. Horse stretched long neck, pulled down on rawhide rope, munched at long grasses. I struggled over rough land, away from trail, toward ravine. Old trail was flattened by many moving wagons, raked by travois poles dragged by horses. I slid down sloping bank. I thrust through tangle of poplar branches. Here I would wait for Horse-dance-maker. I turned to see if he were following me and fell against his sweating chest. So silently he had come.

His arms went around me. He held me tight against him with a fierceness I had never felt in him before. I trembled and rubbed my nose in hollow under his shoulder. All pain of lost nights without him eased away, and I was not holding back my wanting him. Arms locked around each other, we tumbled and rolled down slope into underbrush. My skirt was carried up from my legs. I dropped my arms to untie his breech clout. "Don't let go!" I whispered, although there were only nesting sparrows to hear me. I wrapped my legs around his sticky back. I took him into me, and there was a solidness about it that I had not known with him until this night. In Horse-dance-maker there was an urgency that was new. He was no longer fighting that part of him that had led him to his first battle.

All his life he had been afraid to go on horseraids. He was raised to be a legender and provider. Now his worthiness was making him fight for People. Not a raid against Blackfoot to get horses for the hunt, but a fight for our unborn children: that they might have Tomorrow.

His strong body beat against my breast. He gripped my buttocks. I bit his shoulder. I thrust my hips up and took him deeper into me. I wanted him to make a child, a boy child, but it was not to be so. Horse-dance-maker raised up from my breast, threw back his head. He stiffened, then slumped down on me again. Inside me, he was still beating against my skin walls. I rose higher than sky, like bursting of night light into day. It spread down my legs to make my toes curl. Inside me: small wings beating.

Horse-dance-maker lay heavy on me. His breathing slowed. One of his braids had fallen across my eyes. I held it to my cheek.

Over us, branches weaving in and out, and through them I watched changing sky. Grey clouds drifted over land, shaped like many bodies. A long and uneven line of People lying on backs as if they had been set afloat downriver. An old woman wrapped in wolfskin. Girl-child clutching crow feathers. Warrior, hair unbraided. Old Man with weasel pelts tied to his braids. Warrior with many penises growing out of his head. Woman with grizzled head of bear. New-young-man with hair growing all over his face. They all drifted overhead, on backs, hands folded; and they all were wrapped in blankets or animal skins.

Night was broken by crack of gunshot. An old voice: "Wake up! Wake up!" Then steady galloping hooves.

Horse-dance-maker's body jerked. He rolled away from me, up on his knees. He retied his breech clout. His teeth flashed white in darkness. Then he ran up slope.

My back stuck to wet earth. Cold air washed over my sweating body. I sat up and wiped my face with end of my skirt. I shivered. Bits of last summer's leaves and damp dirt clung to my hair. I crawled up to flat edge of Cut Knife Hill, flat against earth, I looked over edge of ravine. Land stretched away from Cut Knife Hill toward new and sleeping camp. Tents belonging to Stonies and Thunderchild's People around edge, and swallow-tailed cones of Little Pine's and Poundmaker's tents in centre places. Northward, new and dense growth of poplar, silver willow, and chokecherry bush. There, buckskin warriors were hidden. Then light began, rising from grey deeper than horse hide. Sky opened before me, light widening like arms stretching from distant Deer's Rump Hill on Little Pine's land, spreading yellow across grassy valley floor, touching greening bush, until light wrapped flanks of faraway hills in sundance cloth. Eastward, Battle River Trail carved through meeting place of bushland, flatland, and hill country. It moved, crawled toward me from final flattening of land far to east at Battleford. Sound of wood striking stones. Coarse voices. Head of column appeared like nose of cautious gopher poking out of hole. Many wagons crossing creek, middle bulging like gopher swallowing garter snake, its tail twisting back into valley.

So redcoats came at last. Soldier Leader's halfbreed scouts led them up old trail.

Old Man Jacob was running across top of hill, his stiff legs humping as if he were stamping out a fire. "Wake up!" he yelled, "Wake up!" He slipped on wet buffalo grass, slid, tottered, and hollered. He tried to rouse sleeping People.

"Warn them," I whispered. "Hurry, Old Man."

A horseman raced across flat of hill toward camp. First fire from redcoats exploded earth on each side of his pony. Grass and dirt flying all around. Horseman pressed his face close to horse's neck. He disappeared through outer line of tents.

I heard women yelling before I saw them burst from lodges. They clutched babies to bare breasts. They ran, terrified, for deep shelter of ravine. Older children ran ahead of grandmothers who smacked them from behind. I saw Fine Day waving his arms and shouting words I could not hear over second blasts from redcoats' guns.

Raiders broke through north side of circle of lodges, ran, crouched, around neck of hill toward poplar bluff. Looked-after-ones were untying buffalo runners from anchor posts, mounting, and fleeing south. Little Pine's warriors crawled through buffalo grass to face redcoats. Stonies were close to me, racing along edge of ravine and disappearing at south end. They took eastern flank of redcoats, protecting women and children hiding below them.

Medicine men had four fires started in camp. Bags open and ready. Chanting began.

Iron balls exploded earth. Dirt sprayed tent walls. Stones pummelled doorflaps.

Removed from fighting, Poundmaker waited on horse for light to grow into day so he could see battle clearly. Thunderchild and Lucky Man flanked his left side, but there was no Leader on his right. Little Pine died before the fighting started.

Where hill rounded down to Battle River Trail, two

redcoats manned big gun, but they could not see Leaders through gunsmoke. Boys, too big to be hidden with women in ravine but too young to fight, spat on their hands and dug iron balls out of earth.

Flattened against steep slope, I elbowed east toward Stonies and ravine where women and children hid. Below me, ravine plunged into darkness. Iron ball sailed like swift sparrow over my head and crashed into underbrush. I covered my head with my arms. Prickly rosebush scratched my legs. Last summer's burrs stuck to my skirt. New buffalo grass was soft against my skin, but longer tongues of old grass were dry, brown and brittle.

Crouched and running now, I stayed close to cover of dropping land. My toe caught in gopher hole. I fell forward, crashed on by belly. My breath was lost. I gagged on air slowly seeping back into my lungs. My fingers closed around something round and smooth. I squeezed it. It was thin and hollow. It cracked like egg shells in my hand. I opened my fist: bleached skull and claw of gopher. Death sign. I dropped it. I crawled around curving bank to east side of hill.

Patches of left-over-snow melting in hollows. I rolled down, through muddied buffalo wallow, toward Stonies. My back bumped against rock. I turned on my belly, spread my hands through new shoots of sage and crocus. My right hand touched a hawk feather.

"Remember empty bellies!" It was Piyeco, running with bent knees, head thrust forward.

I had eaten nothing, but my belly was heavy as if loaded with shot.

"Remember empty promises!" Voice fading. Piyeco moving through scattered Stonies.

Now I heard women and children crying, but I could not see them in thick poplar and willow. I was just ahead of Stonies. I dared to lift my head.

Cut Knife Hill moved in two directions. On my left it rolled towards ravine. On my right it reached down to poplar bluff where Crees were hidden. In between, redcoats and other across-water-men in brown coats lay flat against bared earth, some facing southwest and Stonies, others firing north towards Crees. Wagons at base of Hill, and redcoats behind them. Two redcoats cranked handle of big gun, sprayed flat of hill in jagged arch of bullets that fell short of camp.

Behind me, Stonies hidden by bank of ravine. Ecteh lay on his belly, on his Coat-turned-inside-out, his gun barrel held up by wooden tripod bound with rawhide. He pointed toward north side of hill. "Ota!" his pointing fingers pressed together and forming imaginary spike on top of his own head. Then Ecteh caught sun's light on trading mirror, flashed sign to Fine Day: get sniper with spiked hat.

Crees fired at big gun. Stonies darted from willow to rock, never fired from same place twice.

A warrior leaped over rise of ravine and showed himself to redcoats. He held eagle-feathered willow wand before his face. Wiskwepitakan. Wand was his protection. Sniper with spiked hat shot him, and bullet went through willow wand. Warrior pitched forward, his legs pumping and feet pawing ground but not carrying him anywhere; he fell face down, lay still. Redcoat crawled over to him, raised himself up on his knees, and his rifle butt came down again and again: he smashed warrior's head to bits of bone and bloody skin and hair.

"Shoot! Shoot!" Strong Body yelled at Ecteh.

Ecteh fired. Redcoat leaped back behind wagon. Bullet hit brown boot.

Shells flew over my head and I ducked down closer to earth. I buried my face in buffalo grass. Big gun rattled. Smoke stung my eyes and made my nose run. This was not like fighting Blackfoot.

Crees aimed high so bullets fell on redcoats spread down trail to Battleford. Redcoats could not see them in poplar bluff, so they shot at anything moving, at grass blowing or twig bending.

In poplar bluff another warrior thrust buckskin dummy over his head. A bullet tore through his hat. He earned a Name this day. Shot-through-hat leaped back into underbrush.

I slumped against earth, holding my belly. Sage smell. I lay there, retching. All totems were no good. Fear stretched my skin, pulled my braids apart behind my head. I was cold. Thunder made by guns, not by Bird, blasting in my ears. It was not like fighting Blackfoot. There would be no ceremony, scalpdance, or feast if we won this battle. Redcoats had power greater than any totem blessed by medicine man. "No Tomorrow," my old father had said, praying even so for protection in battle.

"We have them!" Ecteh pointed to Crees in poplar bluff, pointed to drop in old trail to Battleford where Crees and Stonies were coming together behind redcoats. "Three sides!"

Someone big and clumsy was breaking trail through underbrush behind me, noisily crashing through willow, snapping twigs. Two bearpaws swept branches aside and my mother's massive head appeared. Hands pressing on her knees, she stomped up slope, thighs rolling, shoulders heaving. I thought she was coming after me because I was not hiding in ravine.

"Old Woman!" Ecteh yelled, "Back to ravine!"

Bear Woman chose not to hear him. Hands on immense hips, she stood beside me, not looking at me, facing hill and redcoats. "Kiskikoman otasawapiwin!" Voice rising above gunfire. "That is Cut Knife's Lookout!" Swinging her arms, Bear Woman stomped towards redcoats.

They better look out. Bear Woman was coming. They saw her, stopped firing at Stonies. Spiked Helmet yelled, "*Hold fire! It's a woman!*" Stonies stopped firing too. They laughed at redcoats rolling out of her way. Above her, gunsmoke held, then parted like thin skin sliced with knife. Smoke wavered, drifted south.

Bear Woman cut straight line through redcoats. She was going after big gun. Redcoats rolled sideways, elbowed backwards, or scrambled to their feet to get out of her way. "*Jesus!*" sniper with spiked hat yelled, "*the size of her!*" Then silence and eyes of all fighting men followed her.

Redcoats were fussing around big gun like badgers digging hole. They did not see her coming, seemed not to notice silencing of guns. "*Dammit, the carriage is busted!*" Redcoat, swearing at big gun, did not see Bear Woman coming at him from behind. She tapped his shoulder, and he turned to face too-much-woman.

Bear Woman pushed redcoat. "There are children in ravine!" She pawed him. "Infants by creek!" She shoved so hard redcoat fell backwards, broke his fall with hands, and lay sprawled at her feet. "Trying to sleep!" Redcoat closed his eyes, lips moving as if he were praying, his hands clutching buffalo grass.

Bear Woman shouldered big gun and turned it around so it pointed east towards Battleford. "Stop noises!" she said. "You dog manure!" She stood over redcoat again, her face an owlhead mad at gopher. "Big bangs make my children cry!" Then she was running back to ravine, belly shaking, breasts swaying. "Big bangs do not do any good anyway!" She lifted her skirts, leaped over bank, showed more leg than any man could grip in both hands. Her bulging buttocks disappeared in willows.

"Big bangs make my children cry." I howled, it was so funny, my face scrinched, my fists grinding my eyes; and I was crying, it was so funny. Redcoat could not have understood a word Bear Woman said. His big gun pointed at his own men. He cursed and ordered his man to help him turn it back on a camp he could not see for gunsmoke.

Stonies looked at redcoats, laughing. Redcoats looked at Stonies, laughing.

"*If their bloody squaws start fighting they'll win for sure!*" sniper yelled, "*but I don't think they need'em. Look!*" Redcoat pointed, and I saw it too.

Soldier Leader was calling retreat. Wounded were hoisted into wagons, carried in canvas strung between poles. Slowly, townsmen and browncoats back-stepped down trail, fired without direction at bluff and ravine. They tried to hold up pretense of punishing People for looting Battleford. Retreat was slow, a clumsy falling back into Battle River Valley. Redcoat with spiked helmet wasted bullets, fired rapidly, tried to hold Cree warriors while redcoats pulled away from place of their defeat.

"Over here! Strong Body called from poplar bluff.

Redcoat whirled, fired, missed Strong Body.

"Tight ass!" Ecteh taunted. Stonies hooted.

Redcoat swung rifle, looked for Ecteh.

Stony warrior blasted hole in redcoat's head. "Awahē!" Ecteh yelled, "I got him!"

Piyeco was running up old trail to camp to tell Poundmaker redcoats were giving up and going home.

"Finish them off!" Fine Day yelled.

"Let's go!" Ecteh yelled at Stonies. They scuttled out of

130

hiding places in ravine. Behind them, women and children appeared.

Strong Body gripped sniper's red coat. He dragged body up Cut Knife Hill. Crees followed, yelling and flattening bloodied buffalo grass with stamping feet. Strong Body dragged body, eyes fixed on gaping hole in sniper's head. His lips stretched over teeth, he panted like wolf after rabbit.

Strike-him-on-back kicked redcoat's groin. Yellow-mud-blanket stamped on hand. Finger bones snapped. Then, he struggled with brown boot, tried to force his short square toes into it. Night Traveller swaggered, toes turned outward, redcoat's rifle tucked under his left arm. Stonies waved knives. Crees cried, "Cut him to bits!" Ecteh split yellow stripe with coup knife, cut long red line down pantleg.

Then, Horse-dance-maker was there, standing over dead sniper, one foot on each side of head so no one could touch it. "He is dog!" Horse-dance-maker said, "But when dog is dead it is dead!" We do not cut up dogs!"

"Then kick him!" Strong Body cried.

"Kick him! Kick him!" Stonies cried.

"Let women do it!" Strong Body grabbed my wrist. "Kick him!"

"Cut him up!" women cried.

"I . . . can't," I said.

"Cut him up!"

"I do not want to touch it."

"Kick him! Cut him!" Voices breaking something inside me, something I could not name, only feel, and it was tearing at my belly. Death might touch me. If whiteman's spirit had escaped through hole in head—where could it go? Departed-ones would never accept him in place of eternal dancing. So sniper really was dead.

"It is done," I said. "It will not do any good to kick."

At Battle of Belly River, Blood women cut up bodies. It avenged fighting men who died. This was not the same. In this battle there was no winning.

Sky was turning upside down. Sweat streamed down my face.

"Wait!" Piyeco had come from Poundmaker. He pointed at redcoats pushing wagons down old trail to Battleford. He pointed at camp. "All warriors go to place of gathering," he said.

"We rush redcoats from both sides of creek!" Fine Day said.

"Finish them off!" Strong Body yelled.

"Notintokimawak! Notintokimawak!" Piyeco cried.

"Yei! Yei!" Warriors' cry was as old as Battle River, as old as first battle against Sarcee who was Cut Knife. It carried them back to camp.

"Kakweciyahok!" Horse-dance-maker said. He was afraid to leave me behind. "First Woman!" He called me by name so my spirit would not stay with dead sniper.

Redcoat rose up, brushed twigs and dead grass from his coat, picked burrs from his pants. He stood tall. Hole in his head was closed and healed. His pants and leg were no longer torn. He wore his spiked hat. He shouldered his rifle, and marched down old trail. He was going back to Battleford to tell Soldier Leader all that had happened.

"No!" I cried. I flew across top of hill. "No!" I leaped through willow bunched on edge of camp. "No!" I broke through circle of lodges. I ran faster than Horse-dance-maker.

People were gathered around Poundmaker's lodge. Strike-him-on-back was bearer of Pipestem. He spread buffalo robe on earth and squatted on it.

Fine Day had been talking long. "We have shown them" he said, "that we are not to be put away on left-over-land and forgotten. Buffalo are gone. But we are still here!" He was quiet when things did not go well for People. Now that winning belonged to River People Fine Day was heard. "They will never keep promises!" He had seen forty-one winters on prairie. Deep marks, like scars, on his broad face. Small round eyes had sunk beneath ridges of his forehead, but Fine Day was not ready to take his place among old men. Part Stony and part Blackfoot, he wore knotted braid on top of his head, painted his forehead red. "We cannot trust them!" he said. Thin braids swatted his neck. "We fight! Cut them off at creek! Now!

"Ahhhh-ha!" raiders cried. "Ahhhh-ha!"

"Let them go!" Poundmaker signed for silence. "We have won this battle. But we have gained nothing! Woman Leader has more men than there are stars above prairie!" Speechmaker waited for words to reach those farthest away.

Fine Day would not wait. "Shot is gone! We have no powder!" he cried. "No food! I say we attack redcoats and take their guns!"

"Yei! Yei!" warriors cried in one voice.

"Pipestem," Poundmaker said.

Strike-him-on-back rose, bearing Pipe.

"You want to kill them off," Poundmaker said. "You want to take Battleford and attack Fort. Can you defend and hold it too? Do you think more redcoats will not come? Have you forgotten power of these men? Power behind them!" His voice dropped from ringing tones of speechmaker to sighing of an elder. "You are all brave men! Mina/maka! How long can you hold out against big guns? Without food. Firearms. Ammunition. What will happen to children when fighting is over? Promises will not be kept if we break peace!"

"We are fighting wolves!" Horse-dance-maker cried.

"It is true we know woods and how to fight on prairie," Poundmaker said, "but battle in fort is different!"

"Burn it down!" Fine Day yelled.

"Ahhh-ha! Ahhhh-ha!" warriors cried.

Poundmaker raised his hand. "I say we stay here! Let them come to us. If they want another fight we will give it to them. But if they are ready to keep promises that is good."

"I say let's go!" Strong Body yelled.

"Bodies will float in creek!" Fine Day cried.

Poundmaker raised his arm. He held Pipestem. He placed it on earth. "It is there! If any man walks in front of it or passes it he will die!"

There could be no fighting in presence of Pipestem. Warriors lowered heads to show respect. Poundmaker shuffled away, his thin shoulders sagging under blanket-coat. He was suddenly Old Man seeking quiet place to think and pray. Only bravest man was Bearer-of-pipe. Poundmaker was the Peacemaker.

I returned to my lodge. I thought then that I would never get over fear of redcoats.

Annika

In the bushland, sound often travels faster than light. Farm women, baking bread for a dozen threshers or boiling winter underwear in a copper canner, don't have time to keep watch at windows, but they are always listening for tractors returning from the fields or hoping to hear a neighbour's car.

An approaching car or truck always seems to pull hard at reaching the homestead, transmission straining, gears grinding, the sounds short and intermittent, but a leaving truck always seems to be coasting downhill, the motor churning long and even, but diminishing.

Old Woman heard the car before I did. I looked out the window. Through the early evening light and through the dark caragana hedge a wavering beam of yellow lights.

"It's MacRaw!" I said to Old Woman. "Coming to check up on us!"

By the time I had filled the coffee pot with water from the barrel beside the stove MacRaw was in the doorway stamping snow from his galoshes.

"Shut the door," I said. "You're letting in the cold."

"Came by car," MacRaw said. "Tracks are buried in snow and there's no sense clearin' them before the train comes through on Saturday." He unwound his red and white McGill University scarf, shrugged out of his tweed coat and hung it on the nail on the back of the door.

"You're out late," I said.

"When you get to be my age," MacRaw said, "you don't waste the time you have left sleeping." He pulled a chair out from under the oak table and perched on the edge of it. "How's our patient?" he said. "There's a lot of talk in town about you two."

"It's none of their business," I said.

"Well, now," MacRaw said, "Frank Harse says you never come to town any more except to pick up your mail. The Grahams say you never visit them. I guess they don't much like you living with an old squaw. There's rumours going around that you're becoming tetched in the head."

"Is that why you came to see me?" I said. I reached into the oven for the heated-up vetebröd, gripped the edge of the pan so hard the heat worked through my oven mitt into my hand.

"It's more than that," MacRaw said. "There's trouble on Thunderchild's." He darted a swift look at Old Woman, must have decided she didn't understand what he was saying, then said, "The Indians are mad again. They want all the Treaty promises kept and some of their surrendered land back."

"I'm sure they do," I said, "but what's all that got to do with me?"

"Annika, Annika," MacRaw said, "You live in a dream world. It isn't like it was when your grandfather was farming and hiring Indians and they never came near the house. Now they're breaking in and stealing everything. Smash up the place for you."

"No one ever bothers me," I said. I sliced bannock for old Woman and gave it to her with her tea.

"It just isn't right," MacRaw said, "You living up here all alone with nobody to talk to except a dying old squaw."

"*Iskwew,*" Old Woman said, "not squaw."

"What would you have me do with her?" I said. "Turn her out in the cold?" I slid a plate of *vetebröd* onto the table and poured coffee for us. I knew MacRaw meant well, but my jaw was knotting with anger. I plunked into a chair and crossed my arms.

"Send her back to the reserve where she belongs," MacRaw said. He bent his grey head over the coffee bread.

I turned in my chair and said to Old Woman. "Do you want to go back to left-over-land?"

She dipped her bannock into her tea, then held it up. "This is better," she said, "than bannock on *reserve.*" She sucked the bread, her face unchanging, but I knew she was enjoying my struggle with MacRaw. "You make good Indian," she said to me, slurping her tea.

"Trickster!" I said in Cree.

"What did she say?" MacRaw said.

"She likes it here," I said. "I'm not taking any risks anyway. She'll just get sicker if I send her back."

"Annika, that old heart isn't going to last much longer."

"She has a better chance of making it through the winter with me," I said.

"What do you want to do?" MacRaw said. "Get yourself killed or raped or something? Look where you live!" He pointed his fork at the window, "A stone's throw from Thunderchild's!"

I pointed my slice of *vetebröd* at MacRaw, showing him it wasn't meant to be eaten with a fork. "Why do you think Thunderchild's people are so angry?" I leaned forward, but he wouldn't look at me. "Answer that one!"

"Look!" MacRaw straightened his bent body and pounded his fist on the oilcloth. "They have no way of making it. Never have! Land's too rocky an' all bush. They raise cattle and cut into our market and the municipal council complains to Ottawa. They want their own school, but they're not going to get it." MacRaw pounded his fist, like a drumbeat.

Old Woman's head was nodding over her tea, but she wasn't falling asleep.

"What's worse than that," MacRaw said, "they haven't a doctor visiting them regularly. They grump most about that."

"So you do understand," I said.

"See it the way it is!" MacRaw said. "You won't get Ottawa to do anything, not after a hundred years, and the Indians know that. They hate us so much they're about ready to fight again. Only this time they'll be leaving a great many dead people behind them. Before they're put down again."

"I don't believe it's that bad," I said. "Do you, old grandmother?"

"We fight," Old Woman said, "but not with guns and knives. With words and paper. We turn their own words against them now."

"You're just a bleeding heart," MacRaw said to me.

136

"I thought I was like my grandfather," I said.

"Well, I remember your grandfather's fight over herd law," MacRaw said, grinning now. "Got so mad he didn't speak to his own brother for eight years."

"That'll never happen to you, MacRaw," I said. "You couldn't keep quiet that long."

Old Woman slurped her tea and smacked her gums.

"So tell me what else is new in town," I said.

"Well," MacRaw said, scratching under his chin. "I hear tell in the beer parlour that the government intends to build a jail up on the hill where the Mounties can keep watch and see who's coming out of the hotel."

"Catch more drunk drivers that way, I suppose," I said.

"There's cells in the basement, you know," MacRaw said. "I saw the Mountie taking an Indian prisoner out the back way this morning. To the outhouse."

The building next to the bank has always been the Mountie's house, and MacRaw always has a story about it.

"Did I ever tell you about the time," MacRaw said.

"Probably," I said.

"This Mountie we've got now," MacRaw said, "He's a youngster from back east, you know. Too homespun to know what policing the *west* is all about. Not like the old days."

I was trying to decide whether or not to tell MacRaw about the stories Old Woman was telling me. Her visions of redcoats differed from MacRaw's.

"This is a true fact story," MacRaw said. "I was there when it happened!

"The first Mountie posted in the Livelong District, in the whole of the Northwest Territories for that matter, fired his gun—once." MacRaw looked at me sideways, pausing to see if I was suitably impressed. I looked up at the ceiling.

"His name was Sonny or Buddy," MacRaw continued, "I'm not certain which, but it all happened just after Karna built the hotel. He was locked in the back room with her, asking her some uncomfortable questions about her old country business, and it happened that Johnny Tangleflags, you know the squatter from the flats, who was not more than ten or twelve years old, had come to town to show off the first coyote he had trapped. He tossed the frozen animal through the door. The stiff body stood straight up. Karna screamed. The Mountie whirled, whipped out his gun, and shot at the snarling coyote. The bullet missed the dead coyote and went right through the boot and foot of the Mountie!"

"Well, Dr. MacRaw," I said, "I've really enjoyed your visit."

"No, wait," he said. "That's not all. By the time I returned to town on the jigger, Karna had dug out the bullet with her toenail scissors and had wrapped the wound with strips of cloth torn from her petticoat. Buddy was crying 'Don't tell my mother. Don't tell my mother!' " MacRaw hooted and slapped his knees.

I said, "I hope you can drop in again soon."

Angus MacRaw closed one eye, swiveled around in his chair, pointed a twisted finger at me, "You still haven't told me what you're up to!"

So I told him about the grandmothers' lifelong friendship, about the survival lessons taught by one to the other, about the stories Old Woman was telling me.

"Why didn't you say so," MacRaw said, "and save me a lot of worrying?"

"I would have but you won't let me."

"You've got your grandmother's wit. Same sharp tongue too." MacRaw shoved himself up and out of his chair. His knees cracked when he walked to the door.

I helped him on with his tweed coat. "Do up your overshoes," I said, "or you'll catch cold."

"Say, I almost forgot to tell you. I saw young Arvid the other day." He wound his red and white scarf around his neck. "Still playing hockey for the Turtleford Tigers. Well, I saw him coming out of the cafe arm in arm with a pretty young nurse." He ducked his head and looked sideways at me. "The way they tell it in the beer parlour it wouldn't take much for you to snaffle him away from that nurse."

"That was over, between Arvid and I, long before I went to Saskatoon."

MacRaw tapped me on the nose. "You should get out more," he said. "Maybe look over the stag line at the Christmas dance in the Legion Hall. What do you say?"

I shook my head.

"You've got to do something!" MacRaw said. "How long can you go on living this way?"

I had a side of beef in my locker in Turtleford, plenty of Johanna's preserves in the root cellar. I hadn't touched my savings yet. "I'll make it till spring," I said.

"I'm glad you've come home," MacRaw said. "City life's no good. But if settling down with one of the local boys isn't good enough for you, how about a job?"

"I've thought on it," I said. "I need time. Right now I need to sort things out for myself."

I knew MacRaw meant well, but I was having a fantasy of prying him out the door with a crowbar. I put my hand on the doorknob, but he didn't take the hint.

"A year's a long time to grieve," he said.

"I'm not grieving!" I yelled. "I haven't even cried!"

MacRaw put an arm around my shoulder, but I shrugged it away. "You miss your grandmother," he said.

"Not so much," I said. "I've got her," pointing at Old Woman.

She waggled her head at me.

"You can't replace one person with another," MacRaw said. "Get on with the grieving. It has to be done. Get it over, and then get back to living your own life." He opened the door, and I wanted to shove him out. He shuffled through the door, and I slammed it behind him, then leaned against it.

"He is no' so bad," Old Woman said, " 'though he be a dour Scot." She hooted and slapped her blanketed knees.

"I suppose you're going to take his side now!" I started slamming pots and pans on the stove. I slopped water from the barrel into the reservoir.

"When you are ready," Old Woman said.

"Did you like the story about the redcoat?" I asked.

"Long time ago," she said, "I felt poorly towards one." It was one of the many ways of saying love, but Old Woman was a long way from that part of her story.

That night, she led me back to the first winter of the Cree exile in Montana.

Old Woman

Old Misery is ugly twisting river. Sandbars ambush small boats. Sunken logs float beneath surface. In winter, Old Misery throws chunks of broken bank, uprooted trees and jagged ice at those who dare test his power. Swirling waters spin small boats. Rushing water sweeps them beyond landing. Loose shifting bank is held by frozen snow now. Rocks and willows are no protection for lodges, but we are camped at Rocky Point, halfway between Fort Maginnis and Fort Belknap. Inside tents, People lie still, not speaking to each other. No use to roll out of sleeping-robes when kettles are empty. We cannot move camp. Not without food.

Hoar-frost-moon hangs above lodges. In dawn of day, air is heavy and stilled. I must keep fire going, but I do not want to roll out of sleeping-robe, out of Horse-dance-maker's arms. We sleep wrapped around each other. Horse-dance-maker's arms and legs are twisted around me so tight he is like a snake coiled around me. It hurts my back to move. I poke him. "Fire," I say.

He grunts, wraps robe closer around our child before I slip from under it. Fire is low. I must change smokeflaps and add chopped cottonwood to fire. Outside, I tug at frozen anchor-ropes. Smokeflaps do not change, and I pull harder on ropes, try to let air into tent so fire may breathe.

In centre of camp Little Bear sits before cold outside fireplace. He is wrapped in thinning five-point Company blanket. He listens to Thinman singing Wolf Song for those who go hungry:

World is too small

Wolf said.
So Wesakachak blew on it.
He stretched land and sky
for all men and animals
to live on together.

Song ends with Wolf's long howl. It rises above sound of snapping whips, curses of chilled men, snorts of blanketed horses.

Many men in blue coats. They move closer and closer to our camp. They never stop marching.

I think of Little Bear's long walk from place of his father to place of Old Misery. I remember his father's words. "It is time to go. Take People with you."

He was Big Bear, too-much-bear, and he was locked away behind stone walls. At Frog Lake, he took no part himself, warned Little Bear and Wandering Spirit against making trouble. But after the killing, whites blamed Big Bear for the fighting. "I am old," he said to Little Bear. "So it is better that I should go to their place of stones. People need someone to show them how to go on living. Go south. Take People with you. I am old."

I love this new young Leader, Little Bear, although no words have passed between us. I will take him coals to start his outside fire. I carry embers lifted with fork from my fire, but I watch Soldier Leader. I wonder, not really caring, what this Soldier Leader wants. He comes from the south, long way maybe, because his shoulders are slouched and he takes long strides with heavy feet. I bend over Little Bear's outside fireplace, brush snow from centre. Little Bear does not speak to me.

There are two wagons, each pulled by team of six. Wheels break ice crust, but nothing stops whitemen. Not fierce wind, frozen earth, or Old Misery. Long knives will cross river, they might be swept away, but they will cross river. Little Poplar on other side will be harder to handle than fighting water.

I lay coals in fireplace. Now there are two black boots in front of Little Bear. I do not look at Soldier Leader.

"Lootenunt Robberson Kit-eseykason." It is river trader. He took buffalo-skin-liners for floursack and six

141

lardpails. "Soldier Leader has come a long way to make talk," he says to Little Bear. "All the way from Fort Maginnis."

"So far?" Little Bear says. "Just to talk?"

"He heard you were camped here," river trader says. "He has food. Two wagons full of grain. Tea. Many bags of sugar."

"Tawaw!" Little Bear says. "Tell him there is room for him to sit."

I kindle fire with black birchbark. Soldier Leader asks Little Bear to smoke with him. Little Bear shakes his head.

River trader says, "I think maybe there ain't no tobacco."

Soldier Leader says something to river trader. I know a few white words, but I have to listen to river trader to be sure I understand all of it.

"Soldier Leader says he is sorry," river trader says to Little Bear. "He has brought food."

"There are dried berries and roots!" Little Bear shouts. He points at empty snare wire strung between poles. "Tapakwaneyapi! Wire is fast and little rabbit does not cry!"

I stare woodenly at bluecoats strapping heavy feedbags to horses' noses.

"Soldier Leader wants to know your name and how many wives and children you have," Riverman says. "so I tell him you are young buffalo with many cows." He is good interpreter. He makes leaders from both sides of dividing-line laugh together.

I smile into my blanket.

"Tell him I am very dangerous," Little Bear says, "so he better look out!"

Soldier Leader says something, and I think he wants to know what Little Bear said.

Now I hear bad words from river trader: "*bucks . . . squaws . . . papooses . . . starving . . . we do more trading.*" I have learned enough white words to know Riverman is not saying what Little Bear said to Soldier Leader.

"*No trading!*" Soldier Leader says. He frowns, slips pale hand from leather mitten, turns mitten upside-down and shakes it as if he thinks something will fall into his hand.

"Soldier Leader will send men to Fort for more food," Riverman says to Little Bear. "He is worried about storms and how long a way it is to Fort." He turns to Soldier Leader, " . . . *be bad, eh?*"

Soldier Leader shouts at river trader, *". . . I paid you . . . my own pocket!"*

"Whadda man you are!" Riverman rolls back on his heels. He slaps his forehead. He is not translating now.

Little Bear pokes fire with stick. I have forgotten what I am doing, and wind has blown coals out. I see half moon scar on Little Bear's right cheek turning red, but I know he is not angry at me. I kneel and blow on coals.

"Very good. I give you what you need," river trader says. *". . . pay me later,"* he laughs. *"Very good?"*

Soldier Leader nods. *"Tell Chief. . . . take Indians . . . Fort Assinniboine."*

River trader says, "Soldier Leader says he has orders to move you out right away and take you to Fort."

Little Bear stabs melting snow before fireplace. "No!" he says. "We go to Halfbreed Creek!"

"Without food?" Soldier Leader says.

"So we are arrested," Little Bear says. "What have we done?"

"No," Soldier Leader says. He stares from under frosted eyebrows at his men getting ready to cross river. He says something I cannot understand, and Riverman translates:

"He asks if you think he cannot take you?"

"We have no horses," Little Bear says. "There are many sick people. Many old. We cannot move camp. It is too far to Fort!"

"Wagons," Riverman says to Soldier Leader, holding up two fingers, *"Deal?"*

"Eskosan!" Little Bear says. His voice does not have power like his father's, but he makes both men listen. "All People captured by you are of the same tribe. We are River People. Plains Cree. About all old ones were born north of dividing-line."

After this, I do not catch any of Soldier Leader's white words. So I listen to river trader. Only.

"Soldier Leader wants to know if you are *Canadian* Crees," trader says. "And did you fight in Outbreak?"

"You are Soldier Leader," Little Bear says. "I was once

fighting man and I fought for People. But my father who headed all Real People caught up in fighting and others like him lived many seasons in this land where many children were born."

"He wants to know if your father was Big Bear."

I feel bad for Little Bear, that Soldier Leader and river trader speak Name of his father.

"Often. Before. People walked on this land. They moved freely north and south. But never before were any of them bothered!"

"Soldier Leader wants to know more about Outbreak," river trader says.

Small flames lick dry bark. I break twigs. I breathe gently on fire.

"So! Halfbreeds were fighting. Dumont told us to attack redcoats." Little Bear tells Soldier Leader what he wants to hear. "He told us redcoats would kill us off like buffalo."

Soldier Leader hangs head. He might have burned feeding grounds himself. He is sorry for People, sorry they lost everything under sun.

"So we had to take part in it and we fought in all battles."

Soldier Leader rubs both sides of his wind-blistered face. His eyes circle camp. *"All . . . here?"* he says.

"Only a few did not fight," Little Bear says.

"Soldier Leader wants to know how many," river trader says.

Numbers. Whites are always counting, then Treaty numbers they give people instead of names.

"About three-times-four."

"Why . . . fight?" Soldier Leader asks, " *. . . couldn't win."*

Little Bear closes his face. He does not answer.

Long Knives have found small boat. They push it down shore. Little Poplar on north side of Old Misery will be ready for them.

"I think," Riverman says, *"he can't give . . . as why . . . fought . . . .listened ta Dumont."*

Soldier Leader says something and points across river.

"He wants to know about camp across river," trader

says, "who is Leader there and why don't you camp together?"

Little Bear refuses to answer.

". . . *bad blood between Chiefs*," river trader says.

Little Bear and Little Poplar fight over who is to be Leader.

Now river trader is telling Soldier Leader about Little Poplar, " . . .*Chief in war. killed . . .massacreez . . .plenty hard to get him ta move north. Fort . . .too close. Little Bear I think . . .plenty scared o' rope too.*"

Soldier Leader points north then south, talking big words.

"He wants to know why you camp on this side of dividing-line."

Little Bear stares at open water. Log grasps for shore. "After Batoche, my father, then in captivity, told me to escape," he says. "He told me to take those left—south— where they could get protection from a mighty people."

"Ass-licker!" Riverman laughs.

Little Bear tells Soldier Leader how People crossed over dividing-line three and four lodges at a time. How they traded hides and ceremonial dress for food. "No game!" He stares at ration wagons.

Soldier Leader wants to know if there are any more Crees on this side," river trader says, "and where they might be."

"I know of none except myself on this side. We agree to go south of Missouri."

Little Poplar has relatives on Crow Left-over-land and he wants to go there.

"Soldier Leader has one more question," river trader says. "If you could say what to do, would you take land like Halfbreeds in Judith Basin or would you take left-over-land like Crow People?"

"Left-over-land!" Little Bear says. He has begun to talk about having left-over-land of his own. Land set away from whites and their strange ways. Place where People's Way will survive without white-collars and foodgivers and redcoats.

Soldier Leader runs down to river. His boots crush snow. Water seeps into boot prints and turns snow to slush. He crosses foreshore. He springs into boat. He is fighting man. He will feed People and get us safely to Fort

Assinniboine. There, we will be close to dividing-line, close to starting-place, close to place of stone where Little Bear's father is crying for people behind stone walls. Little Bear warms hands over my fire. He says to me, "We are defeated people."

Soldier Leader drove us north from Rocky Point, one hundred and twenty-three whiteman's miles to Fort Assinniboine. He sent two bluecoats to Fort Maginnis with a paper asking for food for us. He waited two days and food didn't arrive, so he set out for Fort Assinniboine. Many days later, Little Bear asked Soldier Leader at Fort Assinniboine, "Why no food sent out?" and Soldier Leader said he did not know what kind of food to send.

So we were driven north. Thirty whiteman's miles from Fort we found three lodges of People. There was no room for them in river trader's wagon, and we only had seven horses left that we had not eaten. Children who had seen only three or four winters on prairie were forced to walk.

We are a long time walking across frozen prairie to Fort Assinniboine. Soldier Leader says we make camp this night in Fort. But we have long way to go. We are weak. We need food and leather clothing to keep going.

I stumble along frozen trail. I follow crossing pattern of Horse-dance-maker's snowshoes. I jump in big uneven prints. I break through snowcap and sink to my knees in snow. I pull myself up. I keep on going.

Ahead, Little Poplar rides between two bluecoated trail-breakers. He turns his face against blistering wind. He sings Ati astoski, making up words as he goes along.

ati astoski	on your way
ati micisokan	on your way home have a meal
ati ayewipikan	as you go along stop and rest
ati nipakan	as you travel stop and sleep
ati astoski	on your way

Wind carries message, tosses it high and clear over heads of long knives, carries it back to People who understand.

Little Poplar's song is more than promise, more than answer to Soldier Leader. Little Poplar does not want to go to Fort Assinniboine. He wants to stop. His song is a warning.

Prairie People know how to travel long distances. Going must be slow and easy with many stops for rest and food.

Astoski, how I want to sleep, but there is no sheltering pine, no hollow or cave, no soft needles for snowbed. Wind whips my moosehide fringes, lashes at mossbag on my back. Wind is angry because we are hungry, because Soldier Leader drives us close to dividing-line where redcoats wait to punish Little Bear and Little Poplar.

"Stop and reeeeest!" Little Poplar's song is swept away in whirling spiraling burst of flying-up-snow.

I slide on frozen trail. I fall. I struggle to my feet, but wind knocks me down again. It tears at my blanket. It pierces my leggings. No feeling in my hands now, and I tuck them under my armpits.

"Come on!" Horse-dance-maker calls, but I cannot see him three snowshoe lengths ahead of me. He is never tired or cold. He is used to long walks. "Come on!" he yells.

I sprawl on trail. Lucky Man's family drifts by me with heads bent against swirling wind and snow flying all around. I stare at snowshoe pattern in snow. White as flour.

"Come on!" Horse-dance-maker yells.

Riverman's wagon rumbles away from me, its sideboards creaking. It carries too many old and sick People. I stare at snow brushed by Horse-dance-maker's broken snowshoe thong. Crossing lines. It looks like print of beaver tail. Beavertail. Roasting. Feasting at Thunderchild's, our last visit, and Horse-dance-maker let beaver out of its cage. Beaver caught, if it was not dead, was wretched, lost, had nothing; and when they let Leaders out—do they keep men in cages?—no, place they took Leaders to was made of stone.

"Come on! Get up! Come on!"

Flying-up-snow whirls over trail, dances around Soldier Leader's face. He looms over me. His face is fierce, lashes frosted.

"*Cloth?*" He takes bundled medicines from my back. He grabs it in leather hands and my shoulder is wrenched. Sleeping child stirs in mossbag. Her small body twists on my back, but she does not cry.

"Crazy Indian!" Soldier Leader turns bundle over in leather hands. His mouth shapes white words, and wind blows them away. Thick fingers pick at rawhide knots.

"No! No!" I kick Soldier Leader, my rawhide toes hit hard leather boots. I howl. My toes bunch inside stiff moccasins.

Soldier Leader pulls horse blanket around bearded face. He yells something I do not understand, wraps his arms around himself. *"Wrap up!"* he yells. *"Cloth!"*

"Pehta!" I cry. "Pehta!"

Medicines will lose power to heal if whiteman looks upon them.

"Put it on?"

"Namwac!"

"....understand. Cloth! ...freezing!"

"Namoya, neya anima pehta! Horse-dance-maker is here. "Aka nantow kita totaman!" His breath is white smoke.

Soldier Leader tosses bundle to Horse-dance-maker. *"Wrap her up!"* he says.

Horse-dance-maker nods, so Soldier Leader goes back to breaking trail. Sweat runs down my neck into blanket. I fall forward. Horse-dance-maker catches me. He presses both hands against my heaving chest. He tries to get me to do—no—say something.

"Safe! Say it!"

I wipe sweat from my forehead with blanket.

"Bundles are safe! Say it!"

"Medicine."

"Bundles are safe! Say it! Say it!" He grips my shoulders and shakes me. "Say it sayitsayit!"

"Safe."

"That is good. Soldier Leader does not know about medicine. He cannot harm bundles. He does not have that power."

"I believe," I say.

Horse-dance-maker lifts me. He carries me. I close my eyes. I think about sun shining and dragonflies mating above bush thick with ripe berries.

I am picking berries. I stuff them in my mouth. Dark skins burst. Juice is filling my belly.

Sun is shining. Wind is quiet. We are at Fort Assinniboine. People are squatting here and there. I lean against riverman's wagon, beside my mother. I hold Yellow Calf in my arms.

We are at Fort Assinniboine. It is too close to dividing-line for Little Poplar. He threatens to shoot any long knife who tries to stop him from going to Crow People's Left-over-land. He swings rifle wildly. He is ready to take many whiteskins with him on last four-day-walk to place of eternal hunting.

Soldier Leader and another bluecoat grab Little Poplar. Soldier Leader knocks rifle out of his hands with leather fist. Bluecoat locks arms around Little Poplar's neck. They tie his hands behind his back, carry him kicking and screaming, "Trick! Trick!" and they put him in empty ration wagon.

Soldier Leader says something to river trader, but trader has to scratch his head and think about how to translate. "He has taken away Little Poplar," he finally says. "He says Little Bear is now your *Chief*, and you better listen to him."

Soldier Leader puts Little Poplar in *guard house*. We are at Fort Assinniboine, and we think we are all arrested.

Annika

It was Christmas, and Old Woman and I agreed to celebrate it on the Eve in the Swedish way. I had made an Advent Wreath from spruce boughs, and we lighted one candle each of four Sundays before the Eve. Now it was replaced by a short thick Christmas tree. We decorated it with brass candle holders and white candles, felt *Tomtegubbes,* the Swedish version of Santa's elves, and a tinfoil star made by Old Woman. A sheaf of wheat was set high on a pole for the birds. The centrepiece for our table was a nativity scene carved in miniature by my grandfather. I made *chiltbuller, krumkake,* and of course *vetebröd.* Now the fat was hot enough for the rosette irons. I dipped the hot irons into the cookie batter, then quickly dunked them into the sizzling fat.

"The only thing we're missing," I said to Old Woman, "is *lutefisk.* Johanna used to soak it in a bucking tub of lyesalt for two days before she cooked it." I lifted the irons from the pot and tapped the ends with a wooden spoon. Two light and flaky and golden rosettes tumbled onto the wax paper. Shaking powdered sugar over the cookies I said, "*Lutefisk* stinks up the whole house. I never could eat it anyway."

"Worse than skunks," Old Woman said. She was busy stitching beads on rawhide. "Worse than roast porcupine," she sniffed.

The grandmother had been grumpy, crabby, and bossy for over a week now, pounding on the wall several times each night and ordering tea. Her humour had improved today, but I was beginning to be impatient with her.

"My pipe," she said, knowing I couldn't leave the rosettes to light it.

"I have to work fast," I said. "You'll have to wait."

"Ohhhhh, shit!" she said, ducking her head over her sewing again. I suspected she was making a present for me but I pretended I didn't notice.

"As soon as the rosettes are done," I said, "we can have our supper and then open our presents."

My gift to my Other-grandmother was a new Bay blanket. It seemed fitting since she had refused Old Horse's blankets. I wasn't sure of the connection, but I suddenly remembered my Swedish grandmother saying, "Cast your bread upon the waters."

Whenever she wanted or needed something she always gave the identical object away so it would be returned to her. Every Christmas she made aprons for all the women in the family and for her *Kaffe Kärings,* and sure enough she always got aprons herself. Cast your bread upon the waters.

We really teased her the year she gave away seven aprons and got six. That was the year my cousin Eric was married and lived in the house on the Reed Place. We went skating on the river and tobogganing on the hill, and all I wanted was a rubber doll that I could feed and it would wet its diaper. Ernie Sommers got one in, but somebody bought it and I thought I would never get a doll so real as that. Then Johanna rocked me in her chair and told me Eric had gone deer hunting only to meet Rudolph—remember that was the year the song came out?—oh, and she said Eric had said yes, to Rudolph, Annika had been such a good girl and carried in wood chips for the grandmother all summer for seasoning. So I knew then that Kris Kringle would get Eric's message from Rudolph and bring me the doll.

I sprinkled the last rosettes with powdered sugar, then placed the oven dishes on the table. "Time to eat," I said.

I wrapped the grandmother in Johanna's blue chenille bathrobe. "When I was little," I said, "we had matching robes, mine made from material left over."

I lifted Old Woman into Johanna's rocker, put a wooden stopper under the bottom rungs so it wouldn't tip.

"More pillows!" she ordered. "At my back!"

She looked like a small girl seated on pillows so she would be high enough to see over the edge of the table. I couldn't seat her on a kitchen chair because of her habit of nodding off during the meal. The pillows and high wings of the rocker held her like a protective nest.

I lit four candles on the nativity scene. "Everything looks just as it must have been that first Christmas in 1896."

"That was same time as Crees come back to Canada," Old Woman said, "Same time as Whites come across water in wooden boats."

"We go in circles like rabbits. That's what she said again and again—and look—the windmills go around forwards but the sheep are going backwards." I turned the windmills right-side-up. "*From och tilbaka,*" I said. "I go forth until I come back."

"You go outside," Old Woman said.

I peered through the frost-clear centre pane. The councilman from Thunderchild's was waiting outside again.

"Has he come?" Old Woman asked. "Give to him," pointing at the tied-up bundle on her cot. The moccasins and beaded deerhide jacket were not for me.

"Yes, he's out here," I said. "What've you been doing? Sending smoke signals to the reserve Hollywood-style?"

"You do it!" she said.

I carried the bundle outside to the councilman.

On the front stoop, I said, "We're just going to eat. Will you join us?"

I hoped he would refuse; I wanted the special supper just for the two of us.

Councilman shook his head, handed me a large package wrapped in brown paper. Presents for Old Woman from her many grandchildren. "Hey!" he said, pulling his red hunting cap from his head. "Tell her that you see me!"

He had braided his hair, but the ends sticking out from the rawhide thongs were still too short, and he looked as if he had tied two whisk brooms to each side of his head. He shoved his hands into his pockets and started off for the reserve.

I shut the door. "Surprises," I said, tucking the parcel under the tree, "for after supper."

Old Woman was breaking up the Swedish meatballs with her fork. "Cold," she said.

"Don't wait for me!" I said.

"Somebody better start," she said. She dunked the *vetebröd* in the gravy, swirled it around, then sucked on it.

"Gufflebitter," I said, forking pickled herring out of sour cream and spreading raw onions over them. "Then oyster soup. The meatballs are for the main!"

Old Woman gummed her lifebread and grinned. Gravy trickled down her chin.

Heat from the candles had the windmill spinning now. The shepherds and sheep, wise men, Mary and Joseph and Jesus were going around backwards. Even the brass angels were facing each other on the top, and they looked as if they were blowing their trumpets at each other.

"The only time in three months you've ever really mentioned Johanna was when you made the joke about Swedes going forth and back instead of back and forth," I said. "Why?"

"You talk enough for both of us," she answered. "I want tea now."

"I listen to you all day and all night. But you don't talk about Johanna—your friend!—all you do is talk about you!"

"You cannot live in the past," she said.

I spluttered, "Live in the past!"

"You ask me to tell you my story," she said, "but now I think I tell it to you no more."

"Don't you care? Don't you even—miss her?"

"She is here in this house with us all the time," Old Woman said, in English, "and I think now that you will never let her spirit go." She looked at me steadily, eye to eye, across the table. "Let her go."

My mouth trembled, and I pressed my lips together.

"You take me inside white house," she said.

I thought of the day I had found my Other-grandmother spinning in the tractor tire, how my skin had prickled, and how I felt dizzy when she screamed my Swedish grandmother's name.

"But I wanted to look after you—I did it—as much for myself as for you." I felt my chest cave in now, my throat tighten, but I couldn't cry.

Old Woman sighed, "My hair is unbraided then."

Cobwebs unravelling. And on the morning of the fifth day, Old Woman had not only spoken to me, she had asked me to comb and rebraid her hair. The mourning was over. If she had been younger, in full health, Old Woman would have danced with bundles belonging to Johanna.

"She is part of me," Old Woman said, "but I do not take skinning knife and cut her out of me. When you talk about going forth and back, ahhhh, I see brown hands, not as brown as mine but strong like mine, and hands are picking wild strawberries for upsidedown cake for our granddaughter. *'Ohtehimina!'* It is heart-shaped-berry!"

"I remember," I said. "We went for a swim by the beaver dam, then picked strawberries on the way home."

"She is apart from me now."

I was shaking. "I won't let you do this!" I cried.

"It is the same thing," Old Woman said. "She is with me and away from me. Both." She placed her hand heartside. *"Ohtehihk!"* then slowly in English, "A part and apart."

"When you say she is with you, I feel as if she is far away, and I'm so terribly alone. But when you say she is apart I feel as if she is close to me."

"Ahhhhh-ha!" Old Woman nodded, "You are getting close to it."

All day, for many days, I had talked about one grandmother to another. I had spoken to Old Woman as if she were Johanna. It was more than trying to remember and live in the past. I had tried to replace one grandmother with another.

Before we opened our gifts, Old Woman and I traded songs. I sang my grandmother's favorite, "Now We Dance Around the Tree", and Old Woman sang "Silent Night" in Cree.

"We were a split people," she said. "On white-collars' Sunday we dressed our children in white robes and they sang hymns. With long faces and sad faces they sang songs about how sorry they were for being bad. Naaaaa! I do not know what this means: sinned. I only know that I am medicine woman because I never go against rules of Creator. So. Next Monday we held secret sundance and sang glorification songs, but both days we pray to one Creator."

"I just realized something else," I said. "You only swear in English."

"There is no way to take Creator's name in vain," she said, "no way to curse in Cree."

"Now open your presents," I said. I carried her back to her cot and arranged her bundles around her.

Old Woman tore at the wrapping paper, and I hastened to fold it into the woodbox. She smiled and sighed and clucked over each one, then said, "For you." Her hands were empty. There was no deerskin bundle on the bed. "Close to me," she said.

I sat on the edge of the cot. Old Woman untied the necklace around her neck: blue glass trading beads strung on rawhide. "Many winters older than I am," she said. "This many trading beads my grandfather's grandfather got for five beaver skins from Company."

I fingered the beads.

"Tomorrow I'll go to my cousin's place," I said. "We'll have turkey instead of smorgasbörd and—well—it won't be the same as when I was growing up. I'm glad now that it won't be."

"You grow like wild strawberry," Old Woman said.

"What? Not like Swedish Ivy?" I laughed.

"You were born on prairie. In winter. Tomorrow you go see all things joined under sun."

"It's so cold I'm afraid to look at the outside thermometer," I said, "much less go out on the open prairie."

"I want my pipe," Old Woman said.

I watched her pack her small clay woman's pipe, waiting.

"This feeling you have," she said. "It does not belong to to you. You were born on prairie. This feeling of not belonging comes from your grandmother. *Moniyaw!* They do not know how to live well on prairie. So they are afraid of open space." She sucked on the pipestem. "Light it now," she ordered.

I lit Old Woman's pipe, suddenly remembering how we all went to the Battleford Fair in the back of the '46 Fargo. When we broke through the bush onto the flatland, Johanna was terrified. Old Woman took Johanna out of the truck, made her lie down, face down, on the earth. Then coming home at night, the driving, slanting rain, and the coulee plunging into darkness. Again, Johanna was frightened, but what did Old Woman do or say then? What did I do?

"Survival," I said, not knowing where the word came from.

"Ahhhh-ha," Old Woman said. "So now I tell you

about survival. I tell you about new way of living in Montana and how it goes with me then."

Telling stories has always been the elder's way of teaching the young. Of course, Old Woman had told stories to Johanna and I before, but now I was listening in a new way.

Old Woman

We have become scavengers. In early morning, we lie flat against banked snow on coulee's ridge. Empty wagon rumbles slowly back to Fort Assinniboine.

Lucky Man's youngest woman peeks over bank. I shove her raggy head into snow. "Not yet," I whisper. "Wait until you cannot hear wheels creaking."

I curl my fingers around handles of snow-filled kettles. Ready to run. "Now!" I yell to women and children. "Let's go!"

Over coulee's rim, shawled heads appear. Women swing buckets heavy with snow, run for dumping grounds. Behind them, children wrapped in rags drag berry pails and cooking pots full of snow. Heavy night mist rises. Grey haze lifts over dark mounds of burning garbage. We dump pails of snow on fires. Steam rises.

First pickings are best. Silently, eyes red and streaming tears from smoking stench, we poke numb fingers into ashes. We sift hot garbage. We take anything we can eat or wear from steaming piles. I pull out blue pants, singed sleeve. I go after oil cloth. My mother finds coffee grounds inside scorched paper. She juggles potato, cuts out rotten centre, gives it to me. Potato is burned. I lick my fingers.

Old Man shuffles around garbage. He wears only his breech clout. He has made a canopy from old yellow necktie, and he runs before wind. He chants language I cannot speak or understand. I have never seen him before. No one knows where he came from or what tribe he belongs to. But he speaks Cree. He beckons to me with twisted pointing-finger. I dart around garbage. I follow fluttering banner Old Man holds over his head.

He scrambles up ridged bank onto Assinniboine Trail. He breaks into trot that would have burst heart of my old father. I wonder how many winters he has seen. He runs as if his knees are hobbled, but pale skin is stretched smooth and tight over legs that are thick as if they were broken but mended poorly. Even so, I cannot catch Walks-in-wind, so fast he runs toward Fort.

He leads me around shooting place, behind stables. At cook house, he stops. He bends under waving yellow banner. "You should not be digging in garbage," he says. Rough loose folds of his forehead almost hide his spider eyes. His cheeks and lips flap against his gums. No eyebrows or lashes protect spider eyes. Two wisps of hair hang from his small head like braided cobwebs. "Wait here," he says, "and I will go away. You will see a man come out of cooking place. He throws away slops and chewed-up-meat." Old Man runs again before wind.

I lean against cook house, but I do not wait long. A bluecoat comes out of shack. He is Cook, bluecoat who hands out flour and tea. He has hair on his face but none on his head. He dumps slops from wooden bucket. I crawl over to pool of brown water. I fish for potato peelings and bones.

"You're that hungry!"

I back away from Cook. I clutch dripping bones. I am afraid he wants them back.

"Wait! Don't go away! Can you—can you wash clothes?"

Staring, I say, "Ni-nehiyiwan."

"Come." He motions for me to follow him. *"It's all right. I'll give you food."* He points to his mouth and makes it go around like he is chewing something. He leads me into shack.

Inside, there is a black *stove* like one I once saw in Foodgiver's house. Snow melts in a big tub. There are piles of different clothes that belong to bluecoats. Cook points at each pile: *"Wash white first,"* and I see shapes of men's arms and legs that must be leggings they wear under blue pants, *"yellow next,"* and I know scarves they wear around necks, *"then socks,"* and I point to Cook's feet.

Cook gives me tin pail full of white strong-smelling powder and shows me how to dump it in water to make bubbles. He gives me a flat board with shiny ribs on it and tells me to work clothes hard over it. Then he gives me pegs that look like small bird beaks; they bite into scarves so they hang to dry on a rope strung between poles.

I carry tubs full of snow to melt on stove. I scrub clothes clean and hang them to dry. Sometimes I do not do it right: I hang clothes up without wringing them. Once I did not dump out dirty water and swish out bubbles from clothes in clean water and Cook told me not to do that again. Outside, legs and arms freeze stiff and I have to carry them inside to thaw by stove. So they get wet again, and I think this is all silly.

Then I split cottonwood, outside, to build up fire inside stove. I hack at a log. Axe sticks in wood. I bash it against stump. Splinters fly, and log falls evenly into split pieces. I spit on my hands. Chips lie around chopping block like chicken feathers. I remember how I used to gather poplar chips in my skirt for my grandmother. She clucked over different piles of wood: some drying, some seasoned for winter, some too wet to burn. I swing at another log, and I think I can tell Cook about wood for burning. I remember how our fathers went to Battleford to chop wood for redcoats.

I am chopping, chopping, tossing split wood in a pile so Cook will see how much I work. I sweat, chopping, sucking blisters, chopping, but always watching grey light above cottonwood trees. Sun is in middle of sky but is hidden behind bank of clouds that moves slowly towards home of cold wind. Now my pile of kindling is large enough to start many fires.

Cook's hairy face turns around corner of shack. He stops my arm with a hand that is clean, even under fingernails. It smells of beef blood. He holds out pieces of boiled beef and fat. I am sweating, panting, and my shoulders heave. I drop axe, rub my raw and blistered hands with snow. I grab meat and stuff it in my mouth. It has been scraped from long knives' plates, taste chewed out of each piece, but fat is sweet and juicy.

Cook gives me small bundle of chopped beef. He takes round piece of metal out of flat leather pouch folded in square. Token looks like *coins* Horse-dance-maker used to get from Little Bearskin in trade for fox furs, but figurehead is not veiled puffed-cheek image of Woman Leader. I tuck bundle under my arm, make fist over coin and run for camp.

I am running along wind-cleared Assinniboine Trail. I

am thinking about laying coin on trader's counter, about flour for bannock, about tea and sugar. If I wash clothes many times, maybe I will have enough *coins* for new cloth or a blanket-coat.

My breasts are bursting with milk, swollen hard, skin stretched too tight. My dress is wet under my blanket. I have been away from camp too long, Lucky Man's children will be nudging their mother's empty breasts. I have been away too long, milk drips from my nipples, and so many children go hungry.

When I duck into Lucky Man's lodge, small ones leap out of their mother's arms and crawl to me, older ones fight for their turn at the breast. Lucky Man's youngest woman is too-much-tired now. She coughs all night. She cries into her skirt when I come into lodge. Too many have coughing sickness now. Too many children are coughing, even my own angry child, and I do not know how this can be: a child who does not go hungry coughs. I will pass medicine tea around circle this night.

Along ridge of dumping grounds now. Bluecoat near his snorting horse, standing taller than his saddle horn, unbuttoning his pants. Two pieces of glass wired to his ears are tilted on his nose. Steam rises from snow between his heavy boots. He is Yellow Hair. I have seen him blow into horn when sun goes down behind Fort, and he makes noises I have never heard from bird or animal. Not even a mating moose makes such sounds.

Yellow Hair does not see me. He swings legs over horse, heels horse's sides. He bolts back to Fort, rides hard, but sits tall in saddle so I know he is not real horseman, his body does not bend low over horse and move with it. He passes me. Curve of his mouth is not a smile.

I hide my face behind my shawl.

Walks-in-wind scrambles up from dumping grounds. He waves his yellow banner at me. "Ahstum!" he calls to me. "Ahstum!"

I look beyond Old Man's pointing-finger and see something moving between mounds of garbage: a small foot, bare and twitching. Walks-in-wind shuffles down between piles, so I only see his yellow scarf fluttering like sacred cloth on a grave marker.

I find footing, take path sideways, slide where there is ice. Trail curves around ashpiles. I see something bright and shining and yellow: brass button from blue coat. Scarf beside it is not yellow rag bluecoat ties around neck. It is woman's green headscarf. I find blue coat, shapeless on packed-down-snow. One sleeve is missing. It has been torn away from shoulder. Yellow Hair was wearing his coat so this one does not belong to him. I do not understand this, but I am following trail of scattered clothing. Maybe last pickers were having fun with cast-off clothing Soldier Leader's men carted to our camp in a ration wagon.

No scavengers in dumping ground now. Someone has dropped a red fringed shawl. I am afraid that maybe man and woman, drunk together, struggled back from Fort and lost themselves in dump. Too drunk to find their way, they froze to death, casting off clothing when their bodies burned with cold. I have seen it happen too many times.

Blue glass trading beads that were wrenched so hard from someone's neck even leather thong gave way. Bits of cloth. Fear flutters in my chest like broken wing of sparrow. I am afraid of what I know I will find between mounds of garbage.

Old Man's banner waves in wind. He chants. He comforts a new-young-woman lying, as if frozen, on snow.

She lies unclothed, body stiff as if in death, her arms rigid and fists pressing against her thighs. Only her toes twitch. She stares, wide eyes of new dead, unblinking even when Old Man flaps sacred cloth close to her face. I know her. She is youngest child of Night Traveller, and she has seen three-times-four winters on prairie. She has not had her first four days in isolating tent, but she has had her first experience too soon. Even before this, she has seen too much too soon. She was with women who raided trader's post at Battleford. Now she is one of many little scavengers who pick for food in dump. I will call her New Raven after this, bless her with a strong name to take away her pain.

New Raven passes blood between her legs. She is torn. It is not first bleeding time. I take from my bundle medicine moss tied in new rag. I ease it between her tight thighs. Her legs stiffen, but she does not cry. Walks-in-wind strokes her unbraided hair, her bruised forehead, her swollen face. His words are soothing as moss, his voice soft as first spring rain.

She does not speak, but eyeskin folds over her eyes, and I think she is staring behind her lids. It would be good if she could cry, but New Raven's song will not be heard while frost explodes on trees. I am afraid it will be many winters before she sings her own song.

"I will take her to isolating tent," I say, "so no one will know."

"I will bring you her blue coat," Old Man says.

"No," I say, "not her old clothing. Not torn things. We must find new for her."

I tie my own shawl around her legs. Old Man lifts her to her feet, but her knees do not bend. She is straight as lodgepole. I wrap my own blanket around her. Walks-in-wind and I carry her between us, but she will not move one foot in front of the other. We drag her like new pole for isolating lodge. Her toes cut furrow behind her like foodgiver's hoe.

We will take her to isolating lodge, and a husband will be found for her. I will call her My-little-sister, because I have found a second woman for Horse-dance-maker.

If camp were made in old Way, crossing distance would be shorter, but Exact People no longer camp in protective circle unless special ceremony is made. Tents are scattered. Our Leaders were taken away and there is no one to pitch tents in centre places. "You see us camped here and there," I say to Old Man. "You see breaking up of People."

Blood trickles from New Raven's nose. I tilt her head back so she will not choke. She gasps for new breath.

Scratcher and bluecoat with split lip duck under skeleton branches. They break into camp. Split Lip wants to go to Fox's sister. He puts something into Scratcher's hand. Scratcher must be paid first.

Another bluecoat crawls out of Fox's sister's tent. He is taller than anchor post. He looks around as if he has lost his directions, then he sees Split Lip, and the movement of his hands is not sign language. He belches and rubs his belly. He staggers toward Assinniboine Trail and the Fort.

Scratcher strides towards tent, toes turned inward, head thrust forward. He is no taller than a new-young-man.

162

He wears white hat tied down with yellow scarf, grey blanket-leggings, and robe. He does not have coup feather or animal tail tied to his braids. He has not earned a Real Name. He has no status among People. He is one of those we call Government-blanket-people or Old-blue-coat-people because he has lived near forts since end of Company's trading days. He is only Scratcher, and he lives by trading women instead of beaver skins. His left eye twitches. He ducks into Fox's sister's tent.

"I have cursed him," Walks-in-wind says.

But it is Fox who will kill Scratcher, kill him for his sister and all women who are traded for burning water. He will shoot holes in his tent and bundles, smash his rifle against rock, and steal his horse. Fox will stop Scratcher's trading, and there will be no returning of things destroyed, no blackened brow of forgiveness for Scratcher.

Scratcher is hitting Fox's sister now. Her head strikes tent wall. Canvas yields, bulges, then tightens again. "You don't like to eat?" Scratcher yells.

Fox's sister hits her head against linings. "No more!" she yells, and I think she means no more bluecoats like Split Lip. Tent wall bulges again, springs back. "No more. Until... tomorrow." Her word fall like robin from nest. Trying to fly away too soon.

"There is nothing we can do," I say to Walks-in-wind.

We tighten our arms around New Raven. Slowly, we shuffle towards isolating tent.

I wish Scratcher had not seen New Raven. I am afraid he will come after her now. Scratcher ties women together on rope, like horses, and he leads them to Fort for trading. He goes after the young, the weak, the hungry. I am afraid for New Raven.

New Raven is in isolating tent now. Medicine took away her pain. But she will not speak to me. So I tell her a story to make her think about it another way.

"I tell you about new-young-buffalo," I say.

"I ate some tongue once," Little Poplar's new woman says. She will be given to Little Poplar when she comes out of isolating lodge. She will be his sixth woman.

"So! In the time when a person could not walk across prairie without sighting large herd, there was a young buffalo who had seen three winters. He was one winter too young to take part in mating seasons, but spring came earlier than usual. New-young-buffalo watched other buffalo fight. Females were very beautiful, worth fighting over, and one beckoned to him. He took her as his wife. But when sun rose for fourth time New-young-buffalo felt an itch behind his ear. He tossed his head. His mate rubbed his ear with her nose. But itch did not go away. Then his belly was itchy. He scratched with his right foot like this."

I rub my own belly, scratching. "Now he was itchy under his fur all over. He rolled in long grass, he roared, he rolled onto his feet. He tossed his head from side to side. He bucked. He chased himself until he was dizzy. Then he ran. He butted at everything in his way. He roared. Small game ran away from him. His fur began to fall out. More and more fell out until he had left a trail of matted clumps behind him.

"Asa! All day he ran and all night he chased himself. Next morning he raced to river. He saw a man out hunting. He chased the man. The man was afraid. He knew he would get the Itch too if sick buffalo bit him. Then he would go wild too. He would crawl on his hands and knees and howl. Women would throw food at him, and he would eat like dog."

"And they would wrap him in wolf skin," Bear Woman says, scratching her belly, "and hang him upside down until wildness went away."

"Asa!" So New-young-buffalo who mated too soon chased man towards river. He climbed up embankment, stumbled—"

"Bull?" Little Poplar's new woman says. She scratches her head.

"No!" Bear Woman cries, "brave man!"

New Raven turns her face to skin wall. It is first movement she has made without help, so I know she listens to my story. I jump to my feet. My shadow leaps up on skin wall.

"Man jumped down," I say, and I crouch and jump, "onto ledge overhanging water." I turn to my mother as if she is buffalo I want to push over edge. I leap at her. New Raven watches my shadow change shapes on skin wall. It is growing taller.

"New-young-buffalo snorted and pawed earth. He tore up reeds and small willows. Then sick buffalo started down bank." I am going at my mother now, head lowered, and I paw my feet on floorhide. She acts afraid of me, and Little Poplar's new woman gasps.

"Man picked up dead branch and poked buffalo's nose so he backed away." Now I am brave man, and I jab with firestick. "Buffalo ran down slope, came at hunter from other side." I whirl around. "Again man poked and poked at him with stick." I fight my shadow now. "Around and around buffalo ran," my hands circling, "trying to get at him from above, then below, from this side and from that side." I dart and dodge my long shadow. "This went on for a long time. Sick buffalo grew weaker and weaker. Finally he fell over." I drop to my knees, roll over on my side. "And died."

Then I leap to my feet. "So man slid down riverbank and ran long shore until he reached his camp." I collapse before fire. "For days on days and nights on nights he was so tired he could not move. And that is why boys must not chase new-young-women too soon. Or they will get the Itch!"

"Does Scratcher really have the Itch?" New-young-woman says.

"He ate meat from sick buffalo and got it," Bear Woman says.

"I think lice make him scratch," I say. "Ocikomasis! He is Lousyman! He ties his hat down with rag. To hide lice! Even so his hat bounces on his head. Lice dance underneath!"

My mother laughs and scratches her back. New-young-woman laughs and scratches her neck. But New Raven is silent. I must try to show her that bluecoat, not New Raven, has sickness and is unclean from mating too soon. I try to think of another story, but many people are suddenly shouting, voices joining in single cry:

"KA-KA-KI-WAA-CHAAY-NAAK!"

"Crow People are here!" Bowboy rides through camp. "Crow People are here!" He fires his rifle.

"Wastes bullets," Bear Woman says. "But it is good Other People have come. You go. I will stay with new-young-women."

Outside, people burst from lodges. They rush down trail. Women wave bright scarves. Some weep, call after an uncle, a cousin, a sister-in-law. They run through dumping ground, crawl up humped ridge on other side.

There, long line of Different People halts. Above them, stars seem to burst into flame as if fires of night-dancers have moved south from Land-of-cold-wind. It is not northern lights; they do not dance here; light is torch waved in greeting by Crow Leader, and lightning sparks are changing colors of porcupine quills glinting on his blanket-coat. He is Crow Leader. Eagle Moon has risen, but he does not make camp. He comes to us under night sky. Once, only bravest would enter Exact People's camp before dawn. We are known to Crow People as Cut-throat-people, but this Leader comes bearing the Pipe.

Outside fires blaze welcome. Crow People ride into camp. Young men lean from horses to touch reaching hands of children. They toss bright ribbons and blankets to young girls. They.race ponies through camp.

Little Bear and Little Poplar and Lucky Man bring Crow People to visit us. They bring food with them.

Now I squat before my own outside fireplace, frying bannock from flour given to me by Little Bear's Woman. We will serve handgame players. I squat before fire, on my haunches, so skirt is above my knees and falling away from my legs. Heat spreads up my legs, between them, and I am wanting to be with a man this night. On such a night, when there is food for children, I want to lie under sky with a man. But it is not Horse-dance-maker I am thinking of, it is Little Bear, and I wonder which woman he will roll into his sleeping-robe. It is not so bad to be thinking about Little Bear, it is only wrong to think about a man before my child has seen three winters. Now, with so little milk for children, old Way is talked about by grandmothers. I must keep my milk for children of mothers whose breasts have shrivelled. It would be wrong to make a new child in my belly when so many go hungry. I will not look at Little Bear when he comes out of his tent to play handgames. I will not let him look at me. I will turn away.

Bannock is ready on one side. I turn it. It is cooked on other side too, and I cannot remember turning it over fire. I slice it and take it to handgame players.

Crees and Crows sit in double line of players, facing each other. Horse-dance-maker signs to drummer that games should start. He takes bannock from my plate, smacks my backside. He loves me as much as he does the horses he wants to win this night. If he wins some, will he come into my sleeping-robe and want more than warming up to my backside?

"Here is my stick!" It is Fox. He thrusts long arm between Horse-dance-maker and Bowboy. He dares Yellow Bird, Crow People's leader of handgames. In flat of his hand, a smooth shaven willow as long as his palm is wide. In his other hand, a stick with a bark band in the centre. "I'll put up my rifle and lodge against your wagon and horse!" he yells at Yellow Bird.

I offer bannock Fox, but he brushes plate away. He only wants horses.

Yellow Bird leans forward, picks up centre sticks, his bright coup feathers dipping and tickling Fox's long pointed nose. His players put up robes, guns, ammunition. Crees offer what they have: ceremonial dress, lodges, knives. Yellow Bird places ten sticks in centre. Fox tosses two sticks, catches them, passes them from hand to hand behind his back, then hides them under blanket spread over his knees. He is singing now, trying to distract Yellow Bird. Drummers hit beaver skins with tufted sticks. Each player sings his own Song.

"Ough! That one!" Yellow Bird points at Fox's right hand.

Fox whips his hands from under blanket. Unmarked stick is in his right one.

"Naaaa!" I say, and Horse-dance-maker says to me, "Tssst! You take players eyes away from sticks! You can pass bannock only if you are quiet!"

Fox throws sticks to Yellow Bird who catches them and shoves them under his own blanket before I can see which one is banded.

"Ough! That one!" Fox is unlucky again. Hand he points to holds banded stick. So Yellow Bird takes handgame-stick from centre and places it on his side, "Kocak! Again!"

Handgame goes on until Yellow Bird wins six of ten centre sticks. I fry bannock and pass it around until my flour is gone. Then rising drumbeats tell me game is over. Fox is quiet, unsmiling. Crows pile guns, tents, clothing, blankets, tobacco before him.

"You play well, jackrabbit," Yellow Bird says to Fox.
Fox rises to his feet without using his hands.
"Mahskesis nit-eseyikason!" he yells. He is thin and sky-reaching.

"Jackrabbit! What long skinny legs you have," Yellow Bird says. "Mistapōs! It must be your Real Name!"

Horse-dance-maker jumps up and says, "That-is-all. Handgames are over now."

Yellow Bird covers his head with his arms. "Don't let little rabbit beat me up!" He whimpers. "I'll give him tobacco. But don't let him hit me!"

Fox shoves Horse-dance-maker aside. He slaps Yellow Bird's head and shoulders. "Stand up and fight!" he yells. Yellow Bird is standing, but he is a head shorter than Fox. "No one calls me little rabbit!" He hits Bird.

"Little Rabbit!" Yellow Bird says.

Now I know there will be a fight, and no getting over it. Wapōs, Rabbit, is Fox's Family Name. It is never to be spoken. So I yell at Yellow Bird, "Do not call him that!"

Horse-dance-maker pulls Fox's arms. He is younger than Fox by several winters, and he is as broad and short as Fox is tall and narrow. He has iron arms. One blow from his axehandle fist and fight will be over.

Horse-dance-maker ducks between players' arching arms, comes up between them so Yellow Bird has to let go of Fox. "Bird is only sore at losing," he says, "but he will get over it."

Yellow Bird beats his elbows against his sides, scratches packed-down-snow with right foot. His cowering head bumps Fox's elbow. He is having too much fun with Fox.

Fox's jaws are knotting. He pulls his coup knife from his belt. Crow has insulted Fox's Family Name, and it means a fight with knives until one man is dead.

"Settle it by running!" I yell.

Fox's eyes glow, his eyebrows are tufted points, his nose pinched. There is nothing Fox loves more than racing, on foot or with horses.

"So-ho! He is jackrabbit!" Bird says. "But I don't think he can run that fast!" He pinches Fox's leg, above his knee. "Soft!"

"Show him!" I yell.

"He needs wings to fly faster than me!" Bird dances around Fox, arms spread like wings, dipping and swooping.

"Do it!" I cry. "Live up to Family Name!"

"When sun is high we meet on open plain," Fox says.

Bird stands on one leg, other poised for flight. "If you win you keep handgame winnings," he says, "and I'll give you my horse. But if I win you give me winnings!"

"It is done!" Fox says.

Bird and Crow players dance away to where women have pitched tents.

"My winnings." Fox says. "They are to be given to those who have no providers. All but tent. It is for my sister."

Women who have no men to bring home winnings swoop down on blankets and clothing.

Horse-dance-maker and Fox stride toward Fox's sister's tent. "Prairie wool turn green, " Horse-dance-maker says.

I drag new tent behind them because this is woman's work. I am happy for Fox's sister. Her tent is made of scorched top skins and smokeflaps that other women have thrown away. It will fall down when wind is angry at People for giving up and not finding a new way to live. But now Fox has a new tent for her.

Fox's sister is screaming. A gunshot. Then a bullet tears through lodge covering and zings over our heads. Only Fox has to duck. Voices rise in single cry: "Kill him! Kill him!" Fox and Horse-dance-maker swoop around tent. I drop new tent and run behind them.

People have gathered before Fox's sister's tent. They make circle around her. She is drunk. Her hair is unbraided and flying all around her face. Her black skirt hangs in two pieces from her waist. Her breasts are bruised, one swollen larger than the other.

Split Lip lies on his back, upper body sticking out tent-door, legs hidden inside lodge. Blood oozes from bullet scratch on his cheek. His eyes are swelling shut from a beating. An empty jug is beside him. Fox's sister tries to kick his face, but she wobbles, and misses. Horse-dance-maker and Fox grab her arms and hold her tight between them. She sways, tries to wrench free from iron hands.

"Let me have him!" Fox says.

"Ahhhh-ha!" People cry. Fox's sister has no husband, so Fox must punish Split Lip.

"He should be tortured!" Fox says.

"So he dies slowly!" Bowboy yells.

"Scratcher!" Fox cries. "I get him too!"

Scratcher does not have his women with him. He has taken all but Fox's sister to long knives at Fort. He darts through women and children. He avoids those who blame him for trade in women. He scuttles away to Fort where long knives will give him protection.

"We have finished with fighting and killing!" It is Little Bear. People make room for him, allow him to make his way through them. He does not look at Fox's sister. "No one is to blame!" he says.

Those who were once providers and remember how it was when they did not watch their women go to long knives for two bits, they shake heads. They blame themselves for what is happening to People. They press forward, some wave knives. Even Little Bear cannot stop them if members of warriors' society say Split Lip must die.

Little Bear is wrapped in five-point-blanket-coat. He wears status topknot. He bears the Pipe. "She only tries to go on living," he says. "He only defends his sister." He points at Split Lip, "He has no woman. He is far from his own people's lodges. Going away does strange things to a man." He points at Company jug, "Firewater is to blame! I have said it!"

On far side of circle, Scratcher and Yellow Hair carve a way through People.

"What's happened here?" Yellow Hair speaks Pwatak, language of Sioux, and Horse-dance-maker asks Fox to translate.

Little Bear says, "Split Lip has had too much firewater. He slapped this woman around when she wouldn't do what he wanted. She shot holes in tent to scare him away."

Yellow Hair stares at Fox's sister. I cannot guess what he thinks. Fox's sister is crying now, Horse-dance-maker has let go of her, and Fox has his long arms around her. He protects her from long knives. *"I see the problem,"* Yellow Hair says to Split Lip. *"You just ain't good enough! Squaws are used to big bucks! Huh?"* Yellow Hair winks at Horse-dance-maker.

Horse-dance-maker drops his head, hides his anger, just as he did when he and I talked to another whiteman, winters later, on River Street in Place-of-settlement we learned to call *Prince Albert*. No, Horse-dance-maker did not trade me for firewater, not me or any of his other wives, and we went away from *River Street* with knives in our hearts.

Split Lip leans on Yellow Hair now. "*Godam squaws!*" he says. "*They go crazy when they drink!*" He holds his head in both hands. He staggers after Yellow Hair. They beat it back to Fort.

"She is no longer my sister!" Fox cannot bear shame brought to his Family Name. He disappears into dumping ground, but soon now he will go after Scratcher.

Horse-dance-maker's anger is smouldering night fire, and it makes him shake all over. "We must leave this place after Fox's footrace," he says to Little Bear, "and we will put away memory of this camp." He lifts tentflap, Fox's sister ducks inside, and Horse-dance-maker follows her.

"He gets himself mixed up in everything!" It is Bear Woman, and she is screeching more like owl, turning her feathered head his way and that way. "He should care more about old ones in his family!"

Tapwe! It is true. Horse-dance-maker is becoming leader of all ceremonies. He makes announcements. He settles things between fighting men like Fox and Yellow Bird, softens fighting words in families, and he tells stories to new-young-men so they will be ready for taking women. Horse-dance-maker knows all about that, now he is with Fox's sister, now that I have found New Raven for him. But I do not want Fox's sister to live in my lodge. It is not because she has been with long knives that I do not like her. Fox's sister is like Fox's Woman: they worry too much about new cloth and ribbons and they are lazy about putting up and taking down lodges when it is time to move camp.

"What is he doing with that woman?" Bear Woman grabs tent-flap and rips it.

Inside, Fox's sister is wrapped in blanket Horse-dance-maker won in handgames. She rebraids her hair. Horse-dance-maker sucks lip of Company jug. He is getting drunk so he can forget People's shame. Nothing will matter to him for now. "I cannot talk to you," he says.

171

Nodding, I leave my mother shouting after me to come and see what my husband is doing with that woman. But, it is dawn of new day and I must wash clothes for Cook and bring home beef. I will buy a new hat for Horse-dance-maker with the *coins.*

I run to Fort, thinking I have not given milk to Yellow Calf all night, but my breasts are not swelling hard. I am afraid my milk is drying up.

All morning I wash clothes for Cook. I learn a new word: *longjohns.* They are boiling in a copper canner on stove. Cook will not let me chop kindling and make fire. I do not understand this because making and keeping fires is woman's work. Whites do everything backwards.

I learn how to smooth yellow scarves with iron boats flat on bottom that Cook keeps hot on top of stove. They have wooden handles that clip on and off with wooden knobs. Cook shows me how to push them back and forth over cloth. I do this on a flat board that stands on wooden legs. I think this is silly until I burn my nose on steam rising from damp scarves. I see scarves look like new, so I think I will make my own headscarf look new when Cook is outside chopping wood. Iron is too hot, and silk shrivels. I lift iron and see I have burned my scarf. Then I see that irons are not so hot on tank that holds water. Cook calls it *reservoir,* and it means saving water and keeping it hot. So I press my own scarf. It smells of sweet flowers I crush and rub into my scalp. I am afraid Cook will smell them too, so I quickly tie my scarf on my head before he comes back, but I am happy that it looks so new. Maybe Little Bear will look at me at footrace, but I am trying not to think so much about him.

Cook gives me a tin plate of boiled potatoes and meat that tastes like dogwood bark. So I take cold bannock from my left-over-bag and eat it beside woodpile. I tie second *coin* inside bag. Then I race back to camp, hoping I have not missed all of Fox's footrace. I feel my breasts filling up with milk.

Away from Fort, along Assinniboine Trail, on edge of dumping ground, I meet Scratcher. He has wavering line of women on rope. He is having fun with women. He lifts their skirts, smacks rumps, tickles them in soft places. As limp as

Walks-in-wind's tattered banner, women flop sideways. Scratcher prods them with poking fingers.

Fox's sister slaps Scratcher's hands. She is robin trying to fly with one wing. Bowboy's cousin crumples into heap of skirts. She vomits. Too quiet to be drunk, they all make sighing sounds, and I wonder what Scratcher puts in firewater to make women give up and give in. Traders gave people *laudanum*. Maybe that is it.

Fox appears over rise of dumping ground. He holds tight to his shoulder his new shotgun. He could have shot Scratcher, but he wants lousyman to see him, to see who is going to kill him.

"Little one hasn't had enough! You can have her for two bits!" He grabs smallest woman's hair, pulls her head back so Fox can see her face.

It is New Raven. He has broken into isolating lodge when Bear Woman was giving bad words to Horse-dance-maker, and he has tied new-young-woman to his string of women. I want Fox to stop Scratcher's trade in women. I want him to shoot lousyman.

Scratcher pushes New Raven toward Fox. She stumbles, falls, lies still. Her tattered blanket hangs loosely around her shoulders. Scratcher kicks her belly, so she rolls over, blanket slipping and showing new wound, blood red, above darker nipple. New Raven has no breasts, only nipples beginning to swell.

"You want her?" Scratcher yells. "Only two bits!"

Fox shoulders his rifle.

"Only one has had her!"

He aims at Scratcher's white hat.

"I'm only having fun," Scratcher whines.

Fox fires. Scratcher ducks. Bullet shoots into dumping grounds, crashes against bare willows. Fox stands tall, and from where I am crouching, his warrior topknot looks like it touches new snow cloud in sky.

"Get him!" Scratcher yells at women.

Women look at Fox out of pale eyes, move toward him, hands clawing for him. Scratcher is laughing. Women are laughing. Firewater and bad medicine are wearing off and women are getting ready for kicking and scratching. Scratcher will take them back to husbands and fathers, but not even an elder can stop their kicking and scratching and screaming. They have the sickness, are unclean, and they are shamed because everyone knows about them.

New Raven does not have the sickness yet. She has not had her first isolation—all of it. She was born in month of shedding leaves. Her old mother went into bush and did not come out. Night Traveller found her dead, took newborn to Bear Woman. As soon as she could walk, New Raven tossed her skirt and flung buffalo chips in boys' faces. Always, she made them chase her into bushes. They tickled her until she cried from too much laughing. Now boys must never play with new-young-woman. They must not speak to her until a husband is found for her.

Fox must kill Scratcher for his sister, for New Raven, for all women. He must stop this kind of trading, and I will take New Raven back to isolating tent. After three more days she will be Horse-dance-maker's new woman, and no one will know what happened.

Fox aims for Scratcher's white hat. If he shoots now he might hit a woman, their weaving bodies are an uneven wall between him and Scratcher. Scratcher is backing away, and I think he will try to run for dumping ground.

"You can have her for nothing," he says.

"He is going to shoot!" I yell at women. "Down! Lie flat on ground!"

I fall face down, on hard packed snow of Assinniboine Trail. I do not want stray bullet to hit me. But women do not hear me, do not turn away from Fox to look at me. Slowly, they move towards Fox.

He shoots high, over women's heads, and bullets crash in dumping ground. I think one hit some old tin or barrel casing. Gun blasts make women fall down. They roll over and over in snow, covering heads and ears with hands. They are shrieking.

Scratcher runs for dumping grounds. Fox shoots. Scratcher's arms fly above his head. His feet fly up too, his body twists in air, and he leaps like prairie chicken over low bushes. He rolls sideways down into dumping ground.

I am afraid to get up and go and see if Scratcher is dead. I hold my hands over my ears, shutting out women's shrieks.

"Come." Long moosehide toe nudges my elbow. "We

174

bury lousyman in garbage." It is Fox's voice, flat and smooth as his totem's tail. "He is not worthy of four-day-feast."

I scramble to my feet and follow Fox into dumping ground. We roll Scratcher's body into ashpile. It sinks. Bits of ash fly up like blowing snow.

"No one will know," Fox says. He means Scratcher, but I think of New Raven.

Again I take her to isolating lodge.

It is steaming in isolating lodge. Bear Woman boils water in many black pots and kettles to take away coughing of my angry child. Yellow Calf is cradled in fishnet, swaying through steam above fireplace. She does not cry.

"I give her rosehip tea, pine needle tea," Bear Woman says, "but my granddaughter spits it back up."

"We need medicine men to touch centre-pole of sundance lodge," I say, "and pray for her."

"I will make promise to dance," Bear Woman says.

There are two new-young-women in isolating lodge now, and they stare rudely at New Raven. She slumps down on sleeping-robe. All the way back from dumping ground she stomped through snow ahead of me, and I was happy to see her angry. She trailed ends of her fringed shawl, not caring if she got it wet, not caring if her shoulders were bitten by frost.

I kneel before fire, take white dried mud from my medicine bundle. I mix it with boiling water and smooth it to a healing salve, careful not to touch it with my hands. I crawl over to New Raven. Gently I slide her shawl away from her shoulders. She stares at me, eye to eye, but I lower my head to show her I still respect her.

"I am unclean," she says.

"No," I say. "I will clean wound, pack it with medicine, so it will not swell red. So it will heal." I work white mud into wound, make it bleed a little so any evil from Scratcher's hands and finger nails will run out with blood. I tie up wound with strips of cloth. "You rest now," I say. "Stay here for three more days and nights." I do not tell her that I have a husband for her.

Now I must give milk to Yellow Calf. I take her from fishnet cradle. She does not nudge my breast, seek with open mouth my nipple. She does not kick or knead with fists. I try to ease my nipple into her mouth, milk drips from it, but she turns her head away and makes a twisted mouth as if milk does not taste good to her. She coughs, spits up blood. I hold her standing on my knees, so she does not choke. There is no strength in her legs, even her toes do not push into thighs. My child who fought so hard to be born is not fighting now.

How can this be so much so? I have never before seen a child who is not hungry. I have pain in my chest. I cry inside.

Bear Woman takes my bundled child from me. "This is too hard for you," she says. "You go to footrace. I will steam away coughing of my granddaughter. I will give her rosehip tea. She will be better when you come back, and then you feed her. Go now!"

I leave isolating tent, wanting to run across prairie, but it is wrong time to look for new roots. I must dream on it. I run to place of gathering for footrace.

I find Horse-dance-maker at finish-butte. He waves his black hat. He stamps his feet and blows on his hands. "It is close," he says.

Fox and Yellow Bird race in breech-clouts. Both sweat, but only Bird seems to be tiring.

I do not tell Horse-dance-maker about New Raven and how I have found a second woman for him. I do not tell him about our child turning away from breast and coughing blood. I do not tell him about Fox shooting Scratcher. I am hurting too much, inside, to tell him these things. It is also not time for talk when People are happy about footrace.

Fox lopes past last marker, lengthens his stride. Single stretch of his long legs covers same distance Bird runs in three strides.

I am thinking it is time for Horse-dance-maker to wrap me in sleeping-robe and make another child in my belly.

Fox leaps across finish-butte. "Wahwā!" he cries. He circles butte, grinning, for first time truly laughing. Fox swallows air. He touches foxtail bobbing on his head. His totem brought him good luck.

"Ayiman! Ayiman!" People cry in one voice. "Fox wins!"

Crow Leader wraps blanket around Fox's sweating shoulders. He gives Yellow Bird's horse to Fox. He will make big talk now. But it is Horse-dance-maker who raises his arms.

"I am poor man, humble man," he says, "but I will try to speak to you." This change in Horse-dance-maker has been like greening of prairie wool. "Fox has lived up to his Name!" he says. "He won handgames and now he proves he is a runner."

"Tapwe! Tapwe!" People cry.

"He has very long legs," Bird laughs.

Fox slaps his thighs. He hops around butte. "It is wrong time for gophers!" he yells. He pretends to swallow gopher lumps. Fox says eating gophers helps him run long distances without water.

"There are others good at handgames," Horse-dance-maker says. "Bowboy can win horse races. All he needs is fast runner."

"I give him one of mine," Crow Leader says. His blanket-coat is worked with red porcupine quills.

Horse-dance-maker lowers his head. "We do not forget our friends, Crow People, who have been kind to us, who have shared food—"

"Tapwe!" Fox cries. "Other People help us all they can!" Fox is good winner now.

"I say we have found new way to go on living until it is safe for us to go back, over dividing-line, to left-over-lands."

"We will challenge all Different People to play games!" Fox's cheeks are blazing from status he has won. "How can we lose?"

"Nahiyiwak!" Bowboy cries. "We are Exact People!"

"And we will return to our own better off than we were when we left," Horse-dance-maker says. "Crow People leave us now. Soldier Leader says we cannot camp together. Crow People's foodgiver has work for them on their left-over-land. When leaves are budding they will plant seeds, but when prairie wool turns green again small birds will call them to go hunting."

So. Last night Horse-dance-maker made up his first Big Talk. "Prairie wool turns green," he said to Fox. He is becoming a leader, but not like Little Bear. It is true both went against teachings of elders, are searching for a new way to live, and fight with words instead of guns. But Little Bear goes to whitemen and tries to get piece of left-over-land to live on here. Horse-dance-maker stays away from them and tries to find a way that will go on apart from them.

"They will be scratching in dirt and picking rocks and weeds and stones from land," Horse-dance-maker says. He holds up tobacco bundle. "Crow Leader has invited us to join them at Sundance. I think we all have promise to keep!"

People lower heads. I have my own promise to dance four days and four nights. Bear Woman promises to dance if life of Yellow Calf is spared.

"We will dance and pray," Lucky Man says, "to make Great Deliverer happy!"

"Ahhhhh-ha!" People cry. "Ahhhhh-ha!"

I run with People back to camp. Scratcher's white hat blurs before my eyes. My child is dying white death. Snow flies up under my rawhide feet. I run before wind.

Bear Woman waits for us outside isolating lodge. "Epwakomohkwet," she says. "She was bleeding from throat and I could not stop it."

Horse-dance-maker throws back his head and raises his arms to sky. Here, changing lights of departed-ones-dancing do not whistle-call among stars. But our child is dead. I feel myself falling forward. Horse-dance-maker catches me and holds me tight against his heaving chest. He pounds my back. I shove him away from me. I beat my own breast. I tear at my hair, unbraiding it. I fall against Lucky Man's grandmother's travois. Horse-dance-maker gathers me into his arms again. He strokes my hair. We drop to our knees. We are crying together, rocking, holding each other. Our pain passes in and through and out of each other.

"This pain of losing your child does not belong only to you!" Bear Woman tears me from Horse-dance-maker's arms. "Child belongs to tribe!" she yells at me. "Go!" She shoves me towards Bowboy's tent. "Call People together!"

So I am telling People, not knowing what I am saying, but they are gathering food and comforts for time of mourning. I run from lodge to lodge, until I am at Fox's sister's tent. It has crumbled, fallen under wind. Misipiwan. It is buried under snow. Wind pushes me. Drummer's call pulls me to Little Bear's tent. It is largest lodge, belongs to Son of Big Bear, and it will hold People for four-day-feast. I hear Death Song rising through smokeflaps.

Bear Woman has hung long strip of braided birchbark over tentflap to chase away Bony Scepter. She has scattered ashes before it. Inside, she has carefully laid out Yellow Calf. People are settled before fire circle. Lucky Man speaks about Blackfoot boy who changed himself from ugly child to worthy-man. I take my place on women's side of tent. I sit still, clench my hands together in my lap.

Fox speaks of Medicine Hat so people will remember power of medicine. Fox never does it right, maybe because he is loneman and is always thinking about women and horses, is always telling stories about horses and women. He should tell story about lost child who brought good hunting to people.

"We must not grieve too long or we will disturb child's spirit and not help her on her way to better place," Walks-in-wind says. "We cannot wish she had stayed longer to know cold, hunger, and coughing sickness. We must not deny her reunion with ancestors. Now she is better off than we who will miss her. We cry together and share sorrow. Now we let her spirit go. Let us be happy for child who will dance with ancestors!"

"I ask you to restore unity between earth and sky," I say to Walks-in-wind, "so my child will find friends to go with her on her last-four-day-walk."

Walks-in-wind wails for my child and for mourners. He asks for Pipe. He mixes tobacco and sweetgrass in clay dish. He cleans his hands with yellow ochre, smooths parted hair, rubs heartside. "Who are relatives?" he says.

"Grandfathers and Grandmothers," Bear Woman says. She makes first link with departed-ones. "Her father and mother," she says. She makes link with the living.

"My father," I say.

"My oldest brother," Horse-dance-maker says.

Walks-in-wind passes Pipe through sweetgrass smoulder four times. He lights it. He kneels on buffalo robe. He holds Stem in left hand, bowl in right, rocking now, arms arching, and he raises Pipe to four directions. He prays. "We have little to offer but we give what we have to child's spirit. We share with she who leaves us for better place." He wraps small body in blanket, loosely so she may walk freely to place of ancestors. "May she live among friends. May she never be cold. May she never know coughing sickness." He places small medicine bundle, woman's pipe and tobacco beside body so Yellow Calf will have what she needs in new life. He presents offering of dried meat. He throws food into fire.

Now there is no separation between earth and sky, between mourners and departed-ones. Outside, wind no longer beats against tent walls. Inside, quiet holds, for my child is ready for her four-day-walk. Feast-for-dead will last four days. On fourth, old women will paint my face, comb and rebraid my hair, and lead me to dance. Women will dance with leather bundles belonging to all departed-ones, and we will leave spaces in circle for them.

Now I feel loss of my child in different way. My breasts are swollen with milk for her. I want to hold her and nuzzle soft neck and sweet-smelling hair. I wrap my arms around myself. I am not afraid for my child, but I will always miss her. I stare at fire, its light folding around me, and faces and voices of People fade into last winter of buffalo.

There was no food. Bear Woman chased me outside. "Ask your father why no food!" she yelled. I found him rekindling outside fire with wind-dried roots. I ran to him, crying, and he sat me between his knees. "Look!" he cried. "Capicipiwasin!" His hands were weaving like wind through long grasses. "See how wind blows snow along top of drifts? You must learn to understand why people do and say what they do." He laughed. "Even understand how it goes with your bear of a mother!"

So now I tell you, my Other-granddaughter, what my old father said to me when I was many winters younger than you are now.

Death comes like sudden blowing up of snow. It threatens to knock down lodges. We cannot see for flying-up-blizzard. But storm passes and quiet returns. In summer, rains are slow and lasting. Thunderbird drenches our lodges and stops us from moving camp. We always fear visit of summer pup most. He has never left lodges.

So I say, my Other-Granddaughter, that I have seen how ways of whites crash against ways of Indians. Misunderstanding will be as long time passing as summer rains. But I have seen People sharing so they could survive without buffalo, sharing even in death. There is always a coming together of all things under sky. What is in People is outside them, and what is outside them is inside them. My first born belonged to People before she was my child. Her going away was no worse than flying-up-snow. Soon I will be ready for my own last-four-day-walk.

I am only visiting here.

Annika

In January I abandoned the sleeping loft, moved my bed downstairs and slept on the other side of the woodbox so I could keep the fire burning in the stove all night. I was up every three hours, adding split poplar to the fire and making foxglove tea for Old Woman.

In January, the month when frost explodes on trees, I began losing my sense of time. I kept the coal oil lamp going long after Old Woman fell asleep; and I slept away a great part of each day.

I started crying in my sleep.

In dream, it was always summer. I was walking through thick blue spruce and northern pine, searching for Johanna. She was just ahead of me, I found her cotton sunhat, like a fallen woodflower on the path, a footprint of crushed brown pine needles; but she remained just ahead; I couldn't find her. I emerged from the bush into a clearing and found myself in a cabbage patch.

Brown earth was humped like a freshly-turned grave, and in its centre a large Copenhagen cabbage lay in a bed of crushed ice. A man, tall as northern pine, with axle-tree shoulders, waited there for me. His skin was neither white nor brown. He wanted to love me, but I cried, "No! Over there!" pointing to the rock garden of woodflowers transplanted from Sweden. He grabbed my hand; and we were running towards the home place; but I was crying, running in my sleep, and crying. My feet thudded on hard-packed earth.

I was awakened by the thud thud of Old Woman's fist banging on the calcimined wall. She wanted Johanna's china pot, but by the time I had stumbled out of bed, it was too late.

She'd wet her bed. I turned up the flame on the coal oil lamp, removed the front and back lids from the stove and shoved three big pieces of poplar into the firebed. Then I fetched a clean nightgown and fresh sheets from the dresser.

"You drink too much tea at night," I complained, moving Old Woman to the rocker so I could change her sheets. "I'll have to wash clothes again in the morning." I stuffed the soiled sheets into the copper canner. It was the third or fourth time I had changed her bed that night. "Call me sooner!" I said.

"I bang and bang on wall," Old Woman said, "but you do not wake up. I call and call but you do not come out of dream."

I tucked Old Woman back into bed, gave her foxglove tea, and crawled into my own cold bed. I laid my parka on top of the covers for extra warmth, hoping to sleep through the rest of the night without dream and without having to get up again.

I fell back into a dream of wading through cat-tails and long green grasses that leaned towards the Turtle River. I followed the river, searching for Johanna. Where the river flowed down to the Livelong Flats, I broke through a tangle of wolf willow onto a wide range of buffalo grass blown in one direction: northeast. My grandfather was striding over the rising land toward me, his face sunny, his hair lifted and teased by wind.

The prairie broke away at our feet, dropped over a rocky cliff. "This is my brother's land," a young Bjorn said, "but there is my home place." From the northeast, the great water rolled and heaved and tossed foaming spray onto a sandy beach that lay beneath another unscalable cliff. Directly across the inlet, thickly wooded land, trees I couldn't name; and in the centre a yellow house with cedar shakes on the slanted roof. The sky was blue; unclouded. Yellow and blue, the homeland colors. Together we stood, young Bjorn and I, buffeted by prairie wind, an ocean away from the yellow house. And in my sleep I was crying, unable to bridge the chasm; I was crying so hard I woke myself up.

The coal oil lamp had burned down. A pale grey light lay behind the frosted windows. Old Woman wasn't pounding on the wall. She was a mound buried under quilts and her new Bay blanket.

I made a tent by sitting up and pulling the quilts over my head, then stuck my arm out the side and groped for my parka and jeans, fingers closing around the wolf fur trimming the hood; then slid my clothes under the covers. I pulled on my jeans, tucking my nightgown into them, then parka, before throwing back the covers. I grasped the oven door and hauled myself out of bed.

The woodbox was empty. I shoved my hands into my pockets and found my sheepskin mittens. Felt boots inside my rubber ones, hood up, and I stumbed to the door, yanked it open, expecting wind and whirling snow, but the outside air was heavy and still.

Cold air burned the inside of my nose, seared my lungs. I turned my head sideways inside the parka hood, breathed deeply until I had adjusted to the temperature. I jumped over the front stoop into snow that caught me like quicksand and pulled me down to my knees. I waded three or four steps to the woodpile, stacked poplar on my left arm, and started a small avalanche of tumbling wood. Arms raised, I climbed the steps back into the house.

It took five trips out to the woodpile before the woodbox was refilled and each time I dumped an armload I expected Old Woman to holler at me, but she didn't even stir in her sleep.

"You wake up only when you want to," I grumbled.

I emptied the ash drawer, crumpled newspapers, and started a new fire in the stove with wood chips and shavings. Then I went out to fill the copper canner with snow, returned, and set it on the back burners to melt water for washing clothes. The reservoir was half empty and I filled it with snow too: warm water for our morning sponge baths.

I did these things by habit, thinking now that I had actually chosen to live in the old homestead, forgetting how oil burners keep my cousin's farmhouse warm all night, how water is pumped up from the cistern, how power lines provide electricity for lights and stove. I went back out for an extra load of wood to stack against the wood box, found myself staring at the split poplar.

Poplar split by her woodsman's axe. Birchbark scrolls to fill her winter. And twice she ran away, once back to Hannas, her village near Malmo, only to return.

"Why?" I had asked her often enough, once in this place, while filling my apron with wood chips, "Why did you come back?"

"So I could someday be father and mother, both, to you," Johanna laughed.

But she couldn't have known that my father's life would be eaten away by a duodenal ulcer before I was two, that my mother would run away with the Watkin's man. Special orders filled: dried lingonberries for the Swedish pancakes and cardomom for *vetebröd*. Then she was gone, my mother, with the Watkins man, and I only remember the heady smell of spices.

The early morning sun spread over the yard and north quarter, turned the snow blue. I shaded my eyes against the glare. Frost exploded on spruce trees and caragana hedges.

I needed more time. I had to go back further, beyond the headiness of spices, over the ringing of old voices in my head; I had to go back before I could go forward.

"Because I love you I let you go."

Who said that?

"Because I love you I do not hold you back."

It was Johanna, yes, and she was putting me on a bus for Saskatoon. It was right to go, and I did; now reaching up, unhooking snowshoes nailed beside the door.

I crouched on the bottom step of the front stoop. Leather thongs were frozen stiff, but I strapped the snowshoes around my feet, careful not to tie them too tight so I wouldn't get blisters. I stepped onto the snowcap, bending my knees, and the ice crust held; I didn't break through, one foot sliding slowly forward, lifting the other; and I took the short slope down, passed the turkey shed where Johanna fed them her own cottage cheese so her turkeys boasted more white meat than those of any other farm wife in the north country; and my arms gently pumping, legs loose now, until I was into the easy swing and forward run; shoulders heaving, snowshoes carrying me beyond the log barn that once housed Lightning-foot and Thor. Behind me, Johanna carried two pails of water up from the well, her arms like wings spread out, balancing the pails, and water slopping over the rims onto the path up to the homestead.

Sunlight like a beacon; and down the pasture, through

blue spruce and birch trees with moss growing on their north sides; until only willows, branches reaching like arms out of snow-buried graves. I found the Turtle River and followed its long winding curve, south, towards the flats and the bridge built by Bjorn and Arvid. My parents' initials were carved on the wooden railing, but I didn't stop, not thinking about where I was going or why, only taking the natural course of the river.

I was sweating, my face burning; and it was summer rising over the hills above the beaver dam. I saw myself skipping on rocks across the river. Dragonflies mated above wolf willow. I gathered tiger lilies growing in the road allowance. My mouth and chin were blue from saskatoons.

I was seven years old. My sun-faded hair was tightly braided and bound with blue ribbons. I wore a grey pleated skirt, a yellow blouse with blue flowers embroidered on the sleeves, new brown and white saddle shoes. I ran up the hill from the bridge, late, licking my lips and chin and trying to clean my face with the edge of my apron before Auntie caught me. I ducked under the barbed wire fence, scrambled over the ditch onto the washboard road.

The '46 Fargo rumbled towards me, Uncle driving on the wrong side of the road and raising up dust. He had his black ball cap pulled down, but I could see he was frowning; I knew he wanted to go on to the Battleford fair without me, teach me a lesson for running off like that, but Auntie wouldn't let him.

"Pump 'em! Pump 'em!" Auntie yelled, meaning the brakes, and the Fargo bounced over the hard ruts, passed me, then stopped in front of the lane into Swain's Place.

Now I was climbing that same hill, sideways, and my right snowshoe stopped against a large boulder. I rested on it, my back to the hill, elbows on my knees; and I watched the full memory of that summer day open before me on the road around the neck of the hill down to the bridge and dam near Swain's Place.

Uncle backed the Fargo into the lane so he could turn it about; and I ran, not to the cab, because I was dusty, my new shoes muddy, blue stains on my apron; and I could see Auntie's mouth going like she was chasing a calf that got into Uncle's wheat. Johanna sat between them, her head bobbing from this side to that side, and I knew she was coming between their argument about me.

I stepped up on the running board, and strong brown hands reached over the cattle railing and lifted me into the wagonbox.

"Siddown!" Uncle yelled through his open side window.

I crouched between cream cans. The truck lurched forward, swung back onto the road, and nosed south towards the gravel highway to Battleford. The Indian woman squatting across from me seemed to be very old to me then, although her hair was not whitening like grandmother's nor was her skin as folded and wrinkled. Her full round face was smooth and gleaming with sweat, but the skin around her eyes was cracked. She wore a long skirt, leggings, beaded moccasins, bright shawl and headscarf.

A half day of rumbling and shaking at thirty miles per hour, over ninety miles to North Battleford. That first time at the fair, I was allowed one orange pop, two rides on the ferris wheel, one on the merry-go-round, and I spent the afternoon watching the Turtleford Tiger ball team get creamed by the Edam team. The Indian woman spent her time with the Battleford River people who had pitched their tents on the fair grounds and were dancing with feathers and bells for the curious white people.

At dusk, Uncle gassed up the Fargo at the garage on the south end of the small city. He slumped behind the wheel, rolled a cigarette from the MacDonald's tin. Auntie leaned against the side door, yawning. The Indian woman and I were settling in the back of the truck for the long ride home. My stomach felt sickish from the warm orange pop. I wanted my grandmother. She was on the edge of the paved road, one hand on her hip, the other shading her eyes from the sunset's spreading orange and purple glare.

I leaned over the cattle railing. *"Mor-mor,"* I called.

Johanna didn't hear me. She lifted her skirts and ran across the highway and its gravel shoulder; head down, she plunged through the open gate onto a summerfallowed field. Beyond that, prairie stretched away forever. My grandmother ran forth and back, holding her head.

The Indian woman was fast climbing down the loading end of the truck. She leaped over the pavement, bounded down the sloping shoulder of the road, and caught Johanna from behind. Thick brown arms wrapped around Johanna's shoulders and arms; the Indian woman held her still. Slowly, she turned them both in a circle, her smooth cheek pressed against Johanna's.

I gripped the wooden sides of the truck so hard my fingers were numb. Uncle puffed his roll-yer-own cigarette, and Auntie dozed with her mouth open.

The hefty, tall Indian woman suddenly thrust my grandmother down to the ground, face down, and pinned her arms above her head. She spoke in Cree, voice low and deep, and I couldn't hear what she said. Then she let my grandmother go, stood back, still talking, but pointing to east and north and west and south.

My grandmother pulled herself up, smoothed her skirt and brushed it with her hands. She lifted her head, wrapped her arms around herself; slowly turned in a circle.

The Indian woman pointed at fixed places on the horizon. "Where earth meets sky," she said.

The grandmothers stretched out their arms, together turned, drawing the long line in a circle around them: the protective circle of prairie.

The grandmothers strolled back to the truck, arms around each other's shapeless waists; and they laughed together about something only they shared.

Johanna tapped on the door. Auntie wakened and clamped her mouth shut, then stepped out to let Johanna sit in the middle. "Oiiii, yoii, yoi," Johanna said, "Too much sun I have had on my head today."

The memory faded behind my eyes, beamed out by the high sun's glare on snow.

I pushed myself up, took the hill sideways, down to the road; then ducked under the barbed wire fence, and fast down to the bridge, passed Swain's Place, cut swiftly across the Livelong Flats; then the longer climb to the homestead. Tomorrow I would return to the coulee.

When I arrived home again, it was noon. Old Woman had bannock and lardpail between her knees. After my own quick lunch of heated-up *vetebröd* and coffee, I gave her her sponge bath and walked her from the west windows to the door, from the door back to the cot. She shuffled, but she was steadier today. I settled her in the rocking chair beside the stove with her beadwork and pipe.

Water was boiling in the copper canner. I shaved castile soap into the water and boiled the flannel sheets until they were white enough to hang on the clothesline outside. I was wringing a sheet with wooden spoons, and Old Woman looked up from her beadwork.

"I tell you about glorification," she said, "about horsedance."

That afternoon, I learned about glorification and what it was like to be counted the first among many wives.

Old Woman

Soldier Leader finds ways to make us earn rations he hands out at Fort Assinniboine. He finds jobs for many with wood contractors. Then he sends some Crees down to Fort Belknap to help with spring planting.

Little Poplar wants to visit his Gros Ventre relatives on his mother's side, Lucky Man wants to dance for his Great 'Deliverer, and Horse-dance-maker needs to make his dance. So we leave twenty lodges at Fort Assinnibone and move down to Fort Belknap. There, we are eight tents pitched in place set aside for visitors.

After spring planting, Gros Ventre and Crows and Stonies make sundance for four days and four nights. Then it is horsedance time.

I am lying on floorhide, tracing horse's head in dust, thinking skins should have been rolled up and put away for summer, but it is late coming, this summer. It is horsedance time and Horse-dance-maker has no ceremonial dress. I try to give drawing wide smiling mouth, long jaw, but my fingers tremble. I slap floorhide and dust is flying up. My elbow hits Company bowl. It skids across floorhide, rumpling it, and it hits Bear Woman's ankle.

She plows through bundles, looking for bone needles so she can mend Horse-dance-maker's shirt. She snatches bowl, sees it is empty, drops it and kicks it in corner. "What did you do with my needles?" she snaps. She burrows into bundles.

Little-people-with-no-noses hide sewing needles or make grandmothers forget where they put them. New Raven hid Bear Woman's stirring spoon. Not her needles.

"Tanakē?" Horse-dance-maker says. "What is

190

bothering your mother?" He unwraps drum and rattle. "Has my little Raven been up to her old tricks?" He pulls her ear.

"She always blames me!" New Raven says. "I didn't do it!"

Hiding things on grandmother and her hunting for them when she knows where they are, this is game children play, but Bear Woman is always going after New Raven now. She never leaves her alone, and this is strange because New Raven has always been her special child. Maybe that is only way my mother can say she is angry about what happened to New Raven.

"She is lousy," Bear Woman says, not turning around.

New Raven makes trickster faces at her lumpy back.

"Only a little," Horse-dance-maker says, scratching her head, "but not enough to make your mother so crabby. I want to know what is wrong."

"Old women are upset," I say.

"I can see that. Hear it too!"

"They wanted to make feast for new woman but there was no food and no new clothes for her. Now it is horsedance time and no one has new clothes."

"So we have come to this." He pulls New Raven down to him and settles her between his knees.

Horse-dance-maker is more of a father to her than husband, always telling stories to make her laugh again. They go for secret walks, but I do not think he has taken her as his woman yet. I have not told him what happened in dumping grounds, only that I found second woman for him. Even so, Horse-dance-maker must have known something was wrong, New Raven would not speak to him, and I thought he was waiting for her to come to him. We work together to heal New Raven's spirit. I call her My-little-sister and teach her how to be woman.

"So now we have new woman," Horse-dance-maker says, "but no food for feast. No new clothes."

"Everyone can see!" New Raven says.

She no longer twists her body away from Horse-dance-maker when he holds her, but she hides her face on his shoulder. He whispers something only she can hear.

Horse-dance-maker is different with women. He pats my rump while I fry bannock. He never beats me when I am grumpy about his going visiting without me. He is not like Fox who slaps his woman for touching his forelock, then strokes her neck and calls her pretty. Maybe Horse-dance-maker never beats me because there is nothing I do that he does not like. Now he cares for New Raven, with a difference I am not sure of because I can only see what it is like with them. I do not think he says things to New Raven that he says to me, say four-times-four ways of loving. But that is because I am first woman.

Horse-dance-maker puts New Raven away from him now. It is horsedance time, and feast for new woman is old women's work. "Tell your mother to do what she can," he says to me.

"Naaaa!" My mother, her owlish face twists over her shoulder. It is like old rawhide seamed with bits of leather. Small face set in large head, deerhide owlhead stuffed with rags. "Naaaaa!" She twists her feathered neck.

"What is wrong now?" Horse-dance-maker says.

I want my mother to be quiet. I am afraid she will tell about New Raven. I lean over my mother, pat her back.

My breasts swing under my calico dress. My belly hangs low this time. I must look more like sway-back-horse than woman making child in belly.

"You do not know?" my mother yells. She knows it is forbidden to speak directly to son-in-law. "Yellow Hair! He forced himself on her. Scratcher took her to Fort and gave her to long knife who brought us cast-off-clothing."

I want to hit Bear Woman.

New Raven opens her mouth and howls more like coyote than singing bird.

"Ayiwakikin!" Horse-dance-maker cries. He looks at horsehair forelock on his nose with crossed eyes.

My mother sags into floorhides, crying, lips flapping. "Kaaaaa! Once. Before. She would be worthy of two horses in trade! She would be carrying first child in belly!"

It is true that New Raven had her first experience too soon, Yellow Hair did it, but she cannot make child until after first time bleeding in isolating tent.

Horse-dance-maker fingers forelock. "Old Women can have feast," he says.

"Naaaaa! Tell your dog-eared husband she wants long

knife, one who is kind and gentle!" Bear Woman elbows into bundles.

I do not know about kind and gentle bluecoat.

"Kisanapewmōstōs!" Bear Woman says. "Not like some in this tent who do not know what it is to be Woman!" She stabs rawhide shirt with sewing needle. "To be old and not cared about!"

Horse-dance-maker's eyebrows shoot up. "What bluecoat?"

"I do not know," I say.

New Raven cries into sleeping-robe.

"She goes to coulee with bluecoat!" my mother yells. "Halfbreed takes women there for trading now."

"I do not believe this about her," I say.

New Raven is gone from camp too often, I know this, but I thought she was gathering wood or picking new berries or going for secret walks with Horse-dance-maker. After what happened in dumping grounds, I cannot believe she goes to long knife for *two bits*.

"She would not have new-young-man!" Bear Woman says.

"So! None of her own are good enough!" I yell, but I will speak to New Raven as eldest sister should.

"So husband was found for her," Horse-dance-maker says. "One with another wife who would be sister and tell her how it is done." He lowers his head, and I think he holds new respect for me. Then he slaps knees, hoots, "Old Man, Shot-in-dark, he should have been the one to do it!" He can laugh at himself when going is hardest for him. "Make feast," he says, "after horsedance."

Bear Woman bunches up ceremonial shirt, tosses it to me. She grabs New Raven's braids and pulls her out of tent. Horse-dance-maker pulls ceremonial shirt over his head and shoulders. I give him tea. I will speak to New Raven, because summer is only just beginning.

Someone scratches at tentflap. I lift it, and Crowman thrusts his shoulders and arms inside, but he is so fat his wide back and buttocks stay outside. He clutches small bundle of tobacco. "I wish to trade," he says.

"Let him in," Horse-dance-maker says.

I pull up tent peg, lift tent skirt. Crow struggles into my lodge on his knees. He is first fat Indian I have ever seen, and I risk punishment from Horse-dance-maker for staring at visitor.

Crow flops onto bulging backside, grabs ankles and pulls feet together so soles of moccasins touch. He cannot sit cross-legged. My jaw drops, mouth gapes, but I do not care. I think of heaping slabs of meat, something-you-eat-with-meat, grease or lard, and pots of greasy broth. Crow People are not much better off than Crees, and I wonder where he finds food.

"I want to trade," Crow says.

"I have nothing," Horse-dance-maker says.

Drum and rattle are all he has left of things belonging to his fathers. Best beadwork he traded for food.

"But now we have horses again," he says, "maybe we can get war bonnets back." He accepts Crow's tobacco. It does not mean he agrees to trade, it means he will talk to Crow.

Horse-dance-maker will trade horses for ceremonial dress because he must appear before women as most dazzling dancer.

"We have power, medicine given us by spirits," he says to Crow. His left eye twitches, jade rings flash on hands. "You know this?"

Crow licks sweat from upper lip. He rocks on haunches, grips knees. "I'll be honest with you," he says. "I have seen power of medicine. Now I see you have drum and rattle."

Crow wears whiteman's coat. It is trimmed with black lamb's fur. Creeping floral design on collar was done by Cree. Deerskin bag hangs from his belt. It is for Strike-a-light steel stamped with Company foxseal.

"Drum is sacred," Horse-dance-maker says. "I need it. Rattle has always been in my family. I cannot trade."

"You need ceremonial dress for horsedance," Crow says. "I work for white-collar in Havre. He collects things and sells them to other whitemen who gather old things and keep them in big showplace. My white-collar will give much for drum and rattle."

If I were new Leader-of-all-ceremonies I would roll

194

Crow out of tent with no more trading ceremony. Crow is something-added-to, hunk of grease, lard gone bad in pail. He adds Cree design to whiteman's coat. He dresses up religion with white-collar-words. He trades things of spirits. He is estranged-one, and he calls himself Crow. Grease melts in boiling water. Crow is bubble swirling in *missionary's* pot.

"I do not need white-collar-money," Horse-dance-maker says. "We cannot trade!"

"Maybe," Crow says. He takes brown interpreter's hat from his head. Under it he wears leather bonnet with raven wings flattened on each side. He wipes sweating face with rag. "Raven-wing-hat is very old," he says. "Cree gave it to my grandfather's grandfather. He wore it on horseraids. Raven protected him, brought him good hunting and many wives. You are Cree. So you know this power."

Crow needs trade so much he will part with ancestral hat, but I do not think it belonged to his grandfathers.

"Kakahkiwatotin!" Crow cries. "I trade it for drum and rattle!" His voice is lumpy. He mixes Cree and Crow words.

Horse-dance-maker turns hat over in hands, strokes raven's wings. Wearing hat, he will make startling sight for women watching horsedance. "No! Drum and rattle are worth more than hat!" he says.

"Hat for drum?"

"Ni-sakitan," Horse-dance-maker says.

Said another way, another time, it means "I love you and want you for myself, so I will not trade you for anything." Horse-dance-maker said it when he gave two horses in trade, for me.

"So give me rattle," Crow says.

"I have medicine bag," Horse-dance-maker says. "It will bring you much from your white-collar!" He fingers long fringes on bag. "Albino calfskin. I am not sure I can part with it."

"Ni-miwayitan," my old father said to Horse-dance-maker, "I am comfortable with my daughter but I do not love her so much I cannot let her go."

"When my grandfather's grandfather saw his woman first time," Crow says, "he was wearing hat, and wings flapped like this!" He sticks thumbs in ears and flaps fat hands, like wings, over his head. "Kaaaaaa! Raven told him to take her!"

Horse-dance-maker balances spirit value of hat against medicine value of bag. But raven's wings will flap and Kaaaa for Horse-dance-maker.

Nicimisayimaw! I think of her as secret love. I want to have secret place with (in) her. Ni-natawayimaw! I want her for myself. Only one. Only her.

"I would like sacred bag," Crow says, "but I will not give hat for it. I'll trade horses instead!"

"There are no more albinos!" Horse-dance-maker hides grinning face behind bag.

In sleeping-robe, he says, "Albino calfskin. Curve of your neck, soft turn of your belly is like that, albino calfskin."

"Two horses?" Crow says.

"I cannot do it."

"Three?"

"There may be medicine in bag."

"Four horses!"

"I wonder if Cree who traded with your grandfather's grandfather got eight horses?"

How could it be so much so? So many horses for one hat. So many horses no man would ever trade for woman.

Ki-kitimakayinitin! I feel humble toward you. Love is not alone. With you, giving and taking will come together. I will unfold lodge cover. It is lined with calfskin. Niwikimakana! My wife is my home.

"Five horses!" Crow cries, "and raven-wing-hat!"

"Bag is yours!" Horse-dance-maker says.

Ni-sawayimaw! I bless you. You make this place blessed. So close, with you, I will open earth, and out of buffalo's last wallow will come Yellow Calf.

"Raven-wing-hat is yours!" Crow rolls out of tent on knees.

"Five horses!" I yell at Horse-dance-maker.

He rebraids forelock for horsedance. "If Crow said he needed bag, I would have given it to him for nothing."

"Horses! I am only woman and not to be asked about it!"

"Tapwe. That is true." He tries on raven-wing-hat. "I will paint my forehead red. Give me paint!"

I throw paint pot at him. "Horses!" I yell. "We have no

food! No new clothes!"

He dips long fingers into paint pot, streaks forehead with red ochre.

"Take hat off. You are getting paint on it."

"There is work to be done for horsedance," he says.

"We wear blankets so full of holes wind blows through. Look at tent! It will not last this summer!"

He looks at himself in trading mirror.

"No hides! No summer linings for rotting tent! Rain will fall on your sleeping face. I hope you get soaked!"

"Ni-miy-askosin.ci? Do I look good?" His forehead is blood red. He turns head this way and that way. "I look good!"

"Horse is most important," I say.

"You pull wagon," he says. "I will load your back and you carry our belongings back to Fort Assinniboine."

"What is worthy? To keep things of fathers or get horses? Sacred bag was dedicated!"

"Make new bag and I will have it dedicated."

"No hide to make bag! No skins for clothing or lodge covers or even rope for your horses!" I am crying, poking fingers through holes in my skirt, pulling at threads.

"I removed medicine from bag," he says.

"Tapwe piko!" I cry.

Horse-dance-maker smoothes hair falling over my face. I strike out at him, wildly, and I knock raven-wing-hat from his head. Fox would kill his woman for this, but Horse-dance-maker picks up hat and strokes wings. He seems to make me disappear. I feel as if I am no longer there for him. Shaking, I leave my lodge. "Look good!" I curse Horse-dance-maker, but he does not call me back.

I go berry picking, try to forget about horses and horsedance time.

I cut through circle of swallow-tailed tents. I run towards horsedance camp. It is horsedance time, and Horse-dance-maker has traded sacred bag for horses. He values Horse above all, and I know he is right to have Dreamspirit. But it is hard not to be loved more than Horse.

In horsedance camp, lodge is up, dedicated cloth flutters, bells sing sacred messages atop centre-pole. This morning, long prayers were chanted by elders, we feasted, and now Horse-dance-maker and his helpers stride around camp. They stop at each tent and call those who wish to dance to bring horses.

Horse-dance-maker learned from his father how to make dance. He wears ceremonial shirt and raven-wing-hat. He leads horse he won in handgame. He dips feathers into paint and ties them to mane and tail. White is color of man's spirit. Yellow for protection. Red for distinction. On horse's forehead, he makes sign of Horse-dance-maker.

Drums call people to dance. I follow women and children to lodge. Outside, new-young-man sits with drummers, small beaver hide drum between his knees. It is Horse-dance-maker's drum. He gave it to new-young-man because he needs it.

Drummers beat out sound of galloping hooves. Song is caught by wind, rises high, circles flight of red-winged blackbirds, mingles with low clouds, falls, then rushes through buffalo grass. Mounted warriors fly around centre-pole. Horses' rumps are painted with symbols of dreamspirits. Hooves cast up clumps of dirt.

"Ayiman! Ayiman!" women cry.

Drumbeats make sound of galloping horses, drop, roll, drop again to sound of buffeting canter. Drummers silence skins. Horsemen jump from horses' backs and dance visions of Miyopayiwin according to directions given them by spirits.

Drummers swing tufted sticks, hit skins, and call horsemen to ride across prairie. Horsemen leap over round swaying rumps. They gallop around streamered centre-pole. Leader snakes away, points of buffalo-horn-hat showing long line of raiders Way across prairie.

"Horse is kind!" Horse-dance-maker cries. He rides alone around centre-pole. Horse is his Friend. Horse is his totem. He honours and glorifies Horse. He rides one with streaming tail feathers and bold brow. He jumps from fringed saddle cloth. He dances beside his Friend.

Horse is dancing. She paws earth, her rump heaving. Mane is fringed shawl around shoulders. She prances. Her neck is damp with sweat. Horse dances. People press forward, sing glorification of Horse.

Someone leans against me, touches my arm, then moves away. It is New Raven. Her hair is parted, her braids tied with new ribbons. She wears new fringed shawl, and I think Horse-dance-maker must have won it for her in handgame. She turns sideways to me, her eyes large and sad.

"Horse-dance-maker," she says.

"Yes, Horse-dance-maker," I say.

We smile at each other and understand things only shared by women.

I lead New Raven away from horsedance.

Summer stretches brown arms around prairie. Bushes are heavy with buck berries, rosehips, and chokecherries. New Raven and I pick berries until sun is too hot on our heads. We find shelter under cottonwood tree. New Raven wraps her long skirt around her knees. She gazes at something only she can see. She has not spoken to me since we left camp. She dragged her toes in dust and looked away from trail as if she were afraid of looking straight ahead.

Hard line to her mouth now, drawn down at corners. Skin of her small round face is tight. Eyes are dark with hating her new place.

"It isn't Horse-dance-maker I'm afraid of," she whispers, turning her head sideways as if someone just struck her. She folds her arms over her knees, hides herself from me. She lies her head on arms. I have never seen New Raven look at anything or anyone straight on. Man-blind-in-one-eye was like that. She is crying, old tears, and I cannot find words to change anything for her. So I say hurting things I do not want to say, "You have to change your ways! You have seen Fox's sister!"

"Horse-dance-maker looks after her!"

"Yes, Horse-dance-maker!" I say.

New Raven is suddenly spilling words, like berries onto blanket for drying in sun, half of them signed, telling me things

I do not want to hear. How Yellow Hair had watched her digging in dump. He sent other girls running back to camp. He chased her around steaming ashes, until, catching hold of her flying hair, he knocked her down. He tore her clothing. He tore her. He made her bleed.

I am glad Fox shot Scratcher, although long knives found a halfbreed to get women for them. I am sorry Fox and I did not take skinning knife to Scratcher's body.

New Raven tells me how, when I took her to isolating tent and tried to keep it secret, new-young-woman who was to be Little Poplar's sixth woman had seen New Raven torn and bleeding. So New Raven was ashamed to be new woman. Even when she had healed between her legs she did not feel put back together, because she was spoiled and unclean, as if she had the sickness, only worse. Her woman's spirit, she says now, is no longer blue. She thinks she can never be a woman to any man.

So it did not matter to her when Scratcher broke into isolating lodge and led her down coulee and sold her. Bluecoat did not touch her, his face all red and his eyes staring, because, she thought, she was so unclean. Later, he asked Halfbreed to bring her to him every day, and still not touching her, he only sat with her under bushes. He told Halfbreed he did not want him to give her to any other bluecoat. Only him.

When new leaves were budding on coulee bushes, New Raven felt it was not right and showed him that he should have her. But he refused, and she thought it was because he was not a man all together. Laughing, he had touched her face, told her things she could not understand because he only knew a few Cree words. So he drew pictures in dust, spoke with hands, not sign language but almost as good. Then she understood that he came from a place where grass was blue. He had a sister who was not much older than New Raven. She lived in a white house that had long rocking benches outside. It swung back and forth at night only. He missed his little sister, and he said if anyone ever bothered New Raven she was to tell him.

Then he was posted at Fort Maginnis. "They get moved around," New Raven says, "and for a long time I thought he would come back." She lifts her head. "He didn't, but it doesn't matter."

"No, it does not," I say.

"He was kind to me."

"Yes."

"I almost forgot Yellow Hair. What he did."

"But not bluecoat who brought us cast-off clothing."

"I don't think about it as much as before."

"But you won't ever forget."

"Not what happened."

"Even so," I say, "it was right that one bluecoat gave you back what another one took away."

New Raven sits up like gopher burrowed out of its hole to smell new spring air.

"You loved him," I say.

She makes cow eyes again.

"Love makes woman's spirit blue," I say.

New Raven says, "I am not unclean now."

"You never were," I say.

"Horse-dance-maker," New Raven says. "He wouldn't have accepted me as second woman if he had known about Yellow Hair."

"I think he would have wanted you," I say. "He does not think poorly of Fox's sister because of what happened to her."

"He understands what is happening to People," New Raven says.

"Ni-wikimankan," I say. "You understand this when he says it?"

"My wife," she says.

"Wiki?" I say.

"Home," New Raven says.

"So he is saying 'My wife she is my home'."

"I didn't know. I didn't understand."

"Now?"

"I go to Horse-dance-maker," she says.

"Yes, My-little-sister, you go to him."

We pick berries again, spread them to dry on blanket for winter eating. Summer is just beginning.

Annika

Because Old Woman and I were snowed in by *misipawin*, Big Blizzard, I didn't make my way to the Livelong Coulee until late in the month of returning hope of spring.

I had always thought that the towns of Livelong and Fairholme and surrounding farmlands were separated by the deep gully, but now, from the vantage point of the hill above the Welshman's house, I saw how the long irregular gouge in the earth joined the hard edges of this land.

The Glaslyn road wound around hills and down into the coulee. It had been cleared by the municipal grader, snow was banked against the cliffs, but the sand trucks had dumped their loads only at the most dangerous curves. Rain-soaked gravel is far more slippery than iced. Once the ruts have dissolved, there is nothing to stop a sliding car or truck from careening over the edge and rolling into the coulee.

I shaded my eyes against the new February sun and tried to see as far as the turn-off from the Battleford highway. I imagined the '46 Fargo bounding like a grasshopper, from side to side, lurching forward, towards me; Uncle pumping the brakes, trying to keep the old truck from rolling into the ditch. I saw myself huddled in the corner between rattling cream cans.

I had slept all the way from North Battleford to the Glaslyn turn-off, my head on a rolled-up blanket. The first distant rumble of thunder wakened me. The truck shook me from side to side, banged my head against the cab wall.

Lightning split the night sky open, and I counted to three before thunder, closer now, applauded the lightning's quick strike. That meant the heart of the storm, its dreadful eye, was only three miles away; and we were headed straight into it.

We drove into a driving slanting rain. Immediately my clothes and hair were soaked. Old Woman and I wrapped ourselves in grey horse blankets and shared a canvas covering our heads. Old Woman began a low chant, a muffled keening: *"Piyeso! Piyeso! Peeeee-yaaaaa-sooooo!"*

I knew it meant Thunderbird. She was trying to keep him away from us. An Indian only calls Thunderbird during the Thirst Dance, never paints the image of Bird on a tent for fear of it being struck by lightning.

I shivered from cold, not fear, because Uncle always said the truck was the safest place to wait out a storm. It had rubber wheels. When electric storms hit at night Uncle herded the family out to the truck. There were lightning rods on the barns to keep them from burning down, but the house, built on the highest rise of land, had none. I had never dared question Uncle, only listened to him reassuring himself and Auntie: "Insulation. Rubber tires keep us from being grounded. Lightning's got to go through into the ground before it can kill you. Even if it hits the truck it can't hurt us because we're sitting on rubber."

Over our heads, thunder sounded like oil drums exploding. I ducked my head out from under the canvas, but counted "One!", and yellow jagged light streaked across the sky in three directions.

"Peee-yaaaa-sooooo!" screamed Old Woman.

Auntie tapped on the back window of the cab. I stood up, gripped the cattle railing, braced my feet. Wind and rain pummeled my face. Auntie waved, her mouth shaping the words, "Sit down!" but it was easier standing up. I bounced on my toes, going with the rumble and shake of the truck.

My grandmother's head was bobbing. She seemed to be rocking forth and back, but she looked back, through the small window of the cab, and I didn't know if she was checking on my safety or wanted her medicine woman.

Outside Battleford, at the meeting place of woodland and prairie, Old Woman had made Johanna face her fear of open space, but the medicine woman was no help now. She crouched in the corner and wailed her fear of thundering Bird.

Again, thunder. Lightning circled the sky. Ahead, the Livelong Coulee.

The old Fargo slid from one side of the road to the other. There was no ditch, only a rock wall on the left and a steep plunge into the coulee on the right. Uncle drove on the wrong side of the road, close to the rock and away from the edge of the gully. The dirt road was so slippery there was no traction at all. Uncle had cataracts, couldn't hit the head of a nail with a hammer. The cab windshield had one wiper.

The grandmothers were singing now: Old Woman chanting to Piyeso and Johanna singing a Swedish hymn.

Uncle pumped the brakes. The truck slid sideways and crunched against the rock wall on the left. Dark moving shapes on the right side.

Indians. Four men on horses, in single file, slowly plodding down into the coulee, close to the outside edge of the road. Their bodies drooped over their horses' necks, soggy blankets clung to their heads and shoulders and backs. Behind them, a team of four pulled a wagon. I looked down, into the wagonbox, and saw many children huddled against three women.

Horses always take the outside of the trail so if they fall it will be towards the inside. Their hooves squished in the mud.

Old Woman stopped chanting and keening. She lifted her head, must have heard the creaking wagon, because she threw off the canvas, scrambled to her feet and climbed out of the wagon-box. She lifted her skirts and ran, head down, to the Indian wagon. Women helped her climb in, and then I could only see dark blanketed heads disappear into the night.

The Fargo took off, like a race horse on its last run, Uncle releasing the brakes; and we coasted down the long slope to the bottom of the coulee, Uncle steering wildly to keep the truck on the road. Across the floor of the valley, gears in bull-low, and the truck groaned and strained, tires spinning; but we made it up the long gravelled incline on the other side to the turn-off near the gravel pits; and northward home.

Outside Battleford, Old Woman had helped Johanna overcome her fear of wide open spaces, of unending land and eternal sky by showing her the unity of all things and the protective circle drawn by the four directions. But Johanna never fully lost her sense of a diminished and unworthy self. She never took communion in the Lutheran church because she believed she wasn't good enough. Johanna faced and came to terms with all anxieties common to immigrants, all but one: her terror of lightning and thunder, perhaps because Old Woman herself was terrified of Thunderbird.

What was stirred in the grandmothers that stormy night was a unifying force that was older than the Livelong Coulee, and it erupted from buried memories older than both women. Only the forms of their expressed fear were different. Who can say that Thunderbird, with spears of light flashing from his eyes, is not a Nordic god in disguise: Thor thundering across the northern sky in his chariot and hurling spears of lightning.

I don't know why, but fear of lightning and thunder is the only fear that wasn't passed on to me by Johanna.

"This fear does not belong to you," Old Woman had said.   I hastened home to tell her what I had remembered and learned.   That night I also learned about how Old Woman was forced to go it alone.

Old Woman

This is how it goes with People. Too many are dying. Too many women are sold to long knives for *two bits*. In Benton and Helena and Havre, trading in women is as bad as it is at Fort Assinniboine. We cannot stop what is happening so we start fighting each other.

This is how it goes with Little Poplar. He cannot accept what is happening to People, cannot accept defeat, and he wants to go back to starting-place and make another uprising. He wants people to demand promises be kept. "It will be more trouble than it was before," Little Poplar says, "because we have guns and horses again." But it is getting of horses that brings trouble to Little Poplar.

He fights Halfbreed Ward over horses. They meet on open plain. Little Poplar has *Colt revolver,* but before he can fire, Ward shoots him three times with *Winchester.*

Now Soldier Leader at Fort Assinniboine wants to get rid of Crees, he says he cannot feed all People living near his Fort, so forty lodges move down to Collin's Ravine in Silver Bow County.

Collins is game warden. When Crees snare rabbits he complains to long knives. He says we go against *game laws,* but Crees do not know what this means. Collins asks Soldier Leader at Poplar Agency to drive Crees out, but Soldier Leader says he has no orders to do that, no food for Crees, and maybe Collins should get us to stop hunting and trapping by giving us frozen cattle downed by blizzards.

So Collins gives us forty head. He has over seven thousand wintering near Milk River, but they belong to Home Land and Cattle Company of St. Louis. *"The cattle are my responsibility,"* he says, *"not thieving Indians!"*

When frozen beef is gone and children are sick again, some men call at Collins' Place. Collins is away, and Crees frighten his woman by carrying away flour and tea and some fresh beef.

Next day, Collins and four cowboys ride into Cree camp. Collins points finger at one man, but he does not look at him. So Collins hits him with club. One of Collins' men says he will shoot warrior. So warrior leaps down embankment, runs creekside, and when his head pops up between bushes cowboy shoots him. Collins and his men leave, but next day they come back and say they have *"planted the carcass." "If you thieving redskins aren't out of the county before sunset,"* Collins yells, *"I'll wipe every mother's son of you off the face of the earth!"*

Crees go away from Silver Bow County. They do not want to camp there again. Crees are scattered all over Montana now.

At Fort Benton, People find white *bootleggers,* Company *rum runners,* Metis *whiskey pedlars* who ran away from Fort Whoop-up after redcoats broke up their trade. There is nothing to do now but wait for ice to break up on Missouri River so they can cut wood for *steamboats.* At night, people fight with knives behind *saloons,* and women wait out front for anyone with money to buy them drink. Halfbreed traders-in-women are busy from dusk to dawn. They do not mind if white man is too drunk to go with woman, but they beat woman who does not take money first.

Soldier Leader at Fort Benton has iron tongue. Crees make trouble for him by drinking, dancing, and chasing women. But sheep stealing, raiding chicken coops and abandoned cabins bothers him most.

Now, *ranchers* and *townspeople,* they say long knives should drive us north over dividing-line. But People do not know about this. They only know about digging in dumping grounds, about eating poisoned coyotes chucked in ravines by *ranchers,* about searching for snowbound cattle, about looking for work in *towns.*

So this is how goes with People for many winters.

This is how it goes at Fort Assinniboine.

It might be ghost camp. No dogsleds race across Assinniboine Trail. No one plays shooting-arrows-game over bushes buried in snow. No outside fires blaze before canvas tents and spectral skin lodges. Thin smoke rises straight up from crooked stovepipes and swallow-tailed cones like Last Breath. Unearthly haze hangs over dumping grounds.

Inside my lodge my family huddle around fire. Bear Woman patches winter-killed antelope skins. She coughs and spits. I serve tea, weak so ration will last longer. I am sorry there is no something-to-eat-with-meat, no grease or lard. Horse-dance-maker sips tea. He breathes in steam, warms his hands on tin cup. He returned from search for small game with empty skin bag.

"I have something to tell you," he says.

Bear Woman grabs tin cup from New Raven. "Gather your things together!" she says.

Horse-dance-maker turns away from her. Everyone fights about things that do not matter so they can turn away from pain and anger of going hungry. "I will miss you," he says. "I will go to Benton. Maybe I can chop wood. There are other things which take me to Crow People."

"Other things!" Bear Woman says, closing one eye like owl. "Like another woman, other things!"

"You think I do not know," I say. I feel like treed lynx spitting at dog. "A woman always knows why her husband goes visiting when there is nothing to hunt."

"It is good that you know," Horse-dance-maker says.

"Dogass!" Bear Woman says. "He abandons you for a woman like that one!" She crushes roots with flat paddle.

Horse-dance-maker cleans gun with rag, a habit because there is nothing to hunt.

"I know that Crow Woman!" my mother yells. "She is worse than Fox's sister! Does flea-bitten, snot-nosed, lice-picking husband of my daughter think he is her first man?" Bear Woman whacks roots. "She has so many blue beads placed between her breasts she cannot walk except hunched over!"

"I wish I had some tobacco," Horse-dance-maker says.

"Looking after family is no longer important!" Bear Woman yells.

New Raven shows Horse-dance-maker snowshoe she is

mending. "Ask grandmother to give you resin," he says. He touches her cheek. "You are too hot!"

"Fox's sister used love potions!" I say. "She crushes loveplant and rubs oil in her hair!" I do not like that woman's medicine. I have never made love potion, love is its own kind of good medicine.

"Ahhhh-ha!" Bear Woman says. She scoops medicine with her paddle, dumps it into copper kettle, stirs with paddle. "And when it wore off your husband found Crow Woman!"

"Is your mother not supposed to do that in spring?" Horse-dance-maker says. "Does she have to do that now?"

"We did not know so many would get so sick," I say.

"Does she have to be so noisy about it?"

"You know he has another!" Bear Woman yells. "You are only one more!"

"But I am first woman," I say, "and that is different."

Bear Woman blows her nose loudly. "It will be easier if you do not fight it. Let him live with *Crows!*" She says "Crows" as if they are not people now but have turned into black scavengers who screech.

"I will be here when he comes back even if he brings six women with him," I say, "because it is my place to be first woman." I do not care about Fox's sister or about this new Crow Woman. I must try to keep family together because that is all that is left of our Way.

"Handgame players have said it," Horse-dance-maker says. "We go to Northern Cheyene Reserve at Rosebud Creek. We go to play handgames with Crow People. Then we go to Benton."

Bear Woman rocks on her flabby haunches. She smacks her gums together. "Forget him!" she says.

New Raven leans against Horse-dance-maker's shoulder. She is in half-sleep. It is the fever. I lean over her, coax her awake, and Horse-dance-maker holds her chin while I spoon medicine tea into her mouth. "My little raven goes with me!" Horse-dance-maker says.

I want to shout, curse him, throw something at him. But I crawl out of lodge. I pull my heavy body up, pull on anchor ropes to lift myself.

Outside, on Assinniboine Trail, two women who once asked help from Horse-dance-maker are digging over-turned wagon out of drifting snow. I wonder if they too have given in to whatever it is that makes Horse-dance-maker so much wanted by women. He never seems to go looking for women, never chases them. They crawl under our tentflap, and he listens to their crying. I have never heard him blame them for what is happening to them. So they come after Horse-dance-maker with wet eyes and bare breasts, maybe because they can talk to him, because he accepts them.

Horse-dance-maker's gentle hand strokes woman's face, his smile says I like you the way you are, all of you, and you are not to blame for any of it. He takes away pain. New Raven said she did not hurt so much after she talked with Horse-dance-maker. I understood because he held me in his sleeping-robe and took away my fear of hungry pup chasing me. His stories make us forget about empty bellies. For me, he drew pictures of Deer's Rump Hill with words until I could see it clearly.

Horse-dance-maker is Leader-of-all ceremonies now. He is Leader-of-handgames. He gives People hope. He settles fights between Crees, yes, between man and woman sometimes too. "No one is so unworthy she deserves abandonment," he says. Even so he leaves his own family, maybe so we can go on living with food and clothing players will win. Or is he just needing new woman as Bear Woman said? Why can he not take me with him too?

Horse-dance-maker goes away from camp. He goes to Fort to trade when there is nothing to trade. He goes hunting when there is nothing to hunt. He goes to see Fox who does not like visiting. Who has a sister.

Fox's sister is not beautiful, not even in ceremonial dress. But she has heavy thighs a man likes, soft skin, softer eyes. She listens and makes him feel like he is Leader, her eyes asking: Are you who we have all been waiting for? So. It was not loveplant. I do not doubt its power because I have seen new-young-man run off into bush when Old Woman rubbed his leggings with crushed seeds. Fox's sister must have something that only he can see. I will try to like her more. But I will never like that cross-eyed Crow.

Dumping ground is almost empty of scavengers. I see a boy, not more than four winters old, he blows on his bare hands. His deerskin bag hangs limp on his bent back. Pickings are poor. He has shredded paper in his moccasins. His feet are bitten by frost, beyond healing, but he never cries because there is no feeling in his feet now. I will rub bear grease on his feet and wrap them in rags.

I will stay. He needs my medicine. Children with coughing sickness need my rosehip and pine needle teas. I will stay for them. I duck back into my lodge. I take my place before fire. I clasp my hands and fold them between my knees, not looking at Horse-dance-maker or Bear Woman or New Raven.

"I go," Horse-dance-maker says, "but only until trees are budding. You must stay for birthing, your mother with you."

I want to say that children are always born when People are moving from this place to that place. I want to say that Yellow Calf was born on night of our leaving place of belonging. But I drop my head.

Spirit of Witago, Greedyman, is near me. But I am not stumble-legged-doe he can eat, not moose he can get inside. Witago eats sick people from inside. The only way to get rid of him is by burning night fires or sliding person he holds under river ice. But I have him in my power. I send him spiraling up smokeflap.

"You use your status to take women," I say.

"He will not come back!" Bear Woman says.

"Who can refuse honour of being chosen by Leader?" I say.

Bear Woman wrings rags in ice water and places them on New Raven's hot face. "Did Poundmaker do such things?" she says. "Maybe, sometimes, but not my brave sons!"

Bear Woman has gone too far with her big words. I have listened too much to her. "No," I say. "Horse-dance-maker is Leader now."

Bear Woman's mouth falls open. She wipes it on blanket. She gums her surprise and her anger the way she softens rawhide.

"He has kept us together," I say. "He showed us how to go on living through handgames. So he goes to Crow People? He will come back and when he does we will be better off than we are now. So we must hold camp together, hold People together until he does come back."

My mother dips her owlhead. She does not look so much like Bear Woman now. "Accept what happens," she say, "that is the only way to do it."

I am thinking more about Horse-dance-maker and women. He has them all. Tall hard ones who kick heads of drunk long knives. Soft fat ones who complain of empty bellies when there is game. Thin childless ones who have the sickness or are so bitter a man can carry wood for them all summer only to find even wood is wormy. Now Horse-dance-maker will have cross-eyed Crow Woman. Strange how he finds something worthy in every one, how he treats them all the same.

I tuck blanket around sleeping Raven. Women need my Horse-dance-maker to go on living. I look at him and old warmth passes between us, so good we warm our hands on it.

"You are first woman," Horse-dance-maker says. "There is only one of you." He holds out his arms to me.

I am crying, my face pressed into his shoulder. I am crying because he is going away. But I am crying because he is Horse-dance-maker and I am his first woman.

This is the way of it, with women.

This is the way of it, with Crees. They are Exact People. They are skilled in everything they do, in preparing pipedance, beading ceremonial dress, in four-days-dancing at Thirst Dance, at shooting arrows, in playing handgames. Once they were Cut-throat-people who carefully slit Blackfoot throats and stole horses.

They always say what they mean and mean what they say. They are Exact-speaking-people.

They are providers, warriors, men concerned with spirits, and they are waiting outside back doors in Benton until they are seen by whitemen. They are chopping wood, hauling water barrels, emptying *outhouses*. They offer women as *kitchen help* and *laundry aides*. I do not want to think about what they do when women are turned away from this work. They are scavengers. They eat poisoned coyotes dumped by *rancher* in ravines. They eat snowbound cattle.

This is the way of it, with People.

This is the way of it, with me. All winter I go alone. I

search sky for magpies circling rancher's snowbound calf. I struggle through drifts, hold my direction by following moss growing on north side of birch. I find coyote, tail tucked down and back hunched. He noses bait, belly of sheep in woolgrower's trap. Jaws are offset so unwanted animals may be freed. Poison is slow. Coyote's back stiffens. He cannot swallow.

All winter I dig in dumping ground. I lift my head often, listen for wagon's creaking wheels, horses' steady hooves. I listen across distance of moons and hear my own voice returning.

All night I hunker down, keep fire going. All night I cry my longing. Coyote's howl carries through winter, it carries through night. It breaks silence of days and brings out great moon of returning hope of spring. Earth heaves and spits female from her den. Coyote cannot hear his echo, her soft-pawed approach. She holds moon.

All night Bear Woman coughs and spits into fire. She says she has seen too many winters.

Moons change. Winds change. I pull on ropes anchoring my lodge. I close smokeflaps. Without ropes lodge will sway before wind and crumble. Horse-dance-maker was anchor-rope for my lodge. Without him holding me, for as long as four winds blow against stretched winter skins, I am coyote howling all night.

I am first woman, needing him, and only he can take away my crying. Even without him I am bound to him tighter than wet rawhide shrinking in sun. It pulls tighter when he is away.

I am too thin to be beautiful now, and I am afraid when Horse-dance-maker returns he will not want me. Even my belly is too flat now I have lost my second child.

The birthing was long and slow. It came too late. Rope was twisted around child's neck. My second child never took first breath. When frost explodes on trees I made feast-for-dead. My mother and I danced, only two of us, all spaces in circle were for Departed-ones.

All winter I am dying inside. I have lost hope of spring returning.

This is how it goes with me for four winters. When Horse-dance-maker comes back it will be spring again.

On this blue morning coulee is touched by whispering shadows. Unravelling clouds are torn on jagged crest like raggy cobwebs. I have never seen clouds so low before. I have my digging stick, and I look for medicine roots. My bare legs brush bottom willow branches that hang untidily like wisps of old woman's hair.

I am thinking about Horse-dance-maker. When he returns I will make new lodge where flatland rushes to coulee's lip. I will lash lodgepole pine and swallow-tailed cone with rawhide. I will open smokeflaps to night sky. On lodge skin I will paint four colours, four levels of sky, four winds, four homes of sun.

I climb, my toes curl into earth, my knees bend into hillside. I follow early morning light that folds palely around my dream of Man-of-all-songs. He says Horse-dance-maker will return and take me back to place of belonging. They are both dreamvisions now, Man-of-all-songs who comes to me at night and Horse-dance-maker who comes to me in dreams of new day. But they fade with light falling over summerless edge of coulee.

I squat on large flat rock. I brush dirt from my feet, wishing I could wash them in creek. I fold my skirt in creases behind my knees. I pick burrs and prickly brown cactus pins from my feet. I rest my elbows on my knees, lift my head, and see horseman.

He wears blanket-coat. On his head raven-wing-hat. He slides from horse and leaps down long slope, takes it sideways. Wind lifts raven's wings. Horse-dance-maker's face is sunny.

I press my palms together, tilt forward, feel myself pulled to him. But I do not rise and run to him. I am afraid trickster has sent him to me. He might disappear.

He is here before me, arms dangling at his sides. He pulls me to him, I fight it, but wanting him is so strong in my head and heart I am outside of myself and springing to him like stretched bow string; then snapping back so what I am feeling stings me quick in my face. I am trembling. He points to nesting place under willows. He signs: I could lie beside you all night but I won't touch you. I drop my head, my lips press together and tie up my answer. If I speak I will cry out. I dig

214

my toes in soft earth, push myself up, balance with fluttering arms, but my knees buckle. He catches my hand, pulls me to him, and my arms are around his neck, he holds me fiercely to him, so I cannot breathe.

He holds me. For long time he holds me.

Dark wings of night close around coulee. Coyotes on opposite sides of coulee howl pain of separation to each other. One carries her pup, curving body dropping from her mouth.

Horse-dance-maker's arms fall to his sides. He turns down, leads me deeper into coulee. I trip on unearthed root, and he waits for me, offers his right hand. I take it with my left, push his shoulder with my right, telling him to go on. He finds shelter for us among rocks clustered around willows and scattered poplar. "I build fire," he says.

"It is not cold," I say. I do not want to let go of his hand. I smooth it between mine. "Tapwe ki-tatamihen," I say, and it does not mean "Thank you" the way I say it. It means "Truly you please me."

He pulls his hand away. "There are no spruce boughs," he says, "or pine needles."

"Are you building fire or making sleeping place?" I say. I break willow twigs against my knee, toss them at his feet.

Together we lay fire, hands touching across it.

I am singing inside. Matwehikew. He makes thumping sound, dancing with feathers and bells. Elk hooves bound with rawhide to long pole rattle-call. Partridge, ruffle-tailed, spreads wings, drumming now inside me, four-times-four loveways. It is song of prairie chicken.

Horse-dance-maker spreads blanket-coat over earth. He lies down, tucks hands behind his head, watches me. He knows he will have me because he wants me, because I am first woman. I followed him here, can still leave, but if I stay it is because I belong with him. He waits for me to come to him, knows I will, because I have always followed him from place to place.

I lie beside him. My breasts part against his back. I press against his buttocks, gently butting, and my long legs shape around him. I rub my nose where his braids part. My lips taste sweat. I straddle him. His hands slide along my legs. I am singing inside: my lodge cover is summer-lined with albino calfskin. It unfolds for him. I untie breech clout. His need springs up, cloth falls sideways. I slide forward, and he pulls me down to him.

His first thrust: in me it is like underside of mushroom separating, soft folds closing around him. My hair falls down my back. Skirt rises over my legs. He is pulled into me, he clasps my shoulders, sinks deeper. My shawl falls from my shoulders. My back arches. He rolls me roughly onto my back.

"So now! Ho! My First Woman!"

Later, we are lying under night sky beside fire. I nestle my head on Horse-dance-maker's shoulder. I rub my nose under his chin. Horse-dance-maker tells me about where he has been and what he has seen. It is all so strange but he makes me laugh.

Of all strange things he saw, dress of white people confused him most. Among People, it is men, not women who show ceremonial dress at gatherings. Man dresses according to directions of dreamspirit, according to society he belongs to. But among white men all drab flanneled men look the same.

Horse-dance-maker saw women with sad faces and flat chests who belonged to white-collars. They wore high-necked brown dresses with white lace or black dresses with white lace. He saw foodgivers' women who worshipped work. They picked stones and weeds, hauled water in buckets. They lifted grey skirts between thick legs and climbed on horse or waded across creek with howling babies on wide hips. Town women stepped aside when wagon hit mud hole, folded brims of wide hats around their faces when Cree or Black walked by them. Other women painted faces and wore bangles. They were upstairs women in place called *saloon*. They piled hair on top of heads. Downstairs women sat on men's knees and slapped their backs. They held their *liquor* better than men.

Horse-dance-maker saw strange dancers. Their legs were covered with what he thought was paint drawn in crossing lines. Ruffled skirts and lace underthings swirled around kicking legs. Dancers had arms around each other like our women in move-along-dance and they hopped on one foot but they did not dance in circle. They held tail feathers belonging to faraway bird never seen on prairie. So it was not religious ceremony. But why dance and sing if they were not

216

glorifying anything or enjoying it? Townsmen, ranchers, miners made bird calls and snorted. They thumped tables.

Outside, our women hid in shadows. New-young-men fought with knives.

"People are drinking so they will forget winter's bony scepter and summer's hungry pup," Horse-dance-maker says now. "If we do not stop killing each other off we will die out like buffalo. New-young-men do not care about anything but grabbing hold of new-young-women and getting so drunk nothing matters anymore."

So Horse-dance-maker told them they cannot live like brown-skinned whitemen, cannot fade brown skin like rawhide stretched under sun. They are Real People and they must join together and dance.

He is Leader-of-all-ceremonies now. He bears Pipestem in right hand and holds left under blanket-coat, but drum does not speak for him. "I am not dancing well," he says. Days have passed when man suffered skewers tearing his flesh in fulfillment of vow to dance if son's life were spared, when woman danced because her provider returned safely from hunt or horseraid. Once, People danced four days and four nights until spirits of earth and sky were joined in them. Now People are not dancing well. Horse-dance-maker is not dancing well.

We make words together, with hands, and I learn more of how it goes with him. He says his dreamspirit told him to people earth with those who know the Way, know how to live for He-who-is-above. He will not give up and return to place of eternal dancing until he has many children living all across prairie.

So I do not mind that Horse-dance-maker has brought with him New Raven, Fox's sister, Crow Woman, and new Halfbreed Woman. I will be eldest sister because I am First Woman.

I do not know about trouble other wives will make for me.

Naaaaa! It is not enough that I must teach New Raven how to be woman. I must stop Fox's sister from going to long knives for *two bits*. I must show Horse-dance-maker that cross-eyed Crow Woman is doing her share of work and no more. Naaaaa! That is not enough bother. Now I am having too much trouble with Halfbreed Woman, one he brought back with him from Judith Basin.

I send her to gather wood but she does not come back when there is fish ready for roasting on sticks. This is happening too many times, so I go looking for Halfbreed Woman.

I find her sprawled on long grasses beside river. She lies with her head on one arm. She stares at willows bunched beside river. She plays with grey goose feather. I squat down beside her. She shudders but does not speak. She looks at me out of unhappy eyes that are greyer than dusklight.

I pull my scarf over my eyes. I sign: now you cannot see me spying on you. She sits up, folds her skirt around her knees, and tucks her hair inside her silk shawl. Her nose is strong. Pouting mouth gives words to a too-silent-woman.

"You Flathead?" I say, cutting swift chopping motion to top of my own head. I fix my scarf.

She does not answer, stares strangely, light in her eyes deepening. I am afraid for her.

"I am Cree," I say, slitting my throat with pointing-finger.

She does not understand sign language. She has seen seventeen winters in Judith Basin. She walks with toes turned inward, but wears nothing on her feet. Even so, her toes do not spread like those of one who goes barefoot. Her small feet are shaped like canoes, big toe pointed and longer than smaller toes.

I squat on flat rock, my own rawhide toes balanced on imprints of leaves pressed into rock by many seasons. I rest elbows on my knees. I wait for her to speak.

Below us, canvas tent is pitched among pine trees. Smoke spirals out of new stovepipe. I hear Horse-dance-maker's crackling laughter. He pokes fun at Crow Woman's swelling belly.

"We have fish," I say. "Do you want cross-eyed Crow to make Horse-dance-maker think she did all work of women?"

Halfbreed Woman always avoids women's side of tent. She places herself in Horse-dance-maker's shadow. She does not squat, cross her legs, or kneel. She is young antelope lying down, leans her body against Horse-dance-maker, one knee lightly touching his. This does not please his other women.

"I have combed his hair," she says, "for the last time."

Every night, before he goes visiting, she combs his hair. She parts it on left side, careful not to touch his braided forelock. She presses her nose in his scented hair. "Smells good!" she says. She tosses his hair, fluffs it, flings it over his head so it falls in his eyes. She bites his neck. He grabs her and tickles her.

Other wives are angry so I have to yell at Halfbreed Woman, "Astimite! This Side!"

She never braids her own hair. She lets it fall straight to her waist. I think she does not know how to wear her hair. This makes Horse-dance-maker angry. He wants her to part her hair in middle because that is how Cree woman must wear her hair. I tell her this but it does no good. She has been with us four summers now, but it does no good. She is too much white and not enough Indian. She cannot do beadwork. She forgets and passes between Horse-dance-maker and fire.

Now she slides her middle finger down spine of grey goose feather and separates soft folds. "I didn't know, the first time he asked me to comb his hair," she says, "I didn't know it is forbidden to touch man's totem, medicine bag, or forelock."

She had reached out to unknot horsehair forelock. He pushed her away, jumped to his feet, and I thought he would hit her. Afraid, she had curled on floorhide. He smashed willow back-rest with fists. I saw that Horse-dance-maker did not know who she was, something blinded him; he could not see Sarah because of his dream to people earth with Cree children.

"I'm Sarah," she says. "I try to tell him, but he says 'No! You are my Flathead Woman!' "

He is trying to make her something she is not.

"He expects too much!" she cries. "He demands too much! I am not his dream!"

She has given up trying to be Indian for him. She folds herself into sleeping-robe and will not keep fire going all night.

"Try!" I say. "I will stack your arms with wood and take you back to camp."

She yells at me, "I try and try and try!" She is crying now. "You can't make an Indian out of me!"

"Tell me all of it," I say.

He is too-much-man, she says, even in sleeping-robe. He is always above her, burrows into her, swells, and pushes out herself. So after, she is emptied, lost woman who is afraid of disappearing in him. She says she is only gold dust in tin plate that miners give black-robe so he will forgive them for taking Flathead women. Her dust blows away when Horse-dance-maker calls her his woman.

"Maybe," I say, "you should be Sarah. Be Sarah for him?"

"No!" she yells. 'I can't be Sarah for him! I have to be Sarah for me!"

"I think he wants you enough to learn how to let you be Sarah and not Flathead Woman," I say.

"When he tells me story of boy called Woman Dress who lived with bear one mountain winter in Blackfoot country," she says, "then I don't hear meaning of words, not because my Cree is clumsy, but because he shapes words into something I can feel, into sacred cloth touching me and turning threads on blanket into bright shapes."

I understand this because of how it goes with me. It is good lying alone with Horse-dance-maker under sky, his body my only covering. After, I lie with him on mossbed and listen to stories of long-ago. He sees long distances, sees through mountains, over rivers, across prairie; his vision is undivided by time or place or happenings. All yesterdays are now, he says, but he can no longer put them together with all tomorrows. Even so, his voice holds me, his stories hold me, until I feel joining of all things under night sky. Horse-dance-maker is sound of someone sneaking around lodges and crawling under tentflap.

I am thinking about Horse-dance-maker and forgetting to listen to Sarah.

She says she feels good only when we all come together in singing. She sways between Fox and Horse-dance-maker, their arms tight and strong around her, Horse-dance-maker's hand pressed against her hip; all of us together like that, and she watches drummer's hands, knowing such hands would quicken a woman like no other's, but she wants Horse-dance-maker's hands. Only his.

That first night with us, four summers ago, she lay awake and listened to Horse-dance-maker's breathing. She could not move closer to him because she was afraid he would take her, and she did not want that, with so many people sleeping—or not sleeping— she could not tell in darkness. Heads were buried in sleeping-robes and uneven rise and fall of mounds played soft rhythm against half light of dying embers. She was cold when Horse-dance-maker rolled towards her, his hands kneading blanket and tucking ends around her. Sarah felt safe then. She pressed her face against his broad back.

Light of her first day with us was tunneling into smoke-hole when, in half sleep, Horse-dance-maker rolled again onto his back, flung his left arm hard against her belly, his hand gripped her thigh. She reached for him, felt his drumming under her own arm. Her fingers curled. She only wanted to touch his face. They lay together like that, her face under his shoulder, but not smothered she felt warmed and protected from dark night.

Now I see myself lying under him, my hands gripping his braids, and ache between my breasts and legs is the same. My mind and heart and body come together so strongly and unendingly in him.

All nights are like that now. All of us rolled into blankets, all arranged around fire like lodgepoles laid on earth for lifting. Horse-dance-maker sleeps in centre place, Sarah next to him because she is last in circle and must keep fire going all night. I sleep on other side of him, buried in robe that smells of too many camps. I roll my blankets around and under so turning either way I am always warm against mound of buffalo man. Solid and heavy and unmoving. Buffalo man.

But Sarah does not like sleeping together like that. It is hard for her to sleep next to him, wanting to put her arms around him, but knowing I am on other side of him, our legs curled together under robe. When Horse-dance-maker rolls her into sleeping-robe she lies unmoving because she cannot accept such a private thing as humping under robes with others sleeping near. They cannot see, but too often she hears Crow Woman giggling.

Crow Woman always finds something funny in things not meant for laughter except between lovers. She never forgets Sarah's first try to say "his wife". Ki-wikimakan. Wiki means where he lives, but Sarah said, "He lives in her." Sarah is hurt when Crow Woman imitates her and makes others laugh.

So Sarah cannot sleep too many nights now. She is glad when Horse-dance-maker pushes her out of his robe to her own place. He wants Sarah to be his Real Woman. She says no. It is trading she cannot accept.

"I'm not horse for pulling wagon, not runner for trading, not racer to be broken in and ridden hard and handled, not breeding mare, not Indian pony that leaps from under him." She ties knots in shawl fringes. "Indians see women as horses!" she yells. "They are cared for like buffalo runners, tied to tentpegs so Blackfoot raiders cannot steal them."

"I want you and need you for myself," Horse-dance-maker always says to me, "and I will not trade you for anything."

"You!" Sara yells at me. "You are too quiet, too patient, too willing to help me change. You accept his chasing after women!"

"He crawls under many tentflaps," I say, "but he always comes back to me."

"I hate you!" Sarah yells. "I cannot be like you! Horse-dance-maker loves only you! You treat me like a sister but I hate you!"

Sarah is yellow Bitteroot, uprooted but reaching for sun. She is not Indian. She is not White. She does not fit in with us.

In hollowed side of mossbank, water snatches cat-tails from loosened soil. Cottonwood branches grow upwards to scrawl of treetops that waver against low turn of sky. In nesting branches four blackbirds quarrel over chosen territory. They wait for partition of promised leaves. "And can you see," I say to Sarah, "as far as place where forks of river flow together?"

"No," Sarah says. She snaps feather between thumb and third finger. "I am going back to Judith Basin!"

"Think of being without Horse-dance-maker," I say.

Without him all days would be summer spreading brown over bottom land, sun sucking moisture from earth and leaving it cracked and dried so only cactus can sprout in clumps. When he goes away he takes something of me with him. I disappear like floating square of cloth weaving in and out of itself, threads unravelling palely from Centre-pole of last summer's sundance lodge.

Sarah is vanishing into her own lodge where nothing can touch her, nothing hurt her again. "Why is it only one man with you?" she says. "Why only one?"

"Why does river flow in one direction?" I say. I try to show Sarah how river carves narrow and winding and deep way through long grasses, its long sweep swift and silent until, beyond arch of wooden bridge, it turns to final joining at forks: a sudden rush over blue stones at crossing.

Sarah is crying. She turns a bundle in her small hands. Unbeaded moccasins are for Horse-dance-maker, and I am to give them to him.

Moccasins are new. They were made by Sarah, and they are unbeaded. Many nights she sat with her mother by coal oil lamp. Will Horse-dance-maker understand when he finds Sarah gone and undecorated moccasins waiting in his place before the fire? Will he be able to see her separating beads, bright blues and greens from yellows and reds, counting them because it was more important to know how many there were than be able to sew them together in shape of Bitteroot.

"There are four colors," I say to Sarah.

"Everything he does," Sarah says, "he explains by four!"

"The Only Number," I say.

"If he goes hunting he says he was away four days," Sarah says, "even when he comes back on fifth or sixth day. If he comes back with six prairie chickens he always says there are four. If he met a man with horses to trade there was always four, never two or seven or ten!"

"But you do know four summers have passed since he found you?"

"Years! Years! Years!" she yells at me. She tears grass with small hands. "For four *years* I have tried to be Indian!"

"But it is no good trying now," I say. "You go to Judith Basin."

"I can never do beadwork," she says. She gives me moccasins. "Ekosan!" she says in Cree, then says, "*That's all!*" The words do not mean the same thing.

I am Eldest Sister to all wives now, but Halfbreed Woman can never be Cree. She can only be Sarah.

Halfbreed Woman goes to Judith Basin. I go to Ghost Dance. There is plenty more trouble for me there.

Annika

By thawing weather I had lost all sense of calendar days and months. Old Woman and I had reversed day and night. I was living too much in her past, thinking in Cree and going with the night story to Montana, then dreaming about Johanna all day. I was still crying in my sleep.

It must have been some time towards the end of Goose Moon that I woke up crying and didn't stop.

The dream drove me out of sleep, out of the homestead; and I was running down the lane, patches of overnight ice cold under my bare feet; I was running southward, down the washboard road towards the Livelong Flats, new mud slipping in the ruts under my feet. Chest heaving, arms pumping, tears and sweat streaming down my cheeks; and I was running over the railway tracks, down the long slope onto the flats; passed Swain's Place, around the curve, and I was at the bridge where the beaver build their dam.

I tried to lose myself in river bush. I wandered through spruce and poplar and willow, followed the curve of Turtle River, stumbled in weeds and cat-tails, but I couldn't find and reach its source. I went forth until I came back, in a circle, until I was at the place where the beaver dam spills whitely under the wooden bridge built by Bjorn and Arvid. There, I collapsed. I curled in long wet grasses, in a nest of last summer's old brown grass and new shoots of green beside Turtle River.

The wooden bridge arched over smooth muddy water. It joined the sons of the sons and their lands. Hooves clattering on wooden planks. Lightning-foot and Thor, pulling an oxcart. It creaked and swayed, its wooden wheels rumbling. And Johanna driving the team, her long red hair streaming behind her. She pulled the reins, stopped the cart, and leaped over its wooden sides. She skipped down the riverbank. She wore a long blue-fringed shawl and a yellow headscarf.

She was bending over me, and her face was neither old nor young. Only her eyes were the same, but they had a transparency, as if a silk cobweb had been drawn over them. They held neither pain nor joy. She didn't speak to me, but she seemed to be trying to reach me without touching me. She was bent on some purpose, trying to tell me something.

"*Mor-mor!*" I cried.

My mother's mother disappeared.

I stretched my legs until my toes dipped in icy water. I spread my arms against the bank. Above me, light of new day rising over brown hills. She was there for me, Johanna of Hannas. Her spirit was blue, was part of earth and hills; and light grew upward from grey until it turned yellow, then burnished orange, so the brown earth and blue sky were coming together under day's new sun.

What Old Woman said was true: Johanna was part of me, and now apart. Also. I then felt the calm that only comes with the feeling of knowing all things are joined inside and outside, of finding a reflection of my inner world in the outside world: *miyopayiwin*, the unity of all things under sky.

I had come home. I wouldn't have to tell Old Woman; she would know.

I lifted myself out of the grasses, crawled up the bank, trotted across the bridge, then strolled past Swain's and emerged onto the flats. On my right, the Turtle River curved away through willow just beginning to bud and rushed across stones under the railway trestle; on my left, Swain's barbed wire fence separated the swamp from the bush; the flats themselves were arranged in a circle by natural boundaries of river and bush. The land was too marshy, not much good for growing anything more than hay, and it had been left the way the settlers found it: a grazing ground of long yellow grass.

The Livelong Flats was the place where Thunderchild's Crees held their sundance every spring, and the skeleton lodgepoles were never taken down. I walked into the flatland, towards the sundance camp, and a memory erupted, not of Johanna, but of Old Woman; I reconstructed it with new eyes.

It was suddenly twenty years ago, the month when trees

are budding leaves, and I had run away from the parked truck, from Auntie, Uncle, my cousins; run through the rows of canvas tents, the smell of rawhide and smoked meat raw in my nose. Flies settled on my scabby knees and mosquito-bitten arms, and I swatted at them. Naked children chased long-eared Indian dogs between the tents. Old men and women squatted outside the tents smoking pipes. The chokecherry and willow bushes were draped with bright cotton and silk cloth. I didn't know then that the cloth was sacred and had been dedicated to spirits. When the dance was over white farm women would steal the cloth and make house dresses and school frocks for their daughters. Now, boys from town were beginning to sniff around Indian girls. I recognized Roy the Rat Rittenberg who boasted in Patchgrove schoolyard that he got at least six squaws last June. "At certain times of the year all animals like to get fucked," he instructed the younger children, "and Indian girls like it best after the sundance." I stayed away from Rat, cut through the inner circle of tents towards the sundance lodge.

It wasn't made of skins or canvas. A great wall of poles had been built in a circle, and the branches were in full leaf. Another layer of brush covered the top so it looked like an over-grown tree. Outside, old men squatted before two fires. I didn't know they were important men, the keepers of fires and pipes.

I ducked inside. Singers sat around a kettle drum covered with stretched hide, and they pounded it with tufted sticks. Drums beat steadily, and chanting filled the lodge.

Indian people dressed in beaded rawhide had rabbit fur and bells tied around their ankles. Some of the men had prairie chicken tails fanned out and tied to their backsides. They all danced, feet skittering, around the centre-pole. I didn't know it belonged to Thunderbird, but I did know the Crees were praying for rain. Uncle had said that he hoped they succeeded, spring planting done and all, we needed rain too.

Then I saw the old woman, the one who traded moosehide mittens for chickens, who helped with cooking at threshing time, who went berry picking with grandmother. Her face was painted white, and I thought it was powder or flour. Sweat ran down her face. She was too old to be dancing, too old to be dancing so fast. I couldn't know she had been fasting for three nights and four days, that she would dance until she dropped, that she had danced every June in fulfillment of a vow she had made in 1885, that she would dance every year in thanksgiving that life had been spared. I only stared, wanting to run to her and stop her, but afraid, she looked so different all painted that way, her eyes rolling up in her head; and then she stiffened, threw up her arms, gave a great cry, a Cree sound I didn't understand, and then she pitched forward on her face, lay still.

None of the singers or dancers moved to help Old Woman. I ran from the lodge—crying "Auntie! Auntie!"—and I found her at the truck. She had an armload of ginghams and cottons and flour sacking dyed many colors. She shoved me towards the truck, yelling at me to climb in, we were going home, and I tried to make her listen, "Old Woman fell down! We must help!" But Auntie shooed me away, and Uncle was revving the old motor, my cousins pushing and shoving and horsing around in the back; no one would listen to me.

We rumbled away from the sundance camp in the '46 Fargo and I clung to the railings at the back, watching the sun spread setting rays over the flats, listening to the diminishing sounds of drum and Indian chanting. We climbed the hill, and below, the sundance lodge grew smaller and smaller until it disappeared into night.

The memory gone, I walked home slowly, feeling strangely not tired but refreshed. I breathed new spring air deeply. I trudged along the ditch instead of the road, looking for and finding new tiger lily shoots, crocus, pine cones, and finally, along my own shelter-belt, buds on the caragana hedge.

Smoke, spiralling out of the chimney was wafted by the spring breeze until it dispersed. Old Woman was up starting the fire herself this morning. She had lived to see another spring, although it was only March, I was no longer afraid for her. I saw her small head at the window and I waved, but she ducked down, not wanting me to know that she was worried about me.

Old Woman was back in her cot by the time I burst through the door. She was munching bannock.

I sank into the rocking chair, not speaking, waiting for her to look up. She did look up finally, coaxed by my silence, and she looked at me eye-to-eye. My upper body lifted, I spread my arms out wide, and I just smiled and smiled.

"It is good," Old Woman said. She lowered her head with respect for me, for the first time. Then she dug through her bundle, took out woman's pipe and tobacco, packed the bowl, lit it, and passed it to me. "You smoke now," she said.

I took the pipe, and the first puff choked me. Old Woman shrieked with laughter, and then I was coughing and laughing at the same time; and we were hugging each other, it ran so well now.

The smoke made me dizzy, but I told Old Woman how I had remembered her at that long-ago sundance.

She nodded, then said, "So now I tell you about Ghost Dance. It is not always so good for us then. On both sides of dividing-line, white people are afraid of Indians gathering in such large numbers. More so after Big Bear's Thirst Dance and Outbreak of fighting. White-collars try to make People *Christians,* they call us *heathens*, and do not understand we pray to Only-one, the same God, but we worship in a different way. They think our sundance is torture, and do not understand how a man must suffer bone skewers tearing at his flesh in fulfilment of vow. So. On both sides of dividing-line, the Dance is outlawed.

"It is 1892, and People everywhere are dying because they cannot fulfil promise to dance. So Crees on That Side of dividing-line join in spiritual revival. It is led by that one, a Paiute named Wovoka. He believes in brotherhood, and he promises a new *Messiah,* return of buffalo, and destruction by natural forces of whitemen. He makes Ghost Dance, and Indian People from every nation pray to Creator for return of buffalo."

Listening to Old Woman, I drifted away, once again, to an older time, aware now that I had made a beginning and an ending this day, and that June of 1892 saw an ending and beginning for Old Woman too.

On both sides of dividing-line, in time past and time present, it was spring, the time of budding leaves.

Old Woman

On this side of dividing-line Ghost Dance is happening. We want to celebrate spring's return with many-berries-feast and sweat baths, but we are joining Different People in Ghost Dance.

Wovoka, he is Paiute, and he believes in love between all men. But Sioux give new dance and song different meaning. Long knives are plenty scared about this, about all People across prairie coming together. Whites who have taken land away from us are afraid we want to give it back to Rightful Owner.

So we are at Sioux Ghost Dance Camp now. Pine Ridge was once good place to hide after raid on Blackfoot. But Crees are afraid of this high place, not like Deer-robes-people who crossed Great Divide to steal Blackfoot ponies. Here, Sioux lodges are too many to count. Ghost Dance Lodge is pitched in middle of camp. Inside, people are dancing. But it is not feast-for-dead. It is not sundance or horsedance or scalpdance. People are not dancing to make ancestors happy.

Wicikokansimowin. It is not cermony as old as northern lights. Sapocikan! Little clown who wears mask is not here to touch people and coax them to join in dance. There are no followers shooting bannock hanging in lodges and putting dried meat in skin bags for feasting. No wrestling and carrying away of those who pretend they do not want to dance. Cikistamowin! No joy in songs. No joy in dance.

Sioux are mourning for dead ancestors. Ghost dancers shuffle around circle. They stare at sacred cloth and Centre-pole. They sing new song. Words are Pwahta, and I do not understand all of it. Singers chant to beat of water drum made of smoked deerskin stretched over iron kettle and anchored with seven stones. Water in bottom of kettle keeps skin damp. In centre place, a beautiful Sioux woman in beaded buckskin dress. Sioux Leader calls her *princess*. Dancers pile gifts at her feet.

A Paiute wears a ghost shirt of smoked deerskin. He has painted on it his vision of new world: whitemen dead under rolling earth. Now I understand this new dance. Sioux pray for great avalanche to bury whitemen and punish them for killing buffalo.

"*Messiah is coming,*" Paiute says to me. "So you should make yourself ready." He points to Sioux squatting in front of wall-of-poles. "Get ghost shirt from them. It will give you protection. Get clay for painting face. Tops of cactus will give you colour, feeling of being one with Manitou." He shoves me towards Different People who are selling white mud wrapped in rags.

"It is sacred! Paint face! Dance!"

Old people crowd, hands clawing for mud. Horses, tobacco, money, things of ancestors are traded for white mud.

"*Stop dancing!*" Bluecoats raise tentflaps of Ghost Dance Lodge. "*This ghost dance must cease!*" They carry guns.

No one obeys them.

"*Burn the relics!*"

"*Destroy these heathen objects!*"

Bluecoats come from four directions. They move in and around and over People; and all around tent they tear sacred cloth from poles. They carry out bundles and totems. Outside, bluecoats push tobacco makers and keepers of bundles away from fires. Then bluecoats burn things of the spirits. In darkening sky, lodges of departed-ones and lights of their fires. On earth, tents of ghost dancers and long knives' fires.

People fall to ground. Women wail. Elders claw at burning bundles, poke in fires for things of their ancestors. They are plenty angry. They curse and threaten long knives. They are thrown to ground by iron arms and rifle butts.

I cannot move my legs. My face is closing. Smell of burning skins smothers me. Hands of Man-of-all-songs close my eyes. All around me People drop to their knees. They raise arms to four directions. They pray for forgiveness. They call to new *Messiah* to roll down mountains and stop long knives with crushing rock and burning night fires. They fall to earth, and only I am standing. My feet deep in earth.

Someone touches my arm. It is Sioux Leader. He wears ghost shirt showing rising sun over returning buffalo. He offers me new cloth. "It has never been used," he says. "You will need it to bundle totem remains for your People."

"Tapwe!" I cry. "Ki-tatamihen!"

"You need it," he says. "It is yours."

Horse-dance-maker is there. He lifts me and takes my body into his arms. He smells of smouldering sweetgrass. Then, swift release, and I duck through tents. Wet grass and shrubs brush against my woman's leggings.

I am at bottom of timberline. I climb. I follow Bighorn's trail through lonepine. My toes curl into moss, my knees bend into mountain. I climb. Man-of-all-songs hovers before me, lips parted to speak, calling me up up up mountain. I follow dusklight that folds palely in and out of itself. I follow my dream.

Many days I walk. I gather new roots and herbs. Man-of-all-songs goes with me and tells me to pick foxglove for healing broken hearts.

Many days I go it alone. In Marias Valley I see place where Blackfoot raiders rolled medicine rock down hillside and offended spirit of rock. I see red paint, beads, tobacco and eagle feathers left by Blackfoot needing forgiveness.

I follow sun through pine that spreads like dark masks over mountains. I go as far as Kootenai Country, turn back, and follow pine ridges along Bear Creek to Hungry Horse, then down winding steep banks until I am in Blackfoot Country west of Kalispell. There, cattle are birthing on valley floor. Ranchers plant trees in rows. I follow Lost-prairie-trail through missionary pine. I find good camping among forgotten poplar and in ravines banked with cottonwood. I walk until I come full circle.

In pines above Sioux camp I rest. I lean against Ponderosa pine, its branches whispering to enclosing mountain. Below, beyond lower slopes, beyond steep cliffs rising from south fork of river, earth rushes toward northern prairie. Beyond Going-to-sun-mountains, over dividing-line, is my place of belonging.

I have medicines now. I will tell Horse-dance-maker we must go back to place of belonging, back to Deer's Rump Hill. I have seen too much on this side of dividing-line. I see Deer's Rump Hill through mist of my longing for unclosed land and open sky.

I return to People with medicines.

Along high ridge above camp is good place for Bowboy to keep watch and see who is coming, I know he is hiding behind large rock, his horse lower down in bush, but I do not see Little Bear's scout. I am close to camp now, smoke of many fires makes grey haze above treetops, and I hear Bowboy's horse snorting, then sound of hooves pounding ahead of me. This is strange, Bowboy riding into camp to tell People I am coming, but maybe Horse-dance-maker worried over my going up into mountains for so many days and nights.

Two heads appear over low bush: New Raven and cross-eyed Crow Woman. They are looking for berries and roots. I am glad to see them, but Horse-dance-maker's other wives do not come out of bush to greet me. They disappear, and I can hear Crow Woman is running so fast she breaks twig under her clumsy feet.

"She comes! She comes!" New Raven, faster on foot than Crow Woman, is yelling and yelling, "She comes back!"

I am so close to camp now, I hear dogs barking and small boys calling. They break out of camp and chase each other in circles around me. Bowboy is riding around camp, yelling: "Medicine Woman! Medicine Woman!"

People are rushing to meet me. My bear of a mother ambles ahead of women, her huge head swaying from side to side, but she does not speak to me or come close; she falls back to side of trail. She lowers her head. This is not like my mother.

"What is wrong?" I say, but she does not answer.

I am afraid some great sickness has fallen among People. I trudge into camp, my medicine bundle bumping on my back, and People are ducking out of tents, rising up and away from outside fireplaces; and they are going along beside and behind me. Lucky Man's grandmother folds her hands together and holds them out to me; they are red and swollen and leaking clear fluid. So I nod at her: yes I have medicine for burned hands. Now I see that all old ones have burns, some up to elbows, burns from digging for totems in hot ashes after long knives left Ghost Dance.

In centre of camp, Little Bear stands before his lodge. He wears five-point blanket coat, his hair is tied in status topknot, and he bears the Pipe. Someone, I think it must be Bear Woman, shoves me from behind, and I stumble toward Leader. He signs greeting, so I am not so much afraid now that he will punish me for going away from People. But I do not know what Little Bear wants from me.

Horse-dance-maker comes sideways at me, his head hanging, and he says, "Leader wants to make Talk with you," close enough to me now so only I can hear him, "You go inside his lodge."

People are silent. I only hear dog barking and going after rabbit in bush. People must see my heart leaping out of my throat.

Little Bear lifts tentflap and ducks inside his lodge. "Tawaw!" he says. "You are welcome here."

I duck inside, move towards women's side of tent, but Little Bear points to willow backrest for visitors. "Api!" he says, so I sit.

Leader lights Pipe before he speaks. Eyes of Bear are upon me, and I tremble. He sucks on stem and I see his angry scar. Like Poundmaker, Little Bear allows women to speak in council. Sometimes. But Lucky Man and Bowboy and Horse-dance-maker and other councilmen are not here now.

"My father," Little Bear says, pointing pipestem to north. "He has power of medicine. But he is not here to do it."

"Walks-in-wind," I say.

"At Fort Assinniboine," Little Bear says, "but People tell me they want medicine woman to do it."

"I have medicine plant," I say, thinking about heart of cactus that will heal burned hands.

"It is good," Little Bear says, but scar grows angrier on his face. "Sioux have been very kind to us, they give us new cloth, but there is no one left among us who has power to rebundle totems. To bring back protection!" Little Bear leans forward, his hands folded around pipe stem and bowl. He gives me Pipe. "Will you do it?" he says.

Now I understand why People gather around me in

greeting but were afraid to speak to me or touch me. Because I have power of medicine, herbs and roots, they believe I have power to heal their spirits. Long knives burned sacred objects, things of our grandfathers, totems, and People are afraid they have lost power of dreamspirits' protection. Ceremony must be made, totems rebundled and kept away from all eyes, power restored to People and their broken hearts mended. But there is no medicine man to do it.

"Manitowew," I say.

"Bundles and totems were exposed to white men's eyes," Little Bear says. "People are afraid of spirits' anger. You must undo it!"

"How do you know I have this power of medicine?" I say.

Eyes of bear slant upward at corners and now they are slits. Pointing-finger taps pipe bowl. "You do it!" Little Bear says. "There is much talk around night fires, about how to die by a man's own hand. Some say river. Others are pointing guns at their heads. This fear. This anger. It must be put away! I have never before seen this in People!"

I put Pipe in clay dish. I take from my bundle yellow ochre for purification and braided sweetgrass. "Tell People to bring me their totems and new cloth."

"You are worthy," Little Bear says. "Once. Before. You would become worthy in ceremony and honour given you. But my father is not here to do it."

For four days and four nights I make ceremony of rebundling totems. Each person comes to me in Little Bear's tent, alone. They bring me singed pelts, bits of feathers, claws from birds and animals, whatever is left of totems. I present Stem to four directions, pray to One-above and to each dreamspirit, asking for forgiveness and a new blessing of protection.

I do this for them, not knowing then that I will make purification ceremony again when long knives throw People's bundles onto iron horse where they will lie among unclean women's things.

So we go on living as before, move from camp to camp, from fort to fort, until four summers and four winters later blue coats stop another dance, many-berries feast. It is same as how they stopped Ghost Dance, but now long knives arrest us for being starving Crees.

234

Annika

Old Woman complained at breakfast that her tea was cold, there was too much milk in it, she wanted it clear; and when I filled her cup with hot water she said it was too weak and too hot. I changed her flannel sheets to cooler cotton ones, and she grumbled about her leg hurting each time I rolled her over. She was annoyed that I had moved back to the sleeping loft.

I gave her a sponge bath. Her right hand twitched on the towel I had laid over the Bay blanket. She tipped the wash basin over, spilled water on the blanket and my jeans.

"You did that deliberately!" I yelled. I pulled off my jeans, tossed them in the laundry basket on top of last night's sheets, and put clean ones on.

"It is spring," Old Woman said. "I do not take bath in little tin bowl. I want sweat lodge. Then I bathe in river."

"Do you want to catch cold again?" I pulled her night-dress over her head, and towelled her dry.

"Oiiiii!" she cried.

I had forgotten about her bed sores. Quickly, I rubbed her with alcohol. "Now your clean nightgown," I said, pulling it down over her head, but her arms came through the neck of it, and she twisted it around backwards. "Hold still!" I said. She tried to put her head in one of the armholes.

"A child is easier to dress!" I said. "Do it yourself!" I dumped the nightgown in her lap.

Old Woman crossed her thin arms over her chest. She shivered, but she refused to put the gown on.

"Do it! I said. "Or you will catch cold again."

Old Woman put the nightgown on.

"It's time for your medicine," I said, but Old Woman buttoned up her lips.

"Take it!" I held out a digitalis pill and dipper of water.

"Foxglove tea," she said.

"It's the same thing, only a pill instead of crushed leaves."

"Foxglove easier to swallow," she said.

I slipped the pill into her mouth, but she spat it out. I picked it up, from the blanket, and Old Woman slapped my hand away. "Take it," I said, laying the pill back on the blanket. "You are stubborn and childish and unreasonable!"

She shook her head.

"If I have to," I said, "I'll force you."

Old Woman coughed. "My pipe," she said. Her breathing was heavier today.

"That's another thing," I said. "No more pipe. Smoke is bad for your heart and lungs."

"Today I go home to reserve," Old Woman said.

"That's fine," I said. "But you take your medicine first!"

"Netch," Old Woman said, popping the pill into her mouth and swallowing it without water. She swung her legs over the side of the cot. "Now I go," she said.

"Put this on," I said, holding open the blue chenille bathrobe.

Old Woman stood up, placed one hand on my shoulder to steady herself. She and I bent over, had to scrunch down to get her left arm through the other sleeve. "Tie it," I said. She fumbled with the cord but managed to tie it loosely around her waist. Then she sank down on the cot, breathing quickly. I let her rest, then said, "Now we walk."

"I only walk to Battle River," she said. "I want to go to Deer's Rump Hill."

"I'll take you there," I said. "But you have to be able to walk to the door before you can walk through it—and it is a long way to Battleford."

Old Woman stood up again, balanced by catching hold of the iron bedstead. She took two shuffling steps, and her bad leg buckled. "Naaaaaaa!" she yelled. She perched on her good leg, her arms flailing until she steadied again.

"Hang on to me," I said, "That's it, now try putting your

weight on your left leg again. Good! Slowly now, we walk, that's it."

"Naaaaaa!" Old Woman slapped my cheek. She wasn't strong enough to hurt me, but my face and feelings stung. I wanted to hit her back, but I scooped her up, her small legs kicking. I put her back to bed, roughly.

Old Woman lay back, said, "I walk up Deer's Rump Hill!" and she refused to speak to me until evening.

For the rest of that day, Old Woman was restless, her movements under the covers jerky, abrupt; arms twitching, her feet pushing against the bedstead, and she tossed her head, coughing. She was struggling, yes fighting, and I realized we were not fighting each other.

Every four hours, I stood over her with pill and dipper of water, she refusing with pressed lips and shaking head, but I forced her to take it each time.

By evening, the digitalis had worked, Old Woman slept without coughing and churning in her bed. Towards dawn, she was breathing evenly again, and she continued with her story: I learned more about fighting for life and how the Crees silently resisted their arrest and deportation by cavalry back to Canada.

Old Woman

We are camped outside Great Falls, Montana. We celebrate return of spring with thanksgiving that we have survived another winter, but many-berries-feast is not going well. There are not enough elders, and women must do it: serve leaders seated before Buffalo-robe's new tent.

One elder is missing. He is Old Bear and he is crying inside his tent made of bad material. He did his best, but Thunderbird was angry because there was no meat for a feast. "Many-berries-feast is next best thing to sundance!" Old Bear roared, "but saskatoons do not grow here. Misaskwatomina! Berry broth must be made with saskatoons!"

So Old Bear is singing his song, prays to departed-ones and asks forgiveness for not making sundance, for making berry broth with minkberries.

Minkberry broth is not as good, but it was blessed, and bowls are full. I serve Horse-dance-maker.

He was first to plunge into river after sweatbath. His braids are dripping. "Watch out," he whispers to me. He squeezes his right braid and points it toward bridge. New Raven is running, toes turned inward, toward us. She was gathering white cat-tail roots, and one hand is hidden behind her back. I do not think she is hiding cat-tails.

Horse-dance-maker drinks, wipes his mouth on sleeve, laughing. He is ready for New Raven. In dawn of new day he washed her face with eggs and sent her looking for more among willows.

"She will spread yolk on your face," I say. "You will get what you asked for!"

"No," Buffalo-robe says. "Something is wrong."

New Raven is crying, and she runs to Horse-dance-maker. "Long knives!" she cries. She points towards river. She says something else but we cannot hear her because Old Bear is chanting.

Horse-dance-maker waits for song to end, for Old Bear to stop drumming. New Raven presses her face into cat-tail roots. Song ends, and Horse-dance-maker says, "Why do you cry?"

"Long knives!" She lifts her face. It is smeared with wet dirt, and bits of root cling to her eyelashes. "Many many long knives! Crossing bridge!"

"We will handle long knives," Fox promises.

New Raven stumbles to our tent and Horse-dance-maker calls, "You forgot eggs!" She stops, balances on one foot, other poised for running. She looks at lardpail full of eggs, places roots on ground, straightens, then hurls egg at Horse-dance-maker.

"You think you are so handsome!" she yells.

Horse-dance-maker covers his head with arms. "You missed!"

"Maka kimayatisin!" New Raven grabs her lardpail. "But you are so ugly!" She throws eggs at him.

Handgame players do not think about egg tricks now. They arm themselves with rifles and knives. They duck into tents, hide clubs under blanket-coats, then return to many-berries-feast.

"I will talk to Soldier Leader," Buffalo-robe says to handgame players.

Bluecoats ride into camp. They are led by Sheriff Dwyer and a Soldier Leader who sees everything. Soldier Leader's gaze is clear, direct and searching. His thin lips cut straight line across his face. He looks for more than chicken thief. Six bluecoats at bridge now. More moving around outside camp. River trail is blocked.

Soldier Leader comes to stop many-berries-feast. Long knives always stop Ghost Dance. Elders can be tough and hard to handle when cermonies are stopped. Old Bear is already plenty bad tempered.

Long knives circle Buffalo-robe's tent. Soldier Leader swings leg over black horse and drops to ground. Sheriff Dwyer signs greeting to Buffalo-robe. *"Tell him I wish to speak to the Chief and headmen,"* Soldier Leader says.

"There is no Leader here," Buffalo-robe says.

Soldier leader stares at feathers tied to Buffalo-robe's braids. *"Aren't you the Chief?"* he says.

"I am only a little leader," Buffalo-robe says.

"Who then is the Big Chief?" Soldier Leader says.

"There is only one Leader now," Buffalo-robe says, "and he is not here." Buffalo-robe is an old informer. He has tent made of canvas.

"Little Bear," Sheriff Dwyer says. *"He is their Chief."* He turns to Buffalo-robe, "Where is Leader?"

I wonder if Soldier Leader comes to tell Little Bear that he has been given a piece of left-over-land.

"He comes here visiting sometimes." Buffalo-robe rubs his eyes with pointing-fingers.

"How many braves went with him?" Soldier Leader says.

Buffalo-robe cannot answer. Numbers are unimportant.

Frowning lines deepen between Soldier Leader's eyes. New-young-bluecoat's skin is burned, marked with spots, and looks prickly. His liphair is not as thick as Soldier Leader's. Soldier Leader sits, crosses his legs the way People do, scrinches up his mouth as if sitting hurts. *"Would you say Little Bear took a hundred braves with him?* he says.

Buffalo-robe shakes his head.

"More than a hundred?" Soldier Leader says.

"Ahhhhh-ha, less than that," Buffalo-robe says, "but there are no more warriors."

"Fifty?"

"Maybe. I cannot say."

Soldier Leader's riding whip lies across his knees. He says to Sheriff, *"Tell the sub-chief I come on a matter of great importance, and I must know where Little Bear is."*

Buffalo-robe shrinks into folds of his blanket. "I am only little leader," he says. "You see us camped here. We are not many. Leader's people number many more than you see here."

"Where are they?" Soldier Leader says.

"Maybe at Crow People's left-over-land," Buffalo-robe says. "I cannot say."

240

"But there must be more than a hundred people here."

"Many children. Yes. Many women. Also."

"How many of these children were born in the United States?"

"I do not know." Buffalo-robe grins. He has two top teeth and one is loose. "Me. I have two children."

"Two? " Horse-dance-maker says. "Not bad for old man."

"Ask him to call his people together so I can speak to them." Soldier Leader rises by pushing on his knees. He slaps his boots with whip.

"Old Bear must do it." Buffalo-robe ducks into tent made of canvas pieces held together by cottonwood lashed with rope. Its smoking stovepipe leans saucily towards southeast. Inside, Buffalo-robe asks Old Bear to call People together.

Soldier Leader is Black Jack Pershing and he twitches his shoulders as if blue cloth is itchy. He shifts his weight from one booted shank to other. He is racer at starting-butte.

"THEY STOP MANY-BERRIES-FEAST!" Old Bear hobbles out of tent. He drags one leg behind him. His heavy face is cracked, skin like creek bottom that has been baked hard and dried by many seasons without rain. His head is shackled to bent shoulders. One foot is twisted behind the other. "PEEEEE-HEEE-TOO-TAAK!" he calls.

New-young-bluecoat giggles. He points at Old Bear's feathered forage cap. Soldier Leader yells at him, *"Fleming! Get hold of yourself!"* New-young-bluecoat's grin retreats behind shaking hand.

"PEEEE-HEEE-TOO-TAAK!" Old Bear bellows.

Berry pickers along riverbank hear him. Heads appear above minkberry bushes.

"PEEEE-HEEE-TOO-TAAAK!"

"There is only one man with voice greater than his," Buffalo-robe tells Soldier Leader. He is Big Bear, but Buffalo-robe will not say his Name. "Old Bear can throw his farther."

"KAKWECIYAHOK!" Old Bear wobbles back to tent. He will not talk to long knives who stop many-berries-feast.

People are gathering together. Children with hollow

chests and swollen bellies suck rabbit bones and stare at Soldier Leader. Women with sagging breasts throw sticks at long-eared dogs. I am afraid for them. I remember our first meeting with long knives and how we almost froze and starved to death walking to Fort Assinniboine.

"I do not give you away," Buffalo-robe says to People. "Long knives look for Little Bear."

"*I wish to speak to your Chief and headmen,*" Soldier Leader says.

No one comes forward. Eleven summers ago Real Leaders were hanged or put away behind stone walls. There is only Little Bear and he is not here.

"*I come under orders from the Father in Washington,*" Soldier Leader says. "*I come as a friend, intending to act in a friendly manner with you. I want you to keep together. I will give you rations.*"

Food. Long knives bring food when they want something.

"*It is time to go back to Canada,*" Soldier Leader says.

People wave back and forth like prairie grass under wind. Fear of punishment spreads like prairie fire.

Horse-dance-maker passes Pipe to me. I duck inside our lodge and put it beside his willow back-rest. Soldier Leader has not asked to smoke. I duck back outside and lean against anchor post.

"*I bring a message from your Queen, the Great White Mother of Canada,*" Soldier Leader says. "*She granted full pardon to all her red children who fought in the Rebellion. She did this in '86 but none of you returned to your own land. This made the Great White Mother very sad. She wants all her children together where they belong.*"

"We do not know about this forgiveness," Bowboy says. He is afraid of hanging rope.

"*I have seen with my own eyes the statute made by the Great Mother of Canada granting full pardon for all acts done in the Rebellion,*" Soldier Leader says. "*Be assured no punishment awaits you in Canada.*"

Bowboy stares at armed long knives blocking bridge. If he runs long knives will shoot him.

"Wait," Horse-dance-maker whispers to Bowboy.

"*Now she wants you all to return to your reservations,*"

242

Soldier Leader says.

"We do not make Talk with men armed for fighting," Horse-dance-maker says. He points at long knives. "Send them away. Then maybe some people will talk. Maybe. I do not know."

Sheriff Dwyer struggles with words, sweats, and wipes his face with a rag. He is poor interpreter.

Soldier Leader smiles. Grey metal hammered into his teeth. *"We have come to take you back to Canada,"* he says. *"We intend no harm to anyone. We have promised both governments we will take you back."*

"If it is safe to go back," Fox says, "then why do you bring so many armed men?" His totem's tail bobs angrily. "Why do you surround our camp, hide in bushes, block bridge?"

"You are all under arrest," Soldier Leader says.

Horse-dance-maker, Fox, Bowboy, they jump to their feet. "What have we done?" Horse-dance-maker says.

"Nothing!" Fox shouts. "Soldier Leader stops many-berries-feast for nothing!"

Soldier Leader raises his hands, palms turned outward. *"Wait! Hold your judgement until you hear what I have to say!"*

"We sit," Horse-dance-maker says. "We listen. But we do not go back to Woman Leader's left-over-lands!"

"I assure you I come as a friend," Soldier Leader says. *"Has the American army not fed and clothed you all these years? Have the ranchers not given you snowbound cattle, wood contractors given you jobs?"*

"Only summer pup is visiting!" Fox shouts.

"Tapwe!" Bowboy yells. "What whitemen say they will do and what they do are never the same thing!"

"You say you come as a friend," Horse-dance-maker says, "but I see guns in hands of many long knives."

"You are not American citizens," Soldier Leader says. *"Your home is in Canada. Among your own people!"*

"People are brothers everywhere," Horse-dance-maker says. "Home is prairie." He points in four directions. "North and East and South and West." He chants his own song:

> One-above gave us land.
> He did not divide it; it is one.

He alone can give; He does not take land back.
Dividing-line is yours, not ours.
Prairie is here is there is the same.
Buffalo here were Buffalo there.

"Tapwe! Tapwe!" People cry in-one-voice. Hunters, scouts, runners, and warriors all shout, "Paskwaw! It is prairie! Paskwaw! It is prairie!"

"*No!*" Soldier Leader says. "*You are British subjects, children of the Queen! You have no reservation here and are entitled to none. You must go back! The Queen will give you food. She will clothe your naked bodies. She will show you how to cultivate the soil.*"

Same old promises, made and broken with scratching-stick. Old men heard them four-times-five summers ago at Fort Carleton. They no longer believe in promises, no longer believe soldier leaders whether they wear red coats or blue.

"*No punishment awaits you,*" Soldier Leader says. *We will take you to the border where you will be met by your redcoats.*"

Fear grows again, spreads, takes shape in angry shouts—"We do not go back!"—and in suddenly-shown knives.

"*Your brothers and sisters will be there to meet you,*" Soldier Leader says. "*All is forgiven!*" He reads from two papers. One says *Canadian* Crees have been given much money to go back to left-over-lands on other side of dividing-line. Second one says Woman Leader has forgiven her *red children.*

People do not understand.

"*I have established my camp beside yours. I have put pickets around it and I don't want any of you to try and go away from this camp without my permission. I want a list of your names and I must know exactly how many are here so I can ration food while you are under my charge and protection.*"

"So you arrest us!" Bowboy shows Soldier Leader his axe handle. "You cannot make me go back where I do not belong! There are many more besides myself who belong This Side!"

"*If any of you have acquired any rights here,*" Soldier Leader says, "*you can obtain them through the courts. No one, I am sure, wants to deprive you of any rights."* He rises. He mounts his black horse. He rides through camp watched by People who are afraid of him.

Soldier Leader did not ask if People want to return to left-over-lands, to Woman Leader's foodgivers, white-collars, and redcoats. He arrested People. In ten winters and eleven summers nothing has changed. People are again under Soldier Leader's protection.

"We cannot live as we choose," Horse-dance-maker says. "Handgame players stay! We talk!"

Fox sends lesser players to bring horses into camp. They are stopped by bluecoats. They say they only want to get horses. Two bluecoats go with them so they cannot escape.

Bluecoats guarding everywhere.

Horse-dance-maker, Fox, Bowboy are sitting around outside fireplace talking about what to do. I rekindle fire with wind-dried roots. Horse-dance-maker fans fire with crow wings.

"This is home!" Horse-dance-maker says, patting earth. "I belong to Only-mother! Not to Woman Leader!" Braided forelock bounces on his flat nose. "No man in blue coat will tell me how to live!" He is horse refusing to cross river. He snorts and pulls on his nose.

"Where will you go?" Fox says. "Crow Left-over-land? Navahos might take you in as husband of one of their daughters." Only Fox can think of women when decisions must be made.

Horse-dance-maker spits. "So! Now you allow long knives to lead you by your pointed nose!" He stares rudely at Fox. "I say this is home!" He smacks earth. "I will rest my head on side of hill!" He sweeps dirt into shape of breast. His fingers are round and long as if Only-mother made lodge painter's hand then changed her mind and blunted ends. "Only-mother knows no boundaries! She does not divide people! Whites do not believe she gives life to all things under sun. So we cannot live with them!" His fingers snap—"That is why I cannot go back!"—silver rings flash. "I have said it!"

"Who will be Leader?" Fox says. "You desert People if you escape this camp!" He whittles now, carves short cottonwood stick into shape of faceless man.

"Maybe you can be Leader," Horse-dance-maker says.

Fox bends over stick, his totem's tail falling over his blackened brow, tip between his eyes brushing his crooked Blackfoot nose. He is Fox, sits higher than Horse-dance-maker's raven-wing-hat, but he hides himself between folded shoulders. He tries to be Leader too late. If he wants status he should run more races.

"People will never starve on prairie," Horse-dance-maker says. "So no use fighting over it!" Gone are soft words of old Leader-of-all-ceremonies. His voice is knife scraping stone. "Wild rosehips will feed my children!" He coughs and spits away from fire. "So! Are children chasing butterflies through buffalo grass because long knives gave them chewed-up-beef?" He wipes his nose on blanket-coat. "There are cat-tail roots and eggs, wild turnips on sandy hills, sap running under poplar bark."

Fox is not shamed. "If you stay, People will have no one to help them go on living." His stickman has two legs now and what looks like *forage cap* on round head. "I think Little Bear and Lucky Man will go north," he says, "but if something happens to them at dividing-line?" Fox wants to be Leader.

Only Bowboy has not spoken. "We all may be arrested and hung!" he cries.

"Stay," Horse-dance-maker says. "Do not go back!"

Bowboys palms sweat on his leggings. "I do not know what to do. There is no more scouting, no looking for Blackfoot camps to raid, no searching for buffalo." He hangs his head. "All I do is look for stray horses in summer." He ties knot in fringes on his leggings. "Frozen cattle in winter." Bowboy's life is no good, but he cannot go back. He shot boatman before we crossed over dividing-line, he shot him for chopping Little-brother's head with axe. "They will hang me by my neck," he whispers.

"It is more than choosing between staying away from our fathers or going back to punishment," Horse-dance-maker says. "We have lost the Way taught to us by our ancestors and dreamspirits."

Bowboy says, "It is all gone."

"So we go home to believing in People," Horse-dance-maker says, "Home to believing in One-above, home to living as He wants us to live."

"White-collars! Black-robes! Foodgiver! Redcoats!" Fox pounds earth. "They take away Real Names so we cannot speak the Way. They say we cannot dance! They will not let us be People!"

Horse-dance-maker clasps his hands and presses them on his head. "Maybe we scratch in dirt for food and raise cattle."

"'If we go back we have to take Treaty!" Fox yells.

"Then do you go or stay?" Horse-dance-maker says.

Fox blinks, shakes totem's tail so it swings on back of his long head.

Bowboy grabs his gun. "There is something I must do!" He runs to his own tent.

"Chased by boatman's ghost," Horse-dance-maker says.

"I am afraid for him," I say.

Without speaking, Fox leaves firecircle.

"He tries too late to be Leader," Horse-dance-maker says. "There is no need for Leader to tell People when to move camp now."

Horse-dance-maker needs to be alone to pray, but he waves me away from tending fire to sit by him. "Nitipayimison!" he cries. "Land is held in trust by Only-mother! Not by Woman Leader!"

I smell blood. Horse-dance-maker smells it too. "Ota!" He points to place between Bowboy's tent and Fox's.

Bowboy has killed badger. Arrow in one eye. Belly split and spilling entrails. Bowboy kneels before blood pool.

"He looks to see how old he will be when he dies," I say, "but I think there are no white braids and no wrinkled skin on face he sees in pool."

Bowboy clutches his neck, rises, his face twisted like hanging-rope. His hands are dripping badger's blood. He ducks into his tent, sings his song, and prays to his dreamspirit for protection.

Horse-dance-maker says, "He will never accept dividing-line or barbed fences. Maybe what he sees is best for Bowboy."

"He is too much afraid," I say. "It will not go well."

"Once. Before. We rode across prairie on fast buffalo-runner. We raided Blackfoot camps. We knew joy of dance.

Now summer pup visits our lodges. He has come to stay."
Braided forelock is thinning. Sharp bones of his elbows and
shoulders jut like handles of hidden knives. Raven-wing-hat is
soft and bent. It has seen too many seasons. "People do not
know what to do," Horse-dance-maker says. "We cannot
bring back the Way. So we listen to whites. But their words
are empty kettles. We see only darkness ahead. We say
nothing. Ways of whites and our ways clash until anger builds
inside people and boils like water in birchbark pot full of hot
stones. Ki-nisitohten.ci?"

"It gets worse," I say. "We fight ourselves now."

Who will be bearer of pipe now that Fox is mixed up
with bad medicine, now that Bowboy makes badger
ceremony?

It cannot be the same on that side of dividing-line as it is
on this side.

That night of our arrest, we gather around inside fires.
Horse-dance-maker's women make bannock and tea. Fox's
Woman brings a steer's head to share with us.

"Water is boiling in Company pot," I say to her.

Fox's Woman spits on her *glasses* and rubs them on her
skirt. She cannot see through them because they were made
for squinting eyes of foodgiver's woman. She brought *glasses*
to Fox's lodge with moonstone earrings, *Bible,* and brown silk
dress. Foodgiver's woman gave them to her for putting up
berries in glass jars. Fox's Woman does not hear me. "They
did not listen to you," she says to Fox.

He is sitting in visitor's place before fire. He is not one
to go visiting. He comes to our lodge because he is talking to
People about who will be Leader.

Fox's Woman wires *glasses* to her ears. She reaches for
cow tongue and drops it in Company pot. "I got steer's head
from bluecoats," she says. She pokes tongue with stirring
spoon.

Tongue sinks. Greasy water rises like beaver's dam and
streams over rim of hot iron pot. Fire and water spit at each
other.

"Too much water in pot," Fox's sister says. "She does

not do anything right."

"I can use brains for tanning," Fox's Woman says.

"Tanning what?" Fox says.

Steer's head lies on floorhide beside Fox's Woman.
Flies and maggots crawl in and out of empty eyes. Blood
drippings on floorhide.

"You butchered inside!" Fox yells. "And in another
person's lodge!"

"I tried to tell her," Fox's sister says.

Fox's Woman stirs and stirs with Company spoon.
"My mother was bush woman," she says, scratching her rump,
"and food-giver's woman showed me how to carve meat on
table."

Fox's father warned him. "She spent too much time
with foodgiver's woman," he said. But Fox wanted her so
much he did not listen.

"You belong to Plains Cree now!" Fox yells. "Respect
tent! Butcher outside!"

Her smile spreads slowly on one side of her face. She
sighs, squeezes her breasts together with insides of her arms so
they spill out of her dress. "I miss bushes," she says.

Horse-dance-maker snorts. He cleans his rifle.

Fox laughs. He cannot break his woman in like he does
his horses. When women are alone together Fox's Woman
tells us she does it her way in sleeping-robe, but Fox never
complains about that kind of bucking.

"Maybe I need to drink," Fox says. He takes stickman
out of his medicine bag and begins to carve eyes with knife. He
waits for his woman to give him firewater, but she scratches
between her breasts.

Fox's Woman tucks breasts into white woman's dress.
She shakes out her hair. Moonstones glint like trickster's eyes
on her neck. "I threw it out," she says. "You are no good to me
drunk."

Crow Woman looks at Fox's Woman with crossed
eyes. New Raven smiles behind her shawl. Fox's sister laughs.
Bear Woman smacks her gums. Horse-dance-maker pokes
rags into gun barrel and does not look at another man's
woman.

"I do not believe you," Fox says. "Your brothers have
taken my Company rum again. Sneaky lizards!" Her brothers
are Saulteaux and they slip under tentflaps to take River

Women. They drink Fox's rum which is worse. Fox stretches his runner's long legs, rises slowly.

Fox hits his woman. He slaps her four times full and hard on both sides of her face. *Glasses* fly from her face, swing from one ear. Wire snaps. Two pieces of glass tumble onto floorhide. Her hair falls over her face. She crawls to pile of skins at back of tent. "Dog Leader!" She yells. So she only hid Company rum.

Grinning, Fox takes firewater out of her hands. He takes long drink, sets jug between his knees. He does not offer Horse-dance-maker firewater because Horse-dance-maker does not drink. Fox's Woman returns to Company pot. She scratches her rump.

"Do not scratch!" Fox yells.

"After we eat I will go to river and bathe," she says.

"You cannot!" Fox says. "We are prisoners in our own camp!" He whittles pointed end of stickman's cap. He carves buttons. He drinks, wipes mouth on back of hand.

"Then we have to go back?" Bear Woman says.

"Some do not care. Nipowiwak! They are dead men giving up!" Fox gives stickman strong medicine. He works gun powder into wood with pins.

"So you decided to be Leader and went around telling People to move camp," Fox's Woman says. She scratches between her legs. "Soldier Leader makes decisions now," she says. "This is not time to be Leader. It is just time to go home."

Fox hurls empty jug through rolled-up doorflap.

"There is only left-over-land on that side now," Fox's Woman says. "But it will not be so bad there if we are together." She tugs his braids playfully. He tosses his head away from her. She grabs foxtail totem and swings it so it slaps his left cheek. She grabs foxclaw necklace. Thong snaps against his neck. Claw is in her hand. She jumps up and backs away as if she is going to run away with it. He slaps her face. Screaming, her hair flying around her face, she comes at him with stirring spoon. He wrenches it out of her hand, grabs her around her middle, bends her over his left arm, and hits her shoulders and back and buttocks with spoon. She bites his wrist, kicking, twists her body. She scratches his leg with foxclaw. So he knees her belly. He slams her against canvas wall. She slumps onto floorhide.

Fox takes visitor's place before fire. He tucks foxclaw and stickman in medicine bag.

"You better stop it," I say to Horse-dance-maker, "before they kill each other."

"I want my tea," Horse-dance-maker says.

"It is gone," Crow Woman says. "My eldest sister drank too much."

"You go and see to your horses?" I say to Fox.

"All he does is look after horses!" Fox's Woman yells. She holds her belly. She is lynx spitting at loneman who does not know how to go visiting.

"I will not take Treaty!" Fox shouts.

"What has that got to do with it?" Fox's Woman says. Her long hair sweeps floorhide.

"If I live like whiteman. If I go back to left-over-land. I will be looked-after-person!"

"Then stay," Fox's Woman says. She leans backwards, resting on her hands, before Horse-dance-maker, and she smiles slowly.

Horse-dance-maker leans towards her, peers at her from under raven-wing-hat, left eye twitching. "Lying on floorhide?" he says. "I cannot talk to you that way."

Fox's Woman lifts herself, her mouth open, crying. She flings her skirt over her head.

"Netch!" Bear Woman says. "Naaaaaa!"

Fox's Woman has soft heavy thighs, but her hair is unbraided and her dress is stained with beef blood.

"I am sorry for you," Horse-dance-maker says.

"Then you can have her!" Fox says. He grabs his woman's hair, pulls her up, and throws her at Horse-dance-maker.

She falls against him, her body sagging sideways across his knees. Horse-dance-maker's arms dangle at his sides. He will not touch another man's woman. She is heavy against him and does not move.

Fox raises fist to strike Horse-dance-maker but he beats canvas wall. "I will not be whiteman's Indian!" he yells. His breath is so strong New Raven covers her nose with shawl. But Fox is not drunk. Leanman can drink more than all handgame players and win footraces.

"He is Leader now!" Fox's Woman says. She lifts herself away from Horse-dance-maker. "He can do anything!" She lies on floorhide and clutches her belly.

"You want to be Leader," Horse-dance-maker says, "but you cannot handle your woman. You could have killed her!"

"I would not have done that," Fox says.

"No," Horse-dance-maker says, "because I would not let you."

Once. Before. Fox's father beat his woman until she was unable to carry sliced meat from hunt to camp. Leader of Belt Society tied Fox's father down with rawhide and emptied pipe on his chest.

Fox's Woman smiles sideways at Horse-dance-maker.

"You want my woman?" Fox says. "Then fight for her!"

"I do not want her," Horse-dance-maker says. He has Fox's sister but Fox will kill him before he can take his woman. "Take her back to your tent!" Horse-dance-maker says. "Take beef broth and give it to your husband," he says to Fox's Woman.

I help Fox's Woman to her feet. She holds her belly. She wobbles to tentflap. She turns on Fox, "Are you coming or not!" she says. She tilts her head so moonstones glint at him. She shakes her breasts, small smile on one side of her face. Her knees are wobbling.

Fox follows his woman.

"Sometimes man and woman need to fight," Horse-dance-maker says. "Fox's Woman will never be handled and that is why he wants her."

"She teased Foodgiver and made him chase her around woodpile," Bear Woman says. Her sagging belly shakes with laughing. "Fox's Woman's skirts were over her head, her bare rump humping, and Foodgiver was under her!"

"Foodgiver's woman caught them," I say. "She was quick as white weasel. She threw Fox's Woman out of her *yard* and gave Foodgiver lashing with horse's *harness!*"

"Fox's Woman never took another man after Fox traded two horses for her!" Bear Woman says.

252

"Not another man," I say, "just bluecoats!"

"I want my bannock and tea," Horse-dance-maker says, but there is no time to drink it.

Soldier Leader calls People to gather again.

Outside, bluecoat faces rising sun. He places shiny horn to thick lips. He is Yellow Hair, bluecoat we knew at Fort Assinniboine many winters ago, but he is stouter now and has more white hairs than yellow. Blasts from his horn scare Bear Woman.

"We are being attacked!" she yells.

Horse-dance-maker ducks out of tent, holds his gun against his chest. I duck around him, slap his legs, laughing. Old women chase dogs. New-young-women run to husbands, clutching newborn to their breasts. But New Raven hides from Yellow Hair inside our tent. Fighting-men crouch behind wagons, wait for long knives to attack.

Laughter bursts from Horse-dance-maker's nose. He squats beside Fox. Bowboy sits beside him. Unlike Horse-dance-maker, Fox and Bowboy cannot laugh at themselves. They stare at wagon train breaking into camp.

Soldier Leader slides from his horse and turns it over to Yellow Hair. *Bugler* drives peg into ground, ties reins to it, and tethers horse's legs. Two bluecoats hoist folding table and camp chair from wagon and set them up for Soldier Leader. Long knife with split lip places leather *book* much like *Treaty Paylist* before him. Soldier Leader takes up scratching stick.

Women gather around ration wagon, holding out bowls for flour and tea. Fox's Woman tickles Yellow Hair's nose with fringes on her shawl. He gives her extra bowl of flour. Fox frowns. He did not hit her hard enough.

"Soldier Leader wants something," Bowboy says, pointing at Post Interpreter who is coaxing Lucky Man's People away from opposite side of camp to place of gathering.

"*Line up!*" Soldier Leader says.

New-young-men rush forward, surround Soldier Leader's *table*. They push long knives. They shout, "Let us stay!"

"This Side I live on now!" Bowboy shouts, but he stays squatted in front of our lodge with Horse-dance-maker and Fox.

Halfbreeds are shouting loudest. They plan to run to Bearpaw Mountains and fight any Soldier Leader who comes looking for them. They are from Judith Basin, and they are what Little Bear calls *American citizens.* We are not sure what this means.

Halfbreed knocks big book from table. Yellow Hair slaps him across chest with riding whip.

"CHESKWA!" Old Bear roars. He points at Lucky Man who stands behind Soldier Leader.

"Is he armed?" Soldier Leader says.

"No," Interpreter says. A Company man left over from trading days, this sounding creature knows People and how it goes with them.

"Ask him his name and where he was born," Soldier Leader says.

"Tan'eseykasoyan? Tante oci kiya? Tante ehociyan?"

Lucky Man refuses to answer. He cannot say his Real Name because it represents his dreamspirit. He lives up to his Name and to his family name.

Fox rekindles outside fire.

"You are a Cree Indian?" Soldier Leader says.

"I am Exact-speaking-person," Lucky Man says.

"You come from Canada?"

"I hunted on prairie on That Side," Lucky Man says, "and I hunted on This Side."

"You fought with Big Bear?"

"He was Leader until redcoats arrested him."

"Do you know his son, Little Bear? Where is he now?"

"He is my friend," Lucky Man says.

"Are you Lucky Man? Is that why you won't answer?"

"Tapwe! Pahpiwiyin!"

"You fought with Poundmaker?"

"Once. Before. Piece of left-over-land was named for me. My land and Little Pine's were together. Near Cut Knife Hill. I refused to fight, but I was forced to take part in small way. I never shot anyone!"

"Then why are you in exile?" Soldier Leader says.

"Why did you come to the United States?"

"Some of Big Bear's People came to Cut Knife and said big army of redcoats from Beaver Hill's House killed many at Frenchman's Butte. So we decided to go to Land-of-long-knives. We asked foodgiver, could we go hunting geese at Tramping Lake for ten days? Then Great Deliverer answered my prayers and helped us escape."

Soldier Leader strokes liphair with thumb and pointing-finger. He smiles between his fingers.

Fox braids sweetgrass. He lights ravelled end. It smoulders in clay dish.

"I would very much like to go back and see my old friends and my old hunting places," Lucky Man says, "but because of foolishness of two of my young men, there is rope ready to be placed around my neck should I return to land Woman Leader has taken away and given to settlers."

Soldier Leader's smile lies flat on his straight lips.

Bowboy covers his face with shaking hands.

"You have your duty. I have mine," Lucky Man says. "We do not go across dividing-line."

Soldier Leader stiffens. He leans back, almost falls off his camp chair. *"They are going back! Read them the proclamation!"*

So sounding creature tries to say Big Paper again. He stumbles over words, searches for meaning. Fox stands beside sweetgrass smoulder. He will do something to stop what is happening to People. He tries to be Leader. Sounding creature wipes sweat from brown face with rag. He speaks words we cannot understand. People lower heads and try to listen with respect. New-young-bluecoat traces sweaty red line around forehead where hat is too tight. He squeezes boil on neck where collar rubs. Even long knives do not seem to understand Paper.

"This part Woman Leader signed herself!" sounding creature says. "She put her mark on it with scratching stick!" He shows People woman Leader's great Seal. "You can trust Great White Mother," he says.

"Now do you understand why you must return to Canada?" Soldier Leader says.

Lucky Man squats on grass now. He is more comfortable than Soldier Leader who bounces on canvas *chair.* "It is true," Lucky Man says, "that some fought Woman Leader's men when they were starving. That is why they cannot be sure it is safe to go back."

"*But they all heard the words forgiving them!*" Soldier Leader says. "*Their Queen's words!*"

"I heard some of her words," Lucky Man says. "She does not blacken brow of those who did the killing. No, I think not all will go back. That-is-all!"

"*No, that is not all! My orders are to take you over the line. There is only just so much money, so much food, and each day we waste talking is wasted travelling time, wasted food!*"

"People never starve on prairie," Fox says.

"*What did he say?*" Soldier Leader shouts. "*What did that man say?*" He leans over table and points at Fox.

Riverman translates, and Soldier Leader stabs big *book* with scratching-stick. He rises, leans both hands on *table,* and his knuckles turn white. "*Now look here! I want to know how many people are here so I can ration enough food. I want the names and birth places of all Canadian Crees so I can tell the Great White Mother all her children have come home.*" He puts ends of scratching-stick to paper, ready to make black marks.

"There are more of us here now than before," Lucky Man says. He speaks of many children born since crossing-over, of Chippewa who have no left-over-land, of Assiniboine and Gros Ventre who never stop wandering. "Some children born here want to stay. They belong This Side. And there are many more who will not cross over to Woman Leader's Side."

"*That's exactly why I need to know where each of you were born,*" Soldier Leader says. "*I will put your names on this paper and you will put your mark beside them. I will tell Governor Rickards that some of you are not Canadians.*"

Fox fans smoulder with crow wings.

"Then those who want to stay may stay!" Lucky Man says.

"*I cannot say what the Father of this State will do, but I think it is safe to say only the Canadian Crees must go back.*"

Fox stretches arms over smoulder. He grips stickman. "Thunderbird is angry at what he does!" he cries. "He is angry

256

because buffalo were killed, angry because we are defeated, angry because we are arrested!" Fox hurls stickman into smoulder. He yells, "Strike him down with nightfire!"

Gun powder explodes. It flashes warning at Soldier Leader. Flames lick stickman. It burns. River people are afraid. Women cover faces with shawls. Old men chant.

"*What's that man doing?*" Soldier Leader says. "*Tell him to sit down!*"

"*He doesn't want to go back,*" Riverman says, "*so he curses you.*"

Fox squats calmly before tent. Sun is in middle of sky. He will be loneman now he has put curse on Soldier Leader. No one wants to know person mixed up with bad medicine.

I cannot make good medicine for People who need to undo Fox's curses because I am herded with People onto *boxcar* and carried away through prairie night back to dividing-line.

Annika

Old Woman cannot get out of bed. The pain has returned to her leg, and she is taking some kind of Indian medicine for it, possibly ratfood.

She suffers the pain of remembering and the pain of her illness. She is so deep into the past, into reliving her story, she talks in her sleep.

There is nothing I can do except go with her. But, can loving overcome death?

.

Old Woman

Elders have said it: before Across-water-people came to prairie, killing oneself was unknown among People. It was against teachings. Before we were forced to live on left-overlands, surviving meant never giving up. Now too many People are dead-men-giving-up. They do not fight foodgivers and white-collars. They do not fight fear of empty life. They do not fight Soldier Leader. They let him drive them like cattle to iron horse.

I see Bowboy perched on wooden railing. He was scout for Big Bear, and he is too-much-afraid of hanging rope. He wants to talk to Soldier Leader. He shreds thistle stem with teeth. Short-barrel *Winchester* between his knees is loaded. Bowboy grips Paper, his only protection now. It will stop long knives from sending him back to that side of dividing-line.

When he was scout for Big Bear, Bowboy found buffalo and led providers to good hunting. He found perfume plants, tea in swamps, wild turnips for grandmothers. He knew where to find Turtlestone Circle left by lost tribe, knew Blackfoot hid ponies in Turtle Hollow. On both sides of dividing-line, he was scout. He knew every rock and bush, every trail and wallow. But Bowboy will never scout again, never break trail again. Not on that side or this side of dividing-line.

Bowboy shivers. He picks at dry seeds. He crushes them between his fingers, spits on them, rubs them into braids. Smell is too strong.

Wind is hot, and it means long dry summer, but Bowboy shivers. Horses are bothered by flies and white hands pushing them onto *boxcars*. They do not want to go to That Side. Long knives are red in faces, sweating, cursing. They do not know how to handle people's ponies. They get kicked in kneecaps.

Buffalo-coat, Hotman, and White Snake squat before fire and kettle of tea. They laugh at long knives.

Bowboy cannot laugh. There is nothing to make laughter about being forced to go back to That Side. He shot boatman, killed him for chopping Little-brother's head with axe. Hanging rope is waiting for Bowboy. Hanging rope is pulling him back.

He has Paper, but if it is no good and Soldier Leader makes him go back, Bowboy will be arrested and hanged. Too many redcoats have been looking for Bowboy for too long. Bowboy holds his neck in sweating hands.

He showed his Paper, his protection, to Woman Leader's man when he came across dividing-line. "*I don't know why you should be afraid to go back,*" he said, "*but if you ask my advice as a friend I would say don't go.*" He twisted words like braided rope.

"You can take me back to dividing-line," Bowboy said, "but I will come back whenever I feel like it!"

Now Major Sanno steps down from iron horse. He straightens hat, clasps hands behind back, and rocks on toes. He signs greeting to Pershing, edge of hand slicing hat.

Bowboy beckons to me. "Tell me what you hear them saying."

I sit on wooden railing beside Bowboy. "Soldier Leader says they did good chasing thieves out of hills," I tell Bowboy.

"*Just have to keep after them,*" Pershing says.

I clean wax from my ear with pointing-finger.

"*That's all it takes,*" Sanno says. "*Let them know you won't give up and they come along quietly.*"

"*It was a long hard drive in the Bearpaws,*" Pershing says.

"He had a hard time getting People to come out of mountains," I say to Bowboy.

Pershing stands tall, pulls ends of blue coat so it tightens across his shoulders. His lips shape sounds Bowboy cannot know. Bowboy drops head, listens only to my interpreter's soft sighing, but words and meanings do not come together for me. It always happens this way.

"*We'll have 'em back in no time! The Canadians*

haven't got the men to keep them in hand! Look what happened in '91."

"He led batch of people to dividing-line," I whisper, "and they got back to Post before he did. They were dancing in streets in Havre."

Sanno laughs, but my words do not make Bowboy laugh.

"Sassy! Tricky-ones playing tricks. They slip back into Idaho." I point toward mountains where Deer-robes-people and Flatheads live.

Pershing's arm makes chopping motion. *"Only the pickets around the camp keep these rebels in hand! We lost one hundred and fifty of some three hundred camped near Great Falls, and if we can't hold them I don't know how pretty-boy redcoats will!"* His voice holds ring of steel rolling on steel.

"Bunch got away." I nudge Bowboy. "So there is still hope! Soldier Leader says he has hard time keeping People together and getting them to dividing-line. He is afraid redcoats cannot stop fighting-men from escaping back to This Side. Woman Leader has not got the men to do it."

Bowboy says, "Woman Leader always has enough redcoats."

Pershing chews liphair. *"Their petition for a Writ of Habeus Corpus is set to come up in District Court tomorrow and I've been called as defendant. The bastards even asked the Commissioner in Havre to intercede for them!"*

"He is talking about your paper!"

Little Bear is fighting with words now, but Bowboy does not trust lawman helping him.

"Tomorrow!" Sanno shouts. *"Then the only thing to do is start them for Canada before the law can intervene."*

"Some of them have Certificates of Intent to become American citizens," Pershing says.

Sanno blows into yellow rag, wipes nose. *"You can't tell me Buffalo-coat and The Snake have any real intentions."*

"Sixty were born here!"

"So they say. But they can't prove it. The Court won't do anything."

"And the Canadians? They say the word of an officer," poking blue chest with riding whip,*"—me—was used to lure them into a trap!"*

261

"Long knives and redcoats fight each other," I say.

Bowboy bites thistle stem. It is too green. It tears between his teeth. It must taste bitter.

"The Governor and Secretary of War will support you. Won't be any proof the redskins were unlawfully detained."

Bowboy rises, takes four long steps to long knives, Paper gripped in one hand, gun against his leg.

"I'll handle him," Pershing says. His eyes are round and grey as trade balls. He looks at black markings on Paper. He smacks it with back of hand. *"It's no good!"* He turns to me, *"Tell him the State Court has no jurisdiction over a federal officer. Tell him he's not an American citizen and he has no rights in this country."*

I do not know how Soldier Leader can know that I interpret to Bowboy his white words. I am so afraid my mouth sucks stone, but I say to Bowboy, "Paper is no good. You do not belong This Side."

"Lawman says he will stake his name on it," Bowboy says. "Paper says long knives cannot hold me."

I am afraid to try and translate into *English.*

Boxcars couple. Heavy doors slide open. Rumbling of steel rolling on steel and humping of house on wheels at end of iron horse.

Long Knives snatch bundles and totems from brown hands. They throw them into *boxcars.* People fall to knees, raise arms to four directions. They cry to spirits for forgiveness. They are afraid of dreamspirits' anger.

Bowboy's chest caves in as if iron wheels are sliding over him and crushing him. Rumbling begins in his throat like steel balls rising up: "Ayiwihk!" He thrusts end of *Winchester* at Pershing. "You gave us no time!" he roars. "No time for purification ceremony! No warning!"

Pershing tears up Paper and tosses pieces under iron wheels. He pushes Bowboy toward iron horse. *"I don't know what lies you were told by your lawyer but your deportation was arranged by both governments! Get on that train!"*

"Sipwatay!" I say, "go away." I cannot translate now. "Ahkamitipaskan," I try, "over dividing-line."

Horse kicks wooden walls of *boxcar.* People sit and refuse to move. Pershing whips air with riding crop, shouting, *"Get up! Move!"* Long knives lift People and throw them onto flatcars.

Bowboy shuffles through People, his legs heavy, his arms dangling. Pain in his throat is so bad he cannot breathe. His hands are swelling, his fingers thicken around gun. He crawls over hitching post to other side of iron horse. He stares at sun.

People cannot help themselves, and Bowboy has failed them. He was wrong to trust lawman when long knives held people prisoners in their own camps, separated families, and herded them to iron horse.

"*Amnesty Proclamation does not include those guilty of cold-blooded murder,*" Woman Leader's headman said.

So Paper is no good. It does not protect those who killed at Frog Lake. It does not protect Bowboy. He shot boatman. At dividing-line he will be arrested and hung.

Rope is always around his neck, drawing tighter and tighter, choking him while he sleeps, stretching across prairie; and Bowboy is always running, rope above him, circling hiding places, twisting his vision, so staring now at summer sky, Bowboy sees rope stretching downward out of sun, pulling him by his neck all the time.

Gun barrel in left hand. Butt gripped in right hand. Slowly he turns *Winchester,* and stretching his arms, he points it at his heart. His right thumb hooked on trigger. He lifts his face to sun, yellow light melts into light behind his eyes, turning circles, and face in sun is his own, badger pelt tied to braids his own.

Bowboy is lost into yesterdays of scouting and trail-breaking and looking for Blackfoot camps to raid, lost into looking for snowbound cattle and digging in dumping grounds, lost and falling into all tomorrows of eternal hunting.

Thumb jerks. Bullet slams into him. It splits skin and shatters bone joining shoulder to neck. His arms are flung wide. He drops gun. He crashes against hitching post. His body slumps and slides down to earth. He stares at blood pouring out and spreading on his chest. It is badger's blood.

Face in blood pool was face of Bowboy at time of death, braids black and tied with badger's pelt, skin brown and smooth.

He is Bowboy, Rainy-bow, Daybow, and he did not do it right.

Right hand gropes, clutches pebbles, fingers stretch

until they touch and close around rifle butt. He pulls it up his leg, reaches with left hand, grabs barrel; and slowly, he turns gun on Bowboy. He turns gun upside-down. Hand pumps. Thumb pulls. Blast of gun in his ears. Dull thud against his chest.

Bowboy stares at sun turning in sky. Sun holds face of Bowboy, and out of mouth roaring of buffalo.

People see it: streaming out of sun, thousands upon thousands of buffalo. They are blotting out sun and closing sky.

Bowboy is scouting always.

There are no dividing-lines in place of eternal hunting, but at whiteman's *border* redcoats are waiting to arrest Little Bear and Lucky Man.

We left Great Falls without Bowboy. White people lined iron road and waved to bluecoats playing cards in *passenger coach.*

All day and all night we were sick. Before dawn, iron horse slowed down because redcoated Leader is afraid to meet Bowboy's band except in daylight.

The Alberta Railway & Coal Company train, bulging with one hundred and ten people, one hundred and seventy-six horses, and thirty wagons steamed into *junction* one and one half whiteman's miles out of Coutts.

We were met by another Soldier Leader in red coat.

Iron horse is not rumbling and shaking and rolling on steel now. It has stopped, but it is dark inside. People are sprawled on straw heaped with their own dung. They lie on bales of hay, on rotting wood. They lean against shining milk cans. It stinks in here. There was no stopping so People could find over-the-hill or out-of-sight-places, and sickness has poured from all openings of their bodies.

I crouch near large square opening or ironhorse. I press my burning face against iron bar. I try to breathe cool outside air. Ironhorse spurts steam. It bolts, strains against hitchings, then pulls over steel tracks to *siding.* I look up at sky. Clouds look like bundled belongings of Departed-Ones. My head is spinning. Ironhorse has stopped, but I feel as if I am still moving.

"Welcome to the Northwest Territories."

I hear two men talking, one voice deep and old, other higher and making faster sounds. They are not speaking Cree, but I understand them.

I ease my body closer to edge of floor, using my elbows, and I look out of iron horse. I see a redcoat. He is thin, not so old, but his shoulders sag. He has hair the colour of broom straw and long drooping liphair of one who has seen many winters.

So we are on That Side of dividing-line. We must have crossed over at night. Redcoat is talking to long knife. *"I won't be stayin',"* long knife says. He tucks his hat under his arm. His forehead is soft and white, his cheeks burned by sun. *"My orders are to turn the Indians over to you then return to Great Falls,"* he says. *"There's a bunch of them giving the authorities a hell of a pack of trouble. Money's running out already and there's hundreds left to ship. Looks like we'll have to march a couple hundred overland."*

"Rough trip?" Redcoat says.

"We had a time with them!" long knife says. He gives Redcoat papers, hits his forehead with edge of his hand, turns on booted foot, and strides away. I cannot see where he is going, but I hear gravel crunching under his boots. He has delivered People into hands of Woman Leader's man. Redcoat squints and peers into iron horses's black insides. His cheeks are caved in, his skin slack, his eyes lined and shadowed.

Horse-dance-maker crawls over beside me. He drops his head over the side and throws up.

Redcoat backs away. *"Corporal Clopp!"* he yells. *"Mountain! Sergeant Davis!"*

Horse-dance-maker rolls down onto rain-soaked gravel.

I dare to look outside again. Redcoats pull at sliding doors of cattle cars. Two new-young-redcoats climb into next car. They throw out wheels, sides and ends and middle pieces of wagons folded tents, lodgepoles, Company pots, black kettles, and bundles. A stooped redcoat frees ponies. He strokes noses and forces his fingers into their mouths.

New-young-redcoat leaps up and into cattle car. *"Holy shit!"* he says. *"Look at them!"*

I lean against wooden wall. I hear redcoats yelling.

265

"McEachran! I want Doctor Mewburn down here!"
"He's occupied in the next car!"
"Tell him to come as soon as he can!"

Redcoat lifts Crow Woman's youngest girl. Her nose is running, her eyes open now, but lids are heavy and crusted. Redcoat hands her down to Soldier Leader. He lies her on wet and wild grass struggling to grow among settlers' weeds. She clutches blanket, leans against Horse-dance-maker. He wraps his arms around her, lays his cheek on her head, and picks bits of straw from her face.

Soldier Leader places long-fingered hand on her forehead. His own face is sad, shaped like upside-down tipi, and it is white as new canvas. *"We'll look after your little girl,"* he says. He covers his nose with white cloth.

People jump and stumble and push their way out of cattle car now. Redcoat helps old ones and children. People fuss over bundles. Redcoats move in and around and through them. Small boy with badger pelt tied to his braids is crying because he cannot find his mother. Two handgame players fight over a horse. Crow Woman sits beside Horse-dance-maker now. She is singing, thanking One-above that no one in family walks towards place of eternal dancing.

Redcoats tug on ropes and try to pull horses to river. Tails flick at flies. Feet stamp in mud. Horses toss heads and pull down on ropes. They do not want to go with men who smell of soap and boot grease. They reach for buffalo grass. Then they smell river and bolt. *"Whoa! Whoa!"* redcoats yell. They run after horses, waving arms. *"Halt! Halt!"* They shake fists at runaway horses. *"Whoa! Godammit! Whoa!"*

Iron horse is almost empty now. I do not want to jump out yet. I need to be sick. Howling women grope in heaps of bundles. Old men give plenty bad words to redcoats. "NI-TOTEM!" Old Bear roars. His bundles landed in mud.

Bear Woman is stuck in prairie mud. My oldest son tries to push her from behind, but she does not budge. So he runs around her, grabs her hands, pulls, then lets go. They both fall backwards into mud thick as berry broth.

"Davis! Hourie! Mountain!" Soldier Leader is yelling again. *"Mountain, I want blankets for the old, the sick, and the children. And tea. Tell Cook we need kettles and kettles."*

Mountain runs across tracks to redcoats' camp. I

wonder how he earned his name. He is not as big as mountain.

"Peter, I want you to find out what reserve each man belongs to."

I have seen Redcoat's halfbreed interpreter before, somewhere, long ago. His belly has never felt summer pup's bite. He has never eaten smoked skunk meat. He is Sounding Creature.

"Davis, you and your men bed them down by the fires. I want you to divide them up into two camps, one composed of those wishing to go to eastern points like Battleford and the other made up of those wishing to go to Edmonton."

My throat works up and down, my belly heaves, but nothing is coming up. I cough.

Redcoat hears me. *"Let me help you,"* he says.

I try to fall deeper into shadows.

"Come on, now," he says.

I do not want help from redcoat. I grip wooden wall. I pull myself up. I leap from cattle car.

"Watch out!" redcoat yells.

I fall sideways, but my right leg is twisted behind me. I lie still. I am afraid to move my leg. Someone rolls me over. My lips shape a scream, but I cannot make sounds.

"It's broken! Badly!"

"Get splints and bandages!"

Iron hands hold my shoulders, press them into wet earth. Iron hands grip my hands. I want to kick redcoats, but I am afraid to move my leg.

"Got her? Okay, hold tight. I'm going to straighten it."

Hands are pulling and pulling at my leg. I bite my lips. I taste blood. Metal against my mouth. I toss my head, and iron hands grab it. I clench my teeth. Fingers hold my nose so I cannot breathe. I hold my breath until it explodes. Bad-tasting liquid spills into my mouth. Hands push my chin up, so I have to swallow. Liquid burns my throat, feels hot going down to my belly. My face is wet.

"Hold the splints against each side of her leg. Don't move it! Now we just get this tied up good for her."

My leg does not hurt so much now. I think I will sleep. Hands roll me into blanket. It is tied to two poles.

"Lift together now."

I am swaying in blanket-cradle, being carried somewhere. I hear redcoats talking.

"Horses are a fine healthy lot. Good stock. I wonder where they got them."

"What's the matter with the Indians?"

"Travel fatigue. Colds brought on by poor ventilation in the cattle cars. Mild congestion in most cases. They're all suffering from malnutrition. Mouths full of cancre sores. No Koplick's spots, thank God."

Redcoat carrying my feet turns his head around to look at redcoat carrying my head. He has curled bottom lip and pinched nose. If People have covered-with-sores-disease, he is afraid of getting it. *"How soon can they travel?"* he says.

Big voice at my head says, *"Give them some stiff doses of cod liver oil, lots of tea, and I'd say in a day or two."*

"I expected trouble. Rebels! Deserters! But not this! I swear one little girl has measles!"

"One communicable disease would save both governments a lot of trouble and expense."

Soldier Leader trudges by, his red coat hanging from his shoulders like empty flour sack sagging on anchor-post. Redcoats carrying me stop talking. They lay me beside fire. Old one who makes big words is horse doctor, and he wraps me in blankets. I see kettle hanging over fire. Redcoats lift it and carry it between them, swaying. Old women should make tea instead of redcoats lugging steaming kettles from one camp to another.

How will Horse-dance-maker find me?

I fall into dream of walking up Deer's Rump Hill. I drag one leg, twisted, behind me.

Beside steel tracks I watch bluecoats push Little Bear's People into camp. I am afraid for Little Bear, afraid redcoats will take him to place where bones lie and hang him.

Trail-breaker rides forward, passes Little Bear at head of long line of People, and stops before Redcoat. *"Little Bear and Lucky Man have been identified by Inspector Morris,"* he says.

"Come forward," Soldier Leader says.

Sounding Creature holds brown hat over his heart. He asks Little Bear and Lucky Man to make talk with Redcoat.

Lucky Man tightens striped blanket around shoulders.

He sits on edge of iron road. Where is his Great Deliverer now?

Little Bear ambles forward on flat feet wrapped in many strips of old rawhide. He has seen forty winters now. His black frockcoat is covered with mud, bits of straw and dried vomit. He lifts *cowboy hat* from his head. He still wears status topknot, and two braids bound with beaded rawhide hang down to his shoulders. I have never seen a face as strong as Little Bear's.

"It is my duty as an officer of Her Majesty the Queen," Soldier Leader says, *"to arrest you on charges of participation in the Frog Lake Massacre."* His cornsilk liphair is drooping.

Corners of Little Bear's wide mouth turn down, his thick bottom lip trembles. "I was told by long knives that I would not be molested," he says. His voice is an echo of his father's word and all his teachings. With Wandering Spirit, he killed eight men and captured forty prisoners. Now he thrusts paper at Soldier Leader.

"Leader of long knives gave me this and promised safety!" he says. Scar on right side of his nose throbs. "Are these promises as false as Treaty my father signed?"

Soldier Leader's pale eyes seem to sink deeper into shadowed sockets. He is thin, shrivelled as if he has just healed after long sickness. Maybe he knows great loss. *"I don't know what you have been told,"* he says, *"but your deportation was not brought about by the wishes of the Canadian government. It is the Americans who don't want you. We only take you back at their request."*

"I have more papers!" Little Bear shakes papers clenched in his fist. "These words were put down by other whitemen in Land-of-long-knives! Men who gave me work many times to cut hay and chop wood!"

"I think the terms of the Amnesty have not been explained properly to you," Soldier Leader says. *"Those who fought in the Rebellion have been pardoned, but those who are guilty of cold-blooded murder are not exempt."*

Sounding Creature swabs his bloated face with rag. He interprets slowly. Maybe if he did not stuff his fat face so much he would not sweat so much. He is Halfbreed, his mother Snake Woman, his father Company factor. He did not fight during Outbreak because he knew who would win. He was interpreter for Middleton. He has never known what it is to have summer pup in his tent.

Soldier Leader says. *"My orders are to arrest you. Not judge you. A preliminary hearing has been set for July eighth in Regina. Your guilt or innocence will be determined then."*

Two redcoats clamp chains on Little Bear's and Lucky Man's ankles. They must carry iron balls in their hands. Little Bear takes heavy steps. His small eyes, like his father's, show pain and grief deeper and sharper than cut of knife. Lucky Man is led away by another redcoat. He is Laughing-man no more.

Redcoats and long knives are working together to wipe out last of our Leaders.

Little Bear climbs into iron horse. He goes to place where bones are piled white under sun. He bears chains of his father.

This night, blankets and tea are small comforts to People. We wonder why Woman Leader has betrayed us. Horse-dance-maker and I plan to escape back over dividing-line.

Redcoats give Lucky Man's and Little Bear's People food and start them off for Onion Lake. Four women belonging to Little Bear and Lucky Man want to go to their men but interpreter, Peter Hourie, tells them Leaders were taken to Pile O' Bones to be tried for being in Frog Lake Massacre.

Summer is hard for us now. Fire spreads across prairie. We help ranchers smother fires by skinning cattle, soaking hides in slough water and dragging them over flames. Cactus blooms in dry river bottoms. Water is scarce and is hauled in barrels by teamsters.

More and more people are driven over dividing-line. Sounding Creature keeps numbers all the time, People do not want to give him names, and he is trying to find out who is planning to escape. Too many People have escaped back across dividing-line and long knives must chase after them again and bring them back to redcoats. All this is costing too much, and money is running out.

Last batch of people are marched overland, three

hundred and fifty whiteman's miles, by Black Jack Pershing. On cloudy, rain-drenched day of August sixth they are turned over to Soldier Leader in red coat. They are pushed, prodded, and driven into camp by fifty bad-tempered long knives. Most have escaped before and they will try it again, so Sounding Creature is flying about and keeping numbers all the time.

I am trying to catch dragonfly now.

He is Sounding Creature, dragonfly who hovers over People. He has to take numbers of People, keep track of them to see they are not slipping out of redcoats' camp and tail-tucking it back to Montana. I have seen him flitting from fireside to fireside, from People's camp to redcoats' camp. He tries to find out who is planning to escape, and he says he has big friends in both camps. So I am trying to catch dragonfly.

I hide behind water tower. I am long and thin, and I flatten my back against it. So Sounding Creature does not know I am here and listening to all he says to Railhand.

Sounding has one foot on iron rail. He watches last long slow-moving human train coming into camp. It seems to move out of place where earth meets sky. It separates clouds. "*Last batch,*" Sounding says to Railhand, "*long time coming.*" He thrusts thumbs into vest pockets.

Old Railhand lifts his cap, scratches his dusty head. "*You see 'em at Shelby Junction? Damdest thing I ever saw! You know, those that came from Havre on the Great Northern?*"

Sounding nods, shoves thick neck into coat. Wind promises more rain.

"*We had to transfer them onto the C.R.C. train. The Americans bedded down and the Indian refused to work. Of course most of them were too sick anyhow. So we had to move all those horses from the broad gauge cars onto the narrow ones.*" Railhand pulls up his pants and shows Sounding a large black and red bruise on his knee. "*One nearly kicked me clean over the border! Them Indian ponies hate redcoats so much we had to haul them onto the boxcars one by one, with two hands pulling front legs and two hands pushing rumps!*"

Sounding Creature rubs his liphair. It grows down each side of his face and across his upper lip, but it will not grow on his chin. Snake blood says stop no more of that.

"*We finally telegraphed Fort Assinniboine and sure as*

the cows come home we got military assistance after that! But we had most of them in ourselves by the time the order was wired back."

I did not see that. I would like to have watched bluecoat with split lip pushing ponies from car to car. I would like to have seen Sounding kicked, but not in kneecap.

"Well, like you say, old Pete, this'll be the last of them."

Redcoat and halfbreed slog through mud towards Sounding. *"Better give them a hand,"* Railhand says, and leaves.

Redcoat is Peachpie Davis. He takes dried peaches to redcoats' cook, but he will not give People fresh beef. In time of disappearing buffalo he moved Grizzly Bear's Head and Poorman from Fort Walsh to Eagle Hills. They did not want to go, so Peachpie refused them food. They went with him, but Stonies were afraid to cross fast-flowing-river because of river spirits. Peachpie went ahead with women, made fire and cooked beef. Then many more than a thousand People crossed river. Stonies called redcoat Always-angry-man. Dog stole beef from ration wagon and he shot it. He said he would shoot any Indian who stole food too. He always says, *"Give an Indian food and you can get him to do anything.'*

Halfbreed is follower of Little Bear but he does not belong This Side of dividing-line. Sounding Creature keeps numbers but he missed this one.

Sounding bellies toward redcoat and halfbreed. He takes short steps, toes turned outward, pants flapping between knees. He starts talking before he stops moving. *"I know every last mother's son of them, and my count was right, not counting those that got scarlet fever, and all of that bunch was started off, promising faithfully that they would go. And they did go, taking flour and bacon and tea and tobacco Tom Dickinson got them from Whittington's Store, but bucking because they got no sugar or fresh meat. Indians are always bucking about something, but it was a pretty show, they were well-clothed, white people over the line being kind to them, like Captain Deane who preferred to have them around. Not like over the line where they get the cold shoulder and are passed by with a look."*

People were uneasy, having to stay so long in camp, and some wanted to escape and go to their relatives on Flathead

Left-over-land. So Sounding hovered over and around fires, making talk about escaping. People were sick about broken Word, about being driven north at point of bayonet. They were promised protection, but Leaders were arrested and taken away.

"*I got them all together,*" Sounding says to redcoat, "*with their horses. And I handled the whole lot of them for the coloured cavalry and for the dark mule skinners who drove the ration wagons. Confound them! It is not my business to run after Indians all the time!*"

Sounding will handle halfbreed now. "*He is one of them from the last bunch!*" he says to Peachpie. "*So he thought he would escape!*"

"*I don't belong here!*" halfbreed says. He thrusts paper in Sounding's fat face. "*I'm an American!*"

"*I can't understand him,*" Peachpie says. "*He talks too fast. I can't even get his name from him.*"

Sounding's chest swells. He rubs his chin the way Soldier Leader does and looks down on halfbreed. "*What's all this bucking about?*" he says. "*Why weren't you started off with the rest?*"

"*Ask him his name,*" Peachpie says.

"Louis Thomas!" He blurts out his name, so I know he does not belong with Indians. People will starve before saying Names.

"*These rebels,*" Sounding says, "*are afraid of saying who they are for fear of being hung for crimes they committed during the Outbreak.*"

"*Where were you born?*" Peachpie says. He thumbs through raggy pages. He looks for deserter's name.

"*Pembina,*" Thomas says, "*on the 'merican side.*"

"*Is or was your father an American citizen?*"

"*My father lives in Dakota on south side of Turtle Mountain. Everyone from Turtle Mountain to Fort Benton knows him!*"

"*And your mother?*"

"*'Cept for her we Thomases are all 'mericans.*"

"*Where is your home now?*" Peachpie says.

Louis Thomas points southward, his knuckles knotted, his veins twisted and running blue under skin like many forks of hard-driving river. "*I got house and ranch at mouth of*

Musselshell!"

Peachpie stops scratching on paper. *"Then how do you happen to be here?"*

Pointing-hand becomes fist. It slams into left hand. *"I was cuttin' cordwood! I have one hundred cords ready for the boats, y'know?"*

"I know," Sounding says, *"I'm a poor man like yourself."*

Thomas's moccasins are beaded in creeping floral. Sounding wears hard leather.

"Look here," Peachpie says, adjusting hat strap. *"This is unfortunate, but can you prove it?"* His hair is shorn up past ears, and little red hat looks silly perched on bushy hair.

Thomas shoves wrinkled paper at redcoat. Peachpie holds paper flat, at slant to tearing wind. Sounding closes his poor eye, stares at paper with good eye.

Now Soldier Leader is here. He tells Sounding to pick out Thomas's horses and send him back to Montana. *"What do you say, Peter? Shall we see how many Louis Thomases we can find in the next lot?"*

Sounding nods. He cannot speak now, because Thundering Bird is angry again. Bird opens sky with slashes of light. Sounding bends brown hat into slanting rain.

At meeting place, long line of People is pulled back by trail-breaker. He rides forward on black horse. Rain slithers down leather blanket-coat. *"The last consignment,"* he says.

"I will formally receive the Indians as soon as you can deliver them in column of route outside my camp," Redcoat Leader says.

"Like all the rest," Long Knife Leader says, jerking whip over shoulder, *"they want to go back."*

"I have no anxieties on that score," Redcoat says. He wrings rain from drooping liphair.

"He will settle their hash," Sounding says. *"Like that time Breaking-through-ice refused to set out with the band going to Beaver Hills. 'You better do as you are told,' I said, 'or the redcoats will arrest you, put you in jail, and maybe punish you for disobeying orders. You better simmer down an go,' so Breaking-through-ice went."*

"I hope you can hang onto them better this time!" Black Jack Pershing says. *"Half the batch from Havre we caught*

roaming around Dakota!"

"You may consider your duty fulfilled," Redcoat says.

"After we round up deserters from this batch!" Long Knife tightens leather ropes around horse's neck.

"I'm sure you will drive them out of the hills."

Soldier Leader in red coat turns away from Soldier Leader in blue coat. *"Now, let's get these names down and find out where each family wants to go,"* he says to Sounding .

First man in long line, he has grey facehair. "Isbister *is my name!"* he says, smacking chest.

"I have seen him before," Sounding says, *"when I alternated between being a free trader myself and working for the Company."*

"His name doesn't sound Cree," Redcoat says.

"Where do you come from?" Sounding says.

"I go obber dere. Montana. Den I come obber here."

"Yes, but where do you live?" Redcoat says.

"Calgary."

"Then what are you doing here?"

"I go obber dere. Visitin' Soldier, dey tink I a son a' bitchin' Indian!"

"I am tired of your kind," Redcoat says, *"tired of cavalry rounding up everyone with dark hair and eyes."* He offers Isbister food, clothing, and a horse to take him home.

Widow from last bunch, one I saw sneaking into Sounding's tent, she drags two children through mud. She plucks at red sleeve. *"I was earnin' me own livin' when the bloody soldiers came!"*

"Just go home, mother," Redcoat says.

"We took dah scrip," next halfbreed says. *"I was earnin' good money when dey move me an' my woman offa dah lan'! De rain she come down, an' no tent for our heads!"*

"Wire Lethbridge and get those three old pack tents sent down," Redcoat says.

People shiver, wipe noses on sleeves, cough and spit into mud. Soldier Leader talks about crossing-over, and they listen with lowered heads.

"It's not the Canadian government who doesn't want you. It's the people of Montana who have objected to your living in that state. You were sent over by the American authorities, and if the Canadian government won't have you—

where do you have to go?"

"Long knives want to get rid of you," Sounding says, "as you were among the ranchmen, killing their stock, and so on like that."

"You must plainly understand that although you are going home now, you will not be allowed to settle along the railway. Nor can you infest towns and cities. You will be required to settle in some of the northern reserves. You must devote yourselves to hard work so the government will be relieved of the necessity of supporting you entirely. This way you will, in time, be as prosperous as your kinfolk who never strayed away."

Sounding translates like this: "You better go instead of being made to."

"Do you see these American officers?" Redcoat says, pointing to Long Knife who grips horse's sides with booted feet and to new-young-bluecoat who looks like girl blushing. *"If I say anything which is not true they can contradict me. If these halfbreeds object to coming with me I cannot coerce them, but they are dependent on me for food."*

"I hadn't t'ought o' dat," Halfbreed says.

His Indian woman hides behind his back, but she jabs him with pointing-finger. "Konitacitwet!" she says, "mere words!"

"Go to Regina and see the Indian Commissioner," Redcoat says.

White woman wearing Crow dress decorated with glass beads and porcupine quills carries slant-eyed-boy on hip. *"I'm married to an Indian now,"* she says. *"Can you get me a divorce from the bastard who got me this kid?"*

"I'm sorry," Redcoat says, *"No."*

"Then you ain't as important as you think you are!" She shifts slant-eyed-boy to other hip. *"Wipe the snot offa your face!"*

Redcoat wipes slow smile from his face with rag.

"I charge de gourvenmont ten dollar par jour for dis!" another halfbreed shouts.

"I sincerely hope you get it," Redcoat says.

Sounding pulls rain-battered hat over his ears. He signs for People to move forward. "Where are you going?" he asks storyteller from Poundmaker's. "Go to that camp. Right side for River People."

Woman with no husband rattles up to Sounding, her kettles and pots and pans clanging on string tied around her middle. She goes to Onion Lake. "Where is Little Bear?" she says. "I want to go to him!"

Redcoat hears trouble. "*You will be glad to know,*" he says, "*that Little Bear and Lucky Man were tried in a preliminary hearing before Superintendent Perry at the Regina Police Barracks. There wasn't enough evidence to warrant a trial and they were sent home to Onion Lake.*"

"Wife of Sioux Speaker," Sounding says, "she wouldn't point out Little Bear or Lucky Man as the ones who did the killing."

"*The authorities wanted to show them,*" Redcoat says, "*that the old indictment hadn't been forgotten and that its quashing lay in their future good conduct towards good order and morals.*"

Little Bear's Woman goes to camp on left side of iron road. Stony takes her place before Redcoat and Sounding. He wears breastplate of bones sewn on rawhide.

Top-hatted brother of Four Sky Thunder carries Black-foot medicine lance, a *bayonet* tied to a pole and painted red for blood of men he killed in battle. It has never touched earth.

"*My father had a scar on his side from a sword,*" Sounding says, "*and I grew up playing with his sword. My father used it in the Battle of Waterloo. It was the only thing I ever had that was his. Some of the loyal halfbreeds borrowed it in '69 and I think the rebels must have got it somehow. My father was an Orcadian. From Kirkwell. He was in the Battle of Waterloo.*"

"*Get on with it,*" Redcoat says.

"*But I've been looking for that sword,*" Sounding says. "*Peter!*"

"*Yes, sir, Captain Deane, I'll handle the rebels for you!*"

Blackfoot warrior is followed by girl whose face is smothered with rags. Family of five, led by older sister with bare feet and legs swollen with red sores. Long-eared dog with bones poking through skin pulls travois laden with three children who sit between Company pots. "Touchwood Hills," eldest sister says.

"Between '40 and '52 I was in charge of the Post at Touchwood Hills," Sounding says, *"and the rest of the time I traded at Dirt Hills and Pile O' Bones."*

Blue Hills People trudge on to left camp, their blankets slipping over shoulders shining with rain water. Their stretched moccasins flop and squish in mud.

"All my life I've had a lot to do with Indians and I know every last mother's son of you," Sounding says. "My mother belonged to Snake People. So I'm a poor man like yourselves. I just have to tell you that going against Woman Leader does you no good. Knowing you the way I do, it wouldn't do to try and fool you."

Old Man stares ahead and does not answer Sounding. He sways sideways, his bundled totem swinging on humped back. He shuffles forward, neck stiff, and he cannot turn his head. He is blind.

"It's one of them captured before," Sounding says, *"one of them we started off for Thunderchild's Reserve."*

"I had better speak to them again," Redcoat says. *"It is very expensive to take you back by train,"* he says to People.

"You will all die out if you don't change your living habits," Sounding says, "and the Woman Leader has got to give you a helping hand at it. Or the end is there!" To Soldier Leader now, *"The only way to hold out that hand, as I see it, is to induce them, not drive them like dumb beasts. I know a great many farm instructors who think they can drive humans the same as animals, but that was never managed yet. I lead them by kind words and good example. When a man talks to you like a dog you either try to bite him or you slink away with your tail between your legs."*

"Peter, you talk too much! You are getting paid to interpret, not make my speeches for me!"

"So I always say to them, 'You know you have to do it and so you better instead of being made to do it.' "

"Keep the line moving!"

Horses pulling wagon. Grandmothers and children stare over sides at Sounding. They belong to Piapot. Screaming Red River carts. Halfbreeds from Batoche. A Black who tries to hide under broad-brimmed cowboy hat and body armour made of wooden rods and tufts of hair. Fat Crow trader.

278

"Two hundred and sixty pounds I weigh," Sounding says, *"and that says something! But then we Houries are all big strapping fellows. seven of us. All boys. We get that from our father."*

New-young-women huddle under black umbrellas. They do not know where to go because they are all dancers from *Buffalo Bill's Wild West Show.* Their leader holds *guitar* over her head.

"I don't speak Indian!" she says.

"Where do you come from?" Sounding says.

"Pen-sal-vain-yaaaaaa!" Long knives turn heads. *"I graduate from Indian School. In Pen-sal-vain-eeeee-yaaaaah!"*

"That's the one," Long Knife says to Redcoat. *"She sure gave us a pack of trouble in Missoula! Stirred up the women with her wild dancing. And the men!"*

"Yours or the Indians'?" Redcoat says.

She grins. *"They made us sell our music for food. All I have is guitar!"* She plucks strings.

Calling Hills People, and that is the last of them.

I slog my way into camp. Wooden splints have been taken off, but my leg is stiff. I drag it behind me, a little. I follow Sounding Creature. I do not trust him. I must warn those planning to escape not to talk to Sounding. I think he knows that Horse-dance-maker and I plan to sneak back into Montana. Under cover of this rain.

In camp, redcoats run from fireside to fireside with kettles of tea. They strip away soggy rags and wrap children in dry blankets. New-young-women are afraid to take off skirts. Redcoats look away or get faces slapped by grandmothers.

"I have not had my first experience!" Horse-dance-maker says. He crosses his legs and wraps his arms around his bare chest. "I'm so afraid!" he laughs.

"So is your old grandmother," I say.

Old Women build wall of lumpy backsides for new-young-women to undress behind. New-young-men jump up and down, peek over heads, under skirts, between grandmother's linked arms. They fall over on backs, howling.

Horse-dance-maker and Fox are seated before our fire.

They want tea, and I have only smoking fire to make it on because wood is too wet to burn. I cannot think about what I am doing, because Sounding Creature hovers over fire. "I counted heads," he says to Horse-dance-maker, "and I asked for names. 'Monias!' one man said."

It means dumb whiteman who does not know how to live well on prairie.

"And Sgt. Caudle wrote down Moon-e-yas on the big list. When he asked me what it meant I told Caudle that it meant Brave!"

Horse-dance-maker snorts.

"So I didn't give the man away!" Sounding says.

Redcoats rub down horses, give them pots of steaming mash. Gunshot breaks night air into falling pieces of sound. "Fleming shot a horse," Sounding says. "They have the owner's consent."

Horse-dance-maker's fingers close over skinning knife handle. His jaw snaps like he is cornered fox. Dreamspirit does not forgive killing of horses.

"You still have a long way to go and the money allotted you by the *United States* has run out," Sounding says. "You've held out long enough. You better tell Captain Deane your name."

"Tell him," I say to Horse-dance-maker, "but not your Real Name."

"If redcoats don't give you rations," Sounding says, "who will?"

Horse-dance-maker's face darkens under raven-wing-hat.

"Impudent! Stubborn! Confounding Indians! You get no grub until you answer!"

"We know," I say. "Redcoat has said it. No Names. No food."

"This woman has a great tongue," Sounding says.

"Albino dragonfly!" I say.

"You blame me as why you are being put back on this side," Sounding says.

"I blame you for hovering over us like dragonfly!"

"Indians call me Mosquito Hawk," Sounding says. "I'm as big a muckamuck as anybody in either camp and I have big friends in both camps!"

I pull a skinning knife from my left-over-bag. "I catch you telling Redcoat who is planning to escape," I say, "and I will rip your guts out!"

"I am only giving information," Sounding says, "for your own good. I understand both sides!"

"I will slice your belly and feed it to dogs!"

"I will get Captain Deane to give you a good talking to! You threaten me?" Sounding waves his brown interpreter's hat at Redcoat who is making talk with Long Knife.

"Keep quiet," Horse-dance-maker says to me. "That is not the way to do it."

"Pull in your horns!" Sounding says to me.

"I will cut yours off!" I say.

"*Captain Deane!*" Sounding yells.

Redcoat and two long knives are moving from fire to fire. They give *cod liver oil* to children. People rub medicine on red spots. They cough and hold their aching heads. Redcoat stops before my fire, but he speaks to Long Knife and points at lesser long knife. "*Explain the presence of this man!*" he says.

"*Darn old Indian Queen,*" Sounding says, "*sneaking out like that. They have a* police court house *you can go to! You better tell her, Captain Deane.*"

Redcoat Leader is not listening to Sounding Creature. "*Quarantine!*" he yells at Long Knife Leader.

"*Doctor Tennant is the Quarantine Officer,*" Long Knife says. "*There are a few cases of measles in this batch. But I assure you there is no further risk of infection.*"

"*Peter!*" Redcoat yells.

"*Yes sir, Captain Deane!*" Sounding Creature is ready to handle Indians for his redcoat again.

"*Get Doctor Mewburn down here!*"

"*It's seventy-two miles . . .*"

"*Now!*"

"*. . . to Lethbridge.*"

"*I know how far it is, damn your eyes! I want Corporal Bullough detailed to bring a fresh supply of cod liver oil. At once!*"

"It will not cure red-spots-disease," I say. I put away my skinning knife.

"*Move your fat ass, Peter Hourie, before I get angry!*"

"Next team isn't due for another three weeks," Sounding says.

"Go! This camp is under quarantine!"

Sounding Creature moves his interpreter's weight so fast even dragonfly cannot catch him.

There are spots on People's faces that rags and grease will not take away, spots that *cod liver oil* will not take away. People are getting together, they say I must be Leader now because Little Bear and Lucky Man have been taken away. But making me Leader will do no good. I do not have power of medicine to take away red-spots-disease.

I know fear more stabbing than Sounding Creature's sword, more cutting than skinning knife. Fear. It pulls tighter around my neck than Soldier Leader's hanging rope.

"The only way to do it now," I say to Horse-dance-maker, "is to escape back over dividing-line."

I tell People to hide in Bearpaw Mountains.

Dr. Mewburn travels seventy-two whiteman's miles from Lethbridge in ten whiteman's hours. He and Corporal Bullough, hospital steward, take charge of camp. They put sick People on *Cattle Quarantine Grounds* beside White Mud River.

For many days and many nights campfires are kept burning by redcoats who bring wood down from north. Fresh beef is brought from Lethbridge, but Soldier Leader will not give food to People who will not tell Sounding Creature their Names. *"No names!"* he yells, *"No food!"*

People do not understand. Surviving on prairie means sharing, and no man who needs food is ever turned away.

So Okison escapes. He takes three horses with him.

It rains all night. Next morning camp is said to be free of red-spots-disease. Sounding counts heads, but he cannot find The Rook and one horse, Mooneyas and four horses. Rook was false name for Fox. Mooneyas was name Horse-dance-maker used to fool Sounding Creature.

Mina/maka, now we make our escape.

Under cover of night rain we escaped redcoats' camp.

Horse-dance-maker and Fox hide with horses in Kipp's Coulee. Women wait for them to return to us when redcoat has given up looking for us.

It is not time to be wanting it, I know that, know it is just time to be quiet, careful and watchful. But I am as fidgety as half-fucked fox chased from earthen den by Redcoat Leader's dogs in time of changing leaves. I huddle in wagon, under canvas. I am folded in grey horse blanket. Crow Woman's children crouch against my legs. "Go back to sleep," I whisper. "I will tell you when it is time." I give them maple sugar to suck.

I cross my arms over my knees and drop my head so I do not have to look at that cross-eyed Crow Woman. She pouts because Horse-dance-maker did not crawl into her side of wagon when we stopped for rest and dried antelope meat.

I want Horse-dance-maker. I want fire and kettle of tea. I press my cheek against wet sideboard and smell dust of many summers.

Summer nights always held promises for me. Spruce branches, heavy and moist, brushed against wagon as we returned home from sundance. I was warm then, not shivering in clinging wet dress, and Horse-dance-maker took me for second time under blanket and behind Bear Woman who drove horses. We were going home, not waiting in abandoned wagon for redcoats to find us. It was my first sundance, my first time with a man.

I was gathering brush for lodge covering, watching Horse-dance-maker race back and forth on buffalo-runner. I dropped back from other new-young-women who were fresh from isolating tent. I hoped Horse-dance-maker would choose to carry my wood. He did, but not waiting for night and time for singing and crawling under tentflap to place blue bead between my breast, he made great show of bundling my wood with rawhide. When others were far ahead and raising Centre-pole, he came at me from behind, his arms around my middle and his hands bunched around my small breasts. My buttocks were pressed against his hardness, and he pulled me backwards into bush. He bent his body over mine, so I fell forward and held onto his arms. My hair fell over my shoulders, and I took one braid between my teeth. I did not want to cry out against pain of first experience, and it was quickly done, he leaving me curled under poplars, spill of him and stinging only coming later when I squatted under bush. I was afraid bleeding would never stop.

Woman does not forget her first time, and I am his first woman. I smile crookedly at that Crow Woman. She sucks dried meat.

Being first sometimes means coming last, but Horse-dance-maker makes up for that by taking long time to burst inside me. After having three before me it is easy for him to do that; and I grip his back, heaving, sweat making him slide against me, but he holds firm so my own bursting spreads down to my toes and makes them twitch and curl. After, I press greased end of buffalo horn into me, fold my legs over Horse-dance-maker's, so it seems we will never be apart again.

Because of his other women I do not always get enough pleasuring, and then I go to isolating tent, take my horn with me, burrow into buffalo robe, humping, pretending it is him. Horn is trick my mother showed me. She made me promise not to tell other new-young-women because it is woman's place to await her man's pleasure. But sometimes having to wait until last born has seen three winters is too long. Greased horn helps me stand Horse-dance-maker's taking of other women. Also.

I am first woman, one looked up to, and I give them lessons in how to please Horse-dance-maker. All but Crow Woman. She elbows ahead of me to serve him beef broth. She pretends she made it.

At time of first birthing I show them how to hunker down on buffalo robe. I rub backs with bear grease so pushing is easier. I tell them when to breathe deeply and when to pant and when to hold. Then I make my own coddle of broth strengthened with Company rum. I make mossbags for children. I suckle them myself for first three days until new mother's milk flows. After that they call me My-eldest-sister and bond between women is chanted in our song during medicine feasts when no men are allowed in lodge.

I fold my arms inside blanket. I take nipples between thumbs and pointing-fingers, pinch, tweaking gently. Stirring between my legs makes my knees wobble. After birthing and suckling so many children, my breasts are soft, but nipples are raspberries dropping brightly from heavy branches. Suckling always made me want it, and sometimes I thought that was why Horse-dance-maker kept my belly swollen.

I was looking for arrowheads, combing bleached bones in buffalo jump that time, and my first son was yowling on my back. So I rested on shaded side of ravine and gave him milk. While he sucked, I rubbed between my legs. I was surprised by Black-robe coming upon me between birch trees. His face was swelling red. So I lifted my skirt, spread my legs, and showed him ripeness as life-giving as raspberry nipple. I would have let him have missionary way with me, but I had never known another man, only Horse-dance-maker. Black-robe fled. I was so surprised that any man could fear a woman. I stopped aching in that small place until Horse-dance-maker came. I told him about Black-robe and asked him to nibble emptied breast.

I have never wanted another man, only Horse-dance-maker. Fox's Woman says that is what makes me want it at wrong times. Like now, waiting for redcoats to come looking for us, I want it, but Horse-dance-maker hides in Kipp's Coulee.

He took me before he left rest camp. He crawled into wagon and chose first woman, but it was done as quickly as first time, he afraid to take too long because redcoats were not slow in giving chase. I was pleasured, he saw to that, but he was tired from strain of leading us out of redcoats' camp and he was too swift about it. So I need to finish it.

I am not afraid of redcoat. If he catches Horse-dance-maker and Fox he will only take them back to cattle grounds and keep them under guard until it is time to go on to Little Pine's.

First Okison escaped. Then Ka-te-tipew, He-rolls-over, and Son-of-holding-otter. They disguised themselves as mule skinners and escaped back over dividing-line. I told Horse-dance-maker to take false name because he rolls over better and more often than anyone else, but idea of exact-speaking-person taking name of Mooneyas, dumb whiteman who does not know how to live well on prairie, that made everyone laugh loudest, so he chose it. Fox took name of Rook. I must remember that when redcoat comes and asks me who my man is and where he is. I can say Rook for Fox's Woman. I remember it because of hoarse throat of Foodgiver's woman who told me about those birds nesting under ledges of her house in land across water. But I cannot say Ka-te-tipew, He-rolls-over, without hiding my face behind shawl. I will not be able to say that to redcoat who keeps People together by striding around in big boots that make my own toes curl. His red jacket makes my own breathing hard to do.

Waiting in line for rations he hands out, I stare at tight bulging place in front of him. I am drawn to men with heavy thighs and thick necks, although Horse-dance-maker is lean. But he wears breech clout tighter than others do so he looks good there.

It is wrong time to be wanting it. Wrong time when I line up for rations, because of boots and tight pants. Wrong time when I hunker down frying bannock, because of fire's heat spreading up my thighs. Wrong time when men are hunting, because of suckling at my breasts.

I pinch my nipples hard, trying to stop it before redcoat comes, but pinching always makes me want it more. I am afraid redcoat will find Horse-dance-maker before he can come to me, but there is not much danger of that because redcoats do not know how to travel like Exact-people. They draw pictures of land on paper, draw straight joining line between places they want to travel to and from, then try to cut wagon trail or build iron road across land. They do not think about where to find water, wood, small game. They worry about how long it will take to travel from place to place. People know going must be slow with many stops for rest, many times going away from trail to find food. If they could, whitemen would straighten flow of river instead of following easy curve and turning of it.

I hear hooves thudding against soft earth, sharp quick snap of twigs, swish of leaves brushing horses' hides. Someone breaks trail through underbrush.

I know what to do, how to distract tracker and send him on to dividing-line. Then, when redcoat gives up search, Horse-dance-maker will come out of hiding place and take me across dividing-line into Going-to-Sun mountains. There, long knives will not find us either. Later we will go to Crow Woman's relatives and live with them. It means never returning but Horse-dance-maker says it must be. I would follow him into Sweet Grass Hill where Wesakachak disappeared and left imprints of his buttocks where he slid into earth.

I stretch and bend my stiff leg. I ease away from Crow Woman's children. I crouch under blanket, let it fall, and turning, I tuck it around sleeping children. I stand tall, slow rain cools my face. I sign to Crow Woman that I will talk to redcoat. I boost myself up onto side board, balance, then jump down to soft wet earth. My leg buckles under me, old pain there.

Wooden wheels are buried up to axles in mud. I packed mud around iron rims. Getting wagon stuck was easy, but not easy pushing it under raining sky all night, with Horse-dance-maker leading horses and Fox following, but not trying to cover tracks. We wanted redcoat to follow.

Now I must do it right: make redcoat believe men left us because women make tracking easier and going slow. Redcoat will believe that, and after he leaves Horse-dance-maker will come and take us to safety.

He will come, yes he will come. Through underbrush brown boots appear. Yes, he will come. Then white pants with leaf stains, and yes he is coming, red coat bright even under night sky. Waiting, my arms loose at my sides, my braids wet against my cheeks, and my mouth suddenly dry. I suck my cheeks. I must say it right: Rook and Mooneyas.

In wagon Crow Woman steps out of wet dress. She wraps my dry blanket around her hips, looks down sharp nose at me, cross-eyed. "Want me to do it?" she says.

"No!" I yell, not caring if redcoat can hear me. If I can pull Horse-dance-maker away from Crow Woman's sleeping-robe I can make redcoat look at me. It is soon time of my own changing but I am not so old I cannot turn men's heads.

"What've we got here? Redcoat's dark head appears. He separates and ducks between branches. *"We got them, Peter!"* His wide smile closes distance between us. He is not wearing red coat. He is wrapped in black water cape of shiny leather. He is as dark as sky above trees. His hooded head bends toward wagon. He is so tall he just looks down into it. *"Squaws and papooses, eh?"*

"They make the going slower." It is Sounding Creature. He leads horses. *"High-tailed it back to Montana did they? Left the women and children to fend for themselves*

like always."

"Recognize any of them?"

Closing poor eye, bending knees because there is no crease in his hard belly, Sounding Creature pushes wide face near mine. *"Yes, it's one of them that wouldn't give up their names. Yes, sure, I can see that plump and plain. It's that darn old Indian queen!"*

I turn away from his strong breath, suck ends of my braids. My mouth is so dry. I clench my fist and show it to Sounding. I shake it in his face as if it holds skinning knife.

Redcoat's eyes dart across high yoke of my dress, follow curving line down to my toes that are curling in mud. He licks his dripping liphair as if he would like to munch raspberry nipples. *"Tell her I see she is cold,"* he says to Sounding. *"Tell her I will give her food. But she must go back."*

"Where is your man?" Sounding says.

I shrug, slap my wet sides. *"Kipp's Coulee?"*

"Not very likely," redcoat says, *"and hard to tell at night which way the tracks go. The way they cross and circle."*

He knows, and I cannot breathe now, because he knows.

"Tricky," Sounding says, *"and very nicely done, but I've had a lot to do with Indians and I say they left the women and high-tailed it fast over the line."*

"I've got another one in here somewheres." Redcoat loosens thongs binding his pack. *"And I'll leave tea and some flour with her. Think she knows her way back?"*

"You better go instead of being made to," Sounding says, pointing towards cattle quarantine grounds.

I stare at redcoat's boots. Toes are muddied but they shine to his knees. "Namoya," I say. "I do not go."

"Confound it!" Sounding says. *"It's not my place to be chasing after squaws!"*

"Then go on to the border," redcoat says. *"I'll take the squaws and papooses back to camp, get a fresh horse and meet you as soon as I can. Better wire Inspector Morris when you get to the border."*

"I'll track 'em as far as the line and that's as far as I go!" Grunting, Sounding Creature heaves his interpreter's weight into the leather saddle. It groans. *"Wouldn't live on that side for anything! Confound them!"* Then, soft sucking of hooves

in mud, and Sounding Creature leaves me with redcoat.

He offers me something folded, square, and dry. *"Take it. Take it."*

I clasp my hands behind my back.

"Blanket. Will keep you warm and dry. It's water proof. For horses, but rain won't soak in. Take it."

My arm, stretching for blanket, looks so long and thin in night light. I hold out my hand as if I will take blanket, step backwards, he moving to me, then both unmoving again.

"Napi?" The word is Blackfoot for Old Man, but said another way it means husband, so I know he wants me to give him Horse-dance-maker's Name. *"How many men with you?"*—two fingers held up.

"Two," I nod, "only."

"Tan'eseyekason.ci?" He says, "What is your name?" but it is Horse-dance-maker's and Fox's that he wants.

"Rook." I said it, spoke Across-water-word just right.

"Hey! Now we're getting somewhere! Now the other one. What's his name?"

"Mooneyas." I rub my nose so he will not see grin starting at corners of my mouth.

"Mooneyas! I checked him off with the last bunch! So he got away. Well, we'll get him back for you. I'm sorry."

Then he is following tracks in mud, moving fast around wagon, reappearing on other side. He is quick to my side, dark head close to my face. *"All right! Where!"*

I sweep my arm, hand winging toward underbrush.

"Hiding?"

I lift my clinging skirt to my knees, back up, limping a little, my poor leg buckling. He follows. "Yes. Here. There. This way." I brush leather hood so it falls away to his shoulders. His hair is dry, combed flatly away from high brow, but it curls around his ears. I hook my pointing-finger through knotted ties of cape, pull him slowly into bushes, wet leaves brushing my bare arms. He stoops, his eyes searching for tracks, tufted beard tickling back of my hand. "Ahstum. Ahhhhhstum!" Softly softly, and something rough at my back.

A white birch, its branches sweeping over our heads, leaves spreading cover like patched blanket. Moving closer, he raises his arms so wedge of cape falls open and spreads over me. Red coat warm underneath. Buttons hard against my breasts.

But this is not time to be wanting it, he is not my man, and I must send him in wrong direction by telling him to go in right one. Even so, his hardness is against my thigh, and leaves are turning overhead.

I am forgetting about Horse-dance-maker hiding in coulee because it is my own time of changing and soon I will not be thinking about going with a man under promising night sky into bushes. Then it will be too late to grab hold. Now it is too late for promising. He said he would come back, but I cannot wait like I did before.

His head is on my shoulder. I do not like soapy smell of his neck. I nuzzle under his arm where he smells sweaty like a man should. Cape folds around me, so I am inside and feeling safe, somehow protected by this strange-smelling man. I want to stay here. Hard edge of his chin rests on my covered head, and he just holds me, whispering, "*If you only knew, dark lady, how long it is since I held a woman.*"

Cloth is smooth, his back broad and tightening under my stroking hands, and it is suddenly my turn, my time has come with the coming of this man. Waiting is over.

It is woman's place to wait upon and wait for her man, and I have waited so long, too long, in each camp for Horse-dance-maker. I waited in Benton for him to return from Crow Woman's people. I waited in each lodge so many nights for him to return from hunting. I waited many more nights for him to return from visiting elders. Or other women. And strangely it seems as if I have also waited all my days and nights for this bearded, redcoated man to hold me. It is just my moment, I know that, but maybe it will last all my nights on prairie.

Leaning against me, all hard with wanting me, he just holds me, not forcing his way upon me, so I know he will let me go. He will not make me stay.

Time of changing leaves is freeing me. Grandmothers never told me that would happen, only said—what?—forgetting because I am first woman.

I push against redcoat's chest, and he opens his arms. I duck out from under cape, swiftly brush past him. His left arm catches my shoulder before dropping loosely to his side. I swing my arm up and smack dripping leaves, then turn, stop, dig my toes into soft and watered earth.

290

Leaning sideways against birch, his dark hair limp on his wide forehead, his beard tufted and wet, he looks like buffalo lifting head from watering place. He looks more alone than any person should ever be, eyes darkening so they appear brown, although they are blue dark blue.

He needs me! I am under branches again, under cape, and in his arms; warmth folding around me.

So it is my turn. This time is my time, and for that single time I am the only one. Not one of four.

My arms are caught folded across his chest. I ease down, my hands sliding between his legs and stroking him into hardness again. I push up against him, my skirt rising. He leans me into tree, presses his lips against my neck, soft rub of his tufted beard on my shoulder. My back arches against white birch, and it is quickly done, I slide down and curl over roots.

"I don't want to. But I have to leave you." He wraps me in horse blanket, tucks edges under me.

Rain spatters on leather. Leaves turn wetly above me, singing, and my eyes close. I feel smile spreading across my closing face. And dreaming only of changing light, blue on blue, shading darkly up from dark, greying, light folding out of itself, clearing, palely spreading like cloth drying, then turning is gone.

I awaken, look out of eyes of Man-of-all-songs. I touch my head and feel smooth line of his brow. My hair falls from edge of dark. Taste in my mouth is green, sage blowing along lip of coulee. It is dawn of new day, and mist and light rise together.

Sitting, horse blanket slides over my shoulders, and I reach for lowest branch, pull myself up, then swing my arms and duck out of underbrush. I hear Horse-dance-maker calling me. I see Crow Woman passing last pieces of dried meat to children. New Raven has made tea over small fire.

Arms around horses' necks, his head between them, Horse-dance-maker backs horses to hitching post. "They came after us," he laughs, "but they are missing Rook and Mooneyas!"

"It has stopped raining," I say, "so we do not go to Montana. I have decided we find our way back to place of belonging."

My hand disappears in hand of Man-of-all-songs. My feet start climbing Deer's Rump Hill.

Annika

In the north country, May twenty-fourth has always been too early for spring planting. Frost will burn bedding plants and the farmers' seed, often, well into June. But this year I celebrated the return of spring earlier than usual, and I decided to lay in the garden on the twenty-fourth.

Old Woman had survived another prairie winter, soon we would make berry broth in thanksgiving that spring had come, and now I was loosening the soil around the blue woodflowers and Johnny-jump-ups in Johanna's rock garden.

Sun warmed my back. New leaves on the poplar and caragana danced in its light. I took my trowel to dandelions and crab grass. Not caring if I wasted water, I filled my watering can from the rain barrel and sprinkled the freshly-turned earth around the woodflowers. I was basking in more than sunlight.

I worked all morning, dragging my hoe in rows down the garden, plotting where I would lay in tomato plants and where I would seed the peas and carrots and lettuce and cucumber. When I rested on my hoe, I waved to Old Woman seated at the open window watching me.

She still wasn't pleased with me. She wanted to walk to Turtle River and bathe, wanted a sweat lodge, wanted to make berry broth. But I wouldn't let her.

It was a battle, every morning, giving her her sponge bath and walking her forth and back in the homestead. She wasn't able to walk to the door and back without tiring; she would never make it to the river. I was also afraid she would catch cold again, and my fear always turned to anger. I knew we were never fighting each other, but we couldn't stop the struggle, nor did either of us want to.

Soon I would take her to the river, but in the Fargo, and it would be the Battle River rather than the Turtle. I hadn't forgotten my promise.

Old Woman's head was nodding; she dozed in the sunlight.

I finished the row, then went inside to make lunch.

At the washstand, I scrubbed dirt from my hands and face, splashed cold rain water over my hot neck. Drying with a towel, I said, "Old Woman, it feels so good!"

She didn't answer. Her head flopped sideways.

"Other-grandmother? Are you okay?"

"Annnnnniiiiii!" she cried, her head flopping onto her shoulder.

I ran to Old Woman, knelt before her. "What is it?"

Sweat dripping down the sides of her face, raising up on her forehead. She tilted her head back, and her eyes rolled up. Her face had gone white. Her head flopped down again.

"Pain? Where! Your chest?"

Old Woman waggled her head, "No no no."

Quickly I lifted her from rocker to cot, lay her against the pillows; but she sat straight up, only her head flopping like a raggy doll's.

I dug into her bundle, looking for MacRaw's medicines. I was allowing her to do as much for herself as possible now. She took her own medicine and made her own tea. At night, she was able to get up herself. I found both plastic bottles, the penicillin and digitalis, and both were full.

Old Woman hadn't been taking her medicine, only the foxglove and pine needle teas. The rawhide bundle with the red ribbon was empty. She was out of foxglove, and it was too early in the season to replace it.

I was furious, but I placed my ear to Old Woman's chest. I heard rattling sounds. Her pneumonia had long since been cleared up, and the congestion in her lungs was due to the slow failure of her heart.

I ladled some fresh Turtle Spring water from the pail. I lifted Old Woman's chin, her mouth opened, and I dropped a digitalis pill into it. But before I could place the dipper to her lips she spat out the pill. I took another from the bottle, held her nose and clamped her mouth shut, so she swallowed it.

She sank down into the pillows. There was no fight in her now. She stared at the windows. "Shut it," she said in English. "Shut him out." Then she yelled, "Shut it! Shut it!"

I closed the window. "No one is out there," I said.

Something had frightened her, but I was still angry at her for not telling me she was out of foxglove tea leaves.

"Sweetgrass," she said. "Above door. To ward off Boney Scepter."

I hung the braided sweetgrass from the deer horns above the door.

"Ahhhhhhhh," Old Woman breathing deeply now. "I am looking out window and I see him. I think it is Man-of-all-songs, his head is growing out of top of pine tree, and he wears long robe made from albino skins. His skin is white. His hair is long and white. He holds buffalo skull, and he points it at you. But I do not see you digging in dirt, only Annie, and she is waiting for me to join her. Then I see Horse-dance-maker by caragana hedge. Raven's wings on his head have turned white. I see white faces of all my ancestors sticking out of bushes." Old Woman's hands shook on top of the Bay blanket, and her legs trembled under it.

"No, Old Grandmother," I said. "You do not see Boney Scepter now. You do not see him. Not now!"

"You will not let him in."

"I promise!"

"He might come and get me tonight."

"I'll stay awake. All night! I won't let him in!" I ran to the window. "He's gone. He's not out there now!"

"He will come back." She lifted her right hand and placed it on top of her medicine bundle. "You must destroy anything you do not know by taste. Burn anything which must be mixed with water." Then she lost consciousness.

I stayed by her cot all afternoon. With the windows closed and the fire breathing in the stove, the air was heavy. The clock ticked loudly, and I counted the hours and minutes.

Old Woman was fighting to breathe.

I heard the storm long before it reached the homestead. Wind rushes before a rainstorm, almost seems to be leading it on; and I heard poplar and spruce and pine swaying and tossing their branches.

About four o'clock, the light dropped, suddenly, from

yellow to dark grey. I stood by the window, watching the dark haze move north from the flats, across the north quarter, and finally over my homestead. Then rain, falling straight down, pummelling the shingled roof. New poplar leaves slapped the glass. And the rain. I couldn't see through the wash now, and I left my vigil to put the dishpan under the leak in the sleeping loft.

Again, I sat by Old woman, listening to her breathing, and to wind and rain and clock ticking.

I wasn't afraid of the storm. Outside, rain fell on Copenhagen cabbage patch, battered blue woodflowers until their heads lay on earth, but it lifted orange and black tiger lilies growing in the ditch until they seemed to be reaching for sky.

I knew Old Woman was dying, but I felt as if I were going home. I was on the edge of the Livelong Coulee, and I didn't know how it would be, but it would not be a falling; I would lift, somehow, and then I would, after a long winter, find my own place of belonging. Soon now, I would go home, but unlike the Crees who were rounded up and driven over the border, I would know a rounding out of all things on prairie and cross over into the fullest understanding of the unity of earth and sky that Old Woman had always known and Johanna learned.

All night I lay fully clothed on the bed, listening to thunder gods fight with spears of light. I listened to Old Woman fight for breath. I prayed that she would see, not Boney Scepter, but dawn of new day.

The last time I looked at the clock it was four a.m.

Old Woman

I see them, night-sky-dancers. I see all my
ancestors dancing in northern lights. I turn my face
sideways so I do not look at them face to face. They call
me to come and join eternal dance.

I have never seen lights so changing before, never
seen them drop so close to earth. I have never heard their
call so clear before.

Shrouds of sacred cloth hang from skypoles, long
line of fluttering banners sweeping silently across sky.
Night lights hover over me, waiting for me. Cloth weaves
in and out, floating. Centre light shapes into horseman.
He pulls away from dancers, disappears behind them, then
reappears before them.

The living and the dead move on together. Line
of dancers turns, curving in front of me, and banners are
dropping closer closer closer to earth.

On night of leaving earth, person's spirit
must walk through light.

My head is spinning. I must join them, but earthly
fear hold me back.

Now dancers ride in circle, changing places,
riding around and around me. Lights are spreading tent
over me, blue and rose bursting from Centre-pole, shredded
cloth falling falling falling on me. Pain, here in my heart, it
becomes a longing. My arms are flung wide. I am
stretching open to sky dancers. I find breathing hard to
do. Lights all around me, passing in and out and through
me.

Birdman perches on Centre-pole. He holds out

arms to all who walk living earth. Great-departed-drummer looks after dead ancestors. He rides hard, rushes northward, leads dancers to eternal hunting, his call-to-come softer, fading, but I hear dying.

It runs well now. This night I dance. In lights.

Annika

It was the silence that awakened me. The night storm had passed over my place. Thunder tolled away in the distance, more like a fading rumble of many moving wagons than ringing bells, and it was the sudden silence that frightened me. Newly-hatched robins were not squawking in their nest in the poplar. Gulls hadn't swooped in from the fields to declare war on the barn cats. Even wind was silent.

Old Woman wasn't coughing or groaning in her sleep. There was no rasping breath, no uneven rise and fall to the mound of blankets. She was staring through the window at something only she could see. Her face was white. Air was still and white. Death had re-entered the homestead. But it was the silence that unnerved me.

I leaped out of bed. I fought the impulse to run out of the house, run wild across prairie like Johanna had, run to the end of farmers' fields, then beyond the horizon. I looked out the window.

Outside, Indians were spread out in the yard. Silent. Waiting. I was spooked. How did they know the medicine woman had died?

The councilman from Thunderchild's was squatting on the front stoop, twirling his red hunting cap in his hands. A wagon and team of four Indian ponies was pulled up to the door. Feathers and ribbons were tied to the manes and tails, sacred cloth and bells to the reins and wagonsides. Old women in bright cotton dresses and shawls and scarves were an uneven line of color in front of the caragana. Old men leaned against bent fenders of old cars, rolling cigarettes from a shared tobacco tin. In the backs of battered trucks, children drank cokes and munched potato chips that their mothers had given them to keep them quiet. Young men with full round faces, wearing cowboy hats, jeans and leather jackets, leaned against fence posts and out-buildings. Young women in miniskirts or tight jeans fidgeted with loose strands of hair or traced circles in the dust with toes of their crinkle patent boots. They were all silent. Waiting.

"It is time," I said. I bent over the body. "I promised you I would take you to place of belonging," I said in Cree. "We go now. To Deer's Rump Hill." I folded the small body in the Bay blanket and carried it outside.

The councilman said nothing, remained perched on the stoop, head lowered with respect for the dead. I lay the body in the back of the wagon. Slowly, without a sound, people climbed into their old cars and trucks. The Councilman and an old man who must have been an elder drove the wagon bearing Old Woman's body. Slowly, people formed a procession with the wagon in the middle of it.

I climbed into the cab of the '46 Fargo. I rolled down the window, turned on the truck lights. Last to leave, the Fargo rolled down the lane lined with caragana, passed my Swedish grandmother's garden of reappearing woodflowers. Early morning air was chilled by mist that had drifted up from the flats but it would soon be burned away by the sun.

It was a strange cavalcade that moved, slowly, all day southward to Battleford. People emerged from the bush, pastures, and fields. They ducked under fences and climbed into the back of trucks. At the railway crossing we picked up Old Doc MacRaw who was waiting, bottle of Scotch waving us down, with his jigger. The long line of cars and trucks grew longer as the morning and miles wore on. One Indian who was summer fallowing spun the tractor around and drove it straight off the dusty field, rammed it through the barbed wire fence, knocked down a post, and joined the entourage. He dragged the harrow and barbed wire behind him all the way to Battleford.

The word seemed to go on ahead of us: medicine woman died.

At Battleford I abandoned the Fargo. I left the road to Mounties, Indian agents, missionaries and settlers. Old Woman showed me how to see as far as the place where earth meets sky. Now I followed the Battle River.

I was going to place of belonging. To Deer's Rump Hill.

I am thirty whiteman's miles deep into reserve land. Land has been pushed back, willows and poplar cleared away from the Battle River, so fields lie with backs bared and blackly turned. Two granaries lean together for warmth, each window staring into the other like eyes of original settlers that were always turned outward and were searching for something I can no longer name.

I no longer understand why men want to change the face of the earth. Old Woman told me that whitemen leave nothing untouched. They destroy the unity of all things under sky. They defy the order of Earth Mother and change the rules of Sky Father. They are so hungry for land they only take, not knowing that the taking and giving must be left to earth and sky alone. Left alone, they are one, sharing, so the circle of their love dance is never ending.

Far ahead, the funeral procession moves on without me to Little Pine's where People will make the feast for the dead. Here, yellow foxtails blow in one direction, and I wade through them to steep and muddy banks of Battle River. In willows, ducks are nesting. I turn west with river. Here, there are no squared fields, no fence posts strung together with barbed wire. Here is the meeting place of bushland and flatland and hill country. I struggle through chokecherry bush, prickly rose and wolf willow. I smell sage. For first time I know what it is to smell river.

Above me, a bank of expanding clouds. One shaped like the squatting figure of an old woman smoking a small pipe.

I stumble over rocks buried in long grass. Yellow foxtails brush my bare legs. Then I am running; I cannot stop the flow of land beneath my feet, cannot stop the flying by of blue hills banked against the sky; I cannot stop the turning of days that have led me here. I'm sweating, my jeans damp, my blouse sticking to my heaving sides. I suck air, running, my lips stretched tight, my teeth gritty with dust. My eyes are stinging and I blink back tears. My face is hot against wind. I am running, and memories that don't belong to me are pushing at my back, like hands shoving me forward. Silver willow bursts on either side of me, and I run wild until prairie is again broken by wide steep banks of Battle River. Where Poundmaker's and Little Pine's lands meet the valley opens before me. Panting, I trudge through a long line of white poplar, through a hollow where Old Woman told stories to her children about what happened to new-young-people who ate *mantaskotask,* so the children never touched poison horseplant and wouldn't eat little snake berries growing near maples. "They belong to frogs!" she said, "not to you!" Mushrooms make warts on children's hands. Here, they made a feast of running poplar sap. Red willow bark is dry and ready for crushing and mixing with tobacco, but my Other-grandmother will not be there to do it.

Prickly rose bushes grow thickly on riverbank. My knees buckle. I wobble through low bush, my running shoes catching burrs and thorns. My hands reach for rosehips.

The edge of Battle River is steep and muddy. It drops sharply away from flatland. I sink down to earth. My legs dangle down the bank. My head is spinning and I catch it, hold it steady between my hands. I press my hands on my hot and damp head. Wind pushes at my back. I slide my hands down my forehead and wipe sweat from my nose and cheeks.

I dare to lift my head. My breath is caught. I try to swallow but I have no spit. My breath escapes, but my chest is caving in as if someone has just stepped on it. My shoulders fold around the pain of losing my grandmothers. I dare to look upon Old Woman's place of belonging.

Here, Battle River turns a swift and sharp angle west from Poundmaker's into Little Pine's land. Black poplar roots push out of dark earth, reaching for water. "They like to get their feet wet," Old Woman said. Here is the place where grandmothers caught fish in weirs, where grandfathers snared skunks. Here is where Old Woman jumped naked into water and chased frogs up the banks. I dare to turn my head to the left.

"*Waskicosihk!*" I cry. It is Deer's Rump Hill. It does touch sky. It stretches from the east, across the horizon, to the west; links two homes of sun. I am crying. I have followed the words of Old Woman, and they have led me to the place of belonging.

Bunching my knees, I push myself up and away from the river, take three steps backwards before turning and running back to the trail. I wade through summer grasses. I follow the easy flow and turning of river, pass a new graveyard. There is a freshly-turned mound of waiting earth. At the head of the grave, paper flowers stuck in a tin cup. Strips of sacred cloth flutter on chokecherry bushes. I follow an ancient wagon trail through weeds and rock. It is over-grown with bush and branches that reach out and slap my face and arms. I turn down, to river, sliding and falling and stumbling down the bank. I jump on rocks, crossing the river, then dig my toes into earth to climb the slope on the other side.

The first houses built by farm instructor crowd the riverline. In those early years the people lived in tents all summer and moved into the government shacks in the winter. Now they are empty, roofs folding into themselves, support beams split by lightning or caving in with age. Once, gardens were scattered between these shacks but now weeds choke the earth. No hoes are needed here.

The last house has split poplar stacked against its mud-chinked wall. A slop pail. A wagon wheel. A rusted mower. The walls of this winter house are older than the trees budding leaves above the sod roof. Sacks are tacked over the windows. The door leans on one hinge, half open. No smoke spirals out of the stovepipe chimney.

Inside, the dirt floor has been packed down and swept. A kettle and rawhide bundles lie on an unpainted table. In the corner, a mattress with springs and stuffing poking out of one sagging end. A grey horse blanket crumpled on top. Beside it a chipped cup.

"My Other-granddaughter," the voice wavering and fading in my head. I see through the broken glass of the north window. My hands grip old wooden frames.

Outside, along riverbank, children play willow tag. One boy has taken enough beating with switches and he falls to earth so the others leave him alone. Two long-eared dogs fight over a bone. I listen to the call of distant drums. I hear the fragmented chanting of elders, voices cracked but thrumming. On the long back of Deer's Rump Hill, women dance the feast for the dead, shuffle in a long line towards the Rump. Fringes of their long shawls are lifted by wind. Long unbraided hair swings around withered cheeks. In the middle of the line there is an open space for Old Woman. The dancers descend, weave through poplar, and disappear. Leaving a lone figure on Deer's Rump Hill.

I boost myself up and over the window ledge. I roll down, through long grasses. I scramble to my feet.

On the shoulder of the Hill he stands, bared feet straddling earth. He wears only a breech clout. His hair falls from a high brow. His arms, stretched wide, touch two homes of sun and, turning, he circles four directions.

I kick off my running shoes, stepping on canvas heels, not waiting to untie the laces. My toes touch warm earth. I begin to climb, short grasses brown and soft under my feet.

Behind him, sky holds no clouds. Dusklight is blue and clear. Now he sees me. His face does not change, but eyes catch light so I know he is surprised by me.

Before me, a blue shape stretches in and through and out and around me: a long silk cloth weaving in and out of itself. The edges are bound in satin. Cloth is transparent, there is one tear in the centre, and it goes ahead of me, pulling me all the time.

He holds out his arms to me. He calls me to come to him. I hear the chant, and it holds all words to all songs. He catches the end of the cloth and pulls me to him, cloth unwinding around me.

I am turning, slowly, in a circle, moving all the time, slowly, up Deer's Rump Hill.

He holds the cloth, ends in both hands, and stretches it so it touches all homes of sun and wind. He lets it go, it flutters, then caught by wind, it rises and floats above the Hill.

Slowly, I climb. I am singing inside, and I know the words to all the songs.

Byrna Barclay was raised in Livelong, Northern Saskatchewan, the area where her grandparents homesteaded by the Thunderchild Reserve. She was educated at the University of Saskatchewan and later worked as a research-writer for the Council on Indian Rights and Treaties. In 1977 **Summer of the Hungry Pup** was a winner of the Saskatchewan Culture and Youth Novel Competition.

Her stories and poems have been published in numerous journals and more recently, she edited two books of poetry for Thistledown Press and taught Indian studies at Wascana Institute in Regina. She is at present working on a sequel to **Summer of the Hungry Pup.**

Credits:

Editor: R. Silvester
Publisher: J. Lewis
Cover and Design: D. Lamontagne
Production: L. Solis, M. Wiebe, and N. Miller
Printing and Binding: Co-op Press Ltd., Edmonton
Financial Assistance:
     Alberta Culture
     The Canada Council
     NOVA: An Alberta Corporation
     Saskatchewan Culture and Youth